The Dark Twin

By the same author

Argyll – The Enduring Heartland
A Field Survey of Mid-Argyll

and for children
The Squire of Val
Young Hugh
The Wide Blue Road
Lances and Longships

The Dark Twin

Marion Campbell

To
ROBERT GRAVES
who first re-opened
the long-barred door

Copyright © Marion Campbell 1998
Introduction © Naomi Mitchison 1998

First published in 1973 by Club Leabhar
This edition published by House of Lochar 1998

Cover illustration and design by Sophie Moorish

British Cataloguing in Publication Data
A catalogue record for this book is available from the British Library

ISBN 1 899863 41 9 (hb)
ISBN 1 899863 52 4 (pb)

The publishers acknowledge subsidy from the Scottish Arts Council
towards publication of this volume

Printed in Great Britain by SRP, Exeter
for House of Lochar, Isle of Colonsay, Argyll PA61 7YR

FOREWORD

All historical writing has to be based on guesswork and on the ability of the writer to see deep into the period about which he or she is writing. Even when the people of the past have left plenty of evidence, written or built or painted, we are still unsure. Go back even beyond this kind of evidence and build on the necessities of climate and soil and the probabilities that these people, our ancestors, had certain kinds of hopes and fears and perhaps love and thinking parallel to our own. When this is mastered there comes, at least for some people, the necessity to dream and plan, to let the words come and write them down. If the dream goes right, you may have made a true contact with the past and this, I think, has happened here.

The evidence in whispers and traces of a very early culture in the Highlands is there, but so deeply lost that only the poetic imagination can reach it and make it come alive. In this book tiny shreds of evidence have come together into the flow of a story which, to my mind, presents not only a historical possibility, but a gripping story. Are we entitled to make this jump into the past and write as though we had experienced it? I read it at a time when I was working for two Government bodies; both the chosen members of these bodies and the civil servants who were supplied to us were deeply anxious to do whatever we could for the people of the Highlands, perhaps undoing some wrongs which had been done to them in earlier times. I read this book on my way to a meeting in Inverness. For a moment I noticed Marion Campbell sitting beside me. I had only just finished the book and it had me strongly in its grip. I began to ask her about the end of the book – I would like to have seen a few more firm knots tied. Perhaps you may feel that too. But she was, in fact, not there. Yet that was the strength of the writing. I wonder if this kind of thing may happen to other people who go head and shoulders under into this book.

How close, then, has she taken us into the past? It is not always an easy road. We have to adapt ourselves to certain other beliefs and ideas which may be under our own skins, unnoticed until they are called up. But do not fight them. Let them come and you will have an experience of the past – more especially if you are a Scottish reader – which will give you an extra eye for many things you will see and hear. Go to it then.

Naomi Mitchison

It won't be long now.

I knew as soon as I saw this place that it would be soon. I might perhaps go back to them once more, before it happens: they are kindly people, like my own, and then there's the child who's been looking after me—I don't want her to feel unhappy or distressed. It was a sign to me when they chose her for the work; she's called Yssa, you see. I have never met another woman with your name, since . . .

Yssa! Little Yssa, so willing and gentle and kind—but not my Yssa. Never again my own Yssa till we meet under the laden boughs—how soon, now?

It's sheltered here on the cliff, with the milk-soft sea at my feet, and the little flowers of the turf all round me to scent the warm air. Gulls float below me, the sun reaches deep into the rocks, into my old bones, everything is one here. The sea is one with my home sea. My mother gathered these flowers when she carried her son to the Long Strand riding on her hip. From here a road runs to the Orchard and I am ready to follow it—my feet are shod for it, as someone said once long ago.

I must sit quietly and think before I start. I must try to remember everything properly, as it came, and put it all in order, or nothing will be any good. Every link in the chain must lie in its right place. I have no means to know how long that chain must last before I finger it again, and perhaps you will find it before me. We had so little time—how can I be sure you will remember? You remembered more than I did, but this time we shared so little, so little, my darling.

Only our love. Always, waking, sleeping, standing, walking, the world is full of you: now at last there is only this shell called Drost and all else is you, and the shell will break, the husk will split, and I shall come home. Fire of my heart, I shall leap like flame to you. But we who broke the circle, we are not free yet: hooded and husked we shall return, and if I leave no landmarks for us we may return alone. Or if I let my heart go free to find you, then our two hearts would dance away together, two white butterflies under the sun, and we would go our way without hearts . . . Not so, but by leaving an echo, by leaving my chain, that's the way. By calling up every sight and sound and scent and silence, and leaving them here in the mist at the world's end where we shall find them as we return, that is the way. Whatever happens before then, the sea will beat here, the thyme will blow, the birds will fly, the air will brush the cliff, the rocks will stand or crumble, the mist will cover the sea. Remember for me, rocks and sea and flowers—remember for me, when the white bones forget. Remember what I am going to tell you now.

Part One

I WAS the only child my mother bore, and she was the Middle Priestess. I was called Drost, the son of no man, and she was Malda, the Dweller Among Houses. She had other names at other times and places, but of these I shall speak in due course.

Malda then, living at the edge of the western sea, at the river-mouth in the Land of the Boar, Malda gave me life and the breast in the Hearth-house.

Warmth and firelight and the scent of herbs, milk in a bowl at the hearth and the cat watching it, the spindle twirling and the wool stretching, a voice singing and a foot rocking, and stars above the smoke-hole—so it begins, for I was winter-born and my second winter echoes the first.

Spring brought the feel of a woollen cloak, the warmth of the shoulder below, sunlight and the beat of the sea. These were the days when she went to gather herbs from the grazings, while a little way off the herd-boys turned away respectfully. Towards evening, when the women came out to the milking, they would offer us foam-topped milk warm from the pitchers. The boys would bring rush-baskets with an egg or two, and these she would bless and return, knowing that boys are hungry animals; for the milk also she gave a blessing.

On hot summer days the cattle go down into the water and

I

the boys lie at ease along the sands or hunt for shells to string. We would go home over the dusty cattle-track, the women talking with my mother from a distance and their children staring at me out of the rolled cloaks. And behind us the birds piped along the sands, and the herd-boys whistled.

Our house, a white one as was seemly, was much like any other except that its court was large and cleaner than most (for we had no need to own cattle). The first part, as one entered from the court, was the Hearth-room where the holy fire burned slowly, and behind it was the inner room where we lived and where she taught the young girls. Off it were the little warm nests for sleeping. The Maiden of the Year was with us there, and the Old One herself at times, coming and going under cloud of night. Till I was six I lived there, running among the mysteries, knowing and uncaring what songs were sung and what boughs were burnt on the Hearth.

The other women came at times, about their own matters or to the feasts; but it was part of the sickness of my people that few men came, even to the feasts. The men, through one or two of them, had cut themselves off from the things that would have healed that sickness, and the evil grew on their fault. But I knew none of it—I played a little with children who followed their mothers, but I did not even think of stepping outside the charmed ring round the house.

I suppose I saw Ailill, for I remember a thin child with hair so fair it was almost white. Within that ring is neither queen nor slave, and if I saw a jewelled woman with him I paid no heed to her. But I remembered Ginetha when I saw her again, so she must have been there sometimes. Ginetha the Queen was devout not by habit but only in emergency; more often it would be some plump smiling soul from the household who would lead him to throw his flower-wreath with the rest of us.

I do remember Ginetha now, once. It was a showery spring day, and she pushed through the curtains and flung herself down at the Hearth where I was helping my mother tend the fire. She lay twisting herself and sobbing—I stared at her tears —and my mother took the branches from my hands and gave me a little push towards the inner room.

Ginetha snatched at her bracelets and the gold around her throat and thrust them towards the Hearth. My mother knelt

2

by her and tried to take her hands, but the Queen raised herself and gazed wildly about, her grey eyes like wet pebbles in a stream, and cried in a voice of hatred—

'You! What have I to do with you, who have stolen my desire?'

'Sister and daughter, I have stolen nothing,' said my mother. 'Feed the fire and make your prayer to the Mother. But take up your jewels; she has no need of gold, and these will be missed. Come, let us tend the fire together and pray to her.'

But Ginetha only wept more bitterly, bowing herself and stretching her hands towards the flames, and at last went out still weeping, leaving a forlorn pile of gold on the hearthstone.

My mother gathered it, shaking her head, and carried it into the side room where the offerings lay, and there it remained.

Our year arranged itself round three festivals, neither so well attended nor so splendidly celebrated as they ought to have been, but great days to me. The spring feast brought all the girls in their garlands, and my mother used her arts to divine which of them might remain to learn the mysteries. Most of them were troublesome chits, and they were often sent packing before long. It is desirable, though not essential, as my mother would tell them, that the Maiden should remain in the Hearth-house all the year before her dancing; hers is the chief part in the spring feast and she must prepare for it. But, as she would tell them, an unworthy representative is worse than none; better for the maid to be chosen on the very night of spring, by the Maiden, than for some false substitute to set out from the Hearth in her robes.

'Have a care,' I have heard her say, 'for if she whom you stand for should be angered by your neglect, she will come on that cold grey wind that is both steed and sword, and strike you down for an appeasing sacrifice.'

Neither they nor I thought it possible that she would come.

My mother was the only priestess to be seen regularly by the people, for the Old One moved out of the hill only by night, and the Maiden must be kept closely hidden; these are safeguards, for the untrained might take great harm from chance encounters with either of them in their times of power.

I loved best the harvest-dancing, my mother's own feast, when we children ate all we could hold, and ran about the threshing-floors late into the night with our little clay cups pierced with holes through which glanced the tiny flickering lights. The spring feast grew too wild for us, and only the first part of it was at the Hearth. There they brought their wreaths and passed them through the smoke, and there the songs began, and the dancing, and the procession wound away to the hill to follow the Maiden. Some of the older women stayed by the Hearth with us, gossiping and taking care of the babies, and giving us mouthfuls of sweet roots and honey saved for this time. We would all be asleep in a tangle of small bodies long before the dancers returned, sated with delight and drooping with weariness, their feet wet with the dew of dawn.

But the winter feast was a time of cold and fear. The winds mourned round the walls, carrying on their backs our forbears, come to see how we were behaving (so said the older girls, left in charge of us); the outer court was full of mourning women, bewailing their dead of the year and of former years, for then the dead part finally from the living and the last rites are performed for them. Far off on the hill-tops the men lit their fires and the flames gleamed wildly across the dark, echoed by fires in the sky, the dancers at the ageless feast. The village was deserted. For us of the Old Way the dead passed, and for the New Way the winter beast who had eaten the sun licked his greedy chops insatiably, driving them to offer him food they could ill spare. It was a time of soothsaying and spell-working, and we huddled round a fire that threw out blue darts of flame to mark the passing of unchancy things.

I suppose I knew nearly as much as most of the women about the three feasts. The spring dancing was the time of the Maiden; Mistress of the Gates, Queen of Skills, they hailed her. This is she whom now I know to be the core of the faith, the vision of life-in-death, the ultimate unobtainable joy of poets, on whom to meditate is the beginning of wisdom, on whom to presume to think is the beginning of madness. The harvest, my mother's time, was the rejoicing of children, the casting off of age and sorrow and the return of joy; the Old One was honoured in winter, with what rites it is not meet for a man to know.

These three are so interwoven in symbol and action that mortal thought may not divide them: the three beasts, roe,

4

mare and sow; the three birds, cuckoo, swan and raven; the colours of silver, blue and red—these are each and all matters a lifetime's thinking cannot plumb. But I am running ahead of my trail.

In my fourth year my mother brought home another child. The mother had died in the bearing, and the father had thrust the babe aside. There were kinswomen who might have reared it, but he chose to offer it in payment for my mother's work; it might have been permissible to dedicate the little thing to the Hearth's service, but blatant trading in flesh and blood was another thing. My mother caught the little creature up and brought her away, leaving neither blessing nor curse behind.

She came in about dawn and woke the Maiden of the Year, a tall fair rather stupid girl—Lada was her name; a good mother of sons later, but then carrying her harvest and sluggish with it. Between them they roused the fire and heated milk, and when I crawled out to the warmth my mother was dipping a corner of cloth in the bowl and holding it to the thing on her arm. A strange thin wailing had roused me; it was cut short and followed by a contented snuffling.

'Is she gone, then?' asked Lada, white-faced.

'Aye, gone to her peace and her joy, my dear. That poor man —neither he nor that sister of his could be bothered with this little lass—ai-ai, but you're hungry; suck, then. You're there, son of my heart? Here's the newest baby you've ever seen. You'll think she's very ugly, but come and see her.'

She put back an edge of her cloak, and I gazed at the small scarlet face convulsed with greed.

'That's not a baby, it's a little pig!'

'It'll turn into a proper baby soon if we can feed it,' said my mother, dipping the cloth again.

'Why have we got to have it? Hasn't it got a mother of its own?'

'Her mother was too tired to stay here; she's gone away to the Apple Orchard, to walk on the soft grass and hear the birds singing and the silver bells ringing in the trees.'

'I don't want it here, I don't like it!'

'She belongs to the Mother as you do. You'll like her when she's big enough to play with you. Lada, you see how to do this? You take her while I make Drost's breakfast.'

5

Lada drew back; I suppose some fear of ill omen troubled her. My mother did not seem to notice; she unclasped her cloak, put it and the infant on Lada's lap, and busied herself preparing porridge for me. The baby wailed and Lada hurriedly dipped the cloth again.

When I looked up from my bowl, she was wholly absorbed in the little thing in her arms.

That was how Cardail came to us on an autumn day. Her father died next spring, caught in his net as he fished alone, but his ungracious offering throve in our house. By my sixth year she was a sturdy stumping child. It was in that year that my mother began to speak to me seriously of the world of men.

She told me I must go out to become a man among men and learn to do as they did, and my heart swelled with pride. She told me never to forget that the Mother was everywhere and in all things, and that nothing man could do could part me from her.

'And see, beloved, I serve the Mother and eat her food, and as far as I am part of her by that service, so far you and I can touch hands whenever you turn your thoughts to her.'

Another time she said, and I was troubled to see tears in her eyes :

'Remember, whatever befalls you, I am here and I love you, and the Mother is everywhere and loves you.'

I wanted to say I would never leave her, but I was burning to wear gold on my arms and carry spears.

She said to me :

'You have never seen women walk straight into the Hearthroom without preparing themselves in the outer court; even so, you cannot walk straight into manhood. Nobody can have anything in life without earning it.'

Yes, that was fair, I could understand that. But I had no idea how manhood was to be earned, and neither, fortunately, had she.

Late one evening by my bed, she said :

'Little son, out there men have found another idea of worship; they pray to gods and not to the Mother any more. Perhaps each of us can only grasp one corner of the hem of her cloak; she has not forbidden them to choose their corner. Do not be troubled, but learn their ways as well as ours; only do not let anyone drive her out of your mind, and remember that nothing can drive you out of hers.'

This and other things that she said I did not at all understand, though later I remembered them when the time was ripe. When she spoke so, I stuck out my chest (my six-year-old stomach rather), and said I would return to her a mighty warrior; but I was troubled to see that this troubled her.

Presently came the spring feast of my seventh year, and the little Cardail was carried in my mother's arms to the first part of the ceremonies. She soon grew drowsy, and my mother beckoned me to take her in. I put her down on her bed and she fell asleep instantly, the wreath of daisies crooked on her dark head, and I went back to the Hearth-room. But the women who stood on the threshold stopped me and said I was too old to watch the dancing now. Puzzled but proud, I went into the courtyard and fed the doves. They swooped and fluttered and cooed round my feet as the singing grew louder, and then the keen grey wind of spring, that marks the Maiden's passage, sprang up and brushed a wing of rain across the court.

The wind brought a sound of other singing. Wondering, I got upon the gatepost and looked down the hill.

The road runs down through the village, a scatter of houses facing all ways, and on to the Great Fort on its rock. Further round are the Old Stones and the graves of the Former People. Within the stones I saw a gathering of men. They hid the middle stone as they stood and faced it, their cloaks shaken by the wind and their spear-heads reddened by fleeting blinks of sun. A thin smoke went up from among them and the chanting rose and fell, now one high voice crying alone and again many answering with a deeper note.

Behind me I could hear the cymbals ring and the clappers beat faster, so I knew the dance had become swift and soon they would come out and go up the hillside. I stood and stared at the men from the wallhead. The dense crowd down there began to re-form into a long snake that wound among the stones. Here was something new: men, too, could dance.

7

The head of the snake turned outwards and began to twist among the houses, working uphill. As it drew nearer I saw it was led by a white-bearded man with something bright in his hands. Younger men dressed like him in white and green came after, and then a splendid figure in a blood-red cloak. They came ever closer until they halted only a few steps from me, and their chanting died out raggedly.

They were all staring at me and I returned their stare.

The white-beard stretched his hands and cried, with a tremor in his voice:

'The Twin! The Dark Twin comes to meet us!'

The men behind him took it up—

'The Twin! The Dark Twin!'

The ring and tinkle and stamp behind me grew louder and louder; at any moment they would come out and I should have to run and hide. The red-cloaked man came forward and brought Ailill with him. Ailill still had the fairest hair I have ever seen, fairer than gold; he had a red cloak too, today, and to my intenser envy a golden collar round his throat.

The tall man said:

'Ailill, call your brother.'

Ailill came a step nearer alone and looked up at me, and said:

'Come, Drost, my brother.'

I scrambled down from the wall.

'I am Drost—' I began, and was going to add, 'and nobody's brother,' but the tall man lifted me to his shoulder.

'You are Drost, my son's twin of the hour and my son,' he said.

I did not want to argue with him, but I knew he was wrong. Oddly enough, neither then nor later did I consider it possibly true.

'I am the son of no man, sir, but of the Middle Priestess,' I said as politely as I could.

The white-beard laughed harshly, but the red man only tightened his arm a little and answered me:

'Yes, you are the son of the Middle Priestess, but we have come to make you a man among men.'

Had not my mother said this would happen? I looked down at him and asked happily:

8

'Then are you going to give me my spears, and a gold collar and a cloak like Ailill's?'

'In the fullness of time, little son—but there are other things first.'

We passed down the middle of the long line which parted right and left for us, I riding on that tall shoulder and Ailill walking ahead, until we were back within the stones.

He turned his face up to me and said very quietly:

'Be steady now, and suffer what must be.'

Then in one swift movement he set me on the middle stone, and the white-bearded one came behind and stripped off my tunic so that I was left standing there mother-naked. I was ready to jump down and run, but the thought of my spears upheld me.

The next instant I heard a thin cry from Ailill, somewhere on my right; a red sleeve tightened across my face and there was a moment's agony in my body. The tall man held me hard but I leaped under his hands.

Next, and worse to bear, while he still held me, every man in that line passed by and each and every one put out his hand and touched me. The gentle touch of those hundred hands returned often and often to haunt me afterwards. I began to shiver and I longed to cry.

At last it was done; they brought me a robe of white wool and fastened a collar like Ailill's round my neck—little I cared by then—and as I still stood on the stone the red man cried:

'Melduin, my brother, behold our son's brother!'

A gaunt, pale, dark man came round the stone from behind Ailill. He too wore gold at his throat, but his cloak was the darkest green a skilful dyer can compass. In his arms he held another such cloak and put it round my shoulders saying:

'Brother of my brother's son, be welcome!'

For a moment his eyes looked into mine and I read in them sorrow and pity and perhaps a warning; certainly deep and abiding sorrow. But I was bitterly disappointed with only a green cloak, and I would not look again at him.

They lifted me down and Ailill came, biting back sobs, and took my hand, and we walked together at the head of the men uphill to the gate of the Fort.

Thus was I taken from my mother without farewell, and

thus I took my place as the brother of the King's son.

There was a feast, and I sat on sheepskins and drank strange sweet stuff from a great horn, but a sup or two from it made my head ache and my eyelids droop. Ailill sat on his father's right hand and I on his left. A harper sang high-sounding songs and they brought us rich food. But I was sore and weary, and wanted my mother, and did not at all understand that all that was gone for ever. At last I must have slept where I sat, resting my head against the King's left arm.

I woke bewildered in a cold dark place, and called out:

'Mother? Mother?'

At once there was light, cold dawnlight from an opened door. One of the younger men of the white robes stooped over me and struck me in the face, and as I began to whimper he hissed:

'That is forbidden to you! Forbidden! Do you understand?' and struck again.

As I drew back in terror he gripped my arm and dragged me out of the hut, shook me and set me on my feet.

'Now be silent! You are under training!'

In that moment of loss and confusion the pattern of the next years was set going on the loom.

Ailill and I were in a small stone fort with two priests and some servants. The slaves never spoke to us except to give an order:

'Eat!' 'Wash!' 'Sleep!'

If we spoke to them, or to each other when they were by, they led us to the priests to be beaten. If we spoke to the priests except in answer to a question, we were beaten. Children who have newly cut their second teeth are full of questions, but we learned to bite on our questions. We were wakened each day at the false dawn, taken outside the fort to wash at a stream, and then set to work. Winter and summer alike we went naked.

From daylight to noon we knelt before the priests, who required us to repeat after them the long verses in which the laws are recorded; at no time did they expound one word. We learned to repeat them without error or comprehension by the simple expedient of a beating for each fault.

At noon we and the priests ate. We were given bowls of meal made into a thin brose with water, and water besides to drink. The learning continued until sunset when we ate again, soup with perhaps a little meat in it, and a bowl of milk with a bannock of meal parted between us. We were taken to wash again, and thrust into the little hut to sleep. It was a low round building of piled stones, the chinks not over-carefully stuffed with moss so that the winds whistled fiercely over us. We crept in on our knees and lay on the bare earth, curled together for warmth. Sometimes one or both of us went without food at evening for lack of learning. Often we cried ourselves to sleep, but softly, head pressed to the other's shoulder, and sometimes we whispered, mouth to ear; we learned to do these things so quietly that the slaves lying against the hut door did not hear.

As the days grew longer our weariness increased so that the day seemed endless, and we stumbled where we had been word-perfect a little before. Of all the training I have known I still think this was the most wasteful, as well as cruel; but now I understand there was need for haste and we had to be driven beyond endurance. The priests must even have found it hard themselves; but if it was hard for them, it was ten times harder for us.

I cannot tell how soon I had the first dream—not for some time at least. But somewhere in that long summer (and our misery was increased by the wet cold weather) I fell as usual into a stunned sleep, but out of it came a dream. I dreamed that I was lying above the sands on the Long Strand, and that a little way off my mother was gathering herbs. The delight was too great; I woke with a start to find Ailill's head a dead weight on my arm; but curling against him I began to tell myself about the strand, and how my mother would go up and down collecting healing plants, laying them carefully in her veil to carry home.

Thereafter whenever I could hold my mind steady for a little before sleep overwhelmed me, I would think of her and of what she might have been doing that day, until I came to long for the night so as to be near her. At first I was sorely troubled because I could not call up her face; it came over me that I had forgotten her, and I was bitterly distressed. Then I remembered what she had told me about the Mother and that nobody could drive me away from her; I called up the image of the Hearth-ashes with all my strength, and stretched my hands to them. At once I saw her come with arms outstretched in answer and I saw her eyes smile, and heard her saying:

'Beloved, you have found your way! I am here, dear heart, I am here.'

With these words which had so often soothed me I fell into the deepest and most beautiful of sleeps.

I tried to tell Ailill, but he had no patience with me. He did not want to dream about Ginetha or about Ailill his father; he preferred to plan his revenge on these priests when he was King himself. He thought it strange that I did not share his plans. He told me many things I had not known: how rich his father was, and how he could have a man killed at the crook of a finger. He told me the gaunt man who had cloaked me was called Melduin, and he was the Dark Twin to Ailill the elder, as I was to him. Here we strayed into wishing we had our cloaks now, but Ailill never strayed far from his planning. He said Melduin had a lesser share in the rituals and the powers, as I would some day. He said the King and his Twin lived in the Great Fort all the time, and feasted and drank honey-wine. He said they could do as they liked with all men, except . . . and his voice faltered.

'Except—?' I mouthed.

'The priest, the one with the white beard—Talorc is his name; he is almost my father's equal in power; far stronger than Melduin. Lurgan, who is here, comes next to Talorc.'

At the name 'Talorc' I felt Ailill shake and grow cold. I wanted to know more; the extent of his powers, and whether he was a favourite of his gods or merely a clever man.

'Why? What does he do? Why are you shivering?'

He said, his mouth to my ear:

'Drost, if a king could be afraid, my father would be afraid of Talorc; even I am afraid of him!'

I was too young and slow and sleepy to pounce on this and treat it as it deserved; I only mumbled drowsily:

'Why?'

Ailill answered in a hoarse whisper:

'He can do anything—anything!'

Then the dreaded moonlight shone in on us as the men pulled open the door and dragged us out to be beaten for our talking.

'The dreaded moonlight!' That was the measure of our misery; the dear moonlight, the cool and peaceful moonlight, the gentle glance of the Maiden as she travels through the starry fields— all brought to this, a herald of blows. So too the sun, the golden chariot, the Mother riding in her glory and scattering wealth on her earth and her children, this had become only a summons back to wretchedness. We staggered wearily through the days and slept wearily through the nights, and at times it seemed we had forgotten happiness.

But all things pass. The year turned and the heather opened, and blew, and filled the air with richness and the thrumming of bees. The nights grew colder and the days shorter, the heather faded and the bracken across the stream flamed gold. One sunset we heard a far sound and looking upward saw a great wedge of birds flying south and talking as they flew. The Mother was calling home her flocks, the time of the Old One was coming.

The harvests were in, it was the time for wars. The days grew shorter and the nights colder and still we knelt repeating the endless verses. Always there was more to learn, and always some fragment of the earlier learning would slip out of place and bring down wrath and blows. But a time came when I could go blindly from end to end, chanting with as much understanding as a stream running over stones. It came more easily to me than to Ailill; I could lose myself in the words and let them run, but he could never forget to wonder how his voice sounded. If I dared to think about the sounds I was uttering, I was lost.

The first snows came, and with them came Talorc. We were kneeling as usual and facing our masters when we heard the slaves behind us making haste to unbar the gate. The priests sprang up and bowed themselves to the ground; someone came behind us and laid a cold hand on my neck. I saw out of the corner of my eye Ailill paler than ever. Then an icy voice spoke above me:

'Well?' said Talorc. 'Have you taught them anything yet?'

The slaves took me away to the hut and held me there till the sun was high; then I was fetched back and bidden to say what I knew. Talorc was in Lurgan's seat, and as I knelt facing him I could think of nothing but his pitiless eyes, cold and grey as a heron's, and his beak of a nose ready to strike. My mouth was full of dust; I could not remember one word of any law. I cried in my heart:

'Mother of all, help me!'

Then I heard a voice saying:

'Begin: This is the Law of the People . . .'

I drew a deep breath and launched out, and went on without sense or thought until I came to the phrases we had learnt last:

'This is the Law, and these are the laws, and they are binding at all times on all men, for so say the Smith, the Swordsman and the Singer.'

I stopped, for I knew no more to say, and let my eyes go back to Talorc. He was nodding his head, and the fingers of his right hand beat a dry drumming on his knee.

'It is well,' he said slowly; 'my sons, you have taught them well. What of your work, Mangan my son?'

The second priest was a thin colourless man who took little part in our training, leaving the blows and the abuse to Lurgan. We seldom heard his voice, even. Now he said quietly:

'The time is not yet, Most Reverend. It will come.'

'It will? Good. Meantime, we travel—fetch cloaks!'

He stood up suddenly; someone pulled me to my feet and cast a cloak round me, the first I had worn since we came there. Night was gathering as they led us out of the fort into a blaze of torches and a line of warriors, painted and armed. They began to move off downhill even as we came to them.

We went down a steep stony trail, stumbling over rocks that hurt our feet, dazed with torchlight and hunger. The men beside me took my arms and hurried me along. When we had walked all night as it seemed, we came suddenly into a level place and the men stood back from us.

We were in a ring of men, a great circle of torches outside them and in the midst a pile of tree-trunks with a dark something flung over it. Talorc took our hands and led us nearer, and when we were very close I recognised the dark thing. It was a crimson cloak.

Melduin came round the tree-trunk pile. He stooped to take Ailill's hands, and said:

'Son of my great brother, sorrowful is the meeting!'

Ailill cried out sharply:

14

'No! No!'

'Yes, little son; but like the warrior he was, and in the hour of victory.'

He straightened himself and lifted something from the pile; it shone coldly in the torchlight. He put it into Ailill's hands, and Ailill stood as if its touch had turned him to stone. It was a long grey sword.

Then I began to understand that we stood by the pyre of Ailill the elder. Before the knowledge had fully entered me, Melduin signed to the priests to draw me back. So I stood among the armed men and the torchbearers and watched as they robed Ailill and girt him with a swordbelt. A wounded man brought a great gold armlet and bent it to fit his thin arm; it must have come then and there from the arm of the dead, but I did not see it taken off for we were on the left side of the body. Talorc himself sheared off Ailill's hair with a golden knife, and gave it into his hands to throw on the pyre. And then Melduin brought a torch and led Ailill to set the logs alight.

As the flames took hold the men around me yelled and clashed their spears and shields, but they could not drown the piercing cry that rose from beyond the pyre. We began all to move in the great ring, the spearsmen stamping and clashing, and when we had made half a circle we came to the women. The Queen stood at their head, wailing and holding out her arms, and behind her I saw my mother standing like a stone, tearless, her eyes on the flames. My heart leaped to her but she did not stir as I passed.

The fire roared with the bitter scent of pines. We circled slowly and as we drew near the women again there came a terrible sign. All our eyes were on the pyre, and there, in the crimson heart of flame, something moved. An arm jerked up, beckoned or signalled, and fell back. The ring froze like hunters round a wounded boar.

Ailill cried shrilly:

'He isn't dead! He isn't properly dead!' and fought in Melduin's grasp. Ginetha flung herself down and beat on the earth. Talorc shouted in a great voice:

'A blessing! The King blesses his son and his people!'

He faced the pyre and launched into prayers.

15

I was shuddering from head to foot and could not stop. The stamping and circling began again, Talorc still praying, but as we came to the same place the ring was broken. Ginetha was writhing on her face towards the pyre, my mother and another woman on their knees trying to hold her back.

She began to shriek:

'He wants me! It was me he called! He wants me with him at last! You shan't take this from me!'

'Sister and daughter, be still; he is gone, he is at peace; it is not yet time for you to follow,' said my mother, and signed to Talorc to help her.

'You shall not have him any longer; he is mine, all mine!'

My mother drew back suddenly; Talorc cut short his prayer and stooped over the Queen in her place.

'Great Lady—'

She rolled on her back, laughing dreadfully, and struck upwards at his face.

As we began to move I had a last sight of her, borne away by my mother and other women into the darkness.

The fire outshone the torches. The men shouted, the remaining women wailed, the earth began to shake. Caught in the rhythm of our mourning the night went by.

Cold dawn found us circling the dead ashes. Two old slaves led me, stumbling with sleep, into a warm place where they bathed me with water from a great cauldron and laid me on a bed of bearskins, and brought me hot milk in a bowl, and I fell into a pit of sleep.

When I woke it was night again. The old men roused me and dressed me in a wool tunic and my green cloak. They combed my hair, and led me out of the sleeping-place directly into the torchlight of the feasting-hall. There sat the men along the walls, and on each side of the hearth was an empty seat.

Before one of them stood Melduin with Ailill beside him. Ailill's face was pinched and grey—I do not know if they had let him rest. When I came they set me on Melduin's left, and he took up a horn of honey-wine and called on all men to drink to the Great Dead. All round the hall they stood and lifted cup or horn, crying:

'To the Great Dead!'

Melduin set his lips to the horn, handed it to Ailill and to me so that we just tasted the heady sweetness of it, and bade Ailill pour the rest on the fire. The golden stuff flowed down, the flames leaped up in answer, and Melduin led us to the steps of the other chair. He left us there and went to his own place, and signed to the slaves to bring food.

He beckoned too for a harper, and at once a slender man stepped forward and knelt, setting his harp on his knee and tuning it with a touch, so ready was it for his song. Looking from one to another, with strange and sparkling eyes under dark brows, he poured out a song of delight and admiration. I had never heard such singing. He sang as if life held nothing greater than his desire to praise Ailill the elder, greatest of kings.

But Ailill the younger, spent with sorrow and shock, began to sway where he sat, so that Melduin beckoned the slaves to lead us out and give us food, and let us sleep again among the warm bearskins.

Three days the death-feast lasted, and three nights we sat in the hall and heard the singers. The dark man would begin and sing as a blackbird sings, without check or artifice; then he would beckon to another behind him who took up the song without a break, while the first made way for him. But it seemed as if he could have sung for ever, as if he only made way for these others because he felt their songs as urgent in their breasts as his own within him. Each night began with the ceremony of the cup and each ended, for us, when sleep overtook us.

On the fourth day we were roused before dawn, and the grey light found us travelling in the hills, back to the Little Fort.

It was hard to return to the long hours and the learning, hard indeed to remember all we had known before. But as our tongues stumbled over the words, our minds (mine at least) began to move again in the accustomed paths, and it cost us not many extra beatings to regain what we had won so hardly. All things became as they had been, and the meaningless chants ruled our days.

Yet not all things were the same; Ailill himself had changed. There was a new air about him, as if over his naked body he still wore the red cloak. The gold armlet was heavy, and his hand would droop, and then he would raise his wrist and look at it secretly, and hold his head higher. He stepped out, when we were away from the priests, as if he were the master and not the prisoner of learning. He had passed through the gate ahead of me many times before I took notice of it.

Lurgan the priest sharpened the barb for me. He began to check me and call me back, to rate me harder and single me out for greater shame, and even to hint that he might a little defer to Ailill over unimportant things. One evening he stood talking to Ailill while our wretched food cooled and my stomach ached for it; when at last they parted, Ailill crossed the cobbles with that new springing walk, turned his head as he sat down, and said to me, kindly, but as a man speaks to a boy:

'Sit then, Drost, and eat.'

'We were waiting for you,' said I crossly.

Instantly one of the slaves struck me sprawling to the ground. I scrambled up, watchful of another blow, and we ate in silence. Only later did I realise nobody had struck Ailill.

A night or two later I was held back from my sleep by Lurgan for some weary fault or other, and when at last I crept shivering into our den I brushed against Ailill, who was lying stretched over the floor. He turned as quick as a cat and pinched my thigh:

'That, for striking the King!'

I cowered from him. He had spoken full loud, and yet no blows followed. It was permitted to him.

Long after his breathing had changed and he was asleep, I lay stiffly against the wall and stared at the dim shapes of stones above me, and wished they would fall and cover me. I think the last of childhood died that night.

A few days later he pulled me to him in the old way:

'Come close, Drost; it's cold.'

We huddled together, but there was a wall of ice between us that no body-warmth could thaw. And that night I had a new dream.

At first all was well; I lay and watched my mother moving about the house and preparing to bake bread. I was well content, lying like a fish below a stone, hardly stirring so much as a thought, till suddenly the curtains parted and in walked Mangan. He was ill at ease, peering about him, but he walked to me and sat down without a word to my mother. His eyes grew big as moons; the room tilted and swung. He took hold of me and drew me into the dark. I tried to call out but my mouth was dry; the thin hard hands pulled at mine and the darkness took us both. I woke shaking, heavy with unshed tears and with a sense of loss no tears could ease. Dawn was breaking and I had lost my dream of home.

When the learning began that day, Mangan spoke first for once.

'Drost, you had a dream last night: tell your dream.'

I hesitated, fearing to feel again that overwhelming loss. I saw Lurgan's hand tighten on the rod; Ailill licked his lips nervously. Mangan signed to Lurgan to be still.

'Tell your dream,' he said again; 'look at me and tell it.'

I looked unwillingly; the eyes were big as moons. I began to stammer out the dream.

When I came to an end, Lurgan said:

'Is it well?'

'It is well; it was as he says.'

'Then is it for you to continue now?'

'A little—now and again. Leave him to me. Drost, sit still and think of anything, anything at all. Open your mind and let it go. Ailill shall speak his lesson first.'

Here was something new indeed. Any breathing-space was welcome; I sat on my heels and let my thoughts go free. They came up with a picture of morning on the grazings—it was spring, and larks were soaring over the Fort. I saw the cattle on the strand, and the birds, and the boys strung out hither and thither.

Mangan's voice was so soft that it hardly reached me:

'Who is the boy by the red rock?'

'I don't know his name; he's got a blue-and-white cloak.'

Mangan sighed and leaned back.

'It can be done, then,' he said to Lurgan. 'Leave it for now. It can be done.'

'Very well. Drost, enough of your daydreaming! Go on where Ailill stopped.'

But I had not heard Ailill, and I blundered and was beaten, and forgot to think about that curious little interlude.

A few days after that, when Ailill was reciting, I heard Mangan bid me fetch him a bowl of water. I got up obediently and filled a dipper from the water-jars in the shade, and turned to find Lurgan staring at me.

'And who gave you leave to move?'

'Let be!' whispered Mangan urgently; but the harm was done. I looked down at my hands and they were empty. I sat down suddenly and was sick at Lurgan's feet.

That night, shaken and disgusted, I strove with all I had to reach my mother. I could not see her, nor the room, nor even the house, for whenever I drew near, Mangan's face hid all else. I struggled in vain, for I had no knowledge to help me, and it was like beating against an invisible wall. So it was for many more nights from full moon to new, but with the new moon the Maiden brought me strength. I thrust against that face, it tore asunder, I saw it was no more than a painted cloth. The cloth split, the firelight shone through, and there sat my mother spinning, fixing her eyes on me with a look of grave enquiry. That was all, but it was enough; I fell into the dream and slept as I had not slept for weeks.

Presently Talorc came again to the Fort. Again he laid his cold hands on us and bade us recite our learning, but this time he slept the night in the Fort, in the room that Lurgan and Mangan usually shared.

Early next morning he sent for me.

He was sitting on a bed-place, his cloak thrown over his back, and Mangan stood against the wall fetching his breath in gasps like a spent runner. Talorc reached forward and drew me to him by one wrist.

'We'll let Mangan rest a while,' said he, 'and you will tell me what manner of dreams you dream.'

'I—I—Most Reverend, I dream a little, sometimes, about my mother's house, and about . . .'

In spite of myself my eyes turned to Mangan.

'So? About the Seer Mangan? And what does he do in your dreams?'

'He comes and takes me away,' I said.

'And quite right too; a mother's house is no place for a boy. What else does he dream of, Mangan?'

'Food, mostly,' said Mangan shakily, 'but every night he strives towards the House of the White Hearth.'

'Hm. And when he reaches it?'

'He watches her, in the inner room.'

'And she?'

'She spins, or prepares food—nothing else. He never dreams of the Hearth.'

'Hm,' said Talorc again—'Drost, there's no harm in thinking of the Hearth, while you know so little of the right ways of worship; I'll have to see you learn them later.' He stopped and frowned for a moment—I suppose this problem had never occurred to him till then. He dismissed it and went on: 'But to dream of the inner room, as if you were a baby—that's unmanly. That must stop. Think of the Hearth and what they do there, if you must—you'll soon grow out of all that.'

Now this I had never done; in all my dreams it had been the inner room I had sought. After my first effort to find my mother I did not dream of the holy place.

Mangan said: 'The door may be closed.'

Talorc made a small angry sound.

'Open it then! What is the good of you?'

Mangan straightened himself and looked at him.

'What indeed? That is something I should very much like to know. What is the good of me? What am I—now?'

Talorc said roughly:

'When you ask unseemly questions you are the fool you always were: at other times you are the Seer Mangan who answers questions but does not ask them. You are the Seer Mangan, and you will go through the gates to your reward and never return.'

'How do you know?' asked Mangan.

There was a stillness like the stillness between lightning and thunderclap. Talorc gathered himself, a cat about to spring: Mangan stood still, but I felt his strength ebbing, just as when Ailill or I had been goaded into answering Lurgan unwisely there was a moment when we knew we had gone too far, and we sank under it and waited. So Mangan sank. After the smallest of pauses he went on his knees and touched his head to Talorc's feet and said:

'It is as you say, Most Reverend: all shall be as you say.'

It was horrible to see him abased, but there was no victory in it for Talorc: almost it seemed Mangan had triumphed in his abasement.

The older man brushed it all aside.

'Show me what else.'

Mangan turned his eyes on me, wide and luminous like the eyes of a moth seeking a flame. Without using speech he said to me:

'Fetch water.'

I went out and towards the jars, and then I remembered that other time. I pretended to fill a bowl and carry it back, but I was only halfway across the court when he came to me in three long strides and knocked me flying. Mangan seldom beat us: that was Lurgan's part: but that time Mangan beat me till I cried for mercy.

'Now come here,' he said, throwing aside the rod and dragging me back to the jars. He forced up my chin and stared through my tears.

I struggled in vain. After a moment:

'Drink!' he said.

I stooped over the water; it was crawling with little vile beasts and flames licked over it.

'Drink!'

'No—no! No, don't make me!'

'Drink!'

I shuddered as I leaned over the foulness, his fingers biting into my neck. There was no help; I stooped till the flames licked my mouth. I pulled away from him and looked again. The jar was full to the top with sweet clear water.

I filled a dipper and drank, looking at him over the brim. His eyes turned to Talorc and I was sorry I had not pretended to be afraid still.

'Are you forgetting your cunning, Mangan? Shall I send you back to train again? Shall I?'

'The metal is strong,' said Mangan. 'The sword will be the sharper when it is forged.'

'Look to it then that the craftsmen do not sleep.'

Mangan sighed, an epitome of weariness.

'Temper the metal a little,' he said at last; 'are there not other things to be learnt?'

Talorc went away looking thoughtful.

One evening after we had eaten, Mangan called me to him. He was sitting against the sunny side of the wall in the last of sunset.

'Drost,' he began, 'do you understand what you are to be?'

I must have looked puzzled, for he went on:

'You know you're the Dark Twin, the other half of Ailill who will be the King when he's a man?'

'Oh, I know he's the King,' I said quickly, currying favour as boys will.

Mangan made an impatient gesture.

'He will be—no child can carry the weight, and few men alone. It needs two; you were born to be his helper. Ailill's a good boy, and he will be a good king if the gods will, but there are some things only you can do. You can dream for him. I am a dreamer; I know how much the likes of us can do.'

'Ailill says he doesn't want to dream,' I said rashly.

'You've talked about it? When?'

I had honestly forgotten we were forbidden to talk.

'Oh, long ago when we first came here.'

'Well, that's for the gods to decide, not for you or for him. But suppose—suppose you were men and at war; you can see it would be useful to send your mind walking through the enemy's camp, can't you?'

'Useful perhaps, but could you do it?' I said doubtfully, not meaning to argue but genuinely finding it unlikely.

His eyes flashed.

'Have I said it would be easy? It is not given to everyone—even when one has the gift, one must learn to use it. Take another case: a councillor plots against the King; you sit over against him and you see the shadows around him. Then you warn the King.'

'A true councillor wouldn't—'

'But there are false councillors—oh, in the name of the Long Hand, must you argue? The point is that I'm here to show you how to use your gifts; it will be more pleasant for you if you consent, so that I do not have to force you.'

'You mean like the maggots on the water?' said I, thinking that I had won that round.

He gave a harsh little laugh:

'Do not flatter yourself, you would have submitted in time.

23

Now heed me. The Most Reverend bids me teach you this trick
—that's what he calls it, a trick. You do not know how to use
what you have, and I am willing to show you. Be shown, and
do not fight me.'

'I don't like maggots,' I said.

'And I don't like bargains, young Drost! Behave yourself and
there won't be maggots. Come, sit by me and we'll try. See if
you can tell me what Ailill's doing.'

'He's probably wondering what you're saying to me.'

'Don't guess—we have no business with guesses. Let your
mind go free—try to feel him.'

Ailill rose up in my mind with a reddish tinge about him; I
saw him standing by the stream talking to one of the slaves.

'He's—he's angry about something,' I began. 'But I can't
really see him from here, can I?'

'Oh yes,' said Mangan easily. 'I can see him too.'

I was suddenly embarrassed, for I knew what Ailill was at.
The slaves had a secret store of honey hidden under the bank
of the burn and Ailill was trying to get some of it as the price
of his silence, because he was there alone.

'Greedy little beast!' said Mangan. 'It's natural for him to
want all he sees—and you boys must be always hungry. Enough
of that. Open your mind to me, Drost, and I'll show you better
things than this. Let it be between you and me; no need to tell
anyone else. Somebody's coming here soon, and I think you'll
like him, but don't tell him either. Out you go and wash, and
get to bed.'

When I ran out to the stream Ailill was wiping his mouth.

I did not like this talk. I could no more dream of home
because he came and spoilt it, and I was no longer free to think
my own thoughts in the little leisure that I had. Presently it
occurred to me to turn my mind to Mangan himself.

This led straight to trouble, for he came at once to the hut
and told me to mind my own business. Ailill wanted to know
what I had done wrong, and pinched and nipped me when I
would not tell him, but I kept silence.

Through time I began to work round the outskirts of
Mangan's mind, and I sensed such a well of misery there that I
could only draw back and pity. I looked at him with new eyes
and saw how his mouth drooped when he sat quietly, and how

24

his hands lay slack before him. Sometimes when he was alone I felt Talorc near him, hovering like a raven above a sick beast. He was in a trap, poor Mangan, and in spite of myself I wanted to help him.

One day he cried suddenly:

'Drost, no! Spare me your compassion!'

I had not known he would feel it.

'I—I'm sorry,' I stammered.

'Spare me that too. Use your gifts, don't waste them. Come, I'll show you something else.'

He filled a bowl of water and made me sit and take it on my knee.

'Now, look down and empty your mind, and tell me what happens next.'

I looked into the bowl and saw at first only the maker's finger-streaks on the bottom. But presently a thin stream of bubbles began to rise, thickening till all the water was clouded, and then the cloud opened and I saw, little and far off, the door of the Hearth-room with its curtains drawn across. A hand came and took the curtains to part them . . .

Lurgan said sharply:

'Ailill, you may be a king but you're also a fool!'

Mangan snatched the bowl off my lap and dashed it to pieces on the cobbles. As he stormed out his voice echoed in my reeling head—

'Fool indeed! You're as false a priest as Talorc!'

As my eyes cleared I looked to see how Lurgan had taken this, but he had not turned from Ailill. That was the first time I read Mangan without his help.

I tucked his words away carefully, for I could scarcely think about them without letting him know I had heard. Talorc and Lurgan, false priests? How? I did not know how a priest was made or trained. Presently I asked Mangan outright. He eyed me curiously.

'One chooses another,' he said. 'They have to be trained, much as you are being trained here but more slowly. Perhaps you were a priest when you were alive some other time and that's why you can use your mind as you do.'

'Oh, I see,' I said; 'my mother chooses the Maiden every year by her arts.'

'That sort of thing,' he said. I could feel his curiosity fairly eating at him.

'What arts does she use?'

He tried to ask it carelessly.

'I don't know,' I said, and that was true. 'There are signs—and something about picking tokens out of a cauldron, I think; at least I know they need the big cauldron for it.'

'Oh,' he said, disappointed, 'I suppose you wouldn't have known anyway. I only wondered how it differed from our own ceremonies.'

I had a sudden vision of the Hearth itself, the smooth grey ash at the centre of the room. It seemed to me that a sharp tongue of flame rippled over it as I watched.

'I don't know any ceremonies,' I said, and I cried to the Mother to bar the door for me. The fire vanished and in its place came a cool blankness. I looked up to the sky and saw across it a thin jerky line of flying birds.

'Look!' I cried; 'look! Cranes going south!'

'So they are,' said Mangan coldly; he knew I had sent for help.

But she had sent more than her birds. A cheerful voice beyond the walls cried out:

'Open to me, you there within!'

The slave nearest the gate ran to a peephole and back to Lurgan. From outside came a sweep of music as sweet as a blackbird at a waterfall.

'That's Felim,' said Mangan. 'Open the gate.'

'Open the gate, Terik,' said Lurgan in a lordly voice, and went forward himself.

As the bars were drawn and the thornbush pulled clear we saw the chief of the bards standing outside, his blue mantle caught under one arm and his harp in his hands.

'Have I to sing the bars down then?'

'Indeed, your Honour, I regret the delay, but I was not informed when I—we—should expect this visitation,' said Lurgan, at his most ceremonious.

Felim laughed, looking round the bare courtyard.

'Faith, I took my own time; and dear mother of mine, if I'd known better I might have taken longer! Have you a cushion at all for old bones?' (His hair was like a raven's wing and his back like a spear-shaft.)

Mangan folded his cloak on a stone and one of the slaves brought a cup of ale. Felim held it aloft, spoke a health of greeting, and drank it off with a wry look.

'High thinking here by the taste of things,' said he. 'And how are the noble boys?'

Lurgan pushed Ailill forward—

'Here is the King.'

'Oh yes, here's Thistledown; where's Charcoal?'

Ailill pushed out his lip and drew himself up as Lurgan cuffed me into sight.

'Hare's bones, the pair of them! The smiths will make their spears light and full light, I'm thinking. What d'ye feed them—chickweed?'

Lurgan said angrily:

'We do as the Council bids us.'

'Hm. Well, you'll have to fill them a little fuller, if they're to go to the Fort of the Girls and come out alive! Have you taught them to sing yet?'

Mangan said drily:

'They have learnt the rules of versification.'

Felim threw up his hands.

'Moon and stars preserve us from the rules of versification! Rhymes in "ng"; stanzas of two hands long with an internal echo on the unstressed beat: that stuff? Here, you poor little brats, listen to me! I made this as I came along: it'll teach you more about poetry than all the rules of versification put into a satiric curse with full assonance and triple cross-rhyme.'

He hitched his harp round, tuned it, and struck up a cantering air to accompany a ribald little ditty. The slaves dropped their work to clap out the beat. Lurgan looked ripe for murder.

So we came under the teaching of a third tutor.

Felim wrought havoc in our orderly lives. He began with a burning interest in food, both ours and his own. Morning noon and night he would crouch by the cooking fire, tasting and criticising, adding a dash of flavour or a pinch of a herb. We ate three times a day, and very differently from before his coming. The slaves caught the inspiration and turned out stews fit for a feast-day. Lurgan might glower, but Mangan began to look less haggard and, as for us, we grew like beanstalks.

That was only part of it: Felim insisted on attending our

27

recitation of the laws, and threw us out constantly by demands to know what they meant. As we dared not consider what we were saying lest we should lose our thread, we never had the slightest idea of the meaning; but here he was, interrupting, prompting, bullying us to think.

'Yes, I dare say it may not mean much to you; the gibberish of it's enough to put anyone off! But what do you think it might mean, put into decent talk? What's the poor benighted soul trying to say? Come away now; how would you explain it to a stranger? Ach, moon and stars defend us, the cuckoo's got your wits! Say it again slowly.'

Thus would he drag meanings out of us until at last we began to see some sense in most of our learning, and even to turn doubtful points over in our own minds before we were asked.

Beside the laws about warfare, theft, cattle-lifting and so on, there were all those about the making of tools and the practice of crafts, the payments of dues to the priests for leave to do certain things, and the laws of versification which Felim had mocked so startlingly on his first arrival. He was, after all, the chief practitioner of his craft, and if he could mock his own laws and live, what justice was there in the long prohibition that opened these laws? Nor did he only scoff and question: he went further and forced us to try our hands at his own art.

'Now then,' he said, squatting between us, 'let's say you're bidden to a feast, and like a decent man you'll take a song with you in case you're called upon to share the entertainment. What sort of a song would you take?'

'A song of praise for the host?' Ailill suggested.

'Well—but what if twenty better are sung before your turn comes? Or supposing the meat's as tough as a storm-cloak and the smoke's been in the kettles? He might take it amiss. Drost?'

'A funny song?' I asked despairingly; it was all very well for Ailill, who had sat within earshot of a hundred feasts.

'Safe enough; or there are the old tales—but they're best learnt off and sung in the proper manner. That's for a bard, not a casual guest at a party. A funny song, then—how would you make one?'

I had been dreading that.

'I don't know,' I said, and waited for the blow.

'The best jokes are old jokes,' said Felim, 'for then the

stupidest man at the table knows when to laugh. And an indifferent song sung with a long face is funnier than a jest of jests told by a giggler. But no, it's not an easy form. Probably the simplest for you is a formal lament. Plenty of rules. You mightn't think it, but I've known them go down best of all in the midst of mirth. Ailill, let's hear you make a lament.'

Ailill looked blankly at him.

'What for?'

'Anything—the year that's away, the good things gone, ill things to come. Sing it to "Green Glen o' mine", or "Love's Weeping", and make it with a catch at the end of the line to twitch their heart-strings: you know:

"Heroes they were, and like heroes they've gone." '

He sang the last line of the famous old lay.

Ailill frowned and scuffled his feet in the dust, and then looked up and launched into a slow sad song. The tune owed many debts and slipped from one to another at need; there were dead kings and drowned queens and parted sweethearts, and if half the lines were well known, even to me, and the others axed out to size, it was still a remarkable effort. He went on and on till Felim held up his hand laughing—

'Enough, enough! You'll have me in tears yet! Oh, you'll get the knack of it soon enough. Mind you, there were crimes enough there . . . but never heed, this once. Drost, can you string words?'

I had been absorbed in listening to Ailill's clear piping voice and in wondering how he could bring lines together so fast. I jumped and blushed.

'Oh no, no, I could never do it!'

'No song at all? Come, will you not try?'

I did try. I tried till my head buzzed with tags of Ailill's verses and with one other that burned its way into my thoughts and hid all else. Felim waited.

Ailill said:

'Poor Drost, he really can't! Let him off, my lord, and I'll go on, shall I?'

29

'You?' said Felim with blistering scorn. 'You—you song-smith! I know your kind—you'll sit capping rhymes with your court bards, of whom the Mother grant I am not one! Drost might have something different for us. Come away, Drost, I can see it's there.'

Under Ailill's scornful stare I stammered out my mastering phrase—

'Creaking of cranes
In a green sky.'

Felim sat back and dropped his hands on his knees.

'Holy Mother of mine! The year that's away and the good things gone. "Creaking of cranes, In a green sky"—what more do you want?'

Ailill said:

'That's not a song!'

'No,' said Felim; 'it's a poem.'

But Felim could never stay long in one place. We woke to find him gone one frosty morning, and back we went to the old grind and two ill-cooked meals. He turned up again at dusk some weeks later in a flurry of early snow, made the slaves build a big fire, and kept us up till the stars were bright with tales of his travels. The chief of his news was that the harvest was keeping badly, for the sheaves had gone wet into the barns and the grain was blackening already.

Lurgan groaned.

'Alas for the people who anger the gods!'

'A bad harvest is a punishment indeed, but we shall see what the spring can do for us,' said Felim. 'If the year turns early and the fishing is good we shall not suffer too much. It might be that certain ceremonies have been neglected of late . . .'

'Such as—?'

'You know best yourself what is done and what is not done,' said Felim.

'The Smith, the Swordsman and the Singer are all duly honoured,' said Lurgan stiffly.

'And which of them makes the grass to grow?' Felim asked with wide-eyed innocence.

Lurgan shot an angry glance towards us and would not answer.

There were several days of light snow showers and then the northern sky grew black and a bitter wind sprang up. The slaves brought in extra fuel and bedded our two cows deep with heather and bracken. Felim left as suddenly as he had come, and before dusk it began to snow in earnest.

It was the start of a long hard winter. Mangan stood it badly, growing more and more gaunt, and coughing as if the smoke of the fire troubled him. Even Lurgan made no bones about letting us sit round the fire; we huddled together, priests, slaves and boys, in the little ring of warmth, and at night we all slept in the byre where the cows kept the air warm enough to breathe. The courtyard was banked deep with a drift the height of the wall on the south, and a path to the gate was kept open by our tread.

Presently there was no need to go out for water; the stream was silent and they filled the kettles from the drift. Mangan lay all day under his cloak in the byre while Lurgan kept us and himself warm with the rod.

At last the snow ceased to fall and the country lay still under its burden for half a moon. Then came two days of sharp thin sunlight, and the first trickle sounded under the ice of the stream. On the third day there was a pounding at the gate. When it was unbarred we saw Felim, rolled in furs, at the head of a column of men.

They were loaded up with firewood, with blankets, venison, cheese, dried fish, all we could desire. They marched in, grounded their loads, trampled a clearing and lit a tremendous fire.

True, when they left next morning they had eaten nearly half their loads, but we were all the better for it.

'Thanks be to the gods who sent you in time,' said Lurgan, standing in the byre doorway after he and Felim had helped Mangan swallow some broth.

'Thank the right one, then,' said Felim shortly. 'Do you not know the frost broke on the first day of the Maiden? We could start no sooner though the loads were stacked ready. She dipped her hands in the river and away went the foster-mother of the cold; you must know that much!'

Lurgan said angrily :

'The Maiden? You mean the wife of the Singer!'

'I mean the one whose day it was,' said Felim. 'And a healer ought to be called to Mangan.'

'The Most Reverend has always made Mangan his own concern,' said Lurgan.

Sure enough Talorc turned up soon after that. He took no notice of us, but went into the byre for a long time, and when he came out Mangan followed him like a sleep-walker. I heard Felim draw a sharp breath. There were purply shadows round Mangan like the underside of storm-clouds; I longed to help him, but did not know what to do, and if I had known I should not have dared.

'There,' said Talorc, rubbing his hands; 'he'll pull himself together soon.'

He warmed himself at the courtyard fire (for it was still bitter), spoke a little with Lurgan, and was gone.

Felim watched him down the hill before he got out a little flagon and warmed a cupful of honey-wine.

'Drink up, Mangan; a sup of that's worth a power of preaching.'

Up to a point Mangan did seem better, but only so far. He made efforts to come into the court and even to take a share in teaching us, but his hands looked too heavy for his arms, and when he walked he seemed to work out anew how to set down his feet. When he sat it was as if I were the very earth on which his bones pressed.

After a week Lurgan ordered us back to sleep in the hut, though he and Mangan kept to the byre and Felim had his little chamber in the wall with a fire at its end. As soon as we lay down Ailill pulled my head towards his—

'Is he going to die?'

'I don't know; he looks dreadful.'

'He might be going to die; I wish I knew how to curse them, I'd make them all die! Do you suppose your mother has cursed him?'

32

I was scandalised.

'My mother doesn't curse people!'

'Don't make so much noise—and don't be stupid, of course she does. Everyone knows that; priests do, so why not priestesses? And my mother says she has power, so I know she can if she likes. Perhaps she doesn't care what they are doing to you. Anyway, I think he is dying. I wish Talorc was!'

'Oh, don't go on about people dying,' I said, turning away.

'You listen when I want to talk to you! I'll say what I like, and do what I like too. I know a trick they do to young slaves who give trouble; Aung told me one day by the stream. Would you like to be shown?'

'Was that the day you got the honey?' said I, too angry to be careful. The next instant he was at my throat like a marten, nipping and scrabbling. Aung himself flung the door open and hauled us over to Lurgan, who thrashed us both for once. He paid no heed to Ailill's angry sobs that I had defied him, and indeed seemed to be thinking of something else. I caught a glimpse of Mangan under his elbow, lying flat in the ferns with his cloak barely stirred by his breathing.

Back in the cell, well warmed and with a bundle of firewood cramping the space between us, I began to wonder if Mangan was indeed dying.

Ailill had fallen asleep at once, as so often he did after a scene. I turned my mind to the byre and had a shock that almost made me cry out. I saw Mangan very clearly, lying there; his head was on my mother's knees and her hands soothing him. His eyelids flickered and drooped and he slept; she did not look towards me, and I was thankful, for I felt I had stolen upon a mystery.

Next day he did not appear. I was with Felim most of the time, and went to my bed peaceful and content. As soon as I had curled myself down I began to think over the night before. It was so unexpected, Mangan and my mother—I puzzled over it for some time before I turned my thoughts to him again. This time he was alone.

I very soon wished myself away. I was no longer watching Mangan; I was Mangan. I was a younger Mangan, cold and alone and in deadly fear, a Mangan whose heart had been taken out of his body and who had nothing left to hold to. He—I—

33

waited in the dark, and out of the dark came a great white animal, the shape of a weasel but the size of a bull. It came slowly and purposefully and crouched by the bed; it lowered its head to the waiting body and began to feed, while the soul that was tied to that body suffered with it. It looked up, the weasel's eyes into the soul's eye, and I saw the weasel had the face of Talorc.

I screamed and arched myself away, waking in a cold sweat with my mouth dry and my shoulders braced against the stones. I lay shuddering as fear of the beast was replaced by fear of questioning and punishment, but nobody came and I realised I had not cried aloud. But I had no longer any desire to know more about the Seer Mangan.

The spring came late that year, and we were hungry before it came. Felim came and went, Mangan grew a little stronger as the days grew warmer, and at last the summer birds began to pass overhead and there were a few plants the slaves could add to our meagre food. There was hunger in the villages too, as Felim told us; they had abundance of one thing only and that was dead meat from cattle that had died of starvation.

'That's what comes of arrogance,' said Felim; 'too many cattle kept, not enough killed and dried, and where are you? Chewing lean beef till your jaws ache, and losing breeding cows right and left.'

'I'm not a herdsman,' said Lurgan; 'do not blame me for the mistakes of ignorant peasants.'

'Ho! And who should teach the ignorant? Answer me that!'

'Those whose work it is; a priest's work is to see proper respect given to the gods, and due reward paid for all their blessings. If the people had not angered the gods they would have been blessed. Drost, let me hear the Law of Offerings.'

It was a tricky brute full of near-repetitions, and Lurgan understandably attached great weight to it. I was still struggling when Aung came and awaited leave to speak.

'I shall flog you in a moment to appease the gods you have insulted,' said Lurgan coldly to me, and to Aung, 'Well?'

'Your Reverence, there are merchants outside who say they

34

have a foreign priest with them, and would your Reverence offer him hospitality for it's not fit for the likes of him down at the huts by the harbour?'

Lurgan's eyebrows rose.

'Why should they think this a fit place to receive a stranger priest? Why not take him to the Temple?'

'Seemingly they've heard your Reverence is here—and seeing you're next to the Most Reverend, and it's so far to the Temple . . .'

Lurgan glowed inwardly.

'We-ell,' he said, trying to frown; 'we-ell, what say you, Lord of Songs?'

'Oh, let's have company by all means!' said Felim, jumping to his feet and making for the gate.

Ailill and I craned our necks for a sight of the strangers, but Lurgan ordered us into the hut. We went as slowly as we dared, looking backwards, but caught only a glimpse of bright cloaks. We heard Felim cracking jokes and gossiping, a rumble of talk, the gurgle of ale being poured, and then some merchants speaking their thanks and Lurgan intoning a blessing.

I wondered how anyone could value a blessing that was reeled out like a trickle of muddy water; more and more in those days I found myself thinking that all priesthood was only a trick, an art of standing and moving, a tone of voice. These thoughts were too old for a boy, no doubt, but my childhood was dead.

Soon afterwards they barred the gate again and we heard Lurgan order food to be made ready. Aung plucked us out, combed our hair and threw old cloaks round us.

'Come to the fire,' he said, 'and be still.'

Lurgan beckoned us to kneel behind him and Mangan.

'You will not understand what you hear,' he said, 'but it is good that you should hear it.'

Presently Felim came from his room and brought the strange priest with him. He was strange, too, in our eyes, a short man and plump with a smooth face and thickly-curling black hair, blacker even than mine. His eyes were so dark that they too looked black, and they darted everywhither. He had on a long white garment and a thick cloak fastened on his shoulder with a knot. The cloak was bleached in patches with sea water, but

35

you could see it had once been the colour of wild violets, though now it was mostly like violets that have faded in the sun.

He came to the hearth stretching his right hand over the smoke and saying something in an unknown tongue that sounded like an invocation; then he bowed, touching his breast, and said:

'Demetroos,'—or some such name, a queer sound to me.

Felim said, pointing:

'Lurgan—Mangan—Felim.'

The stranger bowed again as Lurgan made a place for him to sit between them. This brought him close to me and I could smell the scent of him, a smell of oil and spices, odd but pleasant. He did not look at us boys after one searching glance.

Aung brought a little of our dwindling store of ale; it seemed the stranger would refuse it, but Felim said quickly:

'Barley—it is made from barley, from grain.'

There was another quick glance from those dark eyes and he took the cup and dipped his fingers in it, sprinkling a little on the ground and murmuring something as he did so. Then he raised the cup and drank with the others.

'I have come—' he said carefully, in a rich full voice, 'I have come from my own land, seeking the—the Door of Knowledge.'

'Gate,' said Mangan; 'forgive me, brother and master, but the word is gate. Door is into a room; gate is into a—' he gestured, 'into a wider place.'

'So? I thank you; gate. I learnt only from sailors, you understand? Now, can you help me to find this gate?'

'By what road have you come?' asked Lurgan. It struck me as a pretty stupid question; we all knew he had come by ship to the harbour up the coast.

'I have come by a road marked with white stones.'

'Was the road rough to your feet?'

'I was given sandals.'

'How were the sandals made?'

'From trees that grow by water.'

'How did you walk in them?'

'Backwards, then forwards; the way was long.'

36

'Aye,' said Mangan softly; 'long is the way. How found you the way, you who walked backwards?'

'By the voice of music.'

'How will you know the gate when you find it?'

'By the voice of music.'

'What is inside the gate?'

'Music's self and a well of water.'

Mangan's sigh came from the heart—

'Aye, music's self, and the end of thirst.'

Lurgan said:

'Why seek you this gate so far from home?'

'Because the way is barred to me; with blood it is barred to me.'

'Then why should you find it open to you here?'

'Somewhere,' said Demetroos with a kind of gentle desperation, 'somewhere there is a gate which is not barred.'

Felim said:

'Music is my business. Can you play such toys as this, brother?'

He unslung his harp and passed it to Mangan for the stranger to take and turn it in his hands, considering. He plucked a string, bent his head, tuned the harp and played a few notes of an air that sang to me.

Felim nodded, took back his harp and struck up 'Heroes they were'. The other man almost snatched it from him and played an answering phrase, and they went at it turn about as fast as they could hand the harp between them, while Mangan drew back out of their way. Some of Felim's tunes I knew, others I had never heard, and many I had not heard since I left home: 'The Corn is Fair', 'The Maiden's Welcome', even the baby-song 'Cradle by the Hearth', which I had forgotten altogether. Sometimes the stranger answered with another part of the same tune, sometimes he played something totally different, but their playing had an air of dialogue; at last they stood up together, and as Felim struck the strings the stranger lifted his hands to the noonday sun and sang something that was surely an invocation. Lurgan and Mangan rose with him and we too scrambled to our feet.

The prayer ended with great rolling phrases that I could almost believe I knew, so full they were of beauty; he was blessing the sun and the Rider in the Sun for help in getting here, praying for strength to finish his quest, and drawing strength from the light.

He wrapped his mantle round him as he sat down again, saying to Lurgan:

'You will correct my blunders in your speech?'

'Our speech is honoured in your mouth,' said Lurgan. 'Will you teach us the knowledge of the holy ones of your land?'

He laughed, showing strong white teeth—

'Ah, I must live long to do that!'

Into my mind came a curious picture, almost a memory. I saw a dark blue veil held aside, and beyond it a little mound of earth on which stood a tall pitcher with some ripe ears of corn. Ailill pinched my thigh, just as Mangan was turning to look at me. That was a trick of his lately; he liked to make me start and perhaps earn a beating. Under Mangan's glance he flushed a little and drew away from me.

Mangan said to Lurgan, formally:

'Elder Brother, ought we not to explain why we are here, and who these children are?'

Lurgan, who liked to hear his title, accorded him a little bow.

'But certainly, Seer Mangan, we owe it to our guest. The boys you see here, Most Honourable, are royal children who are receiving training in our laws before they go to the boys' training with others of their age. This fair one is to be our king and this is his Dark Twin; it is our custom that two should carry the kingship, for it is too great to be housed in one body.'

Demetroos turned; his bright glance ran over us and back to Felim.

'I see,' he said. 'This I have heard also—there are those near my land who keep this custom. One goes to war—so?'

'Maybe so; as the gods choose. It is, of course, always possible that the gods will withdraw their favour and give their gifts elsewhere if these two do not please them.'

'Of course,' said Demetroos. A little smile played round his mouth.

I saw Ailill's eyes flash angrily, but Lurgan was not looking at him.

Demetroos remained with us, and we grew accustomed to his watching and listening to our lessons, though I hated to be

38

beaten when he was there. Lurgan knew it well and missed no chance. But most of the time Felim and Demetroos sat together in the sun under the wall, talking or playing snatches of airs and singing softly.

And now I have missed something. That first night, as we were going to the hut, Mangan called me into the dark recess of the gate and set his hands on my shoulders.

'Now, what did you see?'

I had forgotten about the veil and the corn, and it did not seem that I could speak of them.

'Oh, do use your mind, child! I don't want to force it out; when we sat by the hearth and he said it would need a lifetime to tell of his gods—what did you see then?'

'I saw a curtain—a dark blue curtain . . .'

'Wait; don't talk, just look at it,' said Mangan more patiently. 'Yes, now I see; underground, cold and dark, and all those others waiting and fasting—yes, I see. I wonder what his name means? And yet he prayed to the Swordsman, to the Long Hand . . . Can it be that both are together in his country? Why come here, when the Well must be at his very door?'

'He did say something about blood—about blood barring the way,' I said slowly. I could see it, a great red lake spreading into shadowy distances, and I shivered a little between weariness and the sight of that lake.

'Maybe—or maybe he is fated to travel the world to find what lies at his door,' said Mangan. 'You did well, Drost; were you watching for it, or did it come of itself?'

'It came,' I said.

'And you felt neither sickness nor cold after?'

'Oh no, nothing like that; I wasn't trying to see,' I said incautiously.

'Ah! So at other times you have tried? What have you been trying to see?'

'Nothing—nothing,' I stammered, feeling the ground move under my feet.

'You are not yet trained; it will burn out if you use it unwisely. Many a child has it and loses it as he turns towards manhood. Probably you ought to have been sent for training—but may the holy ones grant I never send anyone to that! It is enough to be the Dark Twin without that as well. Have a care;

if you see something that is too much for you, come to me for help. Remember that.'

'Yes, Reverence,' said I, biting back a yawn.

'Oh, go and sleep!' said Mangan with weary kindness, and I went thankfully.

Several times now there had been talk of other training in store for us; I whispered to Ailill to ask what it might be. But he knew no more than I did, except that boys vanished overnight from the villages and young warriors appeared as suddenly, resplendent in deerskins and furs. He said half-angrily:

'You must know, even you, that nobody ever sees a boy in the villages. I never have.'

'You see them on the Long Strand with the cattle.'

'Oh, that! Nobody goes there but women and babies.'

'Anyway,' I said, refusing this opening for a quarrel, 'I don't want to be trained all over again.'

'Nor I, but this isn't making us into warriors, and I want my sword back; when I have that, I'll slit these priests up and tear out their guts and . . .'

But unfortunately he had forgotten to keep his voice down, and the moonlight streamed in on us over Aung's shoulder.

A little after this Talorc came again, at the head of a dozen armed men. We were there when he greeted Demetroos with friendly words, but there were dark colours playing round him and I knew he was uneasy. Talorc was uneasy and Demetroos was somehow disappointed. I did not know why.

At supper, when they were all eating together and we a little way off, Talorc asked suddenly:

'What is it you really seek, brother and master?'

Felim's eyes turned to him as a man's to a boy who has spoken foolishly, but Demetroos answered at once with a long rolling phrase in his own tongue, pulled up and translated laboriously, helping himself out with his hands.

'First, I seek a holy house—the house of him who rides in the sun, his holy house here in the north; Apulu Huperboru' (and may he forgive me if I have mangled that holy name in my memory!); 'I had hoped that you in your wisdom might show me the way, for I think it is near.'

'Indeed!' Talorc's white eyebrows flew up under his thatch

of hair; he looked a bigger man than ever. 'Indeed we have such a house; we call him the Swordsman, the Long Hand.' He bowed towards the sunset. 'He rests his horses yonder in the courts of the sea and sits all night at the ageless feast. Our temple is at the river-mouth; there are few greater. You must visit it, it may be you will find there your desire.'

'May he grant it!' said Demetroos. 'But the house—the house is a sign, not the end of the search. There is a—a gate, and by it a well of water. That is my desire.'

'Oh,' said Talorc scornfully, 'I know that well. It is of no account now; the women have muddied the waters.'

He shot a venomous glance at me, and though I did not understand I felt a sting of anger.

He went on:

'We go tomorrow to the river-mouth, and if it please you to come with us, you will be very welcome at the Temple.'

Mangan's voice came out of a dream—

'The Well is at the end of the world, and the end is not far. The signs are by three and five and seven, and by one. Let him who can see it drink of it. There is no other.'

The voice drooped under its own weight and failed. Felim sprang up and got his arms round Mangan and lowered him backwards.

A whisper slurred on—

'The corn—in the basket—the God—nigh . . .'

His head fell against Felim's breast.

Demetroos was up, trembling.

'What has he said? What has he said?'

Felim said curtly:

'Water, Drost! How do I know what he said, brother? If he lives he will tell you himself.'

Talorc said to Demetroos:

'Forgive the weakness. This young man has gifts at times, but when the God recalls his gifts there is only foolishness. The vessel is flawed—forgive him.'

I came up with the bowl of water and stood by while Felim sprinkled Mangan's face. There rose before me the picture of the little well under the hazels where my mother and Cardail drew their water. A little clear well in a low bank; whenever my mother went to it she took crumbs for the fish that lived in

41

the pool. I looked through it to Mangan's white face and Felim's bowed back and wondered how our little well could so trouble anyone.

Felim held the bowl to Mangan's lips, and I could see he was in the body again and trying to drink.

Demetroos said, as if Talorc had not spoken:

'But what has he said? Will nobody tell me what he has said?'

I spoke without thinking whether I might.

'I think he said "When the corn is in the basket, the God is near." '

Talorc's hand in my face sent me flying.

'Lurgan, take him away! A meaningless babble, brother, I assure you. As for this insolent brat, he shall pay—'

'No, let him be; this is a word of power for me. Leave the child, I beg of you! Felim, keep him here, and let me help you.'

Demetroos swept Talorc aside, knelt by Felim, and put his hands on Mangan's forehead. Felim threw out a hand to check Lurgan, who was bearing down on me as I lay. Past him I could see Demetroos' hands moving gently over the thin dry hair, and I heard him murmur in his own language. Mangan turned on his side and seemed to fall asleep.

'And now—!' said Talorc to me.

I felt his anger like the heat of iron on an anvil, a hand's breadth from me, and I knelt and waited. But instead Demetroos came and bent over me and lifted me up.

'And you heard, young one? Did you—is it possible that you also saw?'

I had to swallow once or twice before I could speak, for I was afraid. Then I managed to say:

'I saw only the well by our house, Most Honourable.'

'Drost!' said Talorc in a terrible voice.

'Let him be if you please, master and brother,' said Demetroos. 'Where is your house, young one?'

'The—the Hearth-house above the river; the Well is where they draw water to clean the Hearth; my lord Felim knows, I expect. I don't know why I thought of it, it's only a little well under bushes.'

'Yes, I know,' said Felim. 'I'll show you tomorrow, brother. Most Reverend, is it necessary . . . ?'

'Yes,' said Talorc. His hand closed on my shoulder and he pulled me away from the others.

When he had finished I thought I must die. I lay where I fell until Aung came in the dusk and carried me to the stream, and then thrust me into the hut where Ailill lay fretting with curiosity. Aung sat against the open door, but I had no desire to speak, and little power. I lay on one side of the hut and at the other Ailill fidgeted, longing to question me. Ailill could never content himself with thinking of something, but must talk it out and know why people were angry, and what I had done. He knew, and I knew, such a beating was not earned by merely breaking silence.

I lay in the dark and prayed to the Mother to help me and to have Mangan in her care. As I fell asleep I thought I saw the flicker of a dark robe, the edge, as it might be, of my mother's cloak.

Next day I could hardly move until Aung and Terik worked on me; afterwards they brought us cloaks and we set out with the men for the village. It was well for me that Mangan could not go fast. He walked with a staff in one hand and the other arm over Terik's shoulder, and Ailill and I followed him. Before us walked Talorc and Demetroos and Felim, and we caught snatches of their talk of foreign places and customs, talk I should have been glad to hear.

We walked through the day, with no more than a sup of water as we forded a stream, until late afternoon, when we came through the high grazings and saw the river, and the village, and the Great Fort. Between them and us lay the Hearth-house, white and welcoming under its curl of smoke. Our road ran past its door.

The priests shook out their cloaks and quickened their pace. As we passed the white walls the door-curtain was drawn back and my mother came out.

I had not seen her in the flesh since the death-fire. She was tall and beautiful as I remembered her, but her face was very pale as she stood there looking at us. We halted in our tracks as if there had been an order.

My first thought was that she had come out to see me, and I was afraid she would know I was sore and would guess the reason. But in the next breath I knew she had not seen me. She looked at Mangan only, her eyes the blue of the sea before storm, and the rest of us stood and listened to our own breathing.

At last, and it was long that we stood, she lifted her arms in the most beautiful gesture I have seen in woman and held them out to him, the blue robe falling from the white. He dropped his hands, swayed a moment, and stumbled to her; his head drooped to her shoulder; I thought he wept. The compassion of the Mother flowed over him; she turned her body between him and us and the curtain fell behind them.

Talorc broke the silence with a hiss.

'Chaaa! This is too much—you saw, Lurgan? You saw the witchcraft at work? Break down the door and pull him out—Aung! Terik!'

'No,' said Felim quietly.

'Did you hear, Lurgan? On your obedience!'

'No,' said Felim.

'First the son, then the mother! How dare they—how dare she defy me? If she doesn't come to her senses by nightfall I'll have the house burnt round her—we'll see who's master here!'

'And who is mistress,' said Felim. 'Come away, my masters—we are weary travellers and we have a guest. Come, Most Reverend, lead your seeker to the Temple. That is of more importance than the deeds of women.'

He began to walk on down the road, saying as he went:

'What are women to you, Most Reverend? Have you not told us many times that they are all beneath your contempt? Here's Demetroos near the end of his quest, longing to worship in your holy place; what if Mangan rests by the way? You know he'll follow you in the end. Come, let us enter the village with singing.'

He swung round his harp and struck up, and Talorc and Lurgan and all of us followed like sheep behind a shepherd. Only Demetroos looked back, as if to remember the place.

By the time we reached the Great Fort half the men of the People were with us. The gathering did something to comfort Talorc. He could always warm himself at the fires of power

even when, as now, another had kindled them. When we came
to the gates he was stepping out almost jauntily.

We swung in through the entrance to the twilight of the
inner courts, and slaves waited to meet us. One of the old men
I remembered from the funeral led me away to a little room,
where he and a younger man bathed me and dressed me and
wrapped my green cloak round me—even to feel its soft
warmth was good. As they finished I heard Ailill cry out:

'Clumsy fool!'

There was the sound of a smacking blow; the two slaves
looked at each other over my head.

For no reason I understood, I wanted to pretend I had not
heard. I asked at random:

'Where's the other one who was kind to me last time?'

'Dead, little lord,' said the old man gently, 'there are many
dead this season.'

'May it be well with him,' said I, and my training took hold,
and I kept silence until they led me into the feasting-hall.

The men stood all round, crowding the great room. Though
the night was warm the fire was heaped high to give light.
Melduin in his green cloak sat in his place opposite the empty
chair. They led me to the left of it and after a moment Ailill
was brought to the right hand. Then there was a long pause
before at last Talorc came in all his robes with the golden collar
and the wreath on his head. Lurgan bore the golden knife
before him.

The men rose as they passed, even Melduin standing as they
went by bowing to him. There was a chair at the head of the
hearth, midway between the kings' seats, and here Talorc sat
with Lurgan standing behind him. When he was seated the
others sat where they could find room.

Melduin drew himself forward with his hands on the arms
of his chair—

'Men of the Boar! You gave your voices in favour of seeing
the boys who have been in the priests' keeping. Here they are;
stand up, Ailill and Drost, and be seen.'

We stood up together, alone of all the people, and felt the
weight of their eyes on us. But indeed we were not tall enough
to be seen by all the men, and a muttering arose and grew as
those by the doors complained of it. Others said that while we

45

were clothed no one could tell if we were well or ill grown. I saw Melduin frown, but he looked at Talorc, who answered the unspoken question instantly.

'But of course, my lord! Let them be stripped and taken round.'

This time I could feel that not Melduin only but many others disliked it, but there were those near us who were quick to pull . off our tunics and pass us from hand to hand. It was no way as bad as that touching at the Old Stones, but loathsome enough. There were some who almost fed on us as they passed us along, and others pinched our arms and legs where the muscles should have been, or hefted us in their hands and grumbled at our lightness. At last we reached Melduin, who drew us to him and lapped the skirts of his cloak around us. I was thankful to lean against him, but Ailill drew away and said, with the fire that was his:

'I shall be glad to have my own cloak!'

I felt Melduin sigh within himself.

'It is coming, son of my brother,' he said peaceably. They were already passing our garments from hand to hand towards us.

When we were dressed again:

'Now,' said Melduin, 'what is your word, men?'

There was a confused outbreak of speech until he held up his hand and beckoned to an old man who sat by the fire.

'What say you, Gerig?'

'They are useless as they stand,' said the old one bluntly. 'They have neither beef nor fibre. They would not live a day on the hill nor an hour in the sea. These are not our kings. What have the priests been at? Have we not sent food we could ill spare, to grow these children into men?'

A growl of approval—Melduin lifted his hand and let it fall.

'Who else? You, Neart?'

'I speak with Gerig,' said a man unseen, on our side of the hall. 'They are fit for nothing; the priests have failed.'

Talorc rose to face Melduin.

'Will you hear me, Lord?'

'Surely, Most Reverend; silence for Talorc the Priest!'

'I am speaking to the lords of the People of the Boar,' said Talorc, at his quietest. 'I am speaking to those who bade us take these boys and teach them the laws. This we have done.'

His voice cracked like a whip.

'Drost! Begin the Law!'

I was on my feet before I knew I had heard him. I stood forward, and stretched my hands to the people, and heard my own voice saying:

'This is the Law of the People; let him who breaks it beware. Let him beware of vengeance from gods and men. Let him who mocks it beware; let him beware of mockery from gods and men. Let him who turns it to his own desire beware; he will be turned from his desire.'

I ran on into the long laws of land-holding and cattle-owning, the laws of war and peacemaking, of crafts, of dues to the priests, of verses, of times and places for worship and feasting. I had never spoken to such an audience nor to such rapt silence. I came at last to the clinching sentence that invokes the three gods, the Swordsman, the Smith, and the Singer, and stopped.

In the stillness I heard a long sigh break from Melduin. Then there was tumultuous noise; the men shouted and stamped their feet, and some struck their spear-butts on the hard earth floor.

Talorc was still standing in his place. He held out his hands and said simply:

'Is it well, ye men of the Boar?'

Through the roar that answered him Melduin said:

'It is well, Most Reverend. Be quiet, all you people, and sit down! Let us take counsel together what to do next.'

'Oh,' said the man Neart, still unseen, 'I am answered! His Reverence has done more than he promised. Let us leave matters in his good hands.'

'No,' said the old Gerig, 'the priests have done their part, but it is only one part. These are to be kings, not priests, as I understand it. Do I understand it, Most Reverend? Or do you train them to take the priesthood into the kingship?'

He spoke most innocently, like a questioning child, but I for one saw the barb as he threw it and in a blinding moment knew the truth to be exactly otherwise; Talorc wanted to swallow the kingship into the priesthood. I remembered the white beast at Mangan's breast . . . as if my thought had reached Talorc, that name was next on his lips.

'I have trained them with the aid of the good Seer Mangan,

47

and Lurgan here, to take their place at your head and serve you in their manner as we serve in ours; but now, men, I have a thing to lay before you, an urgent matter, a new thing. This very day as we came to you we had proof that witchcraft still walks among us. The mother of Drost came out to confront us, bold as you please, and has drawn away Mangan himself with enchantment. Who knows but by this time she has brewed charms of his blood and marrow, to sap the strength of the People and of the kings themselves?'

He won a horrible answer, a rumbling snarl from a hundred throats like the sound of a hunting pack.

'Gently, men and councillors!' cried Gerig, quick on his feet for all his years. 'A man may rest in a house that he passes.'

'Not that house,' said Talorc grimly.

'Went he willingly?' asked Melduin; his fingers moved against my side in kindliness or warning.

'She came out and bespelled him and drew him away from us,' said Talorc; 'was it not so, Lurgan?'

'Even so; the men and the noble boys saw it too.'

'The boys are too young to be heard,' said Melduin. 'Let the men speak.'

'She came to meet us . . .' said one, half shamefaced.

'He went of his own will,' said another.

Talorc broke in—

'But I cry to you for justice, lords! I bring you warning! Here has been hunger and talk of hunger. Those above know why we have hungered, for a hidden sin. Now we see it; I tell you there is open shameless witchcraft among us, the old evil ways of the women's work back again, up there on the hillside. What need to seek further for the cause of our suffering? Burn it out, I beg of you! I warned you long ago it would come to this—burn it out, now when you hear of it! Burn the house and the witch with it! Up, men of the Boar, and cleanse yourselves with fire! It is ten years since we saw this evil so clearly —follow me, all ye who desire good harvests and sons to follow you!'

He swept the length of the hall, and at the door-end caught up one of the torches laid ready for the home-going. Thrusting it into the flames he twirled it round till it blazed, set it on his shoulder like a club, and stormed out. The men poured after him, jostling each other to take torches and light them. Ailill sprang away and caught Lurgan's robe as he passed.

I flung myself against Melduin in an agony. He put both his arms round me and held me tight for one breath before he too rose. His face was stained with a dark flush over its heavy pallor, and his mouth was a hard line.

'Fear not, little son,' he said very softly. 'The Mother is greater than men; when she sends madness she is ready to deal with it. Let us go and see her works.'

Out of the Fort they streamed ahead of us, and by the time we got clear the torches were bobbing uphill. We heard doors barred all through the houses as frightened women shut themselves in; dogs bayed and cattle in the paddocks plunged away from the lights. We swept on up the road we had come down that afternoon, until we were all crowded into the open space outside the Hearth. There they halted, like hounds at check, while Talorc went forward alone to the doorway.

His torch shed sparks as he swung it to bring up the flame.

'Come out, Mangan! Come out you too, witch and deceiver of men, come out and face the judgment of the People! Come out, all ye bewitched and deceived who dwell in the accursed place!'

Silence. The smoke from the Hearth drifted gently towards the stars.

His voice, which had been shrill, dropped into its full melody; Talorc had a beautiful voice, full of influence, when he chose to use it.

'Come out all ye within; in the names of the Swordsman, the Smith and the Singer, come out! I bid ye come forth and be judged!'

Silence.

'Stand round and set alight!' he cried to the men with the torches.

The curtain was drawn back and my mother walked out.

She was shrouded and hooded in her dark blue cloak, only her face showing white. Even her feet and her hands were hidden. She stepped out of the doorway and stood still, and perfect stillness flowed from her and froze the multitude. In the hush we heard the curlews calling on the bar of the river.

49

A shower of sparks fell from a torch as the bearer shook it and swung it to keep it alive; as if that had been a signal, my mother spoke.

'Men of the Boar, you are welcome at your mother's Hearth; what have you come to ask?'

Melduin spoke while Talorc was mustering words.

'Lady, a priest of the New Way rested here today; we seek news of him.'

'News! No, woman, I will tell you what we seek! We seek the death of the witch who has put us all in peril of death! We have come to bring an end to your wickedness for ever and to cleanse the land with . . .'

She answered Melduin as if Talorc had not spoken.

'News of Mangan? Great King, he is in his own place, as far as I know. He was weary, and he rested a little and went on. You do well to be troubled for him, but he is not here.'

Gerig said:

'Well, we are answered, brothers! Mangan's down at the Temple of the New Way, is he? And did the Most Reverend not know that? What are we doing here, men, standing like cattle on a cold hillside when we should be holding council?'

'This is no cold hillside, Gerig, but the door to your mother's house,' said Malda. 'You are welcome within as you have ever been.'

She stepped back, feeling behind her for the curtain.

Talorc was too quick for the others; he sprang forward to stand close to her, and in a low and venomous voice he heaped execrations on her, thrusting his torch towards her at every word. There were things I had never heard even in Lurgan's worst rages, but the tone was fifty times worse than the words. By the torch-glow we could watch spittle gathering on his lips. Melduin gripped my arm, or I might have run at him. He raved on and on, ever more wildly, until suddenly two men walked out of opposite sides of the crowd and took his arms. It was done without word or signal; just that these two could not listen any longer. They pulled him back from her a little and he struggled in their hands.

She had never moved since he began. Now her hands appeared, holding the cloak at her breast.

'The blessing of my mother and yours on you for stopping

him in his madness,' she said without a tremor in her voice. 'Now you see, o men' (a little more loudly), 'now you see what your priests can do. You see how wrong we were, we who served the Mother and never abused you, and how right these are who pour filth over women. I and my mother, and her mother before her, and the Old One before that whom you, Gerig, remember better than I, none of us used this priestly talk to you when you went away from us, or withheld food from us, or neglected our advice for your cattle or yourselves. It must be only great priests who can speak thus; I cannot; I am only the servant of the Mother. But if I have ever helped you or any among you at any time, or if I have helped a calf or a dog of any of you at any time, then I ask you now to take this sick man away, back to his own friends who will heal him and care for him, and spare me at least the presence of the son I bore you when next you come to revile me.'

I felt Melduin flinch; he turned and cried:

'Back! Back all of you to the Fort!'

They stood uncertainly; and as they stood Talorc began again, where he hung between the spearmen.

This time he did not get far. In a sudden gesture she threw off her cloak and we saw the white robe covering her from neck to feet. Her hands went up to her hair and came down again with the two long bone pins that held it up. She jerked her head and over her shoulders and below her waist fell the great dark coils, blue-black in the torchlight, heavy as snakes as they fell and light as mist when they spread about her.

There was a single gasp from the throat of every man there, and as one we fell on our knees. (I saw Lurgan go down among the first.) From the core of my heart I was afraid, and fear ran over us all like rain. This was not my mother, this was Brigitta herself, the Middle One, and we trembled before her.

'I curse Talorc,' she said slowly; 'I curse him for what he has said and for what he has done; for the old theft and the daily thefts thereafter, for the first wrong and the latter wrongs. I curse him for what he has done to Mangan, and for what he has left undone for the people he took into his own hands. I curse him not in soul, not in heart, not in mind, for these are curses in my mother's hand; but I curse him in his tongue, for with that has he assaulted me and my servant. I curse him for

51

the fullness of my time, and with the hair of my head I confirm it to him.

'Begone, accursed, and you who came with him, may you go in peace.'

She went from us so swiftly, while we were still bowed to the ground, that when we dared to raise our eyes there was not a tremor in the curtain to mark her passing, and we were there alone with the torches burning out. By the faint starlight we could make out something white on the ground, struggling between two kneeling men.

Lurgan, may his gods remember his courage, went to help his master. He got his arms round him and raised him, and others came and stood round, but only Lurgan and the two spearmen dared touch him. He was crouping and gaggling with strange sounds in his throat. When he was up he lunged about like a blindfold man, and all drew back from him. Lurgan held him, but could not guide him unaided.

I had turned away, so shaken that I needed to find some place apart from them all, but Lurgan called me by name. Perhaps he thought I should take no harm from my mother's curse.

'Drost, in the name of all the Great Ones, help me get him to the Temple,' he said urgently. I put my shoulder under those dreadful gripping fingers and between us we led him down the hill, the men standing back for us.

I did not know where the Temple was. We went back to the Fort and through it, and out to a little platform above the sea. We climbed down a perilous curving path, hearing the tide chafe below, and came to a wide space with many huts and one great building set against the luminous water.

Men crowded round us; Lurgan muttered some explanation that I did not hear. I could only hear the gagging brabbling sounds Talorc made as we dragged him between us. Someone prised his hand off my shoulder, somebody else led me to a small dark cell much like the familiar one at the Little Fort. There they left me, unfed since morning but with little appetite and small wish to be alone. Ailill did not come, and I fell into a stunned sleep, curled under my cloak and cupping one hand over my burning shoulder.

The morning broke over me like a blessing. I lifted my head and out through the open door I saw the sea new-washed and rippled with little waves, dancing under the first of the sunlight. When I sat up I could see the grass running to the cliff edge grey with dew. I went out and stood on the wet turf and looked round me like one seeing the world for the first time.

A little below me and to one side there was a massive stone building, bigger than a house, dark and forbidding. All around were small huts like the one I had left. Behind me was a black cliff with a path scratched across its face. The sun was striking through a cleft in the rocks and warming the dew with beams that lay almost level on the field. The whole creation was new and clean, and I possessed it alone.

And I was aching with hunger. I remembered yesterday like a bad dream, but chiefly I remembered that I had not eaten. I set out across the slope to find somebody to feed me. When I looked back I saw my footsteps black on the wet grass.

Presently I heard a quern going in one of the huts, and I went to the door and looked in. It was a man who knelt there at women's work, pushing the heavy roller and letting it run back, Brr-tump, Brrr-tump. I came closer and he was startled into letting the roller run over the end of the stone.

'Ow-ai, the little lord! What is your pleasure, little master?'

He spoke like Terik at the Little Fort, and not unkindly.

I said:

'I did not eat yesterday—is there any food?'

He clicked his tongue reproachfully and went to the back of the hut. When he turned he was holding a bowl full of milk curd, and he stirred handfuls of his new-ground meal into it and gave it me all frothing. It was a dish I had not tasted since I left the Hearth-house, and I sat down cross-legged beside him and supped with delight, not forgetting to thank him and speak a blessing over the bowl. Now I had spoken no blessing in the Little Fort, for the sufficient reason that it would have cost me a beating and the loss of the meal; certainly children, like animals, know what is happening round them through their back-hairs without being told. I had talked to nobody, and yet I knew the day was good and old ways were safe again.

With my stomach full my mind could work. I sat against the outer wall of the hut in the early sunshine and sorted out my pictures of yesterday, while the old man went on with his grinding. By and by I noticed people going into the big building, so I asked my new friend what it was.

He rolled his eyes and showed his teeth in a grimace.

'Ow-ai! That the great ones' house! Not go there, little master! Old master very sick there too, not good, ai-ai!'

Lurgan came out as I watched, shaded his eyes and saw me. He had been going elsewhere in a hurry but he checked, thought for a moment, and strode towards me.

'So you're awake? Have you eaten? So; good. You must not wander alone here; come with me.'

He led me towards the big building, walking fast. There was a tautness about him today, something stretched near the limit with anxiety and, yes, a sort of anticipation not altogether unpleasant to him.

'This is no place for you, and I don't suppose you'll be here for long; meantime—are you there, Luad?'

A youth in a short white tunic came from the darkness and knelt to him.

'Stand up, brother,' said Lurgan; 'the Most Reverend lives.'

I almost had it then, the excitement running in him, but I failed to catch it.

'Luad, I want you to look after the noble boy Drost while the Council decides what is to be done with him. Don't take him into the Temple, but anywhere else inside these gates; see he's fed and so on. What were you doing?'

'I was watching the flame, Reverend Master,' said the youth in a simpering voice.

'Then call your next watcher and come back quickly. Drost, you are in Luad's charge; you'll do as he tells you and stay with him at all times. I have too much to do to keep you with me, but I promise you I'll make time for you if you give him any trouble.'

'Yes, Reverence,' I said, trying to see beyond him into the dark.

'Oho, you want to see inside the Temple? It's not for such as you—but wait, you shall see. It is no place for little boys—the Swordsman and the Smith are not easily appeased, nor is the Singer over-gentle when he is angered. Come.'

He took my wrist and drew me in. There was a narrow

54

passage that felt damp and cold, and beyond it more darkness but with space and height. At the far end there was a flicker of firelight glimmering over vague shapes. I was seized with terror and began to shudder; there was horror and evil and the smell of blood and death. I ducked under Lurgan's arm and ran out just as Luad came back with another boy.

Lurgan followed me.

'I told you it was not for little boys,' he said. 'Perhaps you will be more careful in future not to offend them by making mistakes in the laws? Luad, you idle whelp, where have you been? You'll find yourself playing a different part if you keep me waiting again. Mulan, go in and attend to your duty; Luad, off with you.'

He turned abruptly and our obeisances were made to the air.

'Really, how am I to look after you?' said Luad pettishly. 'We can't get food for a long time, and I did want to run through my gestures for the Noon Offering—oh well, if we go down on the cliff you can sit quietly while I practise. Brr, it's cold; have you a cloak? Then let's get it and we can sit on it. Was this where you slept? Ah, what a colour!'

He swooped on my cloak, held it at arm's length, tried it against himself, swept it about, and finally put it round me, saying:

'There, you wear it, and when we get to the cliff I'll show you how to manage it; that was one thing I did learn with those awful people, at least.'

He was leading the way to the edge and talking over his shoulder.

'What people?' I asked.

'Oh, at the Fort of the Girls! You haven't gone there yet, have you? Nothing but spear-throwing till your arms drop from their sockets, and dancing and prancing, and your feet torn to ribbons on the hunting-grounds, and nothing to eat, I do assure you, unless you manage to kill something, and then most likely the older boys take the best of it. I was never more thankful in my life than when my parents dedicated me and the Most Reverend divined my gift for the priesthood. I do all I can to foster it, you may be sure. I should die if he sent me back there.'

We had reached the very rim of the plateau with the sea growling below us. There was a little shelf lower down with a few rough steps cut in the rock leading to it. Luad tripped down and held his hand up to me, but I had already jumped.

'You horrible child, you might have gone hurtling over, and then what would have become of me?' he wailed.

I did not know what to make of him, but I was quite prepared to study him if there was nothing better to do and nobody to make me learn things. I sat against the rock while he walked about, tossing my cloak into a hundred new positions, posturing to show me the ritual gestures he had learnt, and talking, talking, talking. He talked about the Fort of the Girls (whatever that was, he had hated it), and about the priesthood and his gifts for it (though I did not discover what they were), and chiefly about himself. He talked so much that I ceased to listen and leaned back to watch the gulls and the grey fulmars quartering space before me. One big white gull swooped low with a loud raucous cry so like a mockery of Luad that I laughed aloud, and both Luad and the gull were offended.

At last there was a great clamour above us, a brazen bellowing and hammering. Luad sprang up the steps like a fawn, crying, 'Food!' with more human animation than I had yet seen from him.

A slave was beating with a pestle on the side of a great cauldron and the open space was full of people hurrying to him. Luad was heading towards them when Mangan stepped into our path.

'Drost, you mustn't eat with the boys,' he said. 'Luad, my son, you are released from your duty. I will take care of Drost. Come, Drost, and eat with me.'

Mangan's voice was full and strong and his eye clear and open. He looked like a man who had slept and who felt the newness of the day as I had. He took me to a small hut that was his own; I recognised the cloak lying on the bed. The hut was bare and clean, the floor strewn with crushed shells and the bed-place filled with sweet grasses. On one wall there was a scrawl of red paint, and that was all.

We sat on a stone seat at the door and the old slave who had fed me already brought bowls of broth and a platter of meat, and new-baked bannocks.

'Eat, child,' said Mangan. 'I should tell you that this meat is from the sacrifices for the Chief Priest's recovery.'

It was kind of him to tell me but I did not quite know what to do about it. I said a blessing inside my head, and ate, and it was very good. When I had finished, a question popped out of my mouth before I could stop it.

'What's happened to Talorc?'

Mangan bent his thoughtful look upon me—

'But you were there—you saw it. He was cursed.'

'But—is he still—like that?'

'He is dumb,' said Mangan. 'He's over there in a side-room of the Temple, and though I do not think he is going to die, he is speechless and his body is twisted throughout one side. I have been with him all morning but his mind does not speak. We are doing all we can for him.'

I was horrified—

'But she didn't curse his mind! She said that was for the Mother!'

'Then we must assume that others besides the Middle Priestess felt that wrong had been done. It is not fitting for us to talk about it. I have my own share of guilt.'

'Oh no!' I cried. 'Oh no!'

'I have, child; but leave that. Here is a chance for me to show you something more about your gift. I may not have such an opportunity again, so attend carefully.

'I am going to show you how to go free of your body, but first you must know how to return. Try to understand; you are a person, a spirit, that has come to live in a body called Drost. You have lived in other bodies before, and you will live in others hereafter unless and until it pleases the great ones to open the circle and let you go free (and this is something that does not happen easily). While you are in a body you have to put up with all that happens to it, cold and hunger and hurt; this you chose to do when you were without a body, for the sake of the good things you can also enjoy, and chiefly for the sake of walking further along the road that leads to breaking out of the circle. You are not old enough in this body to learn all there is to know about such things, so I am trying to put it very simply for you. Probably in other times and places you knew all I know and more, and the time may come when that knowledge will return to you. Till then do not speak to anyone but me of these things.'

'Demetroos knows.'

Mangan looked sharply at me—

'Yes, Demetroos knows a great deal. Perhaps he will help you some day if he stays here. But this is what I want to tell you at present. You can leave your body if you are careful, and you can return to it again, and while you are free you can go wherever you will. You leave the body lying asleep or resting, and you come back into it by thinking of the place where you left it. You come back over it, you see it as it lies there, you stoop to it, fold yourself up, slide back into it, very gently, very carefully. For the poor body is as good as dead without you, and if it is roused suddenly when you are away or not in full charge of it, it will feel itself deserted, and die. Then you will be left without a shell to live in, and you will have to start all over again inside an unborn baby and wait until it is big enough to start learning.'

I nodded impatiently; it seemed to me that I had known all this long ago.

'Now,' said Mangan, 'as I have told you, you have had many other bodies, and sometimes you cannot remember what sort of shell you are using at the moment—or at least when you begin to train it is difficult, for then doors that have been closed are half-open and you may go through the wrong one. I have been at other times a priest, a woman, a seafaring man— many things. But I have a sign to look for that I have carried with me from shell to shell; sometimes I travel—I used to travel far, and there are few here to call me back. Few—few,' he said almost to himself, 'and many to call me away! Enough; by the way, Drost, there is no limit, except your own power, to the distance you can travel either backwards through former lives or sideways to other places in the present time. But,' and he paused and pointed a stern finger, 'but there are those who do not possess this gift or cannot use it, and they will demand endlessly that you go forwards instead, and reveal the future to them. Do not yield to them, Drost! Nothing but harm can come of it; the way is hard and dangerous and you will not understand what you bring back, nor can one find any interpreter for it. However clearly you remember, it is impossible to explain. So I have found it. If the gods send news of the future, they send the news; it is not for us to go seeking it.

'Look on the wall there at the bed-foot. You see that pattern drawn in red? When I am going out of my body I lie gazing at that pattern, and when I return I see it hanging in the air to guide me back to my body.'

It was a pattern drawn in red pigment, circles within circles within circles.

'Till you find a sign of your own, use that one,' said Mangan. 'Lie here on the bed, so, and we'll put your cloak over you. Now, look at the pattern; what is it like?'

'It's like—like torches whirling—' (I was thinking of the night before). 'No, it's more like those worm-casts you see on the sand; it's like ripples in water, like a stone dropped into deep water—spreading—spreading . . .' And indeed the ripples were spreading and lifting me at their centre until I floated free.

I floated free, free of that prison called Drost with its bruises, out into the dark void where all things have their beginning. I was borne along and desired to see things I had known and loved; but without skill to order my search I was tossed like a twig in a whirlpool, and caught glimpses of here a cool passage into a burning hill, and there tall pillars standing in a brown land. There was a mountain under snow with a river at its foot; there were silvery trees and the voices of doves; for an instant there were misty woods behind a high fence, and the singing of birds mingled with a sweet cold chiming.

So near was I to the Orchard! At that moment I knew I had lost something dearer than life, and I leaned towards the trees to find it, but I knew I must turn away. Ill-trained as Mangan was in that body, he was fortunate that I had known more in the past. I tilted my wings and drifted, and felt him calling me desperately. The darkness cleared a little and I looked down on the feasting-hall.

They were all eating and drinking, no longer holding council but making merry with their decision taken. I saw Felim, and Demetroos in the guest's place, and looked away fearing he would see me. I could make nothing of the talk and began to wish myself away, but I could not recall the sign I was to use.

Mangan knew it, and forced the circles into my mind, so that they took shape dimly and I tilted and slid towards them;

yet as I went I heard one speech clearly, spoken by a man I did not know—

'What if he is dumb? She has been silent all those years— let him take his turn.'

The red circles shone out on the white wall and I was lying in Mangan's bed and shaking with cold.

Mangan worked on me like a slave, chafing my feet and my hands, and lapping my cloak and his own round me. When I was warm again he sat on the edge of the bed and asked:

'Now, little brother, how was it?'

'I'd forgotten so much,' I said; my own words puzzled me as I said them.

'Some forget and some remember,' said Mangan easily; 'it will be better another time. Do not trouble yourself for that. What have you seen? Where have you been?'

'It was dark,' I said sleepily, 'and there was the mountain— and a doorway—and what was that sound when the birds were singing?'

'Aaah, I knew it! That was the ringing of silver bells; you were close to the Orchard and far from Drost then. Keep away from there till you know more; what else?'

'What did they mean about somebody being silent for a long time? That was in the hall, at the end.'

'Men's talk,' said Mangan. 'Never mind interpreting yet; I am concerned only to show you how to go and come.'

A shadow fell athwart the door and Mangan bit his lip.

'Enter, Elder Brother.'

Lurgan stooped and came in.

'So this is where you are! What have you been at, Mangan? I left him in Luad's charge.'

'It seemed to me, Elder Brother (but perhaps I was wrong; I offer you my ignorance), that here was a time when I might show him more of those—tricks—the Most Reverend desires him to learn.'

'Mh! So you want to see him as weak as yourself after these tricks? If I did my duty and followed the will of the Most Reverend as I perceive it (and no wonder you pretend you cannot understand him!) I'd have you scourged before the altars for your share in the night's work—Seer Mangan! Go and wait by him and try to hear him now; he's a little stronger.

As for you, Drost, enough of idleness; come with me.'

As we went one way from the hut I looked back and saw Mangan going the other way, bent in on himself like a man with a mortal wound. Lurgan cuffed me soundly for lagging.

We climbed the narrow path across the cliff and I wondered how we had traversed it in the dark with the helpless old man. At the top Lurgan pushed through a crowd of servants to the doors of the hall, and called Terik out from among them.

'Keep Drost, will you, while I see if the Council is ready?'

I had sense enough not to tell him I knew they were.

Terik drew me aside into an empty room.

'Wait here, little master; I'll fetch you a seat.'

I had no need of a chair; I dropped to my heels as Terik himself would have done, and set my back to the wattled wall. I was still heavy with sleep after my flight.

It was pleasant to have a few moments alone; I was in need of them. But no sooner had I sat down than I felt cold, an icy deadly chill spreading over me; I wanted to spring up and strike out, but I was held. I tried to call Terik back, to beg him not to leave me alone, but I fought for breath in vain. Something smothering, heavy and hairy, lay over my mouth and my nose; my arms were pinned; I threw my head to one side and fought and fought to get my hands up to clear my nostrils. I was going to die—I was choking—I keeled over on the matting—I was finished.

Terik caught me in his arms and carried me out to the sun.

'Little master! Little master! What is it—what's wrong? Terik's here; it's all right now; Terik's here.'

I coughed and gasped and struggled.

Other slaves gathered round us, chattering, offering useless advice, threatening Terik with punishment if any master found us. At last the old man who had tended me before pushed through to the front and clucked at Terik in their own speech. By the waving of his hands he seemed to ask where I had been and to rate Terik for leaving me there. By then my head had cleared and I was sitting up.

'It's all right, Terik,' I managed to say; 'don't worry, I'm all right again now. I was tired, that was all.'

Aung shouted across the yard:

'Terik, hurry! They are calling for him!'

I stood up and straightened my tunic and walked into the hall.

They were all there as I had seen them, sitting back from the broken meats. Ailill was in his usual place on the steps of his father's chair, and Lurgan led me to join him before turning to bow to Melduin.

'Lord, and you men of the Boar, I have brought the boy to hear your decision.'

'It is well,' said Melduin. 'Our word is given for sending them to the Fort of the Girls, young as they are. It seems best to us all, at least until the Most Reverend can direct their training again.'

Lurgan bowed, disappointed of power over us, but with too much else within his grasp to regret it. His mind was busy with a hundred arrangements in which we had no part. All this was clear in that bow.

Melduin beckoned us to stand.

'Hear now, you two boys; it will not be easy for you in the Fort of the Girls where the youngest is a year your elder; but it is the will of your people to send you there, so you must learn what you can and do what you can, and remember all your learning is to be used in the service of the people in time to come. You, Ailill, will be King if the High Gods will, and you will live and die for your people as your father did; and you, Drost, are his Twin and you will live and die for him and for the people, as I have lived and as I will die when my time comes. Go in peace; take them with you now, Regil and Dran, and begin to make them men.'

Two men stood up together and stepped round the fire to us. Though I had not seen their faces before, I knew they were the two who had held Talorc. Certain of the men drew back as they passed, and this confirmed it for me.

Before they reached us Ailill stirred and spoke.

'I will be your king, men, if the High Gods will, and I and my Twin will go and become men; as I obey you now, look to it that you obey me when I return.'

He held his head high and stepped down from his place to walk to the door between the men; I followed after, down the hall, through the court, out of the gate, going I knew not whither.

Outside the Fort they stopped and put us between them, and I had a sight of Ailill's face with the excitement dying out of it, leaving him white and thin-lipped. He was afraid of what lay ahead, and so was I. We went down the path in single file, first Regil, then Ailill, then me and last Dran.

As we took a new road I thought of the little I had heard of this Fort of the Girls, most of it that day from the simpering Luad, and I was afraid. Even Melduin had said it would not be easy for us, and I thought he was a man who measured difficulties by other standards than mine; and in this I was right.

It was a narrow road, running between the Long Strand on our left hand and the rough hill ground above; this was all new country to me. Presently I had something else to think of.

Somewhere on the cliff road last night a stone had cut my sole. It had not troubled me while I walked on grass or smooth ground, but now it began to throb and I struggled not to limp. I could not let the men begin by scorning me; I forced myself to walk evenly and in step, though Regil was setting such a pace that I knew Ailill could hardly keep up.

I had no notion how far we must endure, but suddenly we rounded a corner and saw into a small glen with a river and beyond it a grey wall on a little crag. Far above us sounded a high shrill whistling.

Regil turned his head—

'Not before time, eh?'

'They knew us from far off; would you have them signal so loudly that the stranger knows he is watched?'

'Well—! What ails the dark one?'

'Nothing; a thorn maybe. He can manage.'

I plodded grimly on. My bruised back ached as well, but I was comforted by Dran's words. We forded the cool stream and climbed the slope of the crag, and there at the top in the gateway stood a tall thin boy in a deerskin kilt.

His eyes widened at the sight of us.

'Gerig,' said Regil, 'the Council have sent you Ailill and Drost to train. They are full young but here they are and you must make the best of it.'

Gerig lifted his hand in salute—

'Very well, my lords; what are we to do with them?'

'Train them as far as they're able. Remember they're very

young and they come from the priests' hands, not from home.'

'I see that,' said Gerig drily. I wondered what was wrong with us. 'Well, I'd better get them looking right before the others come home. Come on, you two; we'll have that hair off for a start.'

'Why?' asked Ailill, fear making him bold.

Gerig smiled.

'Because you don't look like a boy, you look like a baby. Shall I take them both into my hut, Regil?'

'One each, you and Culla,' said Dran. 'Eh, Regil?'

'One's enough of a handicap,' said Regil. 'Better separate them. Wait till Culla comes to choose, though.'

'Well, at least I can make them more respectable,' said Gerig. He walked over to a large hut, one of two that stood either side of the yard with a blackened hearth-place between them. We followed uncertainly.

'And by the way, Drost's lame,' Dran shouted after him.

Gerig lifted a hand to show he had heard, and steered us into the hut. It was all spotted and streaked with sunlight shining through the hurdle-walls. There were little piles of belongings down each side, spears and bows hanging from the roof-beams, and more bundles on the pillars of the ridge. Gerig sat on his heels to rummage in one of the bundles, and brought out two soft deerskins.

'Here, put these on instead of those tunics, and then come to the door and I'll cut your hair. Which one's Drost? What's this about being lame?'

I hung my head and mumbled something about a cut.

'Now listen! When I ask a question I want to hear the answer; remember that! What have you done to your foot?'

I did not know how to address him and that made me still more nervous; I said with an effort:

'I cut it on a stone yesterday.'

He knelt before me—

'Show! Nasty; you ought to have cleaned that at once. You must learn to attend to these things; there's nothing clever about going round like that; you might be unfit just when you were needed for a hunt. All right, get dressed and I'll see to it. Come on, Ailill, we'll cut that mop off while Drost's changing.'

Left alone in the hut I pulled off my tunic and knotted the

hide round me as much as possible like Gerig's kilt; I did not know what to do with the tunic and cloak, but I rolled them up and left them at the foot of one of the posts, and as an after-thought I picked Ailill's up and laid them there too. Then I went out to the yard.

Ailill's hair had been cropped short round his head; he looked totally different and rather comical, like a young owl.

'Come on then, Darky,' said Gerig. He sat me on a big stone and went to work with a sharp knife, alarmingly close to my ears.

'Hold still or I'll probably slice a bit off you by mistake!' he said cheerfully. 'Usually before boys come here, their parents make a feast for them and their father cuts their hair and gives them their first kilt and all that. You haven't got fathers, and neither have I, so it's different for us. There, that's better. You'll be allowed to grow it again later as you pass the tests, and when you come back from the Green Glen you can wear it as long as you like—if it'll grow. Mine's been cut so often, I sometimes wonder if it will grow when I can let it!'

'Cut off again?' asked Ailill anxiously.

'Oh yes, when you do something stupid you go back to having it right off,' said Gerig. 'I've lost count, myself. Drost! What in the name of the Mother have you done to your back?'

He was staring at me, horrified. I was overwhelmed with shame that he should see my bruises and know I had deserved such a beating.

Ailill said:

'He disobeyed an order from the Most Reverend.'

'And did I ask you? Poor little animal, something will have to be done about that—Regil, could you come a moment?'

'What's the matter?' called Regil from a passage-room in the fort wall.

'It's Drost—his back.'

'Moon and Stars, I saw it last night and I'd forgotten! Get some leaves, Gerig, and ask Dran for the ointment.'

It was sore; it was desperately sore, and so was my foot, and I was deadly tired after two exhausting days. I sat at Gerig's feet and just as a stream of boys poured in through the gate I dissolved into uncontrollable weeping.

Part Two

IT WAS finished; I was disgraced for ever; they would turn me away from the Fort of the Girls and I should have to go and die alone in the hills. The more I tried to stop, the more thoughts like these overwhelmed me and I broke out again. There was a ring of dusty feet round me; I heard Ailill break into a giggle of sheer nerves. Then Gerig's voice cut through my sobs—

'Have none of you anything to do? What are you all gaping at? Send Arth here to me, and the rest of you go and get the food ready if you've brought any! Culla—ah, there you are, Minnow, I'll explain later, but take this white-top away, will you? Now, Drost—'

Here it comes, I thought, and waited. His hands came down hard on my shoulders.

'That's enough; steady now. I know, you're dead-beat, but you'll be all right when you've had some food. Come on, that's better. I've got some stuff here for your back, it's very cold but it'll help. See if you can manage not to jump when it goes on.'

He laid an icy dressing on my back; the shock of it made me gasp and catch my breath, and though the tears went on running down my face I did manage to check the awful hiccupping sobs. Gerig sat me on the stone again and passed a bandage round and round me.

'Now let's see that foot. Oh, you're there, Arth? This is a great day for you, Fingerling, you're not the baby any longer. Hold this, will you? Here's Drost; he's got a filthy cut on his foot and the little fool walked from the village on it. Drost, this is Arth; he was the youngest here till you came, so he's pretty glad to see you.'

I blinked away a few last tears. Sitting on his heels beside me was a boy with a tousled head of sandy curls and the brightest blue eyes I have ever seen. That was my first sight of Arth.

So in one day I had my first clear flight and my first deep shame, and found my friends Gerig and Arth at the entrance to my manhood; and that was a day indeed.

It was a day to remember, but new things crowded in so fast that I had no time to think about each as it came. I remember how I sat by the fire that first evening, as we ate the stew of hares and birds and drank milk brought in by the herd-boys, and how I wondered if I should ever know all their names. And how I worried in case I was sent to the other group, under the leadership of the heavy thickset Culla, instead of staying with Gerig who now knew, I thought, the worst there was to know about me.

After the meal Regil asked:

'Well, have you settled about the new ones?'

'You choose, Culla,' said Gerig.

'Oh,' said the big boy, 'I'll take the white one; he looks as if he could run, some day.'

'That would be handy for your lot, wouldn't it?' said Gerig, and there was some more chaffing and laughter, and then Gerig said again:

'I don't mind having the other one; he's got spunk.'

I thought for a moment he was mocking me, and then I knew he meant it and my heart swelled. I could have died for him.

When the last scrap of food was eaten, the younger boys made up the fire while the older ones checked their bow-strings and spear-lashings. When Culla had finished his own he inspected the weapons of his group, and then he fetched out the big wooden drum from his hut and began to rub its head with the flat of his hand, 'waking the drum' as they call it.

One by one as the others were ready they gathered about the fire, and Gerig brought a smaller drum and woke it. Someone

68

began to shuffle, another fell in behind him, the two drums spoke, the ring was formed, and the dance began.

I do not remember now what they danced that first night; perhaps the Blackcocks, an easy one that they often used to start with. As they and the drums warmed up together they would go on to more difficult dances, the Stags or the Fishnet or the lovely and intricate Weaving-run; and late and last, Regil and Dran would teach the eldest boys the steps of the Boar Dance or the Dance of the Green Glen. These were different; they were holy dances whose exact perfection was essential. The ring would be checked time and again to correct the position of hand or foot. We younger ones could sit and watch, and some who were too young to dance were allowed to drum for them, so that we all knew the beats and the fingering that called for the changes of step and pace. But when we began to nod Regil would look up at the stars and bid Gerig stop the dancing for that night, and we would go to our beds with the drum-beat still in our minds.

Dran was the finest drummer of all as Regil was among the best dancers of the People at that time, but they were content to teach rather than perform while they were with the boys. Only sometimes as we lay in the huts Dran would finger the light drum softly, talking to it and being answered, and we would fall asleep under that magical sound.

In the mornings it was a struggle to get up from our mattresses of heather, but once outside and racing to the stream we were ready for any wildness. We would jump in holding our noses, or dive from the rocks, and splash and shriek, and tear back to put on our kilts and open up the fire to heat broth for breakfast.

We drank it standing, blowing on the soup to cool it, and looking round us at the weather. For the next thing was to answer Regil's questions about what the day would bring; starting with Arth (for we were left out of account, being too young altogether) he would ask each in turn what he thought the weather would do and what the day's work should be; and he was uncomfortably good at recalling one's predictions in the evening.

Then the work was dealt out, so many to hunt or fish, so many to go round traps, some to work in the Fort at curing hides or making nets; so many to the herding. That first season we were always sent to herd the cattle, being useless for anything else. The cattle were out on the Long Strand, and I loved the warm days above the sands. Ailill hated it, considering it beneath his dignity, and it was not long before he felt the weight of Culla's hand for saying so.

I seldom saw him to speak to; though we rivalled the other gang and taunted them with any mistakes we could discover, and bedevilled them generally, we did not have much to do with them except at the dancing. I was afraid we were too little to dance as well, but as soon as my foot healed Gerig pulled me into the circle and gave me a friendly push to start me off, and I found myself dancing like the others.

On wet evenings, instead of taking the drums out to catch cold, we sat in the huts and one of the men told us tales of old hunts or legends of the gods, while we worked at making snares or plaiting rush-baskets for fish, and the older ones made spear-lashings and arrow-shafts. As the weather grew colder we had another job, gathering baskets of moss to stop up every chink in the hurdles of the hut and plastering it evenly with clay over the outside. I liked this, squelching about in the river-bed to get the clay and slapping fistfuls of it on the wattles and splurging it about with my fingers. Gerig laughed at me, and called me 'Mud-Puddler', and I was in some danger of getting that as my permanent nickname.

Everyone had nicknames; some had several. They were only used among equals or from elder to younger, and we had to be careful to avoid them. I got a few cuffs for mistaking one for a real name, but we soon learned to be suspicious of names with an uncivil or downright rude meaning. Some children, of course, are given strange names for luck, but these are rather different from the names I have in mind.

Gerig himself was 'High-jump' and Culla was 'Minnow', but there were few boys of their year and these names were seldom heard. Arth had been 'Fingerling', but after we came he was simply 'Curly'; everyone liked Arth. I used to wonder what they would find for me. I wanted a nickname, so as to feel completely one of them, but I dreaded earning something really shameful.

But good days they were! There were hard things to bear

and hungry times and cold or weary times, but never cruelty, never a grown man's strength pitted against a boy to hurt or overbear him. When we danced we danced as one, and when we herded we herded in a group, and the weakness of one was a risk to all, for all to overcome.

Besides herding and dancing, we young ones spent our days learning to throw sticks and stones, in preparation for the time when we should be allowed to make real throwing-sticks and eventually spears. This learning was a kind of dancing in itself.

As the days grew shorter the elder boys began to bring in long honeysuckle bines and string birds' feathers on them, and sometimes they came to the beaches with us to collect shells. The night we heard that reaping had begun in the villages there was an outburst of self-adornment, and our elders sat down to supper daubed with coloured earths and gay with feather garlands. Regil said they would frighten the crows white.

The dancing that evening was fairly wild and from time to time people fell out to fasten a string of shells that was coming adrift, or retie a garland, and every night there were more garlands and more daubed faces until the night of the harvest feast.

I had almost forgotten the feast; but that day the older boys came in early and worked furiously to paint each other and bestring themselves with ornaments. Some had long goose-feathers dyed blue and red to thread through their hair-knots. We thought they looked wonderful.

As soon as they had eaten they lined up for Regil and Dran to inspect them, and then off they went into the dusk and we were left behind. It was a warm still night with the full moon shedding radiance even before she rose, and we sat round the fire but nobody suggested dancing. Instead Dran came and sat among us, and said:

'This is the Night of the Mother; do you all know that?'

I almost jumped out of my skin. The Night of the Mother! I had thought that was forbidden. I looked across the fire and saw Ailill sitting open-mouthed.

'This is the Night of the Mother, and your elders have gone to share in the thanksgiving for her gift of a good harvest. She is up there riding in the moon, looking at us, and she is also here and now walking her earth. In the New Way they call her the wife of the Smith, and that may be right; in the Old Way one did not venture to call her anyone's wife, even the wife of a High God like the Smith. She weds where she wishes and the choice is hers. Some of you are children of that choice as I am. After this she makes way for her mother the Old One, who will bring the winter, and she in turn will make way for the Maiden to bring us the spring.'

Ailill said suddenly:

'Who has given the Old Way leave to return?'

'The Old Way has never ceased,' said Dran; 'it is for each one of the people to choose their way and follow it; for me, I choose the Old Way.'

It was long since I had felt another mind at work. The knowledge prickled along my back before I recognised it. Beyond the fire sat Ailill, marking Dran as dangerous, wondering if Lurgan was still his friend, wondering what was happening in the Temple and the Great Fort.

Someone asked what our elders were doing and Dran began to explain about the dancing that would be going on now among the threshing-floors; his questioner was not one of those who had run with a clay lamp in childhood. The jealous mind of Ailill, too old for his body, wrestled on and I wondered what he would do, and then the memory of former harvest-dancings came and filled my thoughts with happier things.

We were most of us asleep before the elder boys came laughing up the slope and stepped over the sleepers to hang up their finery. Next morning there were heavy eyes and drowsy heads and a good deal of cheerful sarcasm from Dran; Regil himself was not altogether awake at first, but in his case the trouble was mostly barley-wine, kept over from last year.

We went down to the cattle-pens, but now we could drive the beasts out to the cleared stubbles and we had only to perch along the turf walls and see they did not break out and stray. There was less to do than on the Long Strand, and we would have been rather bored had not some younger sisters been sent from the houses with cakes and honey left over from the feasts.

The morning went off pleasantly enough with their help until they were called home to eat, when we began to be bored again and passed the time throwing sticks at a mark. We were interrupted soon enough by the village bull, who decided to hoist himself over a wall and set off in pursuit of some penned heifers that had been calling him all morning. We had a brisk time of running and yelling before we persuaded him to give up the notion, and by then several of the men had come down and were shouting too, partly at him but mostly at us.

When the commotion was at its height I saw Cardail coming down the hill with a basket. I yelled at her to mind the bull and she disappeared suddenly. But when the noise was over and the men had gone there she was stumping onwards, till finally she climbed the wall and dodged through the cows to reach me.

'Hey,' said I, 'what d'you think you're doing?'—still the big brother, as if I had never left home.

She looked up at me through her long lashes, dumped the basket and turned to run off—

'For you,' she said.

The others hooted and giggled at me—

'Drost's courting! Drost's got a sweetheart!'

'All right,' I said; I had had time to look into the basket; 'nobody need eat anything that doesn't want to.'

That brought them piling round me for the bannocks and the honey-cakes.

The bull waited till all our hands and mouths were full and then he jumped the wall and trotted through the houses.

That was a leathering all round for the herd-boys, the first I had had, and Gerig made sure we all felt it; not till afterwards did I realise he had had his from Dran first. That was unfair, I thought; he had not been with us; if he had, it would not have happened; the fault was all mine, for mine had been the food. Moreover it was the last of those free-and-easy herding days, for after that one of the older boys had to stay back from hunting and keep an eye on us.

It was some slight comfort to know none of the heifers had actually taken service, but the knowledge came too late to save our skins, and we had to put up with hoots from the other gang and several tongue-lashings from Gerig. Besides, my mother never again sent us food while we were in the fields.

But as far as I could learn not a soul spoke against her for it, where the season before they would all have cried 'witchcraft' and blamed her for the bull's natural inclinations, and ours.

73

Winter drew in. The cattle were housed and we had no more to do with them. Instead even we the youngest went hunting and took our places in the ring, standing still as stones behind Gerig and Culla, carrying a share of the game or even on great days a spear for one of the bigger boys. Gerig had infinite patience in showing us how to move through the dry-leaved woods, how to choose outlook and background, how to mark a bird or follow a blood-trail. Arth and I trotted hopefully at his heels like puppies.

He called us his puppies sometimes; he called us many other things, but this one we took as a compliment. He never told us we were any handicap to him. We did not understand that every deer he killed, every pelt he dried, would be counted by the men when they came. It was Arth who found that out.

We were working by the stream, scraping a hide spread on the bank before pegging it out to dry. He said in an awed voice:

'Do you know about the men coming?'

'No, what for?'

'Dran says they'll come soon to decide if any of the big ones are ready to go to the Green Glen.'

'Is Gerig going away?'

'Dran says it all depends on the men. He says if we spoil this hide they won't count it, and they'll say he's not a good enough hunter yet.'

'Gerig's the best hunter there is!'

'I know that, but Dran says the men won't know unless he has all the skins to show them.'

'I'm wearing one of his skins!' I remembered aloud.

'Dran says we'll have to get some of our own soon.'

We scraped carefully round an awkward angle.

'Haven't you got a kilt of your own?'

Arth said:

'This one came from home, but it's falling to bits. My uncle gave it to me. It's the only thing I brought. He said I could have my father's things when I went back.'

'Why didn't your father give you a kilt? I thought they did?'

'My father's dead. My mother's dead too, that's why they let me come here before all the others. My little brother and my sisters are with my uncle.'

Not having known a father, I could hardly feel for him, but

I knew what it would be to have no mother. I was too young to leave it alone, and asked again:

'Why are they both dead?'

'My father was killed with Ailill the King; my mother died in the big hunger last year. Lots of people died.'

'I know,' I said; but I did not know.

Gerig himself came to watch us, and took the hide away to stretch it. When I thought about him I could see he was troubled these days. He was thinner than ever, he danced harder, he hunted more keenly, he was even more particular than usual about our work. He was always fair and steady, but it was an effort now, and when Regil or Dran checked him for our faults he did not take it so easily.

Then, one evening as we sat hungrily watching the meat grilling, we heard a ripple of music outside the gate. The sound carried me straight back to the Little Fort. Regil said to Gerig:

'You might at least post a look-out!'

He and Dran went to the gate while Gerig looked uncertainly after them. Regil unbarred the door and Felim walked in.

He was the same as ever, raven-dark, spear-shaft-straight, a laughing mouth to greet Regil. He came to the fire sniffing appreciatively.

'The feast of heroes is the food for poets! Give me some of that and I'll sing you a song for it.'

'Lord of Songs, you are welcome!' said Dran.

Gerig took a step forward, faltered and turned away. Regil said:

'Here's Gerig, the eldest of the boys, my lord.'

'Well, Gerig?' said Felim, and held out a hand. Gerig knelt to him silently.

Felim sat among us with his harp on his knee, teasing Culla and the others and laughing like a boy himself, but keeping Gerig near him. When we had eaten, Regil said:

'Now, Felim my lord, can you bear to see these creatures leaping like leg-shackled cows, or will you give us something better?'

'Gladly will I see them dancing,' said Felim, 'but it was in my mind as I came along that I have not sung the old songs for many a day; shall we make a night of it, a song and a dance,

75

a dance and a song? And what of Dran? He has his hands still, I hope? Well then ...'

'But first a song,' said Dran.

'Oh, I've to sing for my supper, have I, poor tramping man that I am? If it's your will—'

He bent his head and struck a chord, and began a piece of nonsense about two men taking fish to market.

He had us whooping the chorus by the second verse, and when it was over he switched to one of the Great Songs, the 'Song of Chariots' from the Cattle-raid. Dran got up and fetched the small drum and wakened it gently with his fingers while Felim sang the opening, so that he was ready to put in the rolls that give you the charging horses. From that they passed straight to the greatest of songs in the Raid, the 'Fight at the Ford' that still brings tears to my eyes; then it was new to me, and as the spears flashed and at last in the cold twilight the otter came down to drink at the ford, my heart was almost out of my body. Old and cold is the man who will not weep to that song.

As the last notes died softly with an echo from the hills, Dran rapped out the beat of the Stag-dance, and up we sprang to stamp round the fire, and next we danced the Blackcocks. Then came a slow thunder from the bigger drum, a ripple from the harp, and we were into the Salmon-leap. Gerig was the best dancer of the Salmon-leap I have ever seen. Perhaps that was why Felim stopped us after it and put out his hand to Regil—

'I've a new song here, brother,' he said; 'may I sing it? I call it the "Song of the Red Spear".'

Regil looked quickly at Gerig.

'Yes, sing it, Lord of Songs.'

Felim moved a little forward, threw back his head, and there and then began for the first time his greatest song of praise; it is greater than any made for Ailill the elder, greater even than the song he made for Melduin at another time. It is the song of a man who went out alone, leaving his wife with her son unborn, and his home and all he loved, to hold a pass and turn defeat to victory, and die among dead foes before help came.

When he began Gerig was watching him like the rest of us; halfway through I saw him bow his head to his knees; at the end he held his head high and his eyes were bright with pride. So I understood that it was Gerig's father who was praised in the song, and had been Felim's dearest friend.

In the silence after the last note Gerig walked into the middle of our circle.

'I thank you, Lord of Songs,' said he in a clear and steady voice, 'I thank you for your song and for singing it here. It is worthy of you and of him.'

'Gerig, you could not praise it more,' said Felim quietly.

Gerig sat down by him.

'Have you sung it to my grandfather?'

'Not yet, son of Grath; I brought it first to you.'

Regil stood up and sent the rest of us away.

I would not have been surprised to find Felim had gone by morning, but instead he stayed some weeks with us, singing nightly from the Cattle-raid and the other great tales of former days. Sometimes he told the whole story and sang the songs as they came; sometimes he sang the songs only and asked us for the story; or he would talk round the story with Regil and Dran while we listened. All these tales teach a boy something about war, or councils, or love or treachery, or the ways in which manhood was attained in other times. It was not by chance that he chose them.

Most of all he spoke and sang of the Boar-hunt, the old Boar-hunt that was a religious ceremony and not only the crowning test of a boy's fitness for manhood. Regil did not care to hear so much said of it, but Dran was as anxious as Felim that we should understand what it had meant to our fathers. Felim would roll off the names of the heroes who took part and what fortune they met, how and why some failed and others were crowned with honour, and Dran would draw him on with questions. Some of this talk was dark to us all, but we sat enthralled by the songs and the stories, while for Culla and Gerig it was like the opening of a long-barred door. Here were the names of men found worthy, who gave their lives to the hunt, or who fell short of glory through greed or falsehood or laziness or cowardice. One could see in the eyes of the elder boys that they were resolved to do better than the best and be worthier than the worthiest of the heroes of old.

It was very near the time of the winter feast, and we had started building our fire for the Night of Fires, when I began to dream again. The talk these nights was fruitful for dreaming; at first I saw little snatches of the tales that had filled my waking thoughts, or fell asleep picturing myself among those great deeds. But gradually I got into a way of sliding into a warm contented rest full of comfort and quiet; it came to me that I had never felt so safe before, not since I had left the Hearth-house on that rainy spring day.

There was something a little odd in my contentment. I trusted Dran and Gerig (but chiefly Gerig) as I had never trusted anyone, but in my dreams I was being led to trust some-one else. There was a tall white-bearded figure that came to me every night and promised me all my desires, a big gaunt figure that stooped over me and bade me hold to him and he would give me mastery of all things. Once a boy near me woke suddenly with toothache and roused us all, and I lay on my heather mattress staring at the unseen roof and pondering on the dream I had left.

It was somehow like gazing into water—into a river pool on a sunny day. There were trees and clouds reflected on the water so that the sky seemed underfoot; as I began to drowse again I was looking at those shimmering clouds. And now, as in a river pool, I saw behind the shimmer a fish moving. A fish in the sky, a cloud in the water—one thing behind another. Suddenly I was sharply awake again.

I had remembered a fish moving under water, the fish in the little well below the hazels. And I remembered when I had seen him last.

Up came another picture all unbidden; Mangan heeling over into Felim's arms and Demetroos flinging aside Talorc to kneel by him, my own voice crying out and Talorc—I shook at the memory of what Talorc had done. I knew now who my white-bearded man had been, and my shaking turned to anger.

I bent my mind on the picture I had seen and presently I saw it again with a difference. I saw the man like a cloud on the water, and behind it stirred the fish; Mangan.

He was crouched over a little fire of smoky twigs, holding his hands over it and staring through the smir. The bones of his fingers showed like rods through the faintly-coloured flesh. His face was so lean that it was only a skull capped with thin hair. He stooped and coughed and the picture wavered. I felt him near me, and behind him something else alive but unmoving. I watched from the corner of my eye and saw a bed-place where Talorc lay under furs.

Mangan said something I did not hear, and then my name.

'Drost? Drost?'

I answered within myself:

'I am here, Reverence.'

'Drost, remember what you have learnt—remember the Most Reverend is your only friend and your sure guide— remember—'

The voice dragged as I well remembered.

Then suddenly he turned his full gaze on me across the smoke, and I heard him very loudly—

'No! The Mother—remember the Mother!'

I just saw him heel over again before mist hid him. I was stark awake and trembling, and I lay till dawn and wondered what I must do.

It was my day to work about the Fort. I found a little moment to go out alone into the hazel wood and hold up my hands to the Mother before I went to find Gerig at the water-side. By then I knew what to do; I said to him:

'I had a bad dream last night; may I speak to the Lord of Songs about it?'

Gerig looked surprised, as well he might.

'You? What kind of dream can you have that deserves to be —well, I suppose you can; I'll find out. Go and get the break-fast ready, Pup.'

A little before noon, when we had finished most of the odd jobs, Felim called me and led the way to a smooth boulder by the stream. He beckoned me to sit beside him.

'Why did you want to talk to me, Charcoal?'

'Because—well, because I'd like you, if you please, to ask Demetroos something for me.'

Felim raised his dark brows.

'What have you to do with Demetroos, child?'

'Please,' I said, 'please ask him to help. Ask him if he can bar a door for me.'

'Dark words! Will he understand you?'

'I think so; I hope he will.' I racked my brains for some token to send him. 'I know—ask him for the sake of the blue veil and what stands behind it.'

Felim laughed a little uneasily.

'That's more of a word from priest to priest than one from boy to man; what have you to do with such things?'

'Please, Felim! Mangan came last night—the Seer Mangan, I mean, and he brought me first one word and then another, and I don't know why, or what I should do, or . . .'

Felim said sharply:

'Here, is Mangan in the habit of bringing you messages?'

'No, lord; he's shown me things sometimes, looking into bowls of water and so on, and once at the Temple he showed me how to go away and come back, only I've never done it again; if Demetroos could come and help me I could perhaps go away and see what it means this time, but I'm afraid to go by myself in case I get to that place where I can't breathe . . .'

The memory of that terror of choking from which Terik had saved me made me rub my hands over my face.

'Moon and Stars!' said Felim; 'somebody's playing with fire! Demetroos must know of this. How did Mangan send you this word?'

'Well,' I said, thinking hard, 'first there was a little fire—no, first there was a picture behind another picture, and it was Mangan sitting by a little fire and the Most Reverend was there too. And Mangan called me and told me to remember—something—and then he said, "No, remember your mother!" or perhaps it was, "remember the Mother"; I think it was. And then he fell over. I don't like it, Felim; ask Demetroos please to help.'

Felim was looking very grave indeed.

'Surely I will,' he said. 'Hold to Mangan's last word, Drost, and remember the Mother. The New Way is not our way; you hold to the Mother and she'll hold to you. Don't let anyone start walking about inside your mind; that's your own private place, and no priest should hold the key to that door. Believe me, I've seen enough harm done in the past ten or twelve years . . .'

'Yes, that's another thing,' I said quickly. 'What did happen, ten or twelve years ago? Somebody said—'

'I dare say they did, but that's a different question. In another five or ten years, if I'm spared till then, I might answer you; not now. It's not my story and I've never told it yet. As for this dreaming business—certainly I'll ask Demetroos. All this going out of your body—I don't like the sound of that. I've seen Mangan—but never mind.'

I wanted to tell him everything now I had begun; I said:

'A white beast comes and eats Mangan's heart.'

'Mother of All! Charcoal, you must not—I had no notion— be a boy while you can, leave all that alone. Tell me, have you made any songs lately?'

'Oh no, I don't make songs; that was Ailill.'

'You made a poem once, about cranes.'

'That was a sort of mistake; it just came.'

'They do,' said Felim; 'they do. One can only be ready to welcome them. Come along, we'd better go back to the Fort; you'll have work to do, and we all have stomachs to fill.'

Felim went away; as far as I thought at all, I thought he had gone to fetch Demetroos. But the days passed and neither of them came, nor did I dream again; so I forgot all about that and ran in the woods with my companions. It was sharp weather with an occasional flurry of snow, and there were birds to be caught by hanging nets from trees and driving the flocks into them. There were traps too to set and lift, and we were busy.

Then, one still and louring day when the sky was hanging with snow (and we were watching the road in case the men came), we saw a little bent figure toddling along the path to the ford. It was muffled in a hooded cloak and walking with a long stick; a wanderer of sorts, one of those who scrape a living by peddling gossip and trashy ornaments, perhaps. Regil was in the Fort; he sent Arth and me to meet the traveller and offer rest and food, for:

'Whoever it is,' said he, 'this is no weather for a poor body to be wandering.'

We raced out like farm puppies round the wall and down the slope to the stepping stones, reaching them while the stranger was still prodding dubiously at the first stone on the far side. We saw a wizened old woman's face under the tattery hood, a brown seamed face with wrinkled eyelids ·and a straggle of grey hair.

'Wait, grandmother! Wait and we'll help you over,' Arth shouted as we plunged knee-deep into the ice-cold water. She stood patiently on the far side, bowed on her staff, her head trembling a little.

'Now,' said Arth, taking charge, 'give me your bundle, grandmother, and we'll go one on each side and you can lean on us; don't be frightened, we'll look after you.'

'Ai, good boys to be kind to an old woman—take care, now, dearies, don't drop my poor little parcel in the water, for where would I get more food? Slow, child, not so fast! My old legs will never carry me over these terrible stones.' I felt her hand shake on my shoulder; the pressure brought back a half-memory of the cliff path to the Temple and I shied; she screeched like a grey crow and clutched again—

'Eeeh, do you want to drown me? D'you want a good laugh when the old wretch tumbles in?'

'Not so, grandmother; go as slow as you like; nearly there now. Mind the next stone, it's a rocker. There now, there you are, safe and sound. Regil sent us to ask you in to eat,' said Arth, jigging on the bank to warm his feet.

'To the Fort of the Girls? Heh-heh, what has the likes of me to do with the likes of them? Still, it was kindly meant; tell the kind gentleman I'm going to shelter yonder in the little cave, but if any of you like to bring a bite of food to an old woman I'll not say no to it. He knows I'm harmless, he'll let me bide.'

'In the cave?' said I. 'It's very dark and rather damp; won't you mind?'

'Eh, laddie, what is it to me where I bide for all the time that's left to me?'

We could not persuade her, so we carried her bundle across to the cliffs and gathered a few armfuls of dry sticks for her, and Arth sent me to the Fort for fire. I went in busily and asked

82

Regil for a firestick, and said she would not come to us. He looked at me pretty sharply, and I supposed he was wondering if we had invited her properly. But he gave me the burning stick and I ran back spinning it and chanting the fire-spell:

'About with that, about with that,
 Keep alive the burning bat!'

till I got to the cave and handed it over safely glowing.

She took it with a mumble of thanks and hobbled inside with it. Arth took hold of my kilt and drew me away.

'I don't like her much,' he whispered.

I shook my head; there was something I did not quite like either, but I did not feel we could go just yet. We waited to see what would happen.

Smoke came wreathing out of the cave-mouth and she stepped through it suddenly, cackling when she saw us startle.

'Run away, children,' she said, 'and tell them I'll not refuse a mouthful of food.'

We took to our heels without delay, back to the safety of the round walls.

The days were very short now and the hunters came in early. We told Gerig about the old woman as soon as we saw him; his eyebrows flew up as he listened.

'Wasn't it right?' asked Arth anxiously. 'We did what Regil said.'

'No, it was right enough; I'm just wondering . . .'

'Wondering what, High-jump?' said Culla.

'If she tells fortunes.'

'Eh? Oh! Hm, we'll take her something, shall we?'

They both began shouting orders; someone fetched a big wooden dish, others piled food into it, picking out the tastiest bits of stew and topping it off with a couple of birds from the spit; we looked on a little sadly at all the best of the food going out of reach. Gerig sent me for a handful of barley-cakes, and while I was getting them I heard Culla's voice rise in anger.

'Keep your thieving fingers out of that! It's not for you or any of us—get back!'

83

Ailill whined—

'But I'm hungry.'

'And if you are? Stealing from a guest is no way to fill your belly. You deserve to be hungry for ever and beg for scraps like a dog. You needn't come with us.'

Ailill said furiously:

'What right have you to speak to me like that? Just because you're bigger than I am, and stronger, you think you can treat me as you like! The men won't think so when I tell them; they won't think you're fit to be a man! And when I'm out of here, don't hope I'll forget you, Culla; oh no, kings have long memories. I shall remember.'

I stood in the store-hut door with my hands full of cakes. Culla had fallen back a step, his face dark with anger. Ailill was scarlet to the roots of his cropped hair, standing over the dish with his hands on his hips and casting haughty glances round him at all the boys.

I was his Twin, his helper, the keeper of half his kingship— I must do something to save him, but what?

Regil walked up to him.

'Kingship is a duty, not a set of self-pleasures; you should not need me to tell you that. You have spoken very ill to the son of a man who served your father all his days, to the King's honour and his own. You cannot unspeak what you have said, and we cannot forget it; all you can do is to give us better things to remember in time coming. Take the trencher now, you and Drost, for you are the youngest. Take it to the old woman, poor and wretched as she is. And you, Culla, remember he is very young.'

'I am remembering,' said Culla through his teeth.

The others jumped into action to cover the silence; I gave Gerig my cakes without meeting his eyes, and took one end of the dish as Ailill lifted the other. The smell of the food turned my stomach and I could feel Ailill's heat beating on me. But the rest of them were stringing out towards the cave and somebody near the front began to clap out the Blackcocks' dance; before we got to the foot of the cliffs a line of dancers was hopping and twirling ahead of us.

We carried the trencher carefully up the bank and Gerig and Culla took it from us, stooping at the cave-mouth.

'Grandmother, we have brought you a present of our hunting,' we heard Gerig say. A deep muttering just reached us. They backed a few steps and led us down.

'Back home and eat, and then she says she'll tell our fortunes,' said Gerig. We looked at each other wide-eyed and hustled into our places.

It was a lean meal and I was not the only one to think wistfully of that laden trencher, but if it was lean it was sooner eaten, and we lost no time in sprucing ourselves up and going back through the gathering dusk to the cave. There was a tingle of excitement through us all; the time of night and the hidden woman (for only Arth and I had set eyes on her) and the promise of fortune-telling, a thing none of us had experienced, all went to draw a ring of magic round us.

Nor were we disappointed. We sat down in our gangs, the eldest nearest the cave, and first Gerig and then Culla went in, and then one by one in order of age till only Arth and Ailill and I were left. It was black dark now and we could not see the faces of those who came out, but the air was full of pleased excitement. I could feel a glow spreading; the old woman was giving good value.

At last it was Arth's turn; when he came out he put his hand over mine and I felt the blood coursing hard and proud.

'What did she say?' I whispered.

'I mustn't tell or it won't come; but oh, Drost, it's fighting and winning and all sorts of things!'

He shivered with delight.

Culla said quietly:

'Ailill.'

I saw him move against the dim glow from inside the cave; Gerig sent a whisper down the rank for me to come up and be ready, and so it happened that I was the nearest, and I heard.

A deep and powerful voice was speaking—

'No, child,' it said gently and regretfully. 'I have nothing for you; a bar of blood and a sheet of still water—a quick end instead of a slow one—that's all, nothing more. Begone with you, whoever you are; it's not for you, the last telling.'

Ailill brushed against me and Gerig's hand thrust me forward. I ducked under the low rock-mouth and into the cold space of the cave. It was dark except for the red eye of fire to

85

my left. I was going towards it when the deep voice spoke from my right.

'Feed the fire,' it said.

I knelt and stretched my hands to find the wood and at once I touched something I knew we had never brought in; whin stems.

I turned to warn her but the words died in my throat; instead I laid the wood on the ashes and said under my breath :

'I am feeding your fire, O Mother.'

I said it whenever I fed a fire, but I was neither brave nor faithful enough to say it aloud. A bright flame lit the cave and as I turned I saw her, sitting against the rock with her cloak thrown back to show her dark red robe. The hooded eyes drew me to her.

'Come to me, child of slaves and father of kings; come and let me feel your hand.' A dry cold palm enfolded mine. 'Yes, this is the one. Father of kings to lead your people when you have left them; so it is, so it will be. You'll break your fate and find your fate, and before that you'll find what you seek. You'll wed young and widow young, and it will be more of her making than of yours. And the wrong one will be the right one at first. Go along with you now, there's no more to tell.'

Gerig said softly from the entrance :

'Will he be a hunter, Great One ?'

'Hunter, fisher, or dreamer, what is that to you ? He will dance to the Smiler and swim in deep waters, and end as he began. Be off; I am weary of you all.'

I scrambled backwards out of the cave and ran to catch up with Gerig. He took my hand or I took his, I do not know which; we were both children needing comfort in face of our heavy fates.

The next day there was no smoke from the cave and our trencher lay on the bank outside it, so we knew she had gone. The matter was not discussed; indeed it went out of my mind. Ailill's anger and the spaeing had sunk together through the floor of my memory and lay somewhere in the depths below, like fish in deep pools, waiting for times not known. And that day the men came.

We were hunting, ringing a high glen to drive a small herd of deer towards the eldest boys waiting at the outlet. We crept and swarmed through the high ground all morning, and worked them gently forward all afternoon, and it was almost too late for clean killing when they came within spearcast. But the hunt went well on the whole and we had a barren hind and two yearlings to carry home.

We were coming down the hillside above the waterfalls, I with Gerig's spear while he took his turn of carrying the kill, when two men stepped out of a fold in the ground. They were in full dress, plumes, fur-trimmed cloaks, bracelets, swords and all. Gerig lowered his beast to the ground and bent his knee to them.

'Three killed and seven let through,' said one of them.

'Two hinds suckling, their two calves, a staggie and two heifer hinds,' said Gerig.

The other man had walked in among us and was turning over the kills.

'One clean spear in the neck, one with three arrow-wounds and a spear-thrust, and one with a broken leg and two arrows in the back; whose spear ?'

It was Lan's, a boy half through his training; Gerig had killed the broken-legged beast with a merciful arrow. The men grunted, signing to us to take up the game.

When we got to the Fort the other gang were home with creels of fish from the river-mouth. Half a dozen men were sitting round the wall watching them work, asking questions and talking to Regil and Dran. Gerig, white-faced, skinned his beast under their eyes and went down to wash. Arth and I got busy preparing the meal. Presently Dran called me aside and told me to put on a kilt of Lan's and take my usual one to Gerig. I went into the hut and found all the eldest boys hurriedly sorting out their trophies and checking spear-lashings and arrows. I went out again as quickly as I could, wishing I had found courage to offer Gerig a word for luck. Instead, I stoked the fire and held out my hands to the Mother for him.

The men and the elder boys made their own ring round a separate fire and we young ones had nothing to do but get the food ready and keep quiet. We heard them asking question after question, each answer received in just such a grudging silence as I had once known too well. When the meal was ready Lan went to Regil and told him, and we carried the meat-trenchers to the men. When they had had their fill we ate, but the elder boys not at all.

After that the drums were brought out and the dancing began. At first we all danced while the drums warmed up, but then Regil made us sit down and the elders danced alone. They danced bare, glistening with sweat that had nothing to do with their training (for they were as hard as leather), and with set faces and clenched teeth. They were taut as strung bows, keen as honed spears, and their feet struck the earth like hands clapping. They danced the Weaving-run flawlessly, and the Stags, and then Dran gave out the beat of the Salmon-leap. This was Gerig's dance of power.

I saw his shoulders ripple as he went into it and then he was off, springing from the earth, curving so slowly that we saw the firelight pass along the length of him before his hands came down to throw him off again over the stooped backs of the others, one by one—in and out, over and over. Each in turn followed him in that loveliest of flowing lines but for me there was only the leaping fish that was Gerig, and Gerig the leaping fish. When the drumbeat slowed to its last roll and he stood still, even the men shouted; as for us, we yelled like hunters.

Regil held up his hand for silence, and one of the men said:
'Well—that's as may be, but what of the Boar?'

So they went straight into the Dance of the Boar, and that went perhaps a little less well (it could hardly go better), and after that the Dance of the Green Glen; and there they stopped and stood with their flanks heaving, waiting for sentence to be passed.

The men spoke together for a little while before one called:
'Gerig!'

The ring closed round him. We heard the beginning of it—
'His hair's short enough; how's this?'
'He's blown!'
'What's this scar? A fall? What business have you to fall?'
Their voices sank lower. Culla leant his hands on his knees and ran his tongue round his lips; another thrust his hands through his hair in an uncontrollable gesture of nerves.

There was the sound of a body thrown to earth, and a single gasp; then silence. After an age the circle opened and Gerig walked out. He moved stiffly into the shadows of the wall and there threw himself down.

'Culla!'

Again the questions, the lowered voices, the sound of a fall, and the timeless waiting—and then Culla walked away into the dark.

Moonlight began to flood the court; I lifted my face to the Maiden and prayed and prayed, wordlessly, for I hardly knew what; for comfort and strength for Gerig and for courage, just a little spark of courage for myself when my time came.

At last it was over and Regil sent us packing to our beds. There were no elders to bid us be quiet, but we were too awed to talk and we huddled under our coverings as fast as we could.

When morning came Gerig's voice called us up as usual and we stumbled drowsily down to the river. It was only when he came up out of the water that I saw him, and I almost screamed. His face was a swollen mass of scars, and so were his shoulders and his upper arms. I glanced away and saw others staring covertly; I looked at Culla and the other elders and saw that they too were scarred but none so terribly. Arth and I gazed at each other and I saw my own horror in his eyes.

But then we saw another thing; one by one the elders fell back before Gerig, and though he hesitated at first, he entered the Fort ahead of them; and he sat to eat with Regil and Dran.

Slowly we came to understand that he had passed in one night through all the stages into manhood and had received all the marks. It was horrible; I have never seen another go through it and I should never wish to see it; but Gerig passed that gate in one stride.

When we understood, we were desperately proud for him and for ourselves, and Arth and I fought the little boys of the other gang. Then we were afraid Gerig would go back to the village at once and leave us to some other leader, but we need not have feared. He chose to stay until the men had come again and again to pass his companions through the degrees, and to go on training with them for the two great dances.

The winter passed and cold winds brought the spring, and at last all the elders were ready. They had a long day's hunting by themselves and made us a feast, and then they put on all their dancing ornaments and took up their spears and their loads of hides, and left us. They were men now in our eyes; their faces and arms carried the same marks as men's; we boys were left to learn what they had learnt.

Lan was our new leader. It took him some time to get the hang of it, but he was good in his own way. And soon afterwards a whole cluster of little boys came and Arth and I found ourselves with a load of work, showing them what they must do. I have never felt so old nor so important.

And about the same time I had another dream.

We had just begun herding the cattle again and they were too weak to stray. Provided we kept watch for the Grey Beasts who were not far away, scenting the weakness of the herds, our work was easy. I was lying one day in a warm nook among rocks, watching a few cows feeding slowly but eagerly on a patch of grass below, when between waking and sleeping I saw Demetroos.

I can remember nothing but the man himself, not where he was nor how he came; there he stood, a man in a faded violet cloak. His arms were folded over his breast.

'Drost,' he said; 'Drost.'

'I am here, lord.'

'Drost, by the sign you sent me, the Sign of the Innermost Mystery, I charge you; I charge you by the Sign of the Grain, bar your mind to everyone and to me as well. Do not open it until I can be with you in the body. I have closed the door, but there are those who would force it open; bar it from within, Drost. This is my word to you by the mystery we share.'

I was saddened. Did he mean I must not try even to reach my mother? I had forgotten to try all these months, but I had been thinking that when we were out on the pastures I might see her in thought if not in life. I wanted to question him but when I tried to frame the words I saw the vision already becoming misty. I made a great effort and called him back but it was only an echo, such as you see if you gaze at a flame and then quickly close your eyes and press lightly on them; Demetroos had gone.

And one of the cows had strayed into a narrow cleft above

90

a drop; I slid down the rocks and herded her backwards (for cattle will never go back of themselves) until she was safely on the pasture again—and there was no chance of reaching out to Demetroos by then. Later, while we were driving the cows back towards the village, it occurred to me that if Mangan had been able, before, to come into my mother's house, he might do so again. I would have to do without all dreams if I wanted to be spared any of them.

A few days later, as Regil was showing me how to finish off the binding on a bow, I felt a sudden leap of fear. Before I could stop myself I had cried out:

'Gerig's binding has slipped!'

'Gerig—what did you say?'

'I—oh, I'm sorry, Regil; I don't know what I meant.' I shivered, for a cloud had hidden the sun.

He spat to avert the geis.

'The gods grant you are wrong, for today they hunt.'

He told Dran what I had said, and Lan took me aside and spoke some hard words about unchancy talk while the others looked sidelong at me. Ailill was heard to say:

'He knows the Laws of Hunting, but you wouldn't think so, would you?'

'And do you?' said Regil, just like Lurgan.

'Of course; but Drost used to fancy himself at them.'

'I've never found Drost guilty of fancying himself much at anything,' said Regil. 'Let me see that throwing-stick, Ailill. I thought so: the shaft's crooked. Scrape it down and let me see it before supper. And tell Moran I want to speak to him about you.'

As Ailill went into the hut he threw me a glance of sheer hatred. I think that was the first time I knew the feeling that was to darken my youth and my young manhood; the feeling that there remained no chance of escape, that I was tied for ever to the daunting duty of backing this animal till death cut me free—without loving him, without even admiring him any more, against all those I loved or might love, however long, for whatever cause. I was not a free man of the People of the Boar; I was Drost, the lesser half of the King.

That evening, as we sat round the fire before the dancing began, we heard the shuffle of feet outside.

Dran and Regil were up as one man to kindle torches and run to the gate. There were six men outside; they filed in slowly.

The first two carried, slung below a pole, a big black boar with the death-foam still on his jaws; and four more carried a hide on which lay something white and still. They passed the bearers of the boar and laid their burden by the hearth, and we saw it was Gerig.

One leg was hidden under a plaster of leaves and clay; a little sluggish blood was seeping through. His head rolled helplessly and his eyes were closed.

As Regil knelt by him Lan went unbidden to fetch ale for the bearers. His eyes flashed as he passed me.

The leader wiped his mouth and gave thanks and said to Dran:

'It was up at the Grey Rocks; you were the nearest.'

'Quite right; where are the others?'

'Gone home with the dogs to carry the news and bring help; is it too late, think you?'

'Still bleeding,' said Regil. 'He'll do, if we can staunch it. Honey, Dran, and ale, and a bag of wool for a pad. How big is it?'

One of the men ran his thumb down his own leg from the turn of the thigh to the knee.

'And how did it happen?' Dran asked, mixing the healing brew of ale and honey.

'Oh, as always; there he was; quick as a hawk—chose his man and broke through three spears to reach him. And the boy's lashings broke.'

'Gerig's lashings broke?'

'They held a little while—see, here's the spear-wound!—but he worked himself up the spear, swallowing it, you might say —you know how he cares nothing for a hurt if he can reach you?—and it was a question if the shaft or the lashing would give first. The dogs got in behind him and hung on, Neart and I speared him here and here, see, on the flanks, and he dragged the whole lot of us up to the boy and seamed him. Without the dogs he'd have gone clean through him.'

Gerig opened his eyes to say in a small polite voice:

'Could I please have a drink of water?'

I leaped for a dipper but he was gone again.

I think we all thought he was dead, except perhaps Regil who had his hands on him; but it took more than that to kill the son of Grath. By next morning he was there all the time, lying weakly by the fire but able to speak and eat; and the day after they took him back to the village. As they lifted him they gave the shout of the Boar-dance, the big 'Ho-ho-*ho*!' that rouses the boar; and that was my first inkling that Gerig had killed, not any boar, but The Boar, and that in his first hunt. I had just enough sense to hide my thickwittedness from the others.

The spring came in slowly that year with long weeks of sleety rain. Hunting was difficult, fishing was poor, and we were glad to eat the shellfish the herders gathered at low tide. Dran told us Gerig had healed and was walking again, but that he had not been able to travel with the others to the Green Glen. That was the first time I knew the Green Glen was a real place and at a distance. I tried a few cautious questions but got the crooked answers I deserved, so I let it be. If there was one thing above all to be learnt at the Fort of the Girls it was that knowledge comes in its own time and not before.

But something else was coming in its due time, something that was to pull me back to forgotten things; I sensed it first when the men talked together gravely, glancing at Ailill and me the while. I felt it again when a messenger from the village came with a notched message-stick, and still more strongly when I saw Dran's face as he ran his thumbnail down the notches.

'Is it worse?' asked Regil, watching him.

Dran handed him the stick.

'As bad as bad can be, I'd say.'

'And nobody's said anything this time? Strange; you never can tell what they'll know and what will miss them.'

And they went their different ways. Now how did I know that someone was desperately ill and that Regil wondered why I had had no sending about it? Perhaps in spite of Demetroos the door was not quite closed. I went off alone and tried desperately to pierce the darkness and see what was wrong; desperately but in vain. Only, all that night and all next day, the skin of my neck prickled as it does when someone watches you from hiding.

The day after, another messenger came and took Ailill and me away without a word of explanation. He merely set off across the ford and along the trail at a run, as he had come, and we had to stretch our legs to keep up with him.

And all the way I felt the prickling at my back and nothing to tell me why.

We came to the village, bypassed the Great Fort, and entered the Temple precincts by the main gate. The priests who met us led us to a room in the guest-hall and as we entered Lurgan came through a side door towards us. He was older and graver; he ran his eye over us hurriedly. We were still in our hunting kilts and splashed to the thighs with mud from the road.

'Get cloaks for them,' he said; and to us, 'in here; he wants to see you.'

He pushed us through the far door. The muscles below Ailill's shoulder blades jerked into knots. Talorc lay before us.

Only his eyes moved as we came in. He was lying by a small fire on a heap of blankets and furs, and he looked withered and faded. We bent our knees to him. The sweat ran down Ailill's backbone.

Lurgan put an arm behind his master and raised him a little. He peered at us with lacklustre eyes and his left hand plucked at the covers. It was like a great tree fallen and turning to bleached timber; I felt nothing, neither fear nor pity for the ruined hulk.

'Come then,' said Lurgan, and led us out.

'Is he—does he never speak aloud?' asked Ailill in a small voice.

'Not yet; only through Mangan. But he sent for you; you are needed. Take your cloaks and come quickly.'

He folded his white cloak round himself and we followed him out and uphill. Neither of us found words to ask where we went or why.

We went straight up through the village to the door of my mother's house. As we reached it the curtain was drawn back and Demetroos met us.

'How is it?' asked Lurgan.

Demetroos answered in a low voice:

'Bring them quickly. What have you told them?'

94

'Nothing yet.'

'It cannot be long. Better tell them.'

Lurgan stopped, halfway through the door, and took our arms.

'When Ailill the elder died in battle there was no time for you to receive kingship from him; all you have, came to you at the fire. If you have learnt anything you must know the kingship is too much for one man, even such a man as Ailill was. Part of his kingship is in his Twin. Melduin is dying; you must receive the rest of your kingship from him before he dies.' .

He crossed the court where the doves flew up as we passed. At the door of the Hearth-room I caught his cloak.

'Reverence, we cannot enter—we are not clean.'

A frown of annoyance ran over his face; he said curtly:

'Well, if you must—be quick. There is no time left.'

I turned aside to the water-jars set ready along the right-hand side of the court and poured water into Ailill's hands, and bathed my face and body as well as I could in my haste, and re-knotted my kilt. There was nobody to offer us clean garments. Quick as we were, Lurgan stood by impatiently; as soon as he thought us ready he led us in.

The fire burned low in its cone of grey ash. He gave us no time to lay wood on it, but I noticed, and wondered, that he made a small obeisance as he passed. Demetroos was holding back the curtain of the inner room; we passed under his arm and came into that remembered place.

The house fire burned brightly; Cardail crouched feeding it and heating something in a bowl. Beyond the hearth a bed had been made up on the floor and two women were kneeling by it. It took me a breath or two to recognise one of them as my mother.

Lurgan bowed deeply as he came in, and stepped round the fire. My mother half-turned, putting out a hand for silence, but when she saw who had come she moved a little aside for him. He stood well back, looking down and beckoning us to come closer. Demetroos remained by the fire with Cardail.

We went to Lurgan and he put us past him so that we looked down at the bed. There lay Melduin asleep, his face the colour of clay and wrinkled like an old man's. His head was turned to the side and his hand held the coverings on his breast. The other woman was at the head of the bed, watching his breathing.

Lurgan touched my shoulder gently and I knelt.

We waited, nothing moving more than the slow lift of the covers that told us he was still breathing. At last there was a tremor in the face and the eyes opened. His gaze wandered and found my mother. She stooped over him to say clearly and softly:

'The children are here; Ailill and Drost have come.'

He turned his eyes to her with a drowsy and wondering look.

'Ailill . . .' he said faintly; 'Ailill and—Melduin?'

'Ailill, son of Ailill, and Drost his Twin.'

He sighed a little—

'What have I to do with them?'

Lurgan signed to ask if he should speak, and when she nodded briefly he leaned forward to say:

'Great Lord, these children will be the kings of the People after you; is it your will to give them your kingship?'

The voice drifted faint as smoke in sunlight—

'Such as I have I give to them; little have I to give them.'

Lurgan said urgently:

'Yet a little longer, lord! Put your hands under his, both you sons of the kings.'

There was a confused movement round the bed. Ailill had to stand aside to let me come closer and Lurgan leaned across to draw out Melduin's other hand and lay it on Ailill's. The little flurry was too much for him; his eyes closed; my mother whispered:

'Is it not enough? Let him rest.'

'He must hand it on; can't you help him? Brother, you at least should understand . . .'

Demetroos took the bowl from Cardail and handed it to the older woman, who raised Melduin's head in the crook of her arm and held the warm milk to his lips. He drank a little and looked at us.

'Ailill, son of my great brother,' he said in the thinnest of voices, 'your share is all that was your father's by right.'

His lids drooped; he roused himself and went on:

'Drost—little son—to you I give all I had; more I cannot.'

His hands lay heavy on ours; he turned his eyes back to my mother and his lips moved a little but no sound reached us. The older woman whispered harshly:

'Wait beyond the fire. This is not for you.'

We drew back with Lurgan and passed beyond Cardail to the door-side, and there knelt again.

We had come far and in haste; with my mind I knew we were in the presence of death, but my body complained of hunger, of cramps, of an itch in a healed cut. I tried to pray or feel awe, but I wanted to fidget and scratch my leg. The smoke stung my eyes and I had to rub them. I caught a glance from Cardail and half-grinned, only just checking myself in time. I was kneeling on the hem of my cloak and it pulled at my neck. I who had learned to freeze on the open hillside as long as need be, I could not be still for two breaths together.

I looked under my lashes at Ailill beyond Lurgan and saw his throat move to swallow a yawn. Lastly I looked up at Lurgan, who instantly pressed his hand warningly against my side; I followed the line of his eyes and saw the group beyond the hearth as he saw them.

There lay the Dark Twin dying. At his head knelt an old woman, becoming more and more the centre of the group as the man faded. At her side was a younger woman, her hair bound back under a blue hood, looking down at the man so that her face was hidden from us. A little to one side stood a girl child, the servant of these women, waiting to hear what she should do, and behind her the stranger priest who was a healer but who could not avert what had to be. The man on the bed lay still, turned a little away from us.

We continued to kneel. My fit of fidgeting past, I let my mind go free. I looked down from above, seeing the inner room and the Hearth-room, and the court now filled with women, and the road outside filling with silent men, and the village empty, even the cattle standing quietly in the outfield and the dogs sitting at the house doors or nudging their masters' legs for comfort in the stillness. Far off I saw the Temple with people going about their work. Last of all I saw the little room where Talorc lay with Mangan kneeling by him and telling him all I saw and more in his low dreaming voice. I saw the sea wrinkling along the cliffs, and the boys herding the young beasts on the strand, and the birds lifting and crying as the tide turned to the ebb.

A low sound by the fire—Cardail was crying. The old woman made a quick angry sign and she went out, her head bent to hide her tears. The other two remained as they had been.

Time passed; I had pins and needles in my legs and wriggled my toes secretly. A log fell into ash with a rattle; Lurgan leaned forward to lay another in its place, holding his hand above the hearth for a moment afterwards.

The weight of silence grew. Demetroos bent to feel Melduin's hands and stepped back. The old woman dipped a cloth in a bowl, squeezed it, and wiped Melduin's brow; the sharp scent of herbs made my nostrils twitch. Then she lifted his head into her lap and settled it there.

My mother gave one loud bitter cry and bowed her head to the ground, then straightening herself she resumed her steady watch.

A gale of cold air blew over us; the fire flared; through the curtains came a third woman.

She was tall and slender and as white as foam, her hair burnished as the red gold traders bring over the sea. She went round the fire and the ashes stirred as she passed. She came to the foot of the bed and held out her hands. Melduin sat up and put his hands in hers, and with a great and happy smile he rose up and stood.

I almost leaped up too in joy that somebody had come who could make him well; but a sharp movement made me turn aside, to see Lurgan throw himself to the ground with his cloak hiding his head. When I looked back the tall woman had gone, and though the Old One still nursed Melduin's head on her knees she was using both hands to stroke the shoulders of Malda, who was lying across the body.

I do not remember moving; we were out in the Hearth-room, shepherded by Demetroos, when next I knew anything. He stopped us there.

'Not straight out to the People, brother,' he said, and led us into one of the little guest-chambers. Here they left us two while he and Lurgan went to the courtyard door. Through the leather curtain we heard the cry of many women taken up from mouth to mouth, and beyond them the murmur and movement of the men.

Ailill leaned against the wall, deadly pale, his mouth working.

'Did he—was that—is he dead?'

I nodded. Something too strong for us both came over us and we wept, as much from fear of death as from sorrow that Melduin had gone, Melduin who had been good and kind and had saved us from the priests.

The two men came back and found us crying, and Demetroos put his arms about us and let us weep. In a little while he said to me:

'See if you can find Cardail and get some food for Lurgan and yourselves.'

So I went out through the Hearth-room to the deserted courtyard and searched for her. I found her at last crouching in a little store-place and mixing meal and milk for bread, and I said in my old brotherly and managing way:

'Demetroos wants food prepared.'

Cardail turned her white face to me; her lips moved but no sound came.

I was trying to get back to everyday things; I said:

'Where's the Maiden? Who is she this year?'

She shook her head.

'There isn't one; she went home.'

'Oh,' said I, and then, 'was it you, then, at—at the end? You did it very well.'

Cardail scrambled up past me; over her shoulder she said:

'It wasn't anybody; it was—her.'

Then at last I understood and my knees gave way under me, and I knelt among the grain-sacks and prayed the Mother to guard me because I had seen the Maiden.

When Demetroos had seen us eat he left us to sleep while he took Lurgan away to bathe and prepare for the ceremonies to come. It must have been late in the night when I was roused by voices.

99

Demetroos was speaking as I woke—

'But are you sure? How can you be sure? A priest does not lightly desert his training.'

For answer somebody groaned.

Demetroos went on:

'I beg of you, do nothing now; give yourself time to think; you cannot—one cannot—think clearly at such a time as this. It has overwhelmed you—let it pass—one may regret bitterly what one does in haste.'

To whom was he speaking? Cardail? I remembered her blanched face and her flight. Could it possibly be my mother? Certainly she had been dreadfully unhappy when all her power and skill had failed to keep Melduin alive, and now Ailill and I would have to be kings in his stead.

The thought struck me with such force that I lost track of the voices; my mind reeled from the idea and I thrust it into a corner and rose on my elbow to listen. When Lurgan spoke, close to our doorway, it made me start up in surprise.

He said most bitterly:

'Surely you have lost something at some time; can you not see I have lost everything?'

'Nobody loses everything,' said Demetroos; 'all things remain in her keeping and she returns her gifts to us when we can use them.'

'I have lost everything,' he repeated as if the other man had not spoken. 'I have been a priest and I have been proud of it, and I thought I had knowledge; and now I am nothing and I know nothing.'

'There is wisdom in that knowing, brother. One can find things by losing them. You are still a priest and you serve the gods. Do not throw all this from you. Wait a little.'

'I am not a priest,' said Lurgan. 'I ceased to be a priest in there, a little before he died. I knew to whom I must pray, and I do not know how to pray to her. She is not served by men; what you have called my gods are shadows in the minds of men, and I have been a servant of shadows.'

'Do not profane the High Gods!' said Demetroos sharply. 'As for shadows—many live happily by the guidance of shadows and prefer them to a light too bright for their eyes. If she, or whoever is most high, has chosen you to be a leader of shadow-men, you must go on leading. Whom can they follow if you leave them?'

'Let others do as they will. I return to her, I take shelter with her. If I die under her anger, I die; but I will not work against her any longer.'

'Ah, that's different. What need to work against any of them? Your feet are on the right path; only go on and do what you have to do and all will be well. Tomorrow when you perform the ceremonies...'

'No! What can I do? How can I perform what I know to be wrong? I do not know how to do what is right; whatever I do I deepen my sin. Let me go!'

There were sounds of a scuffle.

Demetroos said rather breathlessly:

'Be still, you fool; where will you go? Rest here till day.'

'There is madness here for those who have done wrong—let me go!'

Another voice cut across his. It was a deep voice I knew well; the last time I had heard it, it had spoken out of darkness also.

'Children, what is this quarrelling by my Hearth?'

A slight ruffling, the sound of men falling to their knees.

'Demetroos, you who have been living in my daughter's house, what folly is this?'

'Lurgan's heart is sore, Great One, because he has seen matters not in his learning.'

'And is that a reason for brawling? Have you no duties, priest of the New Way?'

'I am no longer a priest,' said Lurgan in a smothered voice; he had hidden his face. 'I am nothing—I know nothing. Kill me and finish it.'

'Kill you? You think yourself worthy of death from my hands? You consider yourself ready for the Orchard, your muddy little spirit fit to play on the clean grass under the apple-trees, dulling the pleasure of the singers with your mutterings? Be off with you, and do what you have to do, and see you do it well! The gods you serve are as much children of the Mother as you are; she has made you a servant to her children; do you think she cannot oversee all the slaves of her household? We want no more foolish talk from you—you'll wake the children, and what is worse you'll trouble my poor child. Go down to your temple, boy, and do as you must; when you've come to a more settled way of thinking perhaps Malda will bother with you some day.

'There now! And what were you thinking of, to let him get to such a state of mind? A healer, you call yourself? Good night to you, stranger, and let us have no more high words in my courts.'

It was the Old One herself. I lay as still as a mouse, hardly daring to breathe in case she knew I was awake and bent her wrath on me too. If Lurgan and Demetroos could be rated like this, what would not she do to me? I held my breath till I was almost bursting, but there was complete silence outside and presently I fell asleep.

The next day the funeral ceremonies began, but we had no part in them at first. Instead, some of the younger men fetched us away to the Great Fort, where we were bathed and robed and led to an inner building I had never seen. To my great comfort we did not pass near that place where once I had almost choked to death.

'Where are we going?' I whispered to Ailill.

'Where are we going?' he demanded in a lordly voice.

The slaves conducting us bowed low and said they were commanded to take us to the Great Lady.

'Indeed!' said Ailill haughtily. 'I have no objection, as it happens, to visiting the Queen my mother, but in future you will be commanded only by me.'

They bowed again and again, touching his feet with their hands, while I wondered if he could really believe he would be allowed to stay here and give orders like a man, at twelve years old.

They brought us to a low wide doorway with a pleasant scent of woodsmoke drifting to meet us. Ailill tossed his cloak over one shoulder and strode in.

A woman cried out as he entered, and by the time I crossed the threshold he was enveloped in the arms of Ginetha the Queen.

'I greet you, Queen,' said Ailill.

She held him at arm's length, murmuring tenderly:

'Little Ailill! My little boy!'

'I'm nobody's little boy now, Queen; and here's my Twin.'

I too was caught in that soft and clinging embrace, and fluttering kisses fell on my face till I drew away embarrassed. She smelt of dried roses and foreign spices and her clothes were soft and floating, and her rings and bracelets clinked as she waved her hands. She put one soft arm round me and the other round Ailill and drew us to a couch near the scented fire. The room was airless and very warm.

'Now let me look at you both!' she cried, sitting down between us. 'How you've grown, my darling, and how thin you are! I told them to make those little cakes you love—where are you, you stupid woman? Isn't the food ready yet? Bring it instantly—you must eat all you can, dearest, because you must at least pretend to fast when the ceremonies begin. There now; isn't that a treat for you?'

A slave woman set a great platter of honey-cakes before us. We had had no breakfast and they looked inviting, but when we bit into them they were so cloying that we could not eat them. I longed for a bowl of broth such as we would have had with the boys. Ailill pushed the platter away and said so out-right and the slave was sent to make some, while Ginetha kept begging us to eat the cakes and nibbling them herself while she talked.

She held Ailill's arm continually and patted it with every second word, and she cooed over him and pitied him for the hardships the men had laid on him, and said he need never again do anything he did not like now that that man was dead.

The inevitable happened quite soon. Ailill pushed her hand away roughly—

'Don't do that, Queen! Can't you understand I'm not a baby any more? I'm the King. I'm going to feast and drink ale, not eat stupid cakes and sit in this stuffy hole. Why did you ask to see me?'

She drew back as if he'd struck her, and indeed he had, harder than any rod.

'Dearest! Dearest!'

He got up and walked away saying:

'Make a fool of Drost if you will, but have done with me.'

Her big grey eyes filled with tears.

'Lady,' I said humbly, 'forgive us; we are weary.'

'Of course, yes, poor child, how tired you must be! Come

and sit down and I won't bother you any more; how like your father you have grown! Don't go yet—somebody is coming here who wants to see you.'

'Who?' demanded Ailill, wheeling round.

The slave brought a steaming dish of beef stew and set it before him. Holding to the principal matter he asked again with his mouth full:

'Who is coming?'

He was answered by the tramp of feet as six temple servants bore in a litter on which lay Talorc.

Ginetha fluttered round them while they set the litter down and helped him on to one of the bearskin couches; he bent his brows and grunted painfully as they settled him. I had knelt to him, but Ailill merely rose in his place and bowed a greeting.

I expected to see Mangan next; I was even anxious to see him, for I discovered a sort of love for him in spite of my fear of most things connected with him. But I was never to see him again in life.

Instead after a moment or two Talorc spoke to my mind.

'I am very skilful at this now; remember that. You will be my mouthpiece while I speak to the Queen. Come here.'

I left the food and went to him reluctantly, under his masterful compulsion. Ginetha looked from him to Ailill and back to me.

'Is the Most Reverend not wonderful?' she breathed.

Talorc moved his one hand and laid it heavily on my shoulder.

'It is necessary to speak fair to this stupidest of women. Tell her I will help her to her desire in return for certain help which I need.'

I said carefully:

'Lady, the Most Reverend says he knows your desire and will help you to it.'

'Does he? Oh, tell him I will do anything—everything— what does he require of me?'

'Tell the fool I'm not deaf as well. Make her get a scarf and lay her bangles and trash on it.'

Ailill said suddenly:

'I'm fed up with this place—I'm going to get more food; coming, Drost?'

He had eaten my share with his own.

Talorc's fingers tightened.

'How can I?' I said.

'You'll do as I . . .' Ailill began, but Talorc took his hand from my shoulder and pointed to the door. The great king of a few moments before grew red and looked down and shuffled his feet, and at last went sideways through the door, a child ashamed. I felt myself grow hot with his shame.

Talorc's mind said to me:

'Was that a king that left us, think you?'

For the first time I realised that Melduin had indeed given me something of his; I lifted my head and met Talorc's eyes and said aloud:

'If he and I are to be kings we need the help of our people.'

He was as much taken aback as I was myself; after a short and ominous pause (when I remembered all too clearly his last dealings with me) he began to laugh, shaking with harsh sounds. Ginetha watched us, fearfully clasping her hands.

He shook off the fit and brought his mind to bear again.

'Cub of the old wolf! You shall have help. Meantime you have not told her my last words; have you forgotten?'

'Lady, he desires you to fetch a scarf or some piece of cloth,' I said.

She pulled off one of her many draperies—

'This? Would this do? What is it for?'

Talorc nodded and pointed to the floor at his feet.

'Now tell her I need gold.'

She was startled.

'Gold? What need has he—what do you want? Oh, why can't you speak instead of looking at me so? Will this chain do?'

She unwound one of her ornaments and laid it on the scarf; he gave no sign that he had seen it, merely fixing his gaze on the broad collar at her throat. She hesitated and with a helpless gesture untwisted the ends and took it off.

He pointed to her wrists—

'All the gold, tell her.'

I repeated this; she gave a little whimper.

'All? But Ailill gave me these! And these I had from—from my father.'

Talorc's mind flashed dark with anger.

'Remind the Lady that I know well what she had from her father. Tell her she can always wear her mother's ornament if she likes.'

There was something so horrible about this that I did not like to repeat it. His fingers dug into my arm. I had a moment's insight into the Queen's mind; she was thinking of a small coffer of blackened wood, hidden somewhere in the room.

'Well done; tell her that,' said Talorc's mind to me.

'The Most Reverend says there's something in the little dark box that you could wear,' I said unhappily.

The next instant she was grovelling before him, stripping off rings and bracelets with shaking hands. She looked up, her eyes brimming over.

'Is it enough? Ask him, Drost, is it enough?'

Talorc looked past her to a chest against the wall.

'Go and open that, Drost.'

When I stood up she was before me, her hands pressed to the lid.

'No, no, I have given you all! Most Reverend, I have given you all!'

'Tell her it may suffice; I shall send for more if I need it. Roll up the scarf and give it here to me.'

I wrapped up the jewels and helped him hide them in the breast of his robe; Ginetha saw them vanish with tears spilling down her cheeks.

'Remind her, this goes to pay for her desire which I know; let her think so. I hope I need not bid you be silent?' and then—

'Call the bearers; I am tired.'

'But how? How will you do it?' she whispered.

'The Most Reverend does not reveal what he will do,' I said. He grunted approval.

I went to the door to fetch the servants while behind me she went on her knees to stare into his face.

When they had borne him out, Ginetha threw her arms round me again.

'Little Drost, dear little Drost, what else did he tell you? What is he going to do?'

'Lady, I don't know; I only said what he bade me say. I'm sorry if I made you unhappy . . . my mother's still got those things you left at the Hearth once; I'm sure you could have them back; she said the Mother didn't want them.'

'Your mother!' Ginetha pushed me away. 'Don't speak to me about your mother! Am not I all the mother you could want, I who am a queen?'

Ailill came in with a honey-cake in his hands—

'Come on, Drost, and see what the men are doing.'

I was utterly spent; all I wanted was a safe place to sleep, out of reach of Talorc's will and Ginetha's clutching hands. I followed Ailill in a daze.

That night saw the pyre burning and the men circling it, but this time it was I who took the torch from the hands of Gerig the Old, and I on whose arm a gold band was twisted; I was still half-tranced and it meant little to me. Only afterwards when they gave me the horn of honey-wine to pour on the flames, and Felim tuned his harp, a fountain of tears broke inside me and I knew my loss.

And Felim sang. He sang the 'Death-song of Melduin', which is second only among his songs to the 'Song of the Red Spear'. I did not understand it then, though now I do when I have no voice left to sing it. Felim sings it yet, maybe, yonder in the Orchard. It tells of a boy who desired priesthood and was turned to kingship by the High Gods; who, turning, found and lost his heart's desire; who, losing, found the service of his people; who gave them safety with his body's pain; who regained in death all he had lost for them.

It is hard and strong and difficult, and one must hear it more than once to know all it has to tell; that night in the death-feast only a few men knew what Felim was saying. But many eyes were bright for Melduin and many voices praised the song.

Then others tuned their harps and sang their songs new or old, and ale-cups were emptied and voices grew loud. We sat each on the steps of the chairs that would one day be ours; we could not yet take our places among the men. I saw Culla, and later Gerig also, among others at the far end of the hall, but the oldest men were around us. There were no priests; they were still busy elsewhere.

The hall grew hotter and hotter till my head buzzed with sleep. I blinked my eyes and shook my shoulders, and looked towards Ailill to see if he thought of going to rest. But he was holding out his cup for a slave to fill, giggling as he held it crookedly. The feast-ale is heady stuff for men and not a drink for boys. As he lifted the cup old Gerig stepped up and took it out of his hands.

'Enough is enough, little king; sleep is your need.'

Behind me a man muttered :

'Now we'll see some sport !'

Ailill jumped up in a fury, but he had forgotten his long red cloak; the skirt of it was caught under a stool and brought him down headlong. As he lay half-stunned at the old man's feet, Lan's father stepped from his place, tossed Ailill to his shoulder as if he weighed no more than a lamb, and bore him out.

Nobody told me what I ought to do; I waited uncertainly for a breath or so (though it seemed long enough to me) and then I bowed to the men and followed.

The same old slave was waiting by the door; he took my hand and brought me to a sleeping-place off the courtyard. When I woke the sun had climbed high into morning.

Doubtless the men of the Boar feasted Melduin for the full three days, but for us the death-feast was over. By dusk we were back at the Fort of the Girls, and the waters of custom closed over my head without a ripple.

I lived those days at full stretch. There were boys older than I who were newly entered and my juniors, to whom I had to show the way; and there were the boys of Arth's group and mine who were two years ahead of me. I had little time to think of what I had seen or heard at the village, or about anything except the demands of each moment as it came. Only at the herding sometimes I could let myself be idle and try to order my thoughts.

On one such day in high summer, when the tide was far out and the cattle had followed it over the warm sands, I lay on the short turf and fingered my newly-gathered handful of shells. There were little yellow ones, splendid dancing ornaments if one could pierce them without breaking, and smoke-blue mussels, and cloudy oysters beautiful to turn in the hand but useless for necklaces. I thought of the winter dances and how we would circle to Dran's drumming, and from that I passed to thoughts of other music.

I played dreamily with my shells and dreamily with memories of Felim singing. What had happened to Melduin, after all? What had the Death-song told us?

If only I knew that, I thought, I would make a song myself as Felim kept asking me to do. It would be fitting, I thought (Mother of All, the pompousness of boys!), if my first song were for my forerunner. With vague thoughts of Ailill I tried to string lines of old lays together, but had to admit I was making nothing of it. 'Music,' I said half-aloud, savouring the word; there was a pleasing phrase somewhere at the edge of thought. Suddenly it came back—

'The voice of music.'

That was it; a day at the Little Fort and Demetroos talking with the priests and Felim—

'How did you find the way?'—'By the voice of music.'

What music had guided Demetroos? How had he heard it? At the furthest back of my mind I half-heard the ripple of a reed pipe. Was he waking or sleeping when he heard it? I had heard once a high sweet chiming . . . from the deepest well of memory came my mother's voice speaking of silver bells ringing above green grass. These were mysteries of the Mother, not of the New Way. And what was this New Way? Why did the men prefer it? How were priests made and why had Felim said Melduin was a priest before he was the Twin? Was he not born the Twin? They said I was born in one hour with Ailill and that made me his Twin . . .

Felim knew so many of the answers—I wished he would come and talk to me. I wished it so hard that I half-expected to see him walking along the sands towards me, but I saw only the other boys straying out to find shells and waiting for the cows to come up for the milking.

A grass cliff shelters the Long Strand on the north. Sometimes one could bring down a gull with a sling-shot when birds coasted down its rocky northern side. Gull feathers were worth having as dancing-ornaments; I tied my shells in a corner of my kilt and ran up the slope of the bank.

But there were no gulls there today; far out to sea they rode in rafts, gorged with fish. The air was still and warm and the short thyme-scented grass was hot to the touch. I lay down and wriggled to the drop on the far side to see what I could see.

At first there was nothing moving; a cormorant flew down the coast and eiders grunted and cooed on the tide. But presently I made out a nearer murmur among the rocks. I worked my way cautiously over the turf until I could see into a hidden gully below me. And there, kneeling on the grass, was a woman in a dark hood.

She was facing the sea and rocking herself back and forth so that at first I thought she was soothing a baby. But then she flung her arms wide and raised her head, and I understood that she was mourning. I had no right to watch; I crawled back and stood up to run, and as I did so I knew who she was and for whom she was weeping.

I fled back to the strand as hard as I could, for I did not want anyone to notice where I had been or to think I had been spying on my mother. But as I ran I wondered whether perhaps Melduin had been my unknown father.

That winter, my thirteenth, was the hungriest I had known. The hot early summer had stunted the corn, soaking rains spoiled the harvest, the grain went wet into the barns and sprouted there, and autumn turned suddenly to winter. The deer changed their ways, as once in a long time they will, and travelled deep into the high ground so that every hunt took us far out. Small game was scarce, the fishing was bad, and the only abundant food came from the little birds that fell to our slings, half-starved with hunger and half with cold.

We danced at nights for warmth rather than for pleasure. With little enough to eat, our dancing was clumsy and we hardly attempted the Salmon-leap or the Stags. Scars were slow to heal, and we were losing skill and hurting ourselves more easily. When Lan took to carrying a sling instead of a spear it was a measure of our condition.

We heard from the villages that many old people were dying. Dran had to go back to bury his mother, and while he was away Regil said one night:

'They say the gods and the Mother are both angry now; who will help a people who anger their gods?'

Lan said:

'How can anyone know what angers them or pleases them? They are up there and we are down here; if they don't bother about us, why should we bother about them?'

Regil turned his head and spat into the fire. I said:

'My mother would say that the Mother is not angry; it's we who don't understand her ways.'

'Well, if she wants us all to die, I'd rather she killed us than left us half-dead like this,' said Lan.

'Isn't there anything one can do to please these gods of ours?' said Neart's son Moran, who had followed his brother Culla into the leadership of the other gang. 'Drost, you ought to know these things; isn't there anything we can do?'

'Yes, Drost,' said Regil; 'you know the laws; tell us what the gods have said about themselves.'

I sat on my heels and assembled the words in my head; to my surprise they came smoothly together and I reeled off the Law of Sacrifices without a check.

'Ugh, it's all priests' work; none of that's for us,' said Lan. 'What are the priests doing about it, Regil?'

'Well, I did hear they'd taken the best of the corn into the Temple, so that people won't be tempted to eat it and leave nothing for the spring sowing,' said Regil.

A flame lit in my mind, a flame of anger. It was for my mother to guard the seed-corn, not for the priests. In my heat I said:

'The spring sowing is the Mother's business!'

'So Dran would say,' said Regil.

Moran said:

'What help will the spring sowing be to us? At this rate we'll not be there by harvest.'

'Oh,' said Regil, 'you're not all that bad yet; you can starve a lot more before you die of it. Wait till you're eating moss.'

'What d'you think we have in the pot today?' said Moran rudely. 'Roots and bark and a few thrushes for flavouring.'

'The spring sowing had better be good,' said Lan.

Arth was sitting with a smaller boy each side of him, huddled together to share their warmth; he looked across the fire to me and said: 'Is there anything we can do to make it good?'

'There's the Maiden's Dancing,' I said slowly; 'very few men go to that; perhaps if more of them went . . .'

'That's not for you,' said Regil hastily.

I had a sudden thought.

'Melduin—I mean the lord who is dead—he saved the people once; what did he do?'

'The great ones forbid it!' cried Regil, and spat again. 'Don't speak of that. Eat your supper before it spoils. I'm going to see if there's a fish on my lines.'

He got up and went out, and Lan shared the food among us, keeping Regil's share; but when he returned he said he had taken one small fish, not worth sharing, and had eaten it. He divided his food between Lan and Moran. Certainly he had moved his lines, as we saw later; but there were very few fish in the river.

That night as others slept round me, one moaning a little and another muttering uneasily, I stared up at the rafters and drove my mind towards the Temple. I had a burning necessity to know what had become of our seed-corn that should have lain dry and safe in the granary behind the Hearth. That need overcame even Demetroos' warning, even my fear of brushing against Mangan's thoughts. I lifted myself out of the body, looked back at it as it lay among the others, and steered myself towards the place below the Great Fort.

There were dark barriers around it; I was not surprised to find them; perhaps Demetroos had made them, or perhaps not. I hung beyond them a while, willing myself to find a way through. Into my memory came a memory of great shafts of golden stone fronting a gateway to wonders at the foot of huge burning cliffs. I saw a dark sanctuary lit by the gleam of golden arrows; what god bore them I did not know, but I stretched my hands to him and to the Mother. Then I saw a little chink of light in the dark wall and I looked through.

Down below me Lurgan the priest knelt by a shallow hearth, holding a wide sowing-tray above the embers and shaking it in the heat.

Someone came out of the shadows into the firelight with a jar of grain on his shoulder; he set it down with a grunt and knelt by the priest. I saw his face; he was Terik, who had been with us in the Little Fort. He held an empty jar for Lurgan to pour in the grain from his tray, and emptied the jar he had brought in its place.

'How much more?' asked Lurgan.

'Five households only, master; the rest belongs to your own people.'

'Five more households! Well for us the harvest was so scanty! If there were more to parch we should need help. As it is—nobody has seen you, Terik? You are sure?'

'The Most Reverend sees me every time I pass with the jars,' said the slave.

'Yes, but after—when you take it to the other store?'

'I do not do that now, master; that's for other times. The danger is only that he who sees in the dark may see me. While you, master, talk to him and hold his mind, he does not look. Then I do it. If he looks now he will see us drying the corn as the order was given.'

'More grain; this is dried. Terik, it is not your life nor mine we carry in our hands; you know that.'

'I know that, master. A life or two is not a great stake to throw on this board. We slaves are all gamblers as you know, master. There is plenty ready to grind and the rest is safe. For every jar I have taken out, I take one back. Three more now, master, and then you can go to your bed and your slave will finish his work.'

Lurgan raised his head and looked about him—

'Quiet! Did you hear something?'

Terik's eyes widened—

'Only the sea.'

But I saw the sweat break out between his shoulders; it was time to go if he could feel me watching.

I woke in the dark hut and lay in fear of unknown evils, unable to read my dream.

When Dran came back he brought beef with him, part of a cow he had killed to make his mother's funeral feast. He told Regil in my hearing that some of the priests had said all meat ought to be laid on the altars, but Lurgan had ordered him to feed his friends instead. He said the priests did not look as lean as most folk.

A few days later Regil went to the village and came back driving two half-grown bullocks. They grazed round the Fort while we watched them like wolves. Regil said they were part of his share of his father's herd, and he would rather eat them now than leave them for his friends to feast on when he was dead. He had also a small bundle hidden under his cloak, and when we were all in, with the bullocks safely stalled and the gate barred, he brought it out and opened it. It was full of fine-ground flour.

We stood round him staring at it; we had not seen meal for months. He mixed it with water and baked small bannocks, one each, and we ate them as they came from the baking-stone. No harvest-cakes could taste better than that bread.

Dran said:

'Bread of the Mother's giving! There's a thing to put heart into a man.'

'To be truthful,' said Regil, 'it's not of her giving but from the Temple. I went to the sacrifices as I told you I would, and that's what they gave each of us as we left.'

'Plenty to grind,' said a voice in my head; 'plenty to grind.' I could not recall where I had heard the words.

Dran sat down slowly, staring at Regil.

'To each of you? How many were there?'

'Not many; most of them are praying at the Hearth these days. My mother begged me not to go to the Temple, but I have always served the New Way; why should I change? Behold my reward.'

'Behold your reward,' said Dran. He threw the last pinch of his bannock carefully over his shoulder into the shadows.

Some time in the next moon, which was the last before the Maiden's, Dran said to Regil:

'What about the Temple? Don't you feel a desire to pray again?'

'They'll not buy my prayers with a poke of meal,' said Regil drily. 'But the gods know all things. Perhaps I will go; I'll go if you'll take me with you to this dancing of yours next month.'

'To the Hearth? But you've never come there before! Gladly, if you will—it may not be much of a dance this year, so be warned.'

'I've taken a notion for it,' said Regil, 'and I fancy some others might like to come with me.' He picked up his spear and went off before Dran could answer him.

In the result, the Maiden's Dancing was so crowded that year (as I heard afterwards) that the men had to wait outside until the women began to come out before they could get into the Hearth-room to pass their garlands through the smoke; so crowded that the line had hardly cleared the courtyard before the head of it was at the hill-foot. There was no chosen girl to lead them; the choice fell suddenly on someone during the dance itself.

Regil and Dran had no business to be away together, but we were so determined to make the dancing a success that we obeyed every rule as if they had been there; and before they came back we had a reward of our own.

On the Day of the Maiden three things happened. The cold grey wind of that day brought down a rotten tree in the woods above the waterfall, and Arth, going for firewood, found the bole full of old ripened honeycomb; Moran and his gang met a badger who had come out into the thin sunshine, and managed to drop a rock on him; and I and the little boys netted the sea pool and took three small salmon, the first of the spring run. So that night we danced, very badly, the Honey-hunters and the Salmon-leap, and Arth and Lan made up a wildish dance they called the Badger-walk. By the time the men got back we were sitting about with full stomachs, baking the badger-hams.

The men had defied Talorc and his gods, but Talorc's time was coming. Twice I half-dreamed of Mangan, and once I saw Demetroos with his shoulder set against a door, thrusting with all his might against Something which I knew to be an ultimate and unbearable frightfulness. I awoke shuddering and lay awake till the false dawn. More and more I needed Felim, but he did not come near us that season.

Instead Neart came with another man, both of them strong for the New Way, and called to Regil to bring Ailill and me out to them (for they could not enter the Fort while their own sons were there).

'What is this?' said Regil, coming down to them with us a few steps behind him.

'There has come a Sending to the Most Reverend,' said Neart;

'the High Gods have shown him how to assure us all of food for this year and many to come.'

'And what part have these boys in it?'

'He said only that we were to bring them to the Temple,' said the other man.

'I wish Dran was back; here, it's—it's not as it was that former time, is it?'

'No, no!' cried Neart at once. 'Nothing like that; he told us himself through the Seer, this is something quite new.'

Regil turned to us—

'What say you? Will you go with the men?'

'What's it for?' Ailill asked; but I, stupidly yielding my will to their pressure—for I think Regil would have resisted if we had refused—I said:

'If it's for the good of the People, of course we'll go.'

'Of course,' said Ailill. 'It is my desire.'

'Very well,' said Regil slowly. He stood watching on the hillside above the ford until the shoulder of the next hill hid him from us.

So again we travelled to the village, Ailill walking ahead with Neart—that gullible man who agreed with everyone—while I went in silence with his companion and wondered what lay ahead. We did not hurry; dusk was drawing in when we reached the village and went round byways to the Temple without meeting anyone.

The gate was standing open as we approached, and waiting in it was a priest I did not know. The men knelt to him in silence, and in silence he beckoned us to follow him.

He took us to guest-rooms beyond the Temple and watched while slaves bathed us and brought us the white robes of priests. When they had finished he led us to the Temple itself and through the outer passages to a gallery on its further side. Here in a little room we found food ready, meat and meal and milk, and we ate, still in silence.

Ailill wiped his mouth and stretched himself—

'Good is the food; do we thank the Swordsman or the Smith?'

'Thank both and the Singer also,' said the priest; 'all three have sent for you, Kings of the Boar.'

He was a fine-looking elderly man with a wise face; I

thought he was a man who might answer questions. And at the same moment he turned to me and said:

'Here am I, dark one; ask me.'

I had not thought he could read me, and was confused. He turned back to Ailill, who was yawning.

'You two brothers must part soon; have you anything to say to each other before that?'

'What should I say to Drost?'

The priest raised his brows—

'Little king, you should be kind to the other part of yourself; he is the storehouse of your learning and the keeper of your wisdom.'

Ailill shrugged.

'If he's there when I need him—' he said.

I began to wonder if there had been something strange in the food. I found my mind running away with me, and Ailill's tongue was betraying his heart.

'I don't want Drost all the time,' he was saying. 'I don't believe all that about the kingship needing two bodies. A really great king has it all in himself. My father didn't need Melduin.'

'Little king, when you are as old as I am you will know how much Melduin held in himself and how much he did for Ailill. One thing that he did you will soon learn: he gave the People safety from hunger, such a hunger as lies on them now.'

'Melduin did?' said Ailill, amazed. 'That was a kingly thing to do; why didn't my father do it?'

'The High Gods chose Melduin.'

'Are they going to choose between us now?'

'Yes,' said the priest. 'They will choose. Rest now, there are hard things to come. Sleep well, little king. Drost, follow me.'

As we left I saw Ailill intent and full of purpose; he and not I should be the saviour of the People.

I said to my guide:

'Reverence, may I know your name, and what we must do?'

'My name is Naas, child; and it is my business to show you what you must do. See, this is where you will sleep. Are you weary, or would you rather talk a little first?'

'No, tell me first, please tell me,' I said eagerly. 'I've wanted to ask so much for so long. Will you tell me everything, or only about what's to happen now?'

'Child!' he said, laughing a little at my vehemence. 'I will tell you what I can of all you want to know. It is your right to know all that touches the People.'

I sat beside him on the narrow bed-place and wondered where to begin; this was not such a priest as I had known before.

'Mangan—' I said; 'the Seer Mangan, is he well?'

'Alas, very ill; but why ask that? Have you not seen him lately?'

'No-o,' I said carefully; 'I have seen—others, but not—'

'Ah, you have of course seen the Most Reverend; that's as it should be. Why ask about Mangan?'

'Because he opened the door to me,' I said; certainly there had been something in the food. My mind was warm and relaxed and words came on my tongue unbidden.

Naas lowered his voice—

'Mangan is a fine spirit with a hard destiny; he might have been many things—I knew him well. His reward will doubtless come. What else, dark one?'

I tried for a moment to hold back the next question but it came out in spite of me.

'Who was my father? I know I'm "the son of no man", but that's in the mysteries, everybody has to have . . . I mean, it's . . . was it Melduin?'

Naas looked really startled.

'My dear child, you cannot ask me to comment on the mysteries of the Old Way! I can tell you this much; wherever you got that idea you can throw it away again; he who is lately dead was the father of no man.'

'And I am no man's son,' I said drowsily; it seemed to make sense at the time.

Naas ran his hand down my back and again laid it against my neck; it was cool and supported me pleasantly. He lowered his voice still further into a murmur while his will overpowered mine with longing for rest. I felt him ease my body down on the bed, just as a little warning flame flickered in a corner of my mind; I tried to sit up and call to Demetroos, but instead I sank under a warm dark wave.

It was not silent under the wave; I felt the pulse of my own blood and heard the sough of my breathing. I was climbing the steps of a high white tower, narrower than a fort and far taller, round and round, up and up, under the wave but rising nearer a greenish glow above me where light beat on the surface of the sea. Far under my feet a single drum throbbed, and as I climbed I heard the waves sigh round me. I looked up to the glow and stretching down through it I saw a pair of hands, immensely long, immensely strong, long slender golden palms and powerful narrow fingers. They reached down to me and I was glad and reached towards them and felt their heat. The fingers curved inward on my either side and I knew they were the hands of the Swordsman, the Rider in the Sun, whose other name is the Long Hand. And suddenly the fingers drove into my ribs, curving between bone and bone to meet round my heart and lift it clear of my breast.

Far underfoot I heard the drum beat twice more, Plon! Plon! and then silence, a painless peace, and a floating free in the green wave.

There was no daylight in the little room to tell me how long I had drifted free; a small lamp burned high up in a niche on the wall and cast a moonglow round the bare cell.

When I returned into the body Naas was sitting by it and watching intently. As soon as I began to stir he drew out of me all I had seen in my dream; he drew out things I had not known I was seeing and hearing. Strangely enough my only fear came from the drum; I dreaded that sound and its cessation. When he was sure I had kept nothing back he passed his hands over my face and the dream went from me a little. He showed me a place where I could wash, and when I returned there was food by the bed.

Naas went away and I ate and lay down. I did not know if I should dress and be ready to go with him when he returned, but until he came I would sleep a little.

As I lay I knew my mind was being called upon to lift itself and go, but it was somehow cumbered; I slept shallowly and uneasily until Naas returned.

Again he said he was willing to answer all my questions, and I tried to ask what it was Melduin had done for the

People, and what Ailill and I were to do; but the words twisted
in my mouth and though he saw the questions in my mind he
gave no answer, merely laying his hand on my neck again.

As I sank into sleep I thought I heard Mangan's voice speaking somewhere near; I struggled on to one elbow and called
out:

'I am here, my lord Mangan—I am here.'

Naas frowned and stooped over me—

'Rest, boy, rest; the Seer Mangan is not here.'

'He was calling me . . .'

He bent his head.

'Yes—it was a mistake, child. Sleep.'

I sank down again. Naas had his hands clasped in his lap and
his eyes were closed. As cautiously as if I were stalking a roe-
deer in broken cover I tried to see into his thoughts, and I
caught an echo of his voice—

'Not now, Mangan, not now! Tell him this is not your time
but mine; let be, be still.'

But I was sliding away into another place.

This time there was a red blaze and heat, unbearable heat. It
was a smithy—why should I suddenly think how all our slaves
hated smithies and would walk a long way round to avoid
passing an open forge door? The smith was forging a spear-
head. He took the iron in his grip of twisted withies and
thrust it deep into the flame, pumping the bellows with his
foot so that the fire roared, and pain broke over me and rose to
torment as the flames leaped up. Then the spear was on the
anvil and the hammer-blows fell, *tink!* on the anvil to steady
the blow and *tonk!* on the beaten iron; and I was anvil,
hammer and spear. From fire to anvil, from anvil to fire—I had
no tongue to cry out to the smith that I was I, and no tool for
his working. The great red-eyed bearded face came louring
over me and greater heat poured from it than from the flames.
Then the spear was ready; through steam and agony of cooling
it was hafted and hefted in his hand, and then—what then?
The spear was ready to be thrown, thrown at the deer running
on the hill and innocent of danger.

I wrenched myself awake, drenched with sweat and shaking
with fear. Naas had my hands in his and was soothing me with
a low comforting murmur—

'There, be still, trust him, the spear feels no wound; trust the spearman who aims you aright—be still, trust him as you have learnt to trust.'

But again as soon as I could speak he dragged out my dream step by step, though the telling was almost as terrible as the dreaming of it.

Again I washed and ate and again he left me to rest; and this time I saw my mother walking far away over the Long Strand among the sea mists, searching, searching everywhere for something lost to her. I tried to run to her, but my feet were clogged with clay (in the common case of such dreams) and before I could overtake her Naas returned and woke me.

There passed several days (I supposed, for I saw neither daylight nor starshine to tell their passing) and all the time I knew with half my mind that there was still more to see. The food they brought me was good and tasted well, and yet every mouthful was drugged. Naas came talking kindly and gently and seeming to tell me many things, but when he went I could never recall a word he had said.

Then there came a time when a slave brought food and hurried away, and before I could begin to eat a clamour arose from outside my cell, men's voices crying and the blowing of horns. I stole to the door and listened to the strange and riotous noise, and in the dark of the passage I saw a vision.

It was like a cloud opening, or a mist, and in its heart a small bright flame. The flame burned among scented branches, pine and apple and whin; and as I looked a hand came and added twigs of rowan. Then I knew I was seeing enchantment, for who but my mother would dare to set that wood on a fire?

I stood stock-still and the firelight showed me Felim and Demetroos and my mother kneeling round it and holding hands in a ring. And I heard all three call me in low voices:

'Drost! Drost! Drost!'

I answered within myself:

'I am here.'

My mother turned her face to me and could not speak for tears. Demetroos called aloud:

'Son of the Great Mother! Remember what you are and what you have been; do not let the priests of darkness have their will. The Great One will guard you from misdeeds of men; call on the Mother of the Grain to guide you.'

And Felim said :

'Singer, by the Mistress of the Flocks I charge you, fast as the cranes fast when they fly to her.'

The mist closed over the fire and the three were hidden. I was alone in that dark narrow place, and I shook with cold, but I carried back with me to my cell three pictures : the grey ashes on the Hearth, and the ears of corn in their veiled jar, and the jerky flight of birds across a clear winter sky.

I stood, dazed, by the platter of food. My mouth was dry with thirst and I was hungry. I shook myself wider awake. I had gone hungry before, a night's fasting need not trouble me; but how to conceal it from Naas? At last I took the platter under my robe to the washing-place—while the shouting and horn-blowing rang out louder than ever—and I mixed the food with water and poured it away and swilled it through the drain-hole in the wall, and splashed the floor with water as if I had been washing myself. And I poured away the milk in the same way, and laid the dish and the cup where they had been before, by the bed.

Then I lay down and drew the covering over me and tried to sleep, hoping I might dream further of the Hearth-house and of my friends.

But that night I learned the power of the New Way, for I had the most fearsome dream of all.

I was walking in a little wood through a grey gloaming and all around was still. From far ahead I heard the note of a pipe playing softly and clearly, a little air like a bird's call, over and over. I went towards it and came to a clearing, and there sat a young man in a rough cloak. His back was turned to me and his fair hair hung over his shoulders, and his arms were raised to hold the pipe to his lips. That sweet fluting bubbled out like spring-water and drew me to itself. I stepped out on to the green moss, and the player turned where he sat and looked full at me with the clearest of blue eyes in a face of surpassing beauty.

Unspeakable terror seized me, so that I ran through the woods stumbling over roots and tearing through thorns, and the piping pursued me, now behind me, now beside me, driving me on. I ran till I was faint, and then I beheld a great grey stone that lay on the ground a little way off. It seemed to promise safety and I staggered to it, meaning to hide beneath it from that terrible sound. As I reached it I saw a golden knife lying on the stone; I put out my hand and took up the knife and at its touch I knew that all the pursuit had been to bring me to this.

I stood over the stone and looked about me, and the player of the pipe faced me and played one last triumphant phrase, and smiled.

I woke clinging to Naas' hands.

'It is over, child,' he said gently. 'It is enough. The High Gods have chosen, as we prayed them to choose between you. They have made their will abundantly clear. It is time to go.'

He put a cloak round me and led me through the dark passages, out into a night of driving rain. We walked over grass and by narrow sheep-paths till at last he stopped me, drew the hood of my cloak over my face, and lifted me in his arms. A pulse in his neck beat against mine. He stooped low, there was a waft of death-cold air, and he set me down on flagstones. He put his hand over my eyes, stripped off my cloak, threw it from him and pulled off the robe also. I saw a glimmer of torchlight from behind me, but as I turned it vanished and Naas with it. I was left alone in a cold dark place that smelt of death.

I stood quite still where he had left me, waiting to see or hear anything that might be there. Nothing happened. I stretched out my arms and moved a step at a time this way and that way, to find what prison I was in.

I walked forward a dozen steps and felt something underfoot that was not stone, while my hands touched rock ahead of me. I ran them up and down and felt a slab of stone standing upright and ending at arm's length above me, where another slab lay across it. Fearing to dislodge that roof I felt to the side instead and there found a great rough sheet of stone, and so also on the other side. Then I crouched down and felt for the thing my foot had struck.

It was narrow and round and smooth, three spans long with a knob at one end—a club perhaps, but not of wood. I kept hold of it, thinking that if anything came through the darkness I should at least be armed, and I groped about with the other

hand. There were many smaller things lying about my feet—
something that might be a broken bowl, a small polished stone,
and a round thing that my hand could barely cover. I turned it
about but could make nothing of it. I gripped my weapon between my thighs and freed both hands, to find below the
smooth top two rounded holes and a jagged edge, and below
it some harder sharp-edged little objects that moved when I
touched them. And suddenly I knew what they were—teeth.

The next instant I was at the far end of the place, pressed
against a wall of slabs, retching and wiping my palms on my
sides. I had dropped that new-found weapon and no power in
this world or beyond would have made me go back for it, for
now I knew. I had been handling unburnt human bones.

The gods know how long I leaned there and shuddered, but
at last the sickness passed and I tried to consider my situation.
I must be in some kind of cave, a cave with an old burial in it,
some place belonging to the Former People, for who else would
have left their dead to fall asunder like a beast's carcase?
Perhaps it was a trap from which the old dead had not been
able to escape, nor should I.

I began again to feel about me, but everywhere the cold
stones turned me back. I wondered how Naas had come and
gone, and it seemed to me that one of the end stones moved a
little when I thrust against it, but there were others in
front, and perhaps more behind to hold it there. Then I
understood so far at least that the priests must have put me
here for a purpose and would fetch me away again when the
time was ripe. So I sat with my back to the wall, as far as I
might from that dreadful thing I had handled so freely, and I
waited.

I must have slept; when next I knew anything I was desperately hungry, and I thought bitterly of the food I had thrown
away. But I took comfort from the memory of my mother and
the others, and remembered the three pictures they had given
me, and hoped they might come to me again.

Instead, after I had waited for an eternity, I heard Mangan's
voice in my ear—

'Drost, the gods have chosen you to serve them. Put your
hand behind you and take the tool of the gods.'

I thought I had explored every crevice, but now when I felt

behind me my fingers touched metal. I tried to draw it out, but it caught on a stone, so that I had to turn about and work it clear. It was a heavy-hilted thing, as long as my forearm, with a razor edge to a hooked blade a little like a reaping knife. The metal was warm in my grasp, not as heavy as iron but heavy enough. I thought the blade was bronze, but the hilt was strange to me until I recalled the feel of my armlet. I fingered it and the hilt together, and I knew the hilt was gold.

I hefted it, wondering, and Mangan said again:

'Stand up now, turn your hand, and strike.'

I swung the thing like a sickle. Mangan said:

'Not so, but away from yourself.'

I turned my wrist and struck outwards and down, and he said:

'It is well. You will offer a sacrifice in this way.'

The voice ceased and I was left alone. I kept hold of the strange knife and swung it as he had said, out and down, out and down, for something to do; and when I slept, I slept holding it.

Again Mangan called me and bade me learn the use of the knife. By this time I was beyond hunger, my whole body was dry and aching, I could not have fed myself if they had brought me food. I slumbered uneasily dreaming of milk and later of water, of a clear spring welling under trees.

And then I saw Mangan. He was walking very slowly away from me, a staff in his hand, going like the oldest of men, a step and a step. He was toiling up a green slope in the morning sun that threw his shadow ahead of him. As he came to the trees he turned himself carefully and I saw his ravaged face. He looked into my eyes—

'Little brother, seer of dreams and hearer of voices, it is finished for me. I have done you much harm, I shall do you no more. I have told her where to find you; I go now to face the mercy of false gods. Farewell, little brother.'

I fell on my knees and dropped the knife to stretch my arms to him. He said slowly:

'May the Mother reward you, child, and not as my gods have rewarded me. I did their will; I sent you the words of Talorc.'

Then he stopped short and cried out:

'I who am going free, why should I lie? No gods' words, but

a man's—Drost, hear me—turn the knife! Turn the . . .'

He choked and fell to the ground and his staff rolled out of his grasp. He gripped the turf and dragged himself forward and I saw once more with his eyes. He was looking into the little well behind my mother's house and as he looked, the fish that lives there to keep the water clean broke surface to snatch at a leaf floating in the dappled shade of the hazels.

Mangan cried—

'A well of water, and the end of thirst! The Well—the Well at the World's End!'

I saw out of the corner of my eye a white thing moving nearby; even as his face fell forward and pressed into the grass, a snow-white doe came to drink at the well.

A terrible trembling filled me; I had heard—when had I not heard?—of the White Doe that carries the dead to the Orchard. The women say those who see her full-face have not long to live, as those who see the Woman at the Ford have not long to live. I had seen her; I had seen her now under two forms; was I to die? I bowed my head on my knees and cried to the Mother—

'Mother of all, be with me and with Mangan the Seer.'

There was a sound of scraping and dragging behind me. Dazzling light fell round me, hands took my shoulders and raised me up. Naas put the knife into my hand, turned me and drew me out into the overwhelming light of the sun.

Stunned by the light I walked forward at the head of the priests. I felt a dense concourse awaiting us among the shadows of high stones, a silent army standing overawed. I did not know who I was, nor where, nor that I was naked; my soul was loose in my body; I held the knife and walked under the hands of Naas.

Shapes rose before me and faded into mist. There were shaven men with great feather fans, and little godheads borne on litters shoulder-high; there was a garlanded bull and the scent of blood; there were trumpets and cymbals and horns. The dust was golden; I walked through it towards the golden pillars of the temple where the Archer waited. The pillars trembled and dissolved into the shapes of the Old Stones. I walked up to the great middle stone where it lay at their centre with the sunlight striking it. Deep in my mind stirred a

126

picture of that other stone where I had sought refuge from the Singer. A white calf lay bound on the middle stone, ready for the knife, passive and still. I raised my hands and my eyes to offer sacrifice to the Archer, and I met the eyes of Talorc.

A shock ran through me. Here was no god but a white-bearded man. His eyes held mine so that I could not look away to the men around us or to the sacrifice laid ready before me. I was under his power.

The silence was broken by the beat of feet flying down the road towards us. The ring moved like grass under the wind; the spell was straining. Talorc held my eyes; I saw his lips move; and suddenly the long-silent voice broke from his throat, croaking:

'Strike! Strike!'

I turned my wrist and lifted the knife. I saw the light gleam red on the blade and yellow as a sunbeam on the hilt; I let the blade fall with its own weight; and I heard Mangan's last words—

'Turn the knife!'

The mists broke open around me. I checked the swing and looked down.

Ailill was the calf bound on the stone.

The blade was falling; with all the remnants of my strength I turned its course and the weight of the haft swept it towards me. There was a scream somewhere in the crowd of watchers, an answering roar from a hundred throats, and a sickening tongue of pain licked through my whole being.

The sun was blotted out in blood, the world spun and fell, I saw Talorc's white robes turn scarlet and far under my feet I heard the drum beat twice, Plon! Plon! and no more.

Part Three

I was free. I was free of the body and its pain, the boy and his fears, the evil and the dreams. I was myself alone. Like a bird homing at evening I turned to fly to the temple, to the golden pillars on the mountain's burning flank where the other half of me walked under the silver trees. Home! Home! I am coming, my darling, I am coming home to the courts of gold, to your Lady of the doves and violets, to my Lord of the bow, to the sickle moon . . .

A pool of blood poured on the lip of a grave, a wall of blood springing in the sun—I sickened and swayed in the void—a dark man stood on my road and said:

'Not yet is the way open for you.'

My heart's darling waited for me below the golden pillars; I struggled against the dark man in vain. From beyond the dreadful veils of red the other half of my heart called me home.

The dark man set his mouth on mine and breathed courage. I trembled in his hands. It was bitter as birth to begin again, to stoop over the wounded body. I went about it seeking a way to escape and finding none. I shrank from it and its pain. I fought to be free.

I felt the spells of women binding me with strands of their long hair, their hands catching at me as I hung above them,

their soft compelling voices calling me down. I turned again to
fly to the burning cliffs to find the rest of myself—

'Not yet is the way open for you.'

As bitter as birth the pangs of re-entering the tortured body.
I recalled the wall of blood that had engulfed me, and I felt the
sickle heavy in my hand, and I cried aloud :

'The knife ! Turn the knife !'

'Little son,' said a woman weeping, 'the knife is turned; come
home to us, beloved, Drost, little son, Drost, come home to me.'

I came a little at her bidding, fearing the blood and the pain,
yearning for the temple of the tall pillars hidden beyond the
dark pool; I remembered many forgotten things, the singing in
the courts and the sorrow of parting, and a white body I bore
in my arms to a cold grave alone . . . and a high thin piping and
the heat of fire and golden fingers plucking at my heart.

The dark man said to the woman :

'They have set great fears about him; he is in the power of
the Lord of the Woods.'

The woman answered :

'The Mother is mistress also of the woods.'

He said : 'If the Old One would come—if she would hasten !'

I was very weary. I folded myself and lay down to rest in
the body, but the pain I had remembered and feared almost
drove me out again. I lay heavily waiting to be set free, and
they forced into my mouth a taste of milk and sweetness, so
that the body yielded and slept.

I lay in a green place at peace. But presently I heard footfalls
and I looked and saw seven tall women, beautiful, wreathed
with dark flowers, walking one by one with downcast eyes to
search in the leaves at their feet. These seven women had one
face, a face of infinite and terrifying beauty, and I knew they
were searching for me. I lay helpless; they were at the other
side of a forest pool, but presently they would come to the
hither side and find me.

But a tremor passed through all seven and one by one they
grew faint as mist and took flight, and down over the leaves,
treading without a crackle of stick or rustle of leaf, came a
great and dreadful beast. He was golden and black and his hide
rippled with his strength. He stooped to the pool and drank, his
wrinkled muzzle rippling the dark waters. When he had drunk

his fill he stretched himself and lay down and I saw his snow-white underbelly and its golden sheen. The huge feet were the feet of a cat and his teeth were terrible as swords. He was the foe of the searching women, and my friend, and I slept.

The dark man said to the woman :

'I have sent the beast of a very great god to guard him from the Lord of the Woods.'

I woke in my own body with my mother leaning over me. She held a drink to my lips, but I could only sup a little before I was back again in the green place.

The beast had gone. In his place, drinking at the pool, was a white doe, and riding on her back a young girl whose name I knew.

'Cardail!'

I stood up in my dream and went towards her and she brought the doe to me—

'Mount up behind me and I will take you beyond pain.'

I mounted gladly, and it seemed to me that I heard the chiming of silver bells. Now all would be well; we rose from the pool and drifted over the forest, and looking down I saw green fields giving place to the sunlit sea; and then she turned to look at me.

Nobody can look over their shoulder without showing their true face. I saw that the face of Cardail was a mask hanging a finger's breadth before the face of a man. The mask vanished, and the face, and the girl, and the doe. I was falling, falling through the air into the deep waves below. They broke over me and I tasted their salt, and they ebbed and left me lying by a hearth, my face wet with tears.

A new voice said above me—

'Where's that milk, girl? I told you to have it ready—do you want him to die of hunger? Give it here; away and weep outside if you can't control yourself. Now, boy, drink this.' One wrinkled brown hand held a beaker to my lips and another raised my head. A compelling dark eye looked down at me. I drank and felt the heat run through me.

'Hm!' said she. 'A pretty work they've made of it between them! Now, understand me, there'll be no more wandering hither and thither; you're back in your right mind and there I'll thank you to stay. As for those that put their ramshackle spells on you, I'll attend to them in due course. Drink the rest of this and go to sleep. I'll be here.'

I drank and slept like a baby, her hand below my cheek.

When next I woke I found the old woman of the cave beside me; I said drowsily :

'You shouldn't put whin on the fire, it's unchancy.'

'Oho! But you put it on with your own hands, child.'

'Arth and I didn't bring it in, though.'

'No, I brought it; it's mine to do as I like with. Are you ready for more milk ?'

'I was hungry in that place . . .' A shudder ran over me and I tried to sit up, crying :

'The bones! I touched the bones!'

'Will you be still?' she said fiercely. 'How dare you move without my leave? And what if you did touch a few bones? The blame's on those that put you there. I'll give 'em bones! Be still; you've bled enough. What have you there, girl?'

My mother came into sight, carrying a bowl. The scent of hot broth was delicious. She put her hand under my head and helped me to drink a few mouthfuls.

Later, much later perhaps, there were voices I seemed to know, beyond the fire. I was troubled because I could not name them. The dark man came to the hearth-side.

'Lurgan is here; he is asking to speak with you, Great One.'

'Lurgan indeed! He'll hear more than he likes from me! What does he want?'

'He asks only speech with you, Lady.'

I brought his name to mind triumphantly.

'Demetroos!'

He came at once and knelt by me.

'Don't go away,' I said; 'make them let me stay here.'

'Certainly you will stay here until you are healed,' he said, and laid a comforting hand over mine. 'Only lie still, and if the great ones will, we'll heal you between us all.'

The old woman said harshly :

'Well, I'd better speak to the fool; tell him, Malda.'

My mother moved uneasily—

'What if—will Drost be safe?'

'Safe, with me here? Bring him in and let him see what mischief his master has made. Safe!'

132

She mumbled furiously to herself.

I lay holding Demetroos' hand and presently saw another known face across the fire. A man in a plain dark cloak knelt to stretch his hands pleadingly to the old woman.

'And what brings you?' she demanded.

'Lady,' he said; 'the seed corn; I have brought it to you.'

'Not before time! Is it fit to sow?'

'It is new grain from the north,' he said humbly; 'it looks healthy. I parched our grain as he commanded, but this is the fresh grain from the north.'

My mother came to the fire running a handful of corn between her palms. She said:

'It is plump, and it smells sweet enough.'

The Old One said:

'What's this about grain from the north?'

'It came with the priest Naas,' he said. 'Sack upon sack, loaded in a ship that came by night under the Temple cliffs. *He* bade me parch the seed and give this out to our own people only; but I gave out the parched grain for meal and this I hid behind the altars, where *he* could not go unaided.'

'So! I had not thought you had that much sense. So he'd have ruined all our harvests, eh? Every field blighted except the ones where he'd performed some of his tricks? Upon your head be it if this does not grow. Take it into your keeping, Malda, and we'll hope for the best. They'll be asking for grain any day now. Why did you bring it here, eh?'

'What else could I do?' he said, and cried bitterly, 'Give me leave to go!'

I saw in my mind the cliffs beyond the Temple and a figure falling from them, falling like a grainsack, turning in the air to plunge into the sea that fretted below. I gripped Demetroos harder.

He looked across the hearth and said:

'Drost bids me keep you from the cliffs.'

Lurgan hid his face.

'Is nothing unknown?' he whispered. 'Why hold me back? What is left but that?'

My mother said:

'To die is easier than to live, Lurgan; if the others have fled, do not you too run from your people.'

Lurgan said, groaning:

'My people! Who are my people?'

'The New Way will have need of a leader now.'

The Old One said:

'Hah, the New Way! Let them come to their senses!'

My mother said:

'But they will need a guide; go back, Lurgan, and be their guide. Bring them here if they will come, but do not tear all down at once and leave them with nothing.'

Lurgan had bowed his head to his knees. She laid a hand on his shoulder.

'Come, child; take strength from your mother's house and carry it to her sons. Bring them home to her. That is her will for you. And you are blessed because you saved the seed.'

He stumbled out shielding his face. The Old One felt my hands and said to my mother:

'Chattering and babbling in here! Enough to send him out of his wits again! Why did you bother with that booby?'

'He too is a son of the Mother,' said Malda.

I held to Demetroos. My mouth was stiff, my eyelids were heavy; I turned my head and let myself slide away.

When next I saw the room clearly it was full of young men. They were crowded together at the far side of the hearth, eating from trenchers set on the floor among them; Cardail was carrying meat to them as my mother cooked it. The smell of venison was inviting. I whispered:

'Is there any that I might have?'

One of the young men jumped up—

'Is he able to eat, mother?'

She came to me at once.

'Would you like some, dearest? I'll get you a little . . .'

'Let me, Lady,' said the young man who had spoken already. He brought a platter and sat beside me; I was vaguely pleased to see him. He cut a piece of meat with his knife and put it into my mouth and it was sweeter than honey to my taste.

I saw a long wavering silver line down the thigh nearest to me; I was fascinated by it and wanted to touch it, but could not direct my hand. I said dreamily:

'The Red Spear?'

'You're a bit muddled, Pup! It's me, Gerig, the son of the

Red Spear. Remember how we used to set snares on the trails above the waterfall? Remember when you fell into the pool because the net was full of fish? Here, another bite, that's the boy.'

'But this isn't the hut! Or if it is, what have they done with my throwing-stick?'

'No, it's the Hearth-house, not the hut,' he said. 'Eat up. They brought you here to be made better. This is a good place; this is where they mended me after the boar got me. Can you manage a bit more? Minnow, another load for him; this lot's gone down like butter. Now, Pup!'

I had not known how hungry I was. My eyes cleared and I saw Culla, and other elder boys I had known, and men I did not know, and I was safe and companioned.

'But if it's not the hut...' I began.

'... why are we here? Eat and I'll tell you. Because we of the Young Men's House have come here to keep guard over you till you're well; that's why. The priests got hold of you, and though Regil and Dran hunted everywhere they couldn't find you, and when we saw you at last we couldn't help quickly enough, so you got hurt; but it's all right now and you're safe. That old seagull of a Talorc won't bother you again, and as for the other one, I warrant he hadn't run so fast for many a day! He's back where he belongs, and that's the last we want to see of him.'

'Don't bother him too much yet, Gerig,' said my mother, but I caught at his hand and said urgently:

'No, I want to know, go on, what happened?'

'Well, you were wounded...'

'Was there a battle?'

'No, not a battle, but you were wounded and the Lady ran and caught you and stopped the blood, and we went after the people who'd hurt you, and some of us brought you up here. And we'll stay until you are quite well. Can you eat more?'

I shook my head. It was becoming difficult to hear what he was saying. He drew the covers over me and went away.

It was after this that the deep wound became poisonous, and for a long time I was whirled about in clouds of heat and pain,

135

and knew nothing but fire and confusion. But at last the women's skill prevailed and I found myself with the Old One near me.

'And that's better,' said she.

I had brought back with me one vision of great urgency; I said, as soon as I could make my mouth form words:

'Mangan ... by the well ...'

'Tuts, that was long ago,' she said. 'Don't fret yourself for him, whatever took him to die by our well. Downright inconsiderate, I call it.'

I said, forcing it out:

'The White Doe came for him.'

My mother said softly:

'Dearest, how could you know that?'

'He said he'd told you where I was,' I said; 'and then he said, "Why should I lie? Turn the knife!" and he fell down and the Doe came and drank, and when I ... when I was out there' (I began to tremble), 'I remembered and I did turn the knife. I did, didn't I? I didn't kill Ailill? Mother, I didn't kill Ailill?'

She said:

'No, my dearest, you didn't kill Ailill; you almost killed yourself but you didn't hurt him. And Mangan did tell me where to find you. I wanted him to come in and rest, but he said I must hurry, so I stayed only long enough to call Demetroos, and I ran—but I wasn't quick enough to save you, my darling.'

I remembered a sound of running feet through a red mist.

'Somebody screamed,' I said.

'Ginetha—poor Ginetha! But it's all right now, beloved; don't think about those things any more.'

'But about Mangan and the Doe,' I said stubbornly; 'he did go away with the Doe, so he's in the Orchard now, isn't he?'

'I think—I think if you say it was so, he must be,' said my mother slowly. 'Great is the mercy. Poor Mangan, safe at last— I'm glad you told me.'

'And it's the Well at the World's End, mother! Didn't you know? He said so; he said it was the Well. Somebody else wanted to know too—couldn't you tell everyone? People go about looking for it.'

'I know they do; but everybody has to find their own well.

It's no good telling them it's here or there; they have to find it and everybody has a different one. It's the looking that's important, not finding one particular well.'

'What does it do, the Well?' I wanted to be a child and lie back listening to her stories.

'It doesn't do anything; it is. The Well at the World's End is a spring of water and the end of thirst. It has seven hazel-trees above it, and five streams rise from it, and a fish lives in it and eats the nuts that fall from the trees, three at a time. And anyone who finds it is never thirsty again, and anyone who drinks from it has his heart's desire, and anyone who ate the fish would have all knowledge, or so they say, but it's only in legends that people are bold enough to take the fish and eat it.'

It was a pleasant story; I fell asleep thinking that I would work out its meaning some other time.

Again I slept; and I went far and far away. I came back from great and unremembered joy, having met my heart's desire beyond the borders of the world, and on my backward path I came by a little ruinous hut. The door was closed with a hurdle, but I could enter.

There were two men huddled over a tiny fire. One was bent and frail, holding one shaking hand to the warmth and nursing the other in his lap. The other man was a little younger; he held in his hands a painted mask. It was night-time as they talked.

The younger said:

'I leave with dawn; it is not safe for either of us here. Are you sure you will not come back with me to the Eagles?'

'No,' said Talorc; 'I remain here. Tell me of the boys. They both live?'

'So I hear from the sailors; I have not been to the village. I am not yet ready to die, even for you. Both are sick; I have tried twice to fetch the dark one away that the sacrifice might be completed. I will try once more while I am here near him, but he is most strongly guarded. You did not tell me he was so well protected; why not? The white one I have not called, for the knife spared him. I have no surety of a blessing from his death.'

Talorc said:

'That is the one you should have called. It was in my Sending at the first that he might be the one to die for the People. Call him.'

Naas said (and now I remembered his name):

'I did not expect either of them would be required to die, until I saw the portents, close to the Day of Offering; I had thought it would be—like that other time.'

'Maybe; but the white one is marked for death.' I saw the bent shoulders move suddenly as if a flaw of cold air had touched them. His own words seemed to startle him a little. He went on:

'Besides, when they lost both their young kings in one day that was the rising of our strength. Let the white one die; then bring Lurgan here to me, and we will do what is next. The dark one must be got out of the women's hands, and purified, and then we shall return. First the white one must die. If Mangan had not died he would have helped you.'

I was weak and confused and heard two voices at once; it seemed that he said in the same breath:

'Fool, fool, why did you blunder? Why did you go your own way and ruin all my work? If Mangan had lived he would have done my will, for I had left him none of his own—but you—!'

Naas said:

'You are sure of Lurgan?'

'Yes, I am sure. He has nothing left else. You will see. He bowed to my commands in the matter of the corn, though his peasant's soul bled. There will be no harvest for our enemies, and they will come crawling to fetch me back to bless them and feed them.'

Naas said:

'Tell me, out of your wisdom, what did you plan to gain by the Great Sacrifice?'

'Prosperity for the People; what else?'

But in my mind I heard him say:

'Power for me and mine; power; power. That is all and ever has been. Power.'

Naas said:

'May the gods grant it even yet!'

He stood up and put on his mask, the mask of Cardail's face.

'I must go soon; but first I will try once more to call the dark one so that it may be finished.'

'With that? What use is that?'

'He is young; they were children together in the Hearth-house; he is coming to an age when she will have some power over him. I have already had him once within my hands through this, but some of their arts came across mine.'

Talorc laughed a little.

'He too! Is he too caught in that snare? I tell you, it is the white one you should call. Call him in my name, not in any foolish girl's. He is well trained to come to my whistle. Mangan saw to that.'

Beyond them and their fire I could still see the grey trees where I had newly found my heart's desire. The sight gave me strength and I grew angry with this work of theirs. I folded my arms over my breast and called up the most terrible likeness I knew, the likeness of that blue-eyed pale musician of the woods. In that likeness I stepped through the smoke of the fire and appeared to Naas, and saw terror flare through him even as darkness hid him from me.

The world fell away under me and I sank into a sea of fiery pain, but at least I knew I had defeated his purpose once and for all.

It was long before I could return into my own body. Many times I approached it to find my way barred by faceless shapes, by omens of fear, or by the shrouded forms of priests or mourners. At last Demetroos forced his way through these shadows and took my hands and drew me safely past. I lay in the bed in the inner room, too weak to lift my head or speak, while he and my mother worked over me with healing spells to guard me.

Weeks may have passed for all I know. At last I heard voices beyond the barriers and turned my head to listen. I knew one, at least, and formed his name with weak lips.

'Felim.'

Demetroos went to the door and beckoned him in—

'Quickly, he calls you.'

'Coming, brother; but it's no use scolding me, mother,' he said over his shoulder in the doorway; 'for once, I know a sight more than you do. Leave her alone and keep your hard words for those who deserve them. Well, Charcoal, you're here again, are you? Have you a song for me yet?'

I said, with what voice I could muster :

'I am no singer, Lord of Songs.'

'You made a poem once; you'll make others. What can I do to please you now?'

My mother knelt to bring me a drink of warm milk—

'Don't tire him, Felim, he's so weak still.'

I found a little more voice.

'Ailill—what's happened to Ailill? Is he safe? Naas said . . .'

'Naas, the Eagles' priest? He'll stay at home if he values his life! Ailill lives.'

Demetroos came into my sight. He knelt by me and questioned my mind without words. I showed him what I had seen of Talorc and Naas together, and the Sending I had made. He asked how I knew such things. I showed him the place of the pillars. I began to fall asleep under his gaze, and while I slept we went together into distant places. When I woke again I felt safe with him, now that he knew how much I had known and how little I knew.

He and Felim were both there when I woke; Felim was saying :

'. . . know how he did it; he must have sent to the north country for all that grain. I would give much to know how he paid for it.'

'What was his link with the north?'

'He trained among their priests; we had no such priests as he in the good days before . . . Priests, yes, a few; Melduin was one of them; but Talorc and his New Way grew strong together after the young kings died and the elder Ailill was chosen. Talorc came back with a message accusing the Old Way of causing the children's death. Ailill upheld him and he upheld Ailill. Why should he try to destroy Ailill's son?'

'Hush, brother, the dark one's awake.'

I wanted to hear more of their talk; I closed my eyes and turned my head away from them.

There were voices in the Hearth-room; my mind passed beyond the door. The room was lit by red anger; my mother, the Old One and another hooded woman stood close together and spoke in furious whispers.

'Begone with you and spare us your noise! We have a sick child within, as well you know!' That was the Old One.

'And I too have a sick child! I have come to tell you—to beg you, even, I who am a queen!—to beg you to take your cruel hands from him; will you kill yet another king?'

My mother said, as the Old One's breath hissed through her teeth:

'Not we, but your priests harmed Ailill; bring him to me, or let me come to him, and I will do what I can for him. My child almost died to spare yours the harm the priests had devised for him.'

Ginetha laughed harshly—

'If you had not meddled no harm would have come to mine; it was your bastard who was to be put out of the way. Think you any man's sword would have slept in its sheath if he had threatened the King with his knife? No, the High Gods turned his devices against himself; they may yet claim their meed of blood and set my Ailill free of spells. You shall not have both my husband and my son, Malda. I have come to tell you so, and to take back my property. I require you to give up my jewels.'

'Jewels?' said the Old One. 'Malda, you did not permit the King to give you her jewels?'

My mother stepped backwards suddenly.

'I, take anything from Ailill's hands? Ginetha offered some ornaments here at the Hearth, long ago; I told her they were unacceptable but she would leave them. Wait here, and I will bring them you—Queen.'

She passed behind the Hearth to the offering-store; the other two remained facing one another.

Ginetha said exultingly:

'Then I was right! This was where he came! You knew it too?'

My mother came back with a bundle rolled in cloth, and put it into the Queen's hands.

'Make sure it's all there,' she said. 'I wrapped them in that cloth the day you left them, and I have not touched them since, but please make sure.'

Ginetha knelt and spread out the bundle. Gold gleamed dully in the firelight. With a little pleased cry she picked up bracelet after bracelet and pushed them over her hands. When she was all adorned again (and she had worn no jewels till then on neck or arms) she stood up, kicked aside the cloth, and walked to the door.

'Now I am free of you,' she said, turning as she reached it; 'set my son free likewise or I will send his men to burn this place over your heads.'

'Did you send them before?' asked the Old One. 'I trow not! Go home, silly creature. Go home, and remember that here is neither queen nor—freed-woman.'

It was Ginetha's turn to fall back; the hiss of her breath was heard in the inner room. My mother walked in to us and sat down heedless of the men's presence, and did something I had never seen her do. She put her face in her two hands and wept bitterly.

Felim said to the Old One, who followed:

'What have you done? How could you? Lady of peace, Lady of beauty, do not weep! Here are your friends, I your brother of the Hearth, Demetroos who loves you, Drost your son—do not weep!'

He knelt and put his arms about her. She dried her eyes on her cloak and bit her lip.

'Forgive me, Felim. She—I was a little distressed. How's Drost?'

I managed this time to move my hands towards her and she broke from Felim and took them.

'How is it, dearest?'

'I'm all right, mother; don't worry about me. She had to get those things back because she'd given all her others to Talorc, last year, and if Ailill's there he may wonder why she doesn't wear any jewellery now.'

'Mother of the Flocks!' said Felim behind her. 'So that's how it was done?'

The Old One moved about the room grumbling to herself. She broke out aloud:

'Fine doings! The Middle Priestess and the daughter of a slave-woman bandying words across the Hearth! And all of it your own fault, my girl, let me tell you that! If you hadn't put yourself in the wrong to begin with, she'd have had no grounds to reproach you!'

My mother let go of my hands. Tears flashed in her eyes. In a choking voice she said:

'If you could bring yourself to believe me . . . ! I can only go on and on telling you the truth. I led the dancing; I did as you had bidden me; nothing more. If there was a sin behind my hope, have I not paid for it? Have I not paid yet?'

I could not bear to see her weep; I tried to raise myself, and a blazing pain went through me and drove me out of the body.

Long after that, I was again lying in my mother's arms. As I woke from a fading dream I heard her voice murmuring softly over me:

'I am here, beloved; I am here.'

A great longing came over me to tell her about my heart's desire. Would she believe me? Would she be angry, or sorrowful, or would she laugh? I lay and wondered, and tried to gather all the smallest crumbs of memory from that dream.

She said:

'What troubles you, Drost? Tell me what troubles you?'

'I'm remembering a dream—' I said. 'Sometimes I have a sort of dream about things that seem to have happened before, and this person is in it—I don't know if it's a real person.' (I was afraid to say 'she'.)

My mother said it for me.

'Someone you loved—before? Is she—is she alive somewhere now?'

I was still uncertain how much I could tell her.

'I think she might be.'

'The Mother grant she is, and that you find her and find her free! Sometimes when people have loved very much they are allowed to find each other and love again, when they come back from the Orchard . . . sometimes not. Sometimes it can be —very difficult.'

She checked for breath and went on gently—

'There's always the Orchard, of course—have you seen her, to know how she looks, this time? Do you know at all where to find her? I'd help you, if I could. One wastes so much time for lack of help . . . is she near, or far?'

'I don't know; I keep seeing her in a sort of wood of grey trees—not alders exactly—not any kind of tree I know. She's

. . . oh, I don't know; I think she's dark, rather like you, perhaps, and . . .'

My mother laughed softly.

'And perhaps not! When next you are with her, ask her for
a sign that you can look for when you meet, waking. You may
be inventing a picture of her, or you may be remembering how
she appeared when you were last together. But oh, my darling
Drost, pray, pray to the Mother as I will, that you may find her
and live out your days together. Not to find them, or to find
them too late, or to live near them and out of reach for ever . . .
perhaps one pays for some past fault by these; great must be
such faults!'

A tear fell on my arm. I turned and kissed her, and knew
more than I could have thought possible. She had found Melduin too late and had never held him, as now she held me,
until he lay dying in this very room.

My heart was ready to break for her; my mind notwith-
standing went on with its endless questions. Why? Why too
late? Why never? And who, if not Melduin, was the father of
Drost?

Felim was the Old One's Son of the Harvest. Even if I had not
heard him call himself my mother's brother I could have
guessed from the familiar way he spoke to his mother. All the
rest of us might go, did go, in mortal awe of her, but Felim
teased her and coaxed her like any other son; they even had
downright quarrels face to face.

From one of these, conducted in not too seemly a manner in
the courtyard, he stormed into the inner room one day and
threw himself down by the fire.

'Women!'

Demetroos, who was scratching little marks like birds' footprints on a smooth piece of clay, looked up and laughed.

'Fine words from a poet!'

'Who should know if a poet does not? She forgets I am anything in the world; a muddy-kneed brat I am to her! I've been
trying to make her less jealous of Malda, but I might have
spared my breath.'

'She, jealous? What need has she to be jealous of anyone?'

'You may well ask! Intolerant old . . . Oh, you're there, are you, Charcoal? Would you not rather be out in the sun? Shall I carry him out, brother?'

'Better not, yet awhile.'

'What are you at there?' Felim was restless; I feared he might be going to leave us on one of his sudden bird-flights.

Demetroos shrugged his broad shoulders and smeared away his marks.

'Thinking what else I could do to keep things safe here; no matter. Sit you down and talk to the dark one.'

'Shall I?' Felim stepped to the bed and looked at me with his head on one side. 'What shall we talk about? You won't sing for me, I suppose? Have you no song in you yet, Charcoal?'

The joke was growing stale. I said fretfully, for my wound irked me:

'Tell me things. I can't sing, you know that. Explain to me. I don't know any of the things I want to know. Who were the kings who were killed? And why did people think the Old Way had anything to do with it? Why did Talorc want Lurgan to damage the corn? Why did . . . ?'

Felim held up his hands.

'King, Lord of the Boar, give your servant time to answer! Talorc tried to spoil the corn so that only his own friends would have any harvest this year. Lurgan didn't do as Talorc wanted, and now there's a fine crop in the fields, may the Mother bring it safely to the barns. What else? The kings who died—a Twin was killed in battle and his king and his own two sons died of sickness soon afterwards. Most people thought it was because of a wrong the King had done, but somebody started a lie that blamed the Old Way.'

'Why did they think my mother had done something wrong?'

'Whisht, child! That was another time altogether. These kings were before all that.'

'But which kings were they? Was it a very long time ago?'

'Not so very long, when you reckon it,' said Felim slowly. 'They were the last before Ailill the elder, who was before Melduin, who was before yourselves.'

'Ailill the elder was chosen King, somebody said—you said

so yourself; why? Wasn't he always the King?'

'Unfortunately not; or rather, unfortunately it was necessary to choose. The kings were dead, as I told you.'

Demetroos said, smoothing his clay again:

'You are hiding either knowledge or ignorance under a
cloud of words. Have your kings no genealogies? Can you give
no account of their descent?'

Felim drew himself up indignantly. (Demetroos glanced at
me, his eyes twinkling.)

'Drost knows better than that! Genealogies are a poet's
stock in trade, his first learning; Drost, you remember that
much of the rules of versification? "These are metres fit to
sing the descent of kings; the beat of eight, the beat of four,
and the coupled beat."

> "Son of kings, brother of kings,
>   Father of kings and a king himself,"

and so on and so forth while the bellows blow the fire. Terrible
stuff it is, and they made us learn it . . . Listen then; I'm not
going through the whole affair from start to finish even for
you; five generations will be enough to throw you into another
fever if you're half the poet I hope you are.

> "Augan had Daran, to Daran succeeded;
>   Daran two sons had, King Brud and his Twin Goll.
>   Brud begat Daran, his brother was Ennis;
>   Ennis left two sons, but no child had Daran."

(And that's one lie, at least; he had a son and a daughter, from
both of whom the Mother save us.)

> "Ennis the Eagles bore down in the dawning,
>   Daran at even lay dead by the young kings."

'Put that way, it scans; Daran and the boys died about a week after the battle.

> "Ailill the swordsman then, son of Goll's son Nest,
> Guided the spearmen who followed the Red
> Spear."

That's Grath, Gerig's father; Ailill brought the remnants of our men to help him hold the pass, after Ennis was killed in battle; Grath was dead before—when they got to him, but he kept the Eagles out of our lands.

> "Melduin the priest then they called from his
> dreaming;
> Melduin the Twin had been Senchan's son, Goll's
> son."

So there you have it. Ailill and Melduin were brothers' sons. Ailill was never reared to be a king, but he was a good war-leader. Melduin was the best king we've ever had (and I'm not forgetting Ennis, but he had to be King and Twin together); Melduin was reared a priest. When he came out into the world again the first thing he saw was your mother, and that was that.'

'But I'm not Melduin's son?'

'Oh no, my lad, you're the same as I am myself, the Son of Harvest, the son of no man.'

'Why did Ennis have to be both at once? I thought you couldn't be.'

'It isn't possible, but he did his best. Daran had—other interests.'

'Hm,' said Demetroos drily. 'A certain lady may disapprove of all this if she hears you.'

Felim chuckled naughtily.

'Which of them? My mother has never minded a bit of scandal since I can remember. Now, if you got her talking . . . ! Well, where was I?'

'King Daran had other interests; what were . . .' said I.

'And no heirs. So Ennis—'

'I thought you said that bit was lies?'

'No heirs; the children of slave-women are not heirs to kings. Do him justice, he had one favourite, whom he made a freed-woman in the end.'

The inner room and the two men were blotted from my sight; I saw instead the small hot room of Ginetha the Queen, and her hands pressed to the lid of a little coffer.

I interrupted Felim without knowing it.

'How do people free a slave?'

'There's a ceremony for it; the main thing is naturally to cut off the slave-collar.'

'And her daughter keeps it!'

I spoke again without knowing.

They turned as one to stare at me. Demetroos was the first to recover; he said something under his breath in his own language, and then to Felim:

'You need not show that chicken where the grain has spilled!'

Felim said to me, deadly serious for once:

'For the love of the Mother, and of your own mother, never say that aloud again! Remember also, Ginetha is half of good blood and half of bad.'

Demetroos said:

'You are a little hard on the freed-woman; for all you know she might have been of good blood in her own country.'

Felim said with a snap:

'I am giving her the benefit of that doubt.'

I could not be bothered to work out under-meanings, but I roused enough to say:

'Never mind all that; when did the New Way start? Was it because somebody thought the kings had been killed?'

'Ailill raised it up; a few of them were here before that; he became one of them and gave them leave to build the Temple. Talorc came home about the same time from training with the priests in the north, and Ailill made him the chief priest.'

'In the north? Not with the Eagles?'

Felim smiled wryly.

'My friend Grath died to defeat the Eagles; Ailill made his

148

fame by defeating the Eagles; and the Eagles made the New Way and sent it to us. At least we do not send our boys to be made men among them, yet; you will go to the Green Glen, to the men of the Bear, as your forefathers went.'

'I? Shall I be worth sending?'

'Of course you will! You do as the women tell you, and rest and heal up, and you'll be there dancing with the best of them. That's enough talking for one day. Lie back and I'll sing something for you.'

He tuned his harp and began very softly 'The Corn is Fair'.

Some weeks later Felim and Demetroos carried me out to lie in the lee of the house, at the edge of the field that runs up to the well. The young men were still around us; Gerig came to talk to me, laying his spear against the wall, and Culla and the others waved a greeting from the ridge.

When Gerig went I had nothing to do but to lie and watch small birds working from the grass to the bushes and back, and swallows swooping over the roof. There is a rhythm in the flight of swallows that just escapes the watcher; over and over again I thought I had it and could guess which way they would throw themselves next, and again and again I was wrong. The steep swing, the check, the headlong swoop and soar, recalled some long-buried beat. What was it that lay under the threshold of my thoughts?

I lay still and waited and presently one line came out—

I was a king, who now am dead.

I tried it aloud; was it from the death-songs of Ailill? No, I could remember no more of it. It seemed to me more fitting for Melduin. I wanted Felim to come.

It was long before he came, and meantime I had dredged up more words and laid them together like shells for a boy to string. When at last he walked round the house-end he found me almost desperate.

'Lord of Songs, come and help; I'm trying to remember a

song, and I don't know when I heard it, even.'

'If you've heard it, I can sing it,' said Felim. 'Tell me.'

'It's something like this—but I'm not sure,' I said, and began:

> ' "I was a man, who am a king;
> I was a king, who now am dead;
> I who was—" (is it "dark when you were red"?)
> "In death regain my maidenhead." '

Felim sat very still, his harp on his knee.

'Go on,' he said; 'go on.'

'But I wish you would! I don't know how it goes—

> "I was a king, who now am dead;
> The wounded boar, the blooded deer;
> The lesser sword, the second spear;
> In death the silver song I hear.
>
> The wounded boar, the blooded deer,
> I sealed your bargain with my pain;
> In death the silver song I hear;
> Mother, receive thy son again!"

Please, Felim, sing it properly; it's bothering me.'

'Very well,' said Felim slowly; he plucked a string.

'How does it start? "I was a man, who am a king"? Not "was a king"—no, of course not.'

He swept his hands over the harp.

Gerig came out of the courtyard to listen. When Felim ended there were several of the young men round us. Gerig asked:

'Is that new, Lord of Songs?'

'It's Drost's song, not mine. For whom do you name it, Singer of the Birds?'

'It's not mine—I only remembered it. I thought perhaps it was a song for Melduin; isn't it?'

'It shall be if you say so; Drost's song for Melduin let it be.

Moon and Stars, of all difficult modes to begin with . . . ! But that's a boy all over.'

He began to sing it again.

So I got my second name and became as I have remained, the Singer of the Birds. I lay all that summer at the Hearth making songs with Felim and learning to polish and perfect them, and seeing and hearing things from my childhood that I had forgotten. Otherwise I was wholly idle, not even bestirring myself to talk with Demetroos.

I saw the lesser ceremonies and my mother's arts of healing, and how she would avert evil from the People by charms. I saw her sometimes, as she sat spinning, lift her head and listen, and then quickly snap her wool round a lifted finger to break a geis she had felt. Whenever she did so Felim and I would mark in the dust the sign of safety.

She was skilful to feel and know geasa, though even she could not always avert them nor ever lift them entirely from those on whom the Mother had laid them. Demetroos asked her once:

'What do you there, Lady? You avert an omen, I think?'

She glanced sharply at him.

'Something I felt pass by me—a geis on the wing.'

'And that is—?'

Felim, seeing she did not want to answer, put in:

'Between an omen and a portent, I think you would say. The Mother lays a condition on some of her children, giving them safety so far, unless and until they meet a certain chance. Some geasa are stronger than others. In the end every man meets his geis.'

Demetroos fingered an amulet he wore in his breast.

My mother said to me:

'Son, kings carry more geasa than other men; it seems strange that we know of no geis for you. The Mother grant you do not offend against your geis through ignorance!'

'I am only the Twin; perhaps there are no geasa for me.'

'No,' she said, 'I do not believe this is so; for Ailill perhaps—but for you there will be, some day. If only I could tell you what it will be!'

'Perhaps it won't come till I'm old, and then it won't matter,' I said.

She broke the wool round her finger to avert the harm of my words.

Harvest came, such a harvest as few could remember. I saw them go out from the Hearth, Felim bearing before him the Silver Branch with its little bells wreathed among the holy flowers, my mother following with her crown of grain to lead the procession round the threshing-floors where the new crop awaited her blessing. The moon shone roundly down and the air was rich with scents. All the People were there, even Ginetha and her women.

I was too lame to follow far, and soon turned back to the Hearth and the company of the little children; the shouting and rejoicing rang through the valley to the Green Glen itself.

The frosts of autumn came hard on the heels of the feast and the sunsets flamed redder than the trees beyond the river. Felim brought word that Ailill was growing stronger as I was. I went down to the Fort once, for the men to decide what I was to do, but they wasted little time over me. I was not fit to go back to the boys. I was beginning to feel I wanted to go, sometimes; but on the whole I was thankful to be at the Hearthhouse.

When we went into the hall, Felim had to whisper to me to salute Ailill. I had not recognised the bleached and haggard youth who sat on the steps and stared past me with sunken eyes.

As we went back up the road (and I was glad of Felim's arm), I asked him:

'Am I like that? No wonder they wouldn't have me!'

'You're not too bad,' he said critically; 'you'll do in a moon or so.'

'But Ailill—what's happened to Ailill? You told me he wasn't wounded, but he's withered like a leaf!'

'He was ill; he'll be all right when you're both with the boys again.'

I think my mother would have known better if she had seen him.

The Old One came again to us, by night as was her custom. She paid small heed to my mother—

'Be quiet, child, I've come to work.'

She summoned all the men to the outer court, Gerig the old at their head, and all the rest down to Lan and the others who had newly joined the young men. I remained with Demetroos in the inner room.

By and by, after a long murmuring of voices, she screeched for me to come out. When I came through the curtains of the Hearth-room there were all the men packed into the courtyard and the old lady haranguing them from the doorsteps. She caught my wrist and pulled me forward.

'Here he is then, your half-king that you want to advise you; judge if he knows more than I! Come, Drost; let us hear what good can come of all your learning; your people want your advice.'

She wrapped her cloak about her and sat down against the wall; she was not angry, merely amused by the childishness of her children in asking counsel of a child.

I bent my knee to salute her and the assembled men.

'Lords of the Boar, what can I say that you do not know far better than I? What am I to answer?'

Gerig (old Gerig, that is) said:

'Boy you are, but King's Twin you are also, and the store-place of our laws. We have destroyed the priesthood of the New Way, but laws are stronger than priesthoods. Tell us this: should we take away their temple, and, if so, how?'

I said:

'There is nothing about that in any laws that I have learnt; what does the King say?'

'Nay, but what do you say?' said a dozen of them together.

It was hard for me to answer. I stood and remembered that cold and hateful place of visions and enchantments and fear. Nothing but fire could cleanse it for me, but then I had never worshipped there; many of those who faced me now must have taken sorrows or hopes there to lay them before the gods as they saw them. I thought how my mother had said once that perhaps each of us could only hold one corner of the Mother's cloak. I cried in my heart:

'Mother, guide me aright!'

To the men I said:

'You have prayed there; if some of the priests were false,

that does not make the High Gods false. The gods are above falsehood.'

In my body as I spoke I felt the long golden fingers drive in below my ribs, and the heat of the furnace on my eyelids, and the cold chill of the Singer's presence on my spine; yes, these were indeed High Gods, though men might worship them amiss. I would ever fear them, but I prayed that the Mother would never abandon me to them. I prayed also that I might have spoken aright to the men.

She answered through the Old One—

'You have spoken well, child. There you have it, men! You will kill all your fires as I have commanded, and you will take clean fire from the Hearth to purify your houses, and you will do all the other things I have told you; but you will not concern yourselves with the place on the cliffs. The Mother permitted its building; let her decide its destruction.'

She stood up and drew me in with her, and we heard the shuffle of many feet as the courtyard emptied.

She held to my arm and looked sidelong at me as we crossed the Hearth-room—

'What made you speak up for the New Way, brat?'

I shook my head and could not answer.

Just before the winter feast there was the worst storm in old Gerig's memory. We spent the night by the Hearth while the heavens cracked over us and thunder shook the earth. There was nobody bold enough to put their nose out of doors that night, and so nobody knew till daylight that the Temple had burned to ash in a fire so fierce that the very stones had melted.

Nothing else was hurt; but Lurgan, the former priest, had not been seen for some days before, and he was never seen again. Whether he lived or died I could not tell; but he was a brave man, and did what he knew to be right in the end, and so may the Mother give him her peace wherever he may be.

When the days began to lengthen we returned to the Fort of the Girls. I was still slow and limped along, glad of Felim's company. Ailill had passed ahead of us; we saw his footprints among those of the men.

Regil had finished his turn of duty and gone back to the village, but Dran was still there, with a new man called Teth. We slipped into the old ways easily enough, a pair of weaklings, tailers in the hunt and dead hands on the nets, but Arth was always near to help me and Ailill's gang eased things for him. The dancing was the hardest.

I happened to make up a song one day at the herding, on a pattering air that came from nowhere; I called it 'Dran the Drummer'. I was humming it as we drove the cattle home, and some of the others took it up. By the time we got to the Fort we were shouting it in chorus, and more verses spun themselves as we went along. Somebody sang it to Dran himself, who took it in good part and even fingered the air on the little drum. The wretched song became a passion with the boys. Everywhere I went I could hear it; behind the driven herds, along the beaches, by the pools where we swam or at the hide-dressing frames—'Dran, Dran, Dran the Drummer'. I was more than sorry I had ever listened to the tune in my head.

. About a month after, I was going alone along a trail to look at some traps, for as I could not hunt with the others these were my main concern. I had leant my spear against a rock, and was kneeling to reset a sprung snare, when a cold wave passed over my back like a sudden flaw of wind. I half-rose and half-turned, as a heavy stone crashed on the trail at my feet. Still on one knee and twisted, I was thrust down and back by a smothering weight that fell on me.

I got one hand free and sought for the thing's throat, while I wondered what it could be—not wolf, for a Grey Beast does not miss the neck-blow; not bear, for it was not heavy enough, nor does the Smiler jump down when he can kill with a scoop of one hand. It was the sharp smell of fear in my nostrils, and the smoothness of the body against my thigh, that gave me the answer. My killer was man.

I got a grip on the hair, tore my other arm free and drew my knee up, as much to guard the wound as to attack; there was something over my face, a cloak perhaps, that blinded and stifled me, and behind it he breathed raspingly. Heavy, hairy, smothering, over my mouth and nose—my arms began to weaken—my head rolled aside—even as I tried for his throat and he for mine, I remembered a horrifying moment in the

Great Fort long before. Had that been a Sending to show me my death? He freed his hand and struck at my muffled head with a stone, but the blow fell on my shoulder. While he was off balance I put out more strength than I knew I had, and rolled above him. I found his face and closed the mouth and nostrils with one hand, and tore away the cloak with the other.

Ailill lay below me on the path.

I think I had known before that. I pulled myself up and took my spear to lean on, and stood over him as he lay limp and gaunt. He fought for breath and rolled the whites of his eyes, but did not try to move. I stood and waited and suddenly he turned his head away and wept.

'Ailill,' I said, 'Ailill, my king and my brother; why?'

He would not answer me.

'Why have I deserved to die? Bring me to the judgment of the People if I have done wrong; don't make another wrong by killing me here in your anger without witnesses. Please, Ailill, what have I done?'

He propped himself on one elbow and coughed.

'You? Is it not enough that you have tried to kill me? You meant me to die; you always meant it, but the priests saved me from you before; Talorc always said I could trust him. Now you've got rid of them, you and your mother, you think there's nobody to help me. Don't think I don't know why I'm still sick; that's her doing. First she arranged the Great Sacrifice to get me killed and you made the only king, and when that didn't work because my mother cried out and broke the spell, she put her eye on me. My mother even humbled herself to ask her to stop, but she only mocked her. She's always hated my mother and now I know why.'

He stopped to cough and fight for breath. I could only stand and listen in helpless horror.

'Well?' he began again. 'Why don't you finish it? There you are with your spear. Why don't you do as your mother would like, and put it through me? You might have a little trouble explaining to your friends, but I am sure she could persuade them that I had been turned into something else—a white boar, say—for the occasion.'

That was the animal he chose to name.

'Ailill,' I said desperately, 'please believe me, my mother

156

doesn't hate anyone, and she doesn't want anyone killed, you least of all. If the Queen thinks so she must be mistaken. And as for the Great Sacrifice, I know who arranged that; I was there, interpreting for him, when he made the Queen give him gold. He said it was to "buy her desire"; perhaps you know what that was; I don't. It was Talorc, Ailill—Talorc and Naas. Don't you remember how Naas told us there were hard things ahead, and that one of us would have to make a sacrifice for the People? I don't understand what they did, but they seemed to make me dream about the gods—'

Ailill interrupted me with a deep shuddering groan.

'Talorc made Mangan send me pictures of what I was to do,' I said. 'It's all Talorc, but I don't know why.'

'But, you fool, that's how she works! She bewitched him long ago. Right from the beginning, when she was called the Maiden, she's bewitched people. She bewitched my father, she bewitched Talorc, she bewitched Melduin. She and that crazed old woman gave out that you were the God-chosen; you weren't, I was. The God came down on my father at the Spring Dancing, and it was my mother he chose, not the Maiden so-called. And after that she made him her lover, for revenge. It's like everything else about the Old Way, rotten and poisonous and vile. Who killed the sons of Ennis? The old hag, of course; everyone knows that, but they're all cowards. I'm not a coward; I'll kill the old creature some day, and your mother too if she doesn't mend her ways. As for you—I'm sorry I touched you. After all, there is a little of my kingship stored in you. You may live.'

I helped him to his feet and he held to me for a breath or so. I left him leaning against the rock that had been his ambush, and I finished setting the trap, and swept the trampled ground with twigs, and strewed it with pine needles, and I went round the rock and cleared up the signs of his waiting; he had sprung the snare and waited, shifting his weight on his heels, knowing I would come.

When I had done everything I led him a little way off and went back to brush out the last footmarks, and we went down the trail together in silence. To the best of my power I closed the whole matter inside my mind and tried not to wonder, even, from what wild grief or frantic jealousies Ginetha had spun this web of fantasy that had caught her son in its mesh.

I was not quite successful in hiding all that had happened, though I told Teth a tale about slipping down a bank and wrenching my shoulder. Dran looked at me a little oddly, I thought.

All summer I carried the load about with me, and sometimes when I was alone I would turn it over and try to understand. I could make nothing of it; only, I took good care never to be alone with him.

The harvest-time came and the eldest boys adorned themselves and went to show off to the girls while we sat under the moon singing the old songs, and even, at Dran's call, some new ones. He had heard that I had been making other songs besides that abominable 'Drummer', and though at that time I had no more voice than a corncrake, he picked up the tune that I croaked, and embellished it while I taught him the words.

One night Ailill surprised us all by beginning a song himself. He had a light clear voice, not of great power but very true and rounded, and he sang first one of the feasting-songs—I think the 'Honey-wine Song'—and then a lament for seafarers. It was an old song, not one that is heard often, but with a haunting turn to the second part.

We all applauded him, with good cause, and after that he would sing almost nightly. He learned some of my songs and they fitted his voice so beautifully that I almost wept to hear them, I who could not bring out the least part of the music that was in me. Once or twice he produced songs of his own, but they were patched-up things, and I remembered how Felim had said he would be a songsmith and a rhyme-capper.

When he sang my songs it healed a little of the wound that divided us, and it healed him too to have our praises. The winter passed quietly enough, and we began to be able to dance again, and to learn the steps of the holy dances, the Dance of the Boar and the Dance of the Green Glen. We still knew nothing about the Glen, except that there we boys would face some ordeal or other.

Early in the spring they prepared us for testing by the men. We were not yet among the eldest, but as usual the Council were pushing us beyond our years. Arth was prepared with us.

The men came and examined us, and allowed us some marks

on our breasts and arms, but not all. Bitter and sharp they were, and still more bitter that we were not accepted as fully ready. Still, when it was time for the accepted boys to go to the Boar Hunt we three went with them.

We were only part of the ring, of course; the boar we roused was young, and charged fast and early, and Lan took the first clean spear. We followed in his train to the village and sat at the feast, and heard for the first time the 'Boar Song' as Felim sang it, and afterwards we danced the Dance of the Boar with the young men. The meaning of the dance was clear to us now, the hunt and the finding, the ring and the charge. Only the inner meaning, the choice that is made in that hunt, was not shown us.

We went also to my mother's house, a little afterwards, for the spring dancing. We went up in our finest kilts and adorned with our shells and trophies, and jumped through the fire in the courtyard, and followed in the long procession that wound away out of the gate when the cry was raised that the Maiden had gone to the hill. The young men at the head of the line began to run, and we followed as hard as we could, but darkness overtook us when we were only a little way up the slopes.

Arth and I sheltered under some rocks from a thin cold rain that swept the hillside. Higher up we could hear the men's voices shouting to each other, and the women at the foot of the hill were singing and snapping their clappers as they danced.

We were cold, and hungry, and we said so; and there was nothing more to say. We huddled closer to avoid the icy trickles that fell on us, and the awe of the time and place came over us. We may have slept a little.

And then, in that time and place, a door opened in my mind and I saw an inner room. It was all hung round with woven cloths and there was a small fire on the hearth, and someone sat by it spinning. She was not my mother, and it was not our inner room, but I was drawn towards the hearth.

The spinner kept her shoulder turned to me so that I saw the knot of her cloak and the white arm below it, and the line of neck and cheek but not the face. I looked down at her hands, and now they moved more and more slowly so that I could see the square palms and the short, slender, blunt-tipped fingers. Something glinted on one wrist and the other hand, and when she laid the distaff in her lap and spread her hands over it, I saw a golden serpent coiled round her arm and a smaller one on her middle finger.

She leaned forward to stare into the fire. I went softly forwards, meaning to put my hands on her shoulders, but suddenly she started up and turned; and in that moment, before I could see her face in the shadow of the firelight, Arth said in my ear:

'Drost—you know Cardail?'

I struggled out of my dream, saying stupidly:

'Cardail? Our Cardail at the Hearth? Why?'

'Do you think she's very—very beautiful?'

'Cardail?' I said again, this time scornfully. 'That little dumpy thing? You don't mean Cardail.'

'How can you call her dumpy? She's little and neat and— You can't have seen her properly.'

'Nonsense, I've seen her ever since she was a few hours old, and a horrible little red-faced thing she was too; of course I've seen her. She's not bad; a bit stupid, but then girls are.'

'Drost, I'll roll you down this hill if you dare say such things!'

'Why? It's true. I've said she's not bad.'

Arth turned away and looked out of our shelter into the misty night. After a moment he said in a new voice:

'She is the moon and the stars to me.'

I sat on my heels and gaped at his half-seen shape. He must be getting old; that was the kind of silly remark Gerig and Culla made when we were not supposed to be listening. I got ready to tease him, and thought how the others would whoop when I told them. Half a man I might be at times, but I was all boy then.

Before I could speak, the night rang with one loud cry from the hill-top, a cry of triumph, worship and joy.

Suddenly the air was full of shouting, men on the hill, women below us; and caught in the common bond of delight we sprang out of hiding and knelt on the ground, and held up our arms to the unseen peak, and shouted with the others to welcome the goddess called up, the god come down.

We danced all the way back to the village with the dawn, and turned off on our own path leaving the women and the young men to dance out of our sight. We came to the Fort before noon, and slept like puppies, where we dropped.

In the next moon the men came again and passed the last of us through our tests and took us away with them, the marks smarting on our faces and shoulders. They took us to a hut behind the House of the Young Men, and we lay there for three nights: on the fourth day they called us out and examined our marks, and when they were satisfied that we were healing they told us it was time to go to the Green Glen.

That night we danced the Dance of the Green Glen once more. In the earliest light of dawn they called us out one by one and gave us our orders in whispers, two men holding each boy at the gate and speaking for his ears alone. We were to go singly up a trail the young men would show us, and on into unknown country. We were to travel alone and in silence, and if we saw another boy we must hide from him. As we entered the strange ground we must beware of hunters; we would be watched and followed and if we were found wanting we would go no further; but if we were permitted to reach the end of the trail it would lead us to the last test of all.

The trail would be faint to find and hard to follow, they said, and we must follow it fasting, drinking water but eating nothing, however long it might take us; and we were on no account to speak or sign to each other, for death would follow.

Ailill went ahead of me. When I passed through the gate the sun was up. Culla was one of my guides with an older man, both of them fully painted and armed. They took my kilt from me and I went with them mother-naked.

We went northerly at first, through the edge of the deer grounds, and bore away for the deep fold where the river runs out from the high hills. We met men returning, and my guides bade me look down and watch the ground as they passed. We went down into the valley above the last fields, where three cairns of the Former People watch the mouth of the gorge, and there they pointed ahead and sent me on alone.

At the corner where the river foams round the rocks and opens its channels over gravels, I saw the first sign that others had passed that way—little more than a bruising of the grasses,

I climbed the shoulder above the gorge, straining my ears to hear anything more than its thunder, and I saw ahead a wild deep valley, its steep sides scored with landslides and its slopes plunging to the hidden and roaring river.

Far ahead I saw something move, another boy going the same way. I crouched among the stunted heather until he was out of sight, lest he should look back and see me, and went on along the faint track of his feet among the mosses.

We were many, moving up the glen that day, but each of us moved in solitude. The high clouds sailed over us, the eagles soared there and the ravens, and the lesser birds flew from the rocks as we passed. The trail led on, no more than a shadow on the slope ahead, hardly traceable when one came up to it. I steered a path from rock to rock and from heather bush to rowan-tree. All morning I walked up the glen, setting my feet down carefully to make no noise, keeping my ears pricked and my eyes open, seeing and hearing nothing but the breath of a wind through the gullies and the flight of birds.

The sun was looking over my left shoulder when I felt the first prick of warning. I went ever more carefully, glancing about me, testing the stones of the screes before I stepped on them, stooping low as I crossed ridges, looking into dips before I went down. I glanced up at the crags when it was natural to do so, as I swung myself across a cleft or straightened to choose my line; I was certainly watched, but I saw nobody. Twice I had sight of the boy ahead of me, but that was all.

Dusk came down, and night. The men had said nothing about travelling or halting through the night. I went more slowly, staring into the half-light, gaining confidence as my eyes widened to owl's eyes. Once I heard someone breathing close to me. I was passing a great mass of tumbled rock; I lay flat in the bog below it and dragged myself past by finger-lengths. Perhaps it was a hunter, perhaps one of us who had stopped to rest.

The grey dawn found me high up in a country of barren hills and water-torn gullies. There was no cover here, only bare hill-sides and shattered rocks and the sharp scars of cloud-bursts. I followed the bed of the river for a time, moving under its banks, until it became a shallow stream and forced me back to the open ground. There were deep mosses now, and no trail to

162

follow, for they swallowed the marks of any passage. For all I knew I might have lost the trail in the night, but I reckoned that the glen itself was the line of the trail.

I went through the mosses like an otter, on my face, first rolling in the peat so that my skin should not show (though it was brown enough already). The sun was high before I had finished that crawl, and ahead of me lay a small saddle and the promise of a stretch of open country, where I should have to cast for the trail.

Before I reached the saddle I knew I was being watched again. I crept and slithered into the shade of a boulder, and round it until I could see the hillside without the dazzle of sunlight to hide it. I picked them up a few moments later when a bird flew down the cliff chattering angrily; two men in brown cloaks, sitting with bows strung and arrows ready. The path over the saddle was not for me.

I was loath to turn back, having come so far, but there was no help for it. I worked back through that weary moss and down the infant river to its first steep feeder stream. Up the stream I hauled myself on forearms and thighs, raising my body to let the water flow under me unchecked, till I came to a small waterfall sheer above me. I came out of cover and crept under stunted bushes, along a little green hollow, and so up to another fall.

I lay there and rested for the next climb, and it was well that I did so, for there was a spear-cast length of naked rock above, hidden by fallen rocks from where I lay. I went up it with a finger here and a toe there in crannies, picked out like a fly on a whitewashed wall. There was a shelf with a deep little pool at the top, and I sank my head and shoulders into it gratefully. Above me was a short stretch of scree, red and newly stripped, and above it the sky and the eagles wheeling.

But the scree was impossible. It slid away under my hands, and twice I was within a hair's breadth of falling back into the pool. At last I had to give up. I lay on the ledge and looked round in something near despair. I lay so still that a little black and white wagtail came down the cliff catching flies, balancing on tiny niches with flirts of his tail. Then he flew up the face and I was alone again.

I looked at the cliff and the wagtail's perches, and it seemed there might be toeholds where the dry grass and the yellow rockweeds clung. The ledge was in shadow, but the sun was bright on the cliff, and I reckoned I must be almost over the heads of the bowmen. I gritted my teeth and set myself to climb.

Once I kicked out a loose stone and hung by my hands fighting for life and a foothold; the stone bounced once on the ledge and went over and I did not hear it strike again. I braced myself not to look down, found my grip, and went on.

The shadow moved over the cliff and it was easier to look up without the glare on the rock. At last, at very long last, I got one hand over the top and drew myself up to lie flat on the grass. When I was ready to go on I opened my eyes and saw a pair of feet a step away.

I pushed myself upright. There were two more men in brown cloaks, one with a bow and one with a spear. So here was the end of Drost, I thought, and I could have spared myself the last half-day's ordeal. I stood still and waited, looking down as our men had commanded, though I longed to face death before it struck.

When we had stood there a great time one of them stepped up to me and took me by the arm.

'Come,' he said, and led me off across the moor.

We walked for a long time in silence, I and the bowman, while the other remained at the top of the cliff. The hill sloped down to the north, and far ahead we saw another man walking and leading a boy. Even at that distance I knew Arth's curly head. So he too was taken; perhaps we could die together. I wondered if those who died here found any way to the Orchard.

As night was falling we came to a stockaded camp and the reek of turf-fires. My captor handed me on to a cluster of men at the gateway, and they pushed me into a cattle-pen already crowded with boys. Looking always at the ground I recognised feet—Arth's a little way off, and Ailill's fair skin scratched and mud-blackened. We had no room to move but stood pressed together, taking no comfort from the nearness of friends. Others were thrust in after us until the first-comers were crammed against the timbers of the pen.

When it was black night the crush began to ease somehow;

164

we heard a murmur of voices nearby, like the voices of the men when they had come to test us for our marking. The pressure grew steadily less, and I felt someone pluck my arm and draw me away.

The blaze of firelight was bewildering when I was suddenly brought into it. Gradually I made out the shapes of men sitting round the fire. Someone came behind me and forced up my chin with an arm round my neck, so that I had to look at them; and a fearsome sight they were.

They were all painted, not as our men paint, but in great streaks and slashes of white and umber, and they wore collars of flat white shiny crescents and cloaks of stiff dark fur. The man holding me began to speak. His tongue was strange, though some words were our words, and it was long before I understood that he was telling the men how he had taken me, and by which way I had come.

When he ceased there was a silence, and in it I was led full circle round the fire. Then a man cried:

'Is it well, men of the Bear?'

A sullen growl answered him, a growl that might have come from the Smiler himself.

He who held me clapped me on the shoulder—

'Well, cub! Come, sit by the fire; tomorrow you dance.'

Then I saw other boys of our people sitting beside men round the fire, and it came to me that perhaps we were not to be killed that night.

Arth came soon after; it was torment to hear the tale of his journey and capture—he had fought the men as I had not had strength to fight, even if I had had courage—and I longed to reach out and touch him. But if I had passed, how could Arth fail? He sat down with his man beyond the hearth.

They accepted us all with longer or shorter talk; I grew faint with sleep and hunger, and hardly knew whether Ailill had joined us. But presently young boys brought bowls of broth, rich with meat, and we ate at the men's bidding. The wound in my groin ached like a fresh sword-cut and I longed to bow myself to ease it, but dared not. They showed us a place to wash ourselves, and brought us back to sleep round the fire, which they had covered with strips of earth to keep it alive till morning. And there we slept till daybreak.

At first light the men woke us and gathered us in a ring round one of their leaders. He was a splendid figure, his fresh paint gleaming, the white necklace catching the light and his skin glistening; there was a strange smell about him, about all of them, that made my hair prickle when I first smelt it.

'Now,' he said, 'today you dance. You dance the Dance of the Green Glen, as you call it; but its right name is the Dance of the Smiling One. It is death, this dance, if you go wrong; he does not forgive nor allow a second chance. Understand, you must dance perfectly or not at all. Four of you will dance the knife-steps and the others the spear-steps. Stand up, you, you, you and . . .'

He walked round the fire pointing to Arth, to an older boy, to a third, and to me. We stood up and waited.

'You four, the knife-steps,' he said again.

Ailill cried suddenly :

'He can't! Drost—the last one—he is the law-keeper to my kingship, the Dark Twin—he mustn't dance !'

There was a shocked silence, and then the man said quietly :

'King of the river-people, they should not have sent either of you if they did not want either of you to succeed; the ring is no safer than the square. Be still; this is in the hands of the great ones; if you withdraw now the Smiler himself will be your enemy for what remains of your life.'

'Drost—' said Ailill.

I turned and looked at him. His face was stiff with anger and, I thought, with pity for me going to death; but looking past that, as Mangan or Demetroos would have done, I saw his desire for my death fighting his desire for my disgrace. Silence had been broken; there was no more reason for me to remain silent. I saluted him.

'Great King,' I said, 'it will be for you and the People.'

He flushed scarlet and said no more.

They brought great tubs of fat and smeared us with it, first we four of the knives, every inch of us except the palms of our hands which they rubbed instead with resin, and next the rest of the boys who were to have the spears. Then they brought us knives, long-bladed curving knives such as they wore, and short spears like boar-spears. The reek of fat from our own bodies choked our nostrils.

The rumour of a warming drum had sounded faintly beyond the palisade all this time; now they assembled us in line, the four knife-bearers at the head, and we began to move out in the stamp-and-hop of the dance. The men danced with us.

The drumming had a strange harsh note that was overmastering. Before we had passed the length of the stockade we were caught up in it, stamping and turning at its command. Two drummers led us along a wide glen and into a side branch, to a level place of smooth grass. There were steep rocky crags shutting us in on all sides. A little way up one side lay a heap of mangled bones that had been a cow.

We made our ring, the four knives in the centre, dancing and drumming without a break. I grew dizzy with turning, till the rock-walls wheeled past me and I stood still among them.

There was a little dark opening high up the cliff; I began to notice it at each turn. And all at once he was there.

He came out into the sunlight and stood on four feet to watch. He reared up a little to see better, and down again.

We danced on. The beat changed to bid the ring open. It was a half-circle now, moving to right and left. We four turned into line and faced him.

Suddenly he decided to join us. He moves very fast when he moves. One moment he was in his doorway, the next he was among us. He swung his head and spoke angrily.

Some of the men shouted to him in greeting; they were all of his kin. He swung his head and watched, and then we saw his great forefeet shift and he reared up and began to dance.

Our own men had never told us that he would dance too; it made no difference, the drum had us in its grip, we stamped and swayed before him and he swayed high above us.

The drums cried:

'Run in! Run in!'

We began the last figure of the dance, the run forward and the leap aside. We ran closer and closer to the great mass of him, passing under the huge forearms one by one. He was caught by the drumming as we were.

The drums cried out sharply as I was running towards him. As I turned under the arm I saw the bare place in the armpit. The drum cried again and I thrust upward with all my strength.

The sky was darkened; a mighty hand fell whistling a hair's

breadth from my head; he cried out in a voice of angry agony, fell as a tree falls, and rolled on the ground. The spearmen closed in, someone dragged me away, and the ground began to tilt under my feet. I wanted to run and hide and weep my heart out, for I had killed the splendour of beauty.

They brought us back to the great carcase a little later, when it was safe. They said Arth and I had struck together, one on either side, and he had died quickly and cleanly. They gave us meat to offer to his spirit and rubbing-sticks to kindle a fire by his head. As the smoke went up, men who had watched from the crags came down and crowded round and began to skin him. They set the hide up on sticks and we passed beneath it, and they gave us his heart and liver to eat.

They led us back to the camp, shouting his praises, and made a feast for the whole tribe of the rest of the meat. The skull they set up by the men's house, the skin they would cure and hang with others inside. The claws were shared among the four of us, and Arth and I were given teeth as well. By next day these things were made into collars and hung round our necks before we set off down the glen. But that night at the feast they sang of bygone dancings, and of the great deeds and misdeeds of the Smiler, how many he had killed, how many he had outwitted, how many he had defied.

I hated every moment of it.

As soon as we were out of sight of the men of the Bear I dived into a deep pool of the river, and washed, and washed, and washed. Arth and I scrubbed each other with earth and grass and leaves, and dived again; we swam in every pool as we came to it; and still we reeked of bear-grease. We said nothing to each other of what we felt, for there was no need. We could have rolled in filth to be rid of that stench.

When we came to our own people again, they roared round us like a swarm of bees. We were led to the House of the Young Men and feasted like heroes; but it was long before I was free of sorrow for that killing.

Now we were no longer boys but young men. We lived in the house on the north of the village, and hunted and fished for ourselves and our families, and those of us who had homes went back and forth at will. On one of my visits to my mother, she said to me—

'Come back and eat with us tonight, Drost; I have a gift to give you.'

I went away into the hills to try for a barren hind, to take her some venison; it is geas even between close kin to receive a gift without making any return. I had my beast by early afternoon, gralloched her and put her on my back, and was coming down the path above the rocks when I saw an old man walking towards me.

My first unworthy thought was a twinge of annoyance that now I should have to offer him a share of my hunting; then I saw who it was. Talorc, a shadow of himself, came along stooping on his staff. I was touched with pity for his ruin, and as we met I gave him the full greeting of his rank and touched my knee to the ground.

He wiped his rheumy eyes and croaked :

'My blessing to you, my son, if you will have it. Stop a breath with me, I have a word for you.'

'A word for me, Most Reverend?'

I was frankly amazed; who would make him a messenger? I saw how he shook, and I laid down my spear and my load and drew his hand through my arm. The lean claws touched my wrist not unkindly.

'I have a word,' he said again. 'Drost, I am nothing; but this I have never known before. A word has come to me. Your mother will give you a gift tonight, and there is a geis on it. It is geas for it to touch rope. That is all; I do not know what the gift is, only that there is a geis on it, and she does not know it. Mangan might have understood . . . but I have never known such a thing before. A Sending—a true Sending! Now that I have told you, let me sit and rest.'

There were flat rocks beside the path; I spread my cloak on them and he sat down, breathing hard.

'Are you sick, Reverence? Shall I fetch help?'

'You can fetch no help to me, child; my feet are shod for the road.'

Then I saw that he had knowledge of his own end, and my heart was shaken for him.

'Rest a little, and we will go on together,' I said.

After a time (and I remember how the larks sang above us) he said:

'Drost, do you know whose son you are?'

'I'm the son of no man, sir,' I answered, thinking that his mind was wandering.

'No,' said he, 'one fault brought all these years of trouble. You should have been the King's son, or the Twin's—a king and the Maiden should have made you. And Daran planned—Daran prepared the way—but Ailill robbed me. Ailill robbed the sons of Ennis, and me. It cost him something; I saw to that; but it cost me more. They chose Melduin—Melduin! When I was there!

'You have king's blood, my son; Daran's blood, better than Ailill had. I would have made you king indeed; I would have taken Ailill out of your path . . . what is the son of a freed-woman's daughter, compared to the son of a king's son?

'Naas ruined it all. Why could he not obey me? If you had been the offering I would not have let Ailill harm you; the marrow of his mind would have split ere he touched you. Ginetha wanted you dead, did she? I took her gold to buy your kingdom. Not you, but Ailill should have died at your offering. He should have crumpled at my feet and died. What could we not have done, you and I? Naas, with his talk of the gods choosing you—he little knew! *I* chose you; I never meant you to be hurt; your blood is too royal to waste . . . when I saw it my own marrow burned. The women were to blame . . . that shrieking fool my sister, and your mother, running in among matters too high for her . . . women should never be permitted to draw near secret things . . .

'Daran; I used to come by night to Daran. He liked to see me. He taught me to bring a little boat in under the cliffs by night. I would sail alone from the Eagles in the dark of the moon. You're clever in a boat too, like me . . . I've watched you with the boys. I came up the cliff that last night—the path was worse in those days, only I used it—and that was how I trapped Ailill. He should have been far off in the hills before then; had I not sent word which way the Eagles would go? He should have been with Grath; he let Grath die.'

'But I thought—' I said. 'I thought he brought help, only it came too late? I thought ...'

'Too late! And why? Because Ennis was dead and he knew Daran had not long to live. He had to clear his way.'

'But the young kings, the sons of Ennis—?'

'I saw his shadow on the wall,' he said. 'I stood quite still and saw his striped cloak at the side gate. I went in, and they lay there. They were pretty boys, men will tell you; they were not pretty then. I looked close, and I saw a shred of his cloak caught in a tooth ... so I knew.'

I was trembling as I knelt beside him. I felt again an old terror that lay hidden in the Great Fort.

'I went in to Daran; there was a secret door. He was dying; he died very fat, very short of breath. I trow the sons of Ennis died short of breath too! He gasped that he had prepared my way; the word he had set running had returned three times to him, the word that the People should choose a priest for the next Twin. They talked of sending the younger boy to be trained, but we knew better than that. I heard the guards stirring and I went quickly. I did not tell him the children were dead; what need? I sailed in again with the dawn and cried as I landed that I had a Sending, that the women had destroyed the boys. They had newly found their dead. It was likely enough; they all knew about Ennis and . . . but never mind that. Daran also had died about sunrise.

'When Ailill returned from his victory I was among the first to greet him. I knelt to him, and put the threads of his cloak into his hand. He drew me aside, saying that he must hear the truth of this Sending from me alone. I told him what I had seen.

'Was it a king, think you, who trembled at that news? He asked what I meant to do. I told him, nothing, if he gave me what I required. He laughed in my face, without mirth. He said the men had already chosen their Priest-Twin.

'There was one thing left for him to give me, and I took that. I took his place on the hill, while he contented himself with my sister. I wanted her—Malda—I was young then; perhaps I loved her. So much talk of love, and they never say what they mean! When you were born I knew my time would come, so I waited; I waited long and long. I had a little revenge on Melduin to sweeten my waiting. And then that fool Naas destroyed it all!

'Let me look at you, now that I claim you at last. You are strong, aren't you? You never gave me your mind; I like you for that, do you know? I thought I had you, but no, you slipped away like water—Ailill now, he was clay to my moulding and of no more account than his father. Yes, they've taught you to hate me; you curse me, do you, you too? It is well—you are strong, as I was. You walk your own way. But I must go down into the dark with you, too, cursing me.'

'No!' I cried, on my knees beside him. 'No, who am I to curse anyone, to hate anyone? I will never be king; that is for Ailill; I do not desire to be king. But if you—if you succeeded, if you led in the dancing, it must have been the Mother's will, she must have meant it to happen; she could have stopped it as she stopped me harming Ailill. Comfort yourself—'

I was going to say 'Most Reverend', but I swallowed the words; instead I put my arms round the shell that was left of him and used words I had never spoken before:

'My father.'

His head fell forward on my shoulder and I felt his tears.

For a long space I held him. We were so still that a young roe came out of the thicket to feed on a bush nearby, not even winding my kill a few feet away. I tightened my clasp to show him this wonder, but in the next breath the creature had moved into the sun, and I saw it shine as white as snow. Moreover it fed on the blackthorn buds.

Talorc moved in my arms, raised his head to speak, smiled, I think, and fell back.

I held him yet a moment longer until I was certain. Then I laid his body down on the rock and folded the hands over the staff. I stood looking down at the man who had been my father, whom I had feared so long, who had confessed so much evil with his last words.

But then I bethought me, and I took my spear and went a little way off, and climbed on a rock to guard the body until someone came.

I had time for long thoughts before I saw a man walking from the village towards me. I raised my voice and cried that there was death in the path, and saw him hurriedly cover his head and take to his heels down the road.

Presently Neart came with bearers and a carrying-frame, and took the body to the hut where he had lived, until the pyre should be ready. I remained behind, and sacrificed the venison I had killed, that the path might be safe and his spirit quieted; and I built a cairn over the place where he had died, and walked round clear of the houses and up byroads to the Hearth-house.

I came to the outer gate and found Cardail standing in the courtyard in a cloud of doves. Her dark hair was bound back with a wreath of white wool; I had not known she was chosen to be the Maiden. I could no longer speak to her as a child to a child.

I gave her the greeting of a priestess, touching my hand to the ground; and was not displeased when she started and blushed and looked away from me. I stood outside the gate, and asked if I might speak with the Middle Priestess:

'For I am not able to enter your presence, Lady.'

'I'll tell your mother,' she said, and ran in.

My mother came out immediately.

'What is it, my son?'

'Mother,' I said, 'I cannot enter your house; I have come from death.'

'The Mother is the giver of life and of death, my child; enter freely.'

She led me formally to the jars that stood ready by the wall, and sprinkled me with water, and brought me a cloak out of her store; and then she took me in her arms and kissed my brow, and said as a mother: 'Come in now, Drost; whose death have you seen? Oh, Drost, is it one of the young men? The Mother give him her blessing!'

I said bluntly, before she could say more:

'Talorc died in my arms.'

She stepped back, wide-eyed.

'Talorc?'

From beyond the Hearth the Old One said harshly:

'Good riddance—pestilent old trouble-maker!'

My mother was trembling; I took her hands in mine and led her to the inner room.

173

'He died in my arms, and he told me my geis before he died, and much else too; and, mother, the White Doe came for him.'

Demetroos came out of the shadows and led her to her own chair. The Old One said:

'Dreams, brat! How could such as he be fetched by the Doe, he who never believed in anything all his life?'

I said doggedly (for I had seen what I had seen)—

'She came from the thorn thicket and waited for him, and when I looked again she had gone.'

My mother stood up. She crossed her hands on her breast and walked to the edge of the hearth. Before our eyes she ceased to be Malda, the Dweller Among Houses, and became Brigitta herself.

She said:

'The Mother is everywhere; she is everything; everything is hers; everyone is hers. Nothing that man or men can do parts them from her. Though a man flee from her, she will go before him; though a man think he has driven her out of his thoughts, he cannot drive himself out of hers.'

I found myself on my knees beside Demetroos.

The golden voice went on:

'All mantles are but a corner of her mantle; all gods are her shadow; all faiths are her faith. Though as children at play you change the names of things, all things are known by name to her. The son of Daran was led far from her in life, but she has shown you that in death he returned homeward.'

She left us and went out to the Hearth, and we were all silent for a space. In that silence we heard a woman weeping softly in the Hearth-room.

Presently the Old One hobbled stiffly to the door.

'Malda, little daughter,' she said gently, 'do not weep for him; the son of Daran is nothing to you now, neither friend nor foe; he is at peace.'

She put her arm round my mother's shoulders and drew her back into the inner room. They sat together beyond the fire.

'Do not weep for him, child,' she said again.

My mother lifted her head.

'I am not weeping for him, my mother, I weep for the end of a long sorrow. Drost, little son, what did he tell you?'

I was ashamed to answer her; at last, holding my head low,
I whispered:

'That—that he was my father.'

My mother drew away from the Old One and said to her:

'Now do you see?'

The Old One said:

'That one? But the King . . . ?'

'Mine was the first sin; I begged you—do you not remember
how I begged you?—to grant that Melduin might be the one;
when it befell as it befell, I took it as her answer to me. And
after, when the New Way demanded of him that we could
never have our joy, still it was her answer. There was no other
for me.'

I knelt by the fire; but my body was cold and the stones of
the hillside cut my feet. I was running alone, under the stars,
one appointed to give herself for the People; behind me
followed the feet of the pursuers and among them one footfall
I strained to hear; and there rose in my path, far ahead of the
hunt, the one I feared above all others.

I shuddered away from the vision and caught at the hem of
my mother's cloak, and the touch of her hand swiftly stooping
to me was cool and healing.

'You see too much, little son,' she said; and to Demetroos:

'Will it pass? Will he be free of the Sight when he is older?
Can you not teach him how to be free?'

Demetroos said sadly:

'Knowledge is knowledge, Lady; no one can forget what
they have desired to know. In another place he desired this
knowledge, and now it is his. It may be, if he finds the one he
seeks, the doors will close.'

'No one can forget . . . Demetroos, what of your own
desires? Have you not begun to forget? After seven years is it
not time to go on with your search?'

'Seven years! Is it possible? A day—a moment! Lady,
where should I go? The Well is here.'

'Beloved, you must find your own well, music's self and the
end of thirst; it is not quenched by drinking at another's well.'

'Is it not? Is there nothing here for me? Can you not give me
—a corner of the mantle?'

My mother said gently:

'Demetroos, look at me; the Well is not here for you. You know better than that. I do not send you away nor bid you remain; but ah, can you not see we should each be looking over the shoulder of the other, to a different face? Wait yet a little and you will find her again in your fields of flowers, as I shall find him under the laden boughs. She waits for you yonder; here you are as near as may be to the road, and no bars will be set across your path as you go; weave your garland here and leave it to put on when you return, but weave no dead flowers into it to grieve her when she comes again.'

Demetroos took her hand and kissed it, and returned it to her lap.

'Shall I go, then? Do you command me to go?'

'Go, if you will,' she said.

'Go if you must,' said the Old One, breaking silence, 'but you have our leave to remain. It may be you can help our people.'

He sighed, and sat down by me once more. His mind was open to me; I saw far off in it a grave in a distant land, offerings laid round it to comfort the spirit and keep it beyond the barriers, and kneeling by it a lonely priest who would have given all his priesthood for one little key to the gates.

Then a new thought came to me; I said to the Old One, but softly, not to disturb the troubled thoughts of Malda and Demetroos:

'If Tal—, if he who is dead was my father, ought I to cut my hair for him, and light the pyre?'

She frowned.

'If he was, and it seems he was, it is not a thing to be spoken of; no one knows the father of the Child of Harvest. Cut a lock of your hair and lay it on the fire, if you like, but do not give the pyre a son's service. See, I will cut a little lock for you, here at the side where nobody will notice; take it where he lies and put it in his hand; it may be his spirit will be the quieter for it. If he were to trouble us dead as he troubled us living, it would cost more than a lock of hair to quieten him!'

She took her knife and cut off a twist of hair and put it in my hand.

'But before you go, child—concerning the Maiden, take this word to the other young men. When I was young, and long before that, the leaders of the Boar Hunt led the spring dancing;

they were marked out for the Mother's service; only those she found worthy to kill her beast were worthy to attempt that other prize. Nowadays they go to that hunt as to any other . . .'

'Lady, forgive me, but we know it is a high and holy hunt.'

'Do ye so? And when has one of you found the White Boar? He has not been seen these twenty years; there is the measure of your unworthiness! When you sight and hunt him, and if and when one of you is permitted to kill him, then you will know that the sickness has gone out of you at last. Remember this, and carry my words to your companions.'

'I will remember, and carry,' I said, kneeling to her, and I rose to go.

My mother sprang up—

'Little son, I had forgotten your gift! Come to the Hearth; it is ready for you.'

'I have no gift to give you in return,' I said; 'I had killed a deer, but I offered it instead when—when that happened.'

'The news was your gift to me; come.'

She took my hand and led me to the Hearth, and I knelt and fed the fire with the wood laid ready. When I looked up she was standing beyond the fire with a long bundle rolled in red cloth in her arms. She unwrapped it, and as she did so Felim came hurrying in with the news of Talorc, checked, and knelt in the doorway.

She took out and held up a broad red sword.

It was a sword of the old times, not such a sword as men carry now with the long grey blades that may bend and cost the bearer his life, but one of the old true kind that will shear through hide or bone; a sword to be kept alive with handling and honing, and polished with hand and oil. The hilt was of white bone bound with gold and the pommel a golden apple.

'Take it, Drost; it has lain long in the Mother's keeping; take it and carry it for her and her people.'

She put it into my hands, stooped to kiss me, and sent me away.

Part Four

I WENT out into the night, a sworded man.

I stood under the stars in the outer court and held the glorious thing in my right hand, and found no words to utter all the high vows that crowded my heart. But presently I remembered the lock of hair, still held in my left hand, and what I had to do.

I went down to the lonely house at the edge of the village, with its hurdle-door open to the dark, and I felt my way to the bed-place and touched the ice-cold thing that lay there, and under its stiffened hands I laid my hair. I could not stay with him, but backed out with my legs trembling, and washed in the stream. Then I went back to the young men, where they lay sleeping, and I crept into my own place and lay down.

And next day Ailill, as nearest kin to the dead, lit the fire to burn the body. There were few men by the pyre, and no women, not even his sister Ginetha. Many things that had been dark to me were lit by the flames of that fire: my kinship with Ailill; the infamy of both our fathers; things to keep hidden for ever.

I kept my hand on the hilt of my new sword all through the rites. When later the young men wanted to discuss it I answered only that my mother had given it me, as was her right (for it is the mother who arms her son), and I turned their thoughts another way by telling what the Old One had said about the White Boar.

Here was a new mystery, and yet half-remembered, for Felim had sung to us of the Silver One for whom the great hunts ranged the land. But no one had seen him, wherever and whoever we asked; we vowed ourselves to follow him to the death if ever we found him, and the older men called us fools to think the great wonders of old would return for our glory.

As for me, I respected the Old One, and I thought it more than probable that in the fullness of time she would somehow show her power; meantime I worked on my sword, rubbing it with oil between my palms, and as always I took care not to be alone with my Twin.

In the deep of winter, when the snow lay over the moors, we young men and the eldest boys went out to the Boar Hunt. First we danced the holy dance, and made our preparations, and we stripped ourselves of ornaments lest hand or foot be checked in the moment of decision; except only that those with swords wore them.

There were many wild pigs about, their trails marked out in the snowy stubbles where they rooted at nights, big and little together.

We were three days in the hunt.

All the first day we went about the edge of the cultivated lands to see where the biggest boars had been, and where they went to lair. By evening we had marked down three trails and chosen one to follow. The next day we began at the patch of scrub where he had harboured, and we found his tracks leading away to the broken country and the rocks above the river. We followed him all that day.

He was a big one. We had no sight of him yet, but the sickle-marks of his feet had cut sharply into the frozen ground and spread apart under his weight where he slipped or jumped. He was a traveller, too, an old bachelor perhaps, or the lord of a herd indignant with the impertinences of younger pigs. Through the early dusk and under the moon when she rose, he travelled and we followed.

He stopped to eat a little here and there—we found his plunderings—but never long enough for us to overtake him. At moonset we rested under cliffs, for ambitious though we were, we were not yet quite mad with desire of death. We slept huddled together, two or three sharing their cloaks, sleeping light and waking often, our weapons under us to keep them dry.

There was a thin cold mist off the snow towards sunrise, the first hint of a thaw. We followed him onward—going more and more carefully, for he was not far ahead; his castings still smoked on the ground as we came to them.

He knew he had been followed. There was the barest hint of a turn in his trail to warn us that at a narrow place between rocks he had sprung aside, to meet us on ground of his own choosing. The first we knew of the honour was one ringing cough from behind the boulders, and then the patter of the neat small feet, a vast arching neck, and the flash of wicked tusks.

'Ugh!' he said as he came. 'Whoof!' he said as he ripped through us; a dozen spears were levelled for him, but they came down after he had passed, however fast they came.

But he was not done with us yet. He wheeled again and the rising sun made a glory of him, every bristle an icicle.

He coughed and swung his head to show us his armoury; all we could see of him was the head and the great wedge of shoulder and collar, and the forefeet primly set together; the dropped hindquarters, and the tail, that would have told us what he was planning, were hidden.

'Whoof!'

There was a flurry of powdery snow, a steaming wheeling mass, and the white turning to red all round. Lan was thrown clear. The spearmen closed in. Ailill ran forward, shouting:

'Let me past! Let me kill him! I'll kill him for you!'

I drew my sword and stood over the struggling heap. The only face I could not see anywhere was Arth's. There was a grey hairy back uppermost; I thrust the sword in as far as it would go, drew it out crimsoned and prepared to thrust again. The mound heeled over; Lan yelled in my ear:

'Mind the feet!'

A razor-sharp hind hoof swung up where my leg had been a breath before. Arth, covered in blood but still gripping his butt, stood up out of the snow and straightened himself cautiously. His spear was in the boar up to the guard-piece.

And the great boar was dead. We stood round him, starting at every twitch of the huge body as it sank down and the blood ran out of the wounds, and in our hearts we knew we had killed the biggest for many a year. Then, as if we had been freed from a spell, we gathered around Arth and clapped him on the back and all wanted to touch him at once, and we shouted and shook our spears. He was not much hurt, though before the rest of us had come to his help he thought the beast would swallow him, so savagely it worked to reach him.

We cut poles from trees, for our spears were not long enough to carry the beast, and we tied its legs together and prepared to carry it back to the river-mouth.

Just as the first four bearers were taking up the load, Ailill said in a puzzled voice:

'I'd always thought they were black.'

'Black or brindled,' said Lan airily, 'or sometimes they're ...'

His voice died away. This one, now that we saw him in full sunlight as the mist lifted, was almost, very nearly, white.

It was an awestricken group of young hunters that came home with the great beast, and an awestricken village that welcomed us, when at last we had struggled back to the edge of the fields and found enough breath to announce our coming with the 'Song of the Boar'.

The elder men had called a council and we were making ready for it. It was a few days since the death of the White Boar, and the next moon would be the Maiden's. Arth said to me in a voice that shook a little:

'Drost, tell me again what she said, about the hunt and—you know—the rest of it.'

'She said that when we sighted him, and if one of us were permitted to kill him, then we should know the sickness had gone from the People.'

'Yes, yes, yes! I know that; what else?'

'Only that the leaders in the hunt were to lead the spring dancing because she would have chosen them. Felim said so too, long ago.'

182

'I know, I know; but did she say if it was the ones who led the trail, Lan and those others, or ... or ...'

'I suppose she meant the first spear; that's you.'

'Mother of All, hear me!' said Arth.

He turned and went out alone.

I thought it a strange ambition in Arth to desire so much to lead the spring dancing. (Before you laugh, my dearest, remember I was still a child asleep. And also this; since I had seen what lay in Demetroos' mind I had remembered, more and more, how in my sickness I had dreamed of bearing your body to a lonely grave under trees; youth lies open to despair; I thought it possible that you were not in the world any more, for I was sure you were nowhere among the People. I had gone with the others to sing with the girls, many a time, but you were not there. So I despaired, and I had no eyes for any other, and I almost enjoyed that sorrow. I remember that I made some songs about it that were praised by the other young men —if not by Felim.)

My wakening was nearer than I knew. We came to the Great Fort, and there were strangers among the servants in the court, small brown men with crested helmets and tunics of painted leather. Ailill glanced at me under his lids and said on a breath: 'What have they been doing while we made our sport up yonder?'

It took me a moment to understand that he had spoken of the holy hunt; by then it was too late to answer, for our ways were dividing round the hearth.

I stopped at the foot of Melduin's chair and waited for Ailill to sit first. Some of the eldest men were standing by his chair, and when he came to them they took him by the arms and lifted him bodily into the seat. I saw a faint flush spread along his cheek.

The hall stood as one, clashed spears, and shouted. Ailill on his throne raised his right hand to salute them.

Now at last he was all king. The red cloak fell open from his shoulders to show the broad embroidered girdle and the sword that had been his father's, and closed again over his knees so that the sword lay not on white but on crimson; the gold collar set off the long throat in which that singing voice was hidden, and the pallor of the skin showed the fine bones of

183

the face. When he raised his head to look across the hearth at me, his eyes flashed as blue as the eyes of that singer I had seen in a haunted wood.

I found words in my mouth and began speaking them softly—'Great Mother, keep this great king . . .'

But my prayer was never finished; the men came to me and lifted me into the other chair, not knowing that they broke my prayer. Fool that I was not to stand forward and pray aloud! But it was still my way to call on the Mother in secret as I had learned to do while the New Way was in power. I was abashed at my cowardice and sat silent while the men cried out around me.

Old Gerig spoke to the King—

'Great King of the Lords of the Boar! The first to greet you are your own men of the Boar; the next to greet you are messengers from the eastern lands with a word for you and for us all. Here they are, the Lords of the East.'

The upper door opened and three men came in.

They were the masters of those we had seen in the court; three short thickset men with heavy beards hiding their throats, in garments of gaudy stripes and cloaks trimmed with the pelts of wolves. They carried short spears, two each, and flat-hilted broad swords with gold on the hilts, and sheathed daggers in wide belts. Their legs and feet were clothed in leathers adorned with gold studs. Rich and barbarous they were to see, and it was beyond question that they were great men in their own country.

They walked down the hall swaggering so that their cloaks swung stiffly, and they greeted Ailill with outstretched hands and rolling sentences in guttural voices. Ailill leaned forward to them—

'Lords of the East, you are welcome to our houses. Bring wine for the noble guests!'

As the horns of honey-wine were carried in, I saw Felim tune his harp. The strangers drank with Ailill and called a blessing aloud, and we all stood and drank with them, and Felim struck his harp and sang the verse of welcome. Then our guests sat down among us and we waited to hear their business.

Their tongues were thick and what they said was hard to follow, but it became plain soon enough.

They were sent, they said, by the Queen of the East; she had two daughters for whom she desired mates, and her choice had fallen on the Kings of the Boar.

There was a mutter of talk round the hall as we grasped what they had said; I did not wholly understand at first, and when I did I was bewildered. I said to myself that doubtless this was a plan for years ahead; the weddings of queens and kings were not lightly arranged; we would be older before the ceremonies took place, and there would be time to learn from someone what these ceremonies would be. And before then— oh, long before!—I would find my heart's darling; gone was any fancy that she was not to be found; I knew she was. I would find her, the other half of myself, my deepest dreaming, and when I had found her neither Queen of the East nor Lord of the Boar would have power to part us whom the Mother had made one heart in two bodies.

But Ailill was replying; he thanked the men and their queen, but the matter must be decided by the Lords of the Boar. They asked his leave to withdraw, and left us.

Gerig called on me for a law concerning the marriages of kings, but there is no such law; there is only the general law that kings must be guided by the Council, and that the children of kings need not be considered for kingship unless they are born of mothers acceptable to the People (this is the rule that may bar the base-born).

'And what is your word in this, my lords?' asked Ailill.

Old Gerig spoke first, as was his right.

'King, it would be strength to us to have the easterners for friends. The Men of the Bear are good fighters, but they will not come out of their own lands unless their backs are covered; they would not come down against the Grey Dogs when your father fought his last war, because neither they nor we had a sure bond with the east. The Eagles and the Grey Dogs are divided now, but if they were to heal their quarrels, then we and the Men of the Bear might have sore need of friends. But, but—there are many ways in which the easterners differ from us. Their queen is a queen, not the wife of a king.'

'If she sends her daughters here they will both be queens,' said Ailill haughtily.

Felim stood up—

'I heard no word of coming here,' said he; 'the easterners fetch husbands for their princesses from all airts, but they themselves may not leave home.'

'But that's ridiculous!' cried Ailill.

'That's their custom,' said Felim. 'And here's another of their customs: queen succeeds to queen, not king to king, and it's the youngest princess who follows her mother to power. The elder sisters are nothing.'

'That may be so with them; it will not be so here,' said Ailill.

'Here or there, it will signify when it comes to succession,' said old Gerig. 'If you two kings marry these two princesses they will be your wives whether they live here or not, and their children will be your children.'

I could not keep my mind on their talk, try as I would; for since that certainty had come upon me a little time before, my eyes were fixed on the smoke and on a grove of grey-green trees beyond it, where my heart's darling walked. This chatter about queens and princesses was in some other time and place; here in my deep dream was my love.

Neart was saying:

'But for the sake of their strength, King, will you not do this for the People? What are their customs to us?'

Regil stood up and said:

'A royal marriage is not a marriage such as other men make; you may travel to their country for the ceremonies, but you will not remain there; what is it to us what they do? And what is it to them, what you do when you return here?'

'That's a twisted word,' said Felim; 'we must know where we stand. If the Mother sends children, whose are they? And where shall we find our next kings? Call the ambassadors back, King, and ask them that.'

'Wait,' said Ailill; 'Regil's right; what is it to them, what we do? It is enough if we go to the east for this marriage, we do them enough honour in that; they have kings, surely, to lead them as my father led you, as I am ready to lead you. If not, then it's time they did. I am willing to go. Drost?'

I wrenched my thoughts back and answered through a dry mouth:

'I must do as the men decide.'

Ailill's lips tightened scornfully.

Old Gerig said again:

'But the children—concerning the children?'

'The children are neither begotten nor born,' said Neart; 'time enough for that when they are there to be seen. It's ill luck planning for sons unborn.'

Ailill said loudly:

'Invite the ambassadors to return!'

They came back, proud and stocky, swinging their short cloaks, and took their seats before Ailill.

'Lords of the East,' he said, 'we are ready to consider your queen's request, but my Council desire more knowledge on certain points; however, on the whole we are inclined to grant your petition. But tell us—when does she desire this marriage to be made? And what will be our position in your country when we visit it?'

'King,' said their spokesman, 'your position will be first among the men, for the Queen's man will stand aside for you when your daughters are born; and as for the ceremony, what more fitting time than the Maiden's Moon that draws near? They are preparing the feast in expectation of your coming.'

This was unforeseen indeed! The talk swelled to a roar, speaker after speaker stood up to protest, besides the main discussion there were a score of lesser arguments all round us.

Dran shouted above the uproar:

'And what of the spring dancing, King? You will not leave us before that?'

The ambassadors were standing too, trying to hear all that was being said; one of them bellowed back:

'If you go to theirs, you need not come to ours! What sort of people are you that do not keep maidens for the Maiden?'

Another cried:

'But are they maidens at all? How do we know how these boys have lived?'

Ailill came to his feet in a swirl of crimson cloak, the gold on his arm flashing angrily as he signalled for silence—

'Hear me!' he shouted. 'We accept the offer; we will go with these men as kings, and as kings we will return to you, as kings and as the chief men in the eastern lands. That is the end of the talk. I have spoken for us both.'

He signed to the slaves to bring in the meat-cauldrons and start serving the feast.

The vision of grey-green trees shivered as a wind shivers reflections in a pool, and slowly and sadly it left me. I sat alone in the midst of the men, in the Twin's chair, doomed to exile like a sold slave.

Within a week we were on the road. We marched in a strong company of spearmen, our own and the easterners' together, while behind us rang the voices of the women and the men who remained, shouting the marriage-cries after us. My mother came out to the top of the village road and blessed us as we passed, the easterners throwing themselves in the dust at her feet to kiss her robes. Felim hitched his harp round on its strap and struck up a marching song to set the step; he never could resist a chance to travel.

We were almost another week in the high hills, kept back by the long train of bearers carrying our gifts and our robes; the men who led us were anxious to hurry us on, for they said their queen would accuse them of delay.

As we walked we were always with one or another of them. I tried to ask about their country, what the land was like, how they lived—anything to fill my mind—but they would only say it was the finest land under the moon (as we would have said of our own), and I had no notion of the look of the place before we saw it. All places were empty for me, anyway.

The east country opened before us one noonday as we came through the last pass of many; we saw below us wide green plains with wreaths of snow holding behind thickets and banks. There were cattle grazing everywhere; I thought at first we had come on a market day. They were heavy cattle too, bigger than ours, and we wondered to see them going loose in the winter-time.

Then people began to gather, coming from nowhere to stand and gaze at us. The eastern spearmen thrust at them if they came too close, and they vanished like mice into holes in the ground. There were no houses to be seen, but smoke came wreathing up from the earth near some of these bolt-holes.

I asked one of the ambassadors where the people lived.

'These commoners? Underground, as is fitting; why should they waste good land with their hovels? Fear not, lord, you will find a great palace awaiting you at the end of your journey.'

We walked through the plains for another day; the easterners' slaves carried tents which they set up swiftly at nightfall and furnished with furs and soft cloaks. They brought us good food too, fresh-killed meat which they took from the herds near the road. The ambassadors pointed out the royal brand on the flanks of the fattest cattle, to show us the wealth of their queen.

The third day, before noon, we saw ahead a great wall on a high rock, the smoke of many fires hanging round it. As we came near, trumpets pealed wildly from the wall and a crowd of folk swarmed out of the gate. All the way up the ramp to the entrance there were merchants' booths, and many foreigners came out of them to salute us.

We were led through the crowd, the guards clearing a way with butt or point impartially—I saw a couple of men fall back bleeding—and inside the Fort was as bad as outside. The place was packed with buildings, as close as gulls' nests on a cliff, and jammed with staring humanity. We threaded our way through, two or three abreast, and came to an inner stockade.

It was grimly adorned; all across the head-bar of the gate sat a row of human skulls. Inside too there were skulls on posts; some of these the easterners saluted as they passed.

'Greetings, bonny fighter!' they said, or:

'Greetings, old warrior, great cattle-driver that you were!'

Ailill plucked the sleeve of their spokesman—

'Is your queen here?'

He looked scandalised.

'You will not enter her presence till you have cleansed the dust of the road from you, and put on robes of ceremony!'

'Naturally,' said Ailill coldly, 'but is this where she lives?'

Like me, he did not care for the decorations.

'She will call you into the presence in due course,' he replied.

Slaves awaited us; they crept to us on their knees and

touched their heads to our feet. I saw Ailill smile at the disgust I tried to conceal.

When we were bathed and dressed in new robes they brought us to a door where the ambassadors were waiting. They signed to trumpeters to strike up, and stood aside for us to go first.

Felim threw back his cloak—

'Our kings are attended by their own music,' said he.

He waited till the clamour of trumpets died down, and then he played us in to the presence with 'The Corn is Fair'.

We came into a long narrow room, dark as night after the wintry sunshine outside, and bitterly cold. At the farthest end there was a red glow, which as we drew nearer proved to be the light of torches burning in alcoves and flickering over red hangings.

I was by now in such a misery of loss that I did not care what became of me; I could not forgive myself the months I had wasted in that insane deception of sorrow. I walked behind Ailill down the long hall without looking about me or ahead; only when he stopped so suddenly that I almost collided with him was I forced to look up.

There were three figures before us, like the figures of the young gods I had once dimly descried in the Temple. These three were shrouded in blood-coloured robes, and out of the robes gleamed three golden masks. They sat on three thrones and faced us as we came.

The ambassadors fell on their faces and beat their heads on the ground. Ailill said to me:

'What are these? Are these their gods?'

Felim whispered behind us:

'Make salutation, lords; these are the queens.'

Ailill and I bowed deeply, giving them the salutation of priestesses, not knowing what else we should do. As I stood upright again I saw their hands crossed on their breasts and knew that they were living women, for all they sat so still.

A grossly fat man came from behind the middle throne, knelt on its steps, and cried in a shrill voice:

'More light! The Queen commands more light!'

The torches blazed up as oil was poured over them. Now the gold masks shone more weirdly than ever, with black eyeless sockets and black slits where the mouths should have been.

The fat man said:

'You have her permission to reply to questions. Which is the younger of the two princes?'

Ailill pushed me forward with his hand. One of the ambassadors crawled a little nearer the steps and bellowed:

'Great Queen, both have come at your command which to refuse is death; they are a benighted and ignorant people without benefit of your august leading; it is their base and filthy custom to consider an elder greater than a younger. This one here is the King, and this is his Twin who is accounted less among them.'

The fat man said in his squeaky voice:

'Impossible! That will not be so here; the younger shall have his due; he shall be permitted to offer himself to the Great Queen's most excellent younger daughter. The elder will be permitted to aspire only to the elder daughter.'

Ailill said angrily over his shoulder to Felim:

'What nonsense is this? They must realise I am the King, whatever customs they have here! If the younger daughter is more honourable . . .'

'Sssh,' said Felim. 'Let me be your mouthpiece.'

He knelt before us and bent himself almost to the ground.

'Great Queen,' he shouted, nearly as loudly as the ambassador but much more melodiously, 'my king commands me to represent to your most dazzling Majesty that he is the chief of his people according to our laws, and it is therefore his right to aspire to the highest honours in any other country. He is deeply sensible of the honour your Sublimity has done him in asking him here, and he begs you to regard him as in all ways worthy of your most noble younger daughter.'

The fat man howled back:

'The Queen decides what is to happen in this as in all other matters; it is impossible to alter her decision. The younger prince is the only possible mate for the younger princess.'

I was too wretched to care how they settled it, but I had a duty to Ailill and to our people; I said to Felim:

'Say to the Queen that we are children of one hour—say too that I am only the King's lawman and the keeper of his memory; say that it would be an insult to their younger daughter to permit me to wed her.'

I could feel Ailill burning inwardly, his mind beginning to thresh like a shark in a net with thoughts of insults and affronts meant or unmeant; there were enough sources of trouble at hand to get all our throats cut and start bloody war as well.

Felim nodded, and while he was intoning at length with every honorific that offered itself to his fertile mind, I glanced again at the three motionless figures and wondered if any of them had skill to read thoughts and to know the fury that was seething so close to them. The hands were the only things that showed they were alive, and now the hands of the left-side figure stirred a little. They were small very white hands, square of palm and with short, slender, blunt-tipped fingers. On the middle finger of the left hand was a tiny mark as if a ring had lain there lately. I wondered what face went with those hands.

'Very well,' the fat man cried; 'the Queen will consider your words. Take the barbarians out of the presence.'

The ambassadors drew us backwards out of the hall, abasing themselves all the way to the door; the three figures sat motionless in the torchlight.

At the door the three ambassadors looked wildly at each other, and one mopped his brow. They hurried us into our own quarters, and departed like men who needed refreshment and a time for discussion.

We sank down on the beds.

'Phew!' said Felim.

Ailill broke out:

'Barbarians! Who are they to call us barbarians? Bellowing like mad bulls—is their queen so old that she's deaf?'

'I think their idea is that she's too far above common mortals to hear them unless they shout,' said Felim. 'It does not concern us.'

He looked sidelong at me, his eyes brimming with laughter.

'Faugh!' said Ailill; 'and that fat creature?'

'I think he must be what they would term the Queen's man,' said Felim delicately. 'But it is not necessary to discuss their ways.'

'Is it not? The Queen's man! Let me tell you, I'll not mate with any of their women to become such as he is! Why, he's ... he looks ... he's not ...'

'He's the father of the princesses,' said Felim hurriedly.

'I don't believe it!' said Ailill. 'And another thing—this rubbish about who marries which—the eldest ought to be the most honourable; if they don't know that, it's time they learnt. And you, Drost, how dare you suggest you're as old as I am? You'll be saying next you're older! I wish some of my mother's women were here to give you the lie in your teeth. Why do they try to fob me off with the elder? Aye, and you helped them, you two! It's for me to choose which I'll have, or neither —aye, or both! I'll see both, and choose for myself. Who gave either of you leave to put words in my mouth? Is this another plot between you and the women to put Drost first?'

Suddenly he was on his feet and whipping out the grey sword; he sprang at Felim, who fell across the bed with the laughter dying in his throat.

'Is it? Is it?'

I might be trapped in a grey web of misery, but I could not let him kill a poet; I threw myself on him and caught his elbows. He fought hard, arching his back, his breath whistling, while Felim put the bed between them.

'King and singer, remember who you are, and where! Why kill your poor fool of a bard? You came to wed one or the other; what is it to you which you have? If the younger is chief here, then she is yours; is not that enough? Put up your sword; there are men at the door. And, King, only consider what fools these people are—hooting and yelling at their queen—banging their skulls on the ground like drunkards—and the fat creature waddling out of his den—and those ridiculous masks! What faces are behind them, think you?'

Felim was calling up the ghost of laughter into a dry throat to save all our lives.

Ailill said uncertainly:

'At least I don't need to hide behind a metal plate ...'

He turned away to ram his sword into the sheath. When he looked again at Felim, his mouth was working. In spite of himself, he began to laugh.

A gale of crazy mirth overran us all three. We fell upon the beds, gasping, wheezing, mopping our eyes, mouthing and waving our hands, and half-sobered breaking out again at the sight of the other two. The fatness of the spokesman, and the round behinds of the crawling ambassadors, and the doll-figures on the thrones, and the shouting—it was all so insane, so gloriously foolish, that we could only roll about and clutch our sides.

In the high tide of our laughing we heard somebody scrabbling on the door. Felim went to open it, rubbing his sleeve across his face, and held a muttered talk with whoever stood outside. When he came back the jest was dead in him.

'The Queen,' he said, 'has sent for me.'

He smoothed his rumpled hair, shook his cloak, picked up his harp, and left us.

We did not see Felim again that day; the slaves brought us food and otherwise we were left alone. Dusk came, filling the corners of the courtyard with violet shadows and smoky veils, and we heard the sounds of the palace beyond, hurrying feet and strange voices and the lowing of cattle. It brought back the days when we had herded cattle ourselves, driving them home with our day's spoil of shells in our hands.

It was airless in the hut. We pulled stools to the doorway and sat out in the twilight. All at once, I was aware of Ailill. He was sitting with taut muscles and clenched hands, his handsome face raised to the stars above the roof, and his thoughts running like frightened squirrels. Fear and hatred and distrust, his old demons, were riding him, and a new one I did not know. It came to me with shame that I, who ought to be his help in overthrowing such things, was instead the unwilling source of them. What help could I give him, though I knelt to him now and begged him to let me help? It would feed his hate that I knew help was needed. Oh Talorc, Talorc, what had you to answer for!

Looking away from him I felt again the grey mist of my own loss. The grey mist, and behind it the grey-green trees bowing twisted stems above the grass, and beyond them a bowed figure walking. I strove towards her, forming words that would not pass my throat. It was a pain like death to see her so near and not to reach her. She came walking towards me through the trees and I saw her eyes wet with tears.

'Never more, beloved! Never more in this life! Our fates are parting. You will not sing for me now. We shall not meet, nor be together ever till we meet in the green fields of flowers.'

She knew it too. The trees were lost in ripples of grey water, and I felt my own tears on my face. Never more; I was only Drost, Drost alone, Ailill's Twin with duties to fill my life till it pleased the Mother to call me home. Well, at least I could fulfil my duty.

I braced my back.

The courtyard glowed faintly as the moon rose, a little less than full. I could see Ailill again, his face a milk-pale oval above the dark cloak.

'King and my brother, what troubles your peace?'

'Where's Felim?' he demanded. 'Why are we left here alone?'

'Perhaps—I don't know—some ceremony—'

'You don't know? You ought to know! What use are you if you don't know anything?'

'It might be some trick of theirs to test us, to see what we'll do if they keep us waiting.'

'By the Long Hand, if they dare—! And as for Felim—!'

'Let's show them we're not troubled by their neglect.'

'How, when they're not here to see?'

'They're close enough to hear,' I said. 'Why shouldn't you sing? I could listen to your singing all night.'

Ailill turned to peer at me in the moonglow.

'What have you in mind now? It's not like Drost to flatter.'

'I'm not flattering anyone; it's true. Sing something—anything. I would sing for you if I could, but you know my voice.'

He shifted about in his chair, coughed, hummed a few notes.

'I don't know what to sing. It seems silly, just the two of us.'

'There's the moon as well,' I said on impulse.

He stood up suddenly, dropped his cloak, and began the 'Invocation at Moonrise'. I stood with him and stretched my hands to the Maiden riding above us through the starry fields. At first he sang very softly, in his breast, clear but low; but at the end he lifted his head and let his full voice ring over the

195

palace. It seemed to me, but perhaps I only imagined it, that all other sounds were stilled.

When he came to an end he turned to me, laughing.

'What now, you foolish Charcoal? I have sung for you; is that enough?'

'No, oh no! Sing more; sing another at least.'

'I don't know what to sing. I don't feel like singing anything I know. Make me a new song, Drost, if you want me to sing.'

Anything to keep him in this glowing mood; I looked out into the shadows and let my mind go free, and words came into it. It was like an old song remembered, not a new one made, and I knew from that that it would be good. I muttered the words to him, and croaked the tune.

We were united, always, by this one thing, that he could sing my songs better than anyone, better even than Felim. I went over it twice for him and at the third time he was ready. It was a simple thing, a song a shepherd might sing on a hill-side, his back against a warm stone and the ground falling under his feet to blue distances.

> ' "Bird in the tree, my love and thee
> Far afield fly, calling to me.
>
> Whither shall I follow and fly,
> Calling her home, lost though she be?
>
> Bird in the sky, lonelier I
> Than ever thou, wander and fly,
> Wander and fly!" '

At the end he did something he had never done before; he threw his arm over my shoulders—

'Singer of the Birds!' he said; 'Singer of the Birds!'

We sat in companionate silence until Felim returned. He came in like an old man, leaning against the doorpost with his harp trailed from one hand.

'Wine, for love of the Mother!'

'Felim, where have you been? We've sat all evening waiting for you!'

Felim drained the cup a slave brought him, shook his head like a swimmer coming up from deep water, and walked past us into the hut. After him trailed the fringes of a strong magic, green and blue smokes and a hint of flame. At that moment I grew afraid, afraid of failing in what we had come for. Ailill had felt it before I had; fear of women's magic.

Felim was already eating breakfast by the fire when I woke next day. His eyes were heavy; he stretched himself and yawned.

'Ai-mai, and the moon not full yet! Mother of All, I have passed through storm and tempest, and a little of it for your sakes.'

'Why? What happened?'

Felim buried his nose in a goblet and laughed.

'You're young, Charcoal, very young at times. But never heed me. We're no further on with "the rubbish of who marries which", as the King calls it. There's one princess yonder weeping because she would rather be a priestess than wed, and the other sitting glum because she mislikes the looks of both of you—at least I think that's it; and their lady mother is ready to eat them both with me for sauce. At least I deserve their gratitude.'

'And ours,' I said; 'but all that's nothing to me; let them settle it to suit themselves.'

'But if you saw them—? Beautiful, both of them, hair as red as the Maiden's own, eyes . . .'

'You sound like a slave-dealer,' I said rudely. 'I tell you, it's nothing to me.'

'Uncommon bitter in one so young?'

'Oh Felim, don't! What does it matter? What am I, besides the Twin?'

'Moon and Stars, is it so with you? Since when? Who?'

Ailill came in and saved me from answering, and soon after we were summoned into the presence again.

This time they led us to a smaller room where the Queen received us alone. She greeted us by name, mangling the sounds in a rough voice, but giving a different greeting to Felim whom she drew down to sit beside her. With her free hand she waved us to stools by the fire.

'And now,' she said, 'a fine work I have to please these two girls of mine! Perhaps it was not so clever to fetch you both here; I should have sent for the King alone, first. But here you are; and what is to be done?'

Nobody spoke, but Ailill looked at me.

'Great Queen,' I said, 'this my brother is the chief man of our country; forget that I am here; I am only his lawman and the guardian of a little of his kingship.'

'So my little Felim says; is that all? Have you nothing else—nothing of your own?'

Ailill said:

'He's a songmaker, Lady, as I am a singer.'

'Indeed?' I saw that he had interested her. 'A king and a singer—it is possible . . . do either of you ever dream?'

'I do,' said Ailill violently. 'Most horribly. Let us not speak of that. I—I dream of our gods.'

'And you?'

She leaned forward, elbows on knees, and drew me to her with eyes as luminous as a moth's. I did not know I had moved until I was at her knees.

'Ah!' she said. 'Who taught you? Man or woman?'

'A seer-priest, Lady.'

'Not a woman, ever?'

There were scented branches burning on the hearth. I remembered another fire, a red eye in the cold heart of a cave. The Queen's hands rested dry and strong on mine.

'Has no woman read your fate?'

'Once, Lady, when we were boys, the Old One told me my fate.'

She looked into my eyes.

'So! You'll dance with a bear and swim in deep waters—that's nothing; ah, but you'll wed young and widow young—the Mother avert that word!—and it will be more of her making than yours; that's as it should be; there's a sign I was right to have you brought!—and the wrong one's to be the right one? A crooked word the Old One gave you! What of the King?'

She released me and turned to Ailill.

'What do you mean, Lady?'

I said:

'Ailill, when the Old One—the old woman in the cave told our fortunes—did she say anything special about your marriage?'

'That stuff? I didn't listen to half of it. Why should I heed the old idiot?'

Under my cloak I marked the dust with the sign to avert evil. I pushed shut the door of my mind against a slow deep voice; it was true, he had no fate.

And I, who had a fate, and a deep dream too, were they never to meet? I wrenched myself back to attend to the Queen's words.

'So there's nothing for it but to find the right one by trial as they did in former times. We have only tonight before the moon's at her strength; we'll hear you sing first, and see if either of you can please my cold-hearted child.'

She clapped her hands and a door opened at the end of the room. The princesses came in together.

They were no longer masked, but their faces were painted white and their hair blazed like fire above the paint. Their eyes, the blue and the grey, shone like jewels under blackened brows. I was reminded of nothing so much as the terrible vision at the death of Melduin, and I bowed myself to its memory. The Queen took it as due homage to her daughters' beauty and was not displeased.

They looked us up and down incuriously and took their places beside their mother.

'And now, sing!'

Felim reached for his harp—

'What song, Ailill my king?'

Ailill thought for a moment and shook his head.

'Let Drost begin; I'll choose my song while he's singing.'

It was kindness, for who would listen to me after hearing him? I looked at Felim, but he was busy with a slack string. I had made many songs that winter, but I could not trust myself to sing any of them now. I chose instead one I had made in haste for a wedding-feast. It had pleased the feasters; it would do very well for these queens. Felim carried the air for me, and I had only to let the words ring as clearly as I was able.

They smiled politely. Ailill said:

'That was one of Drost's songs; I should like with your leave
to sing something so new that even Felim has not heard it
yet.'

He sang the little song we had made together the night
before. At the first note the grey-eyed princess turned to her
mother, suddenly alight.

I loved hearing Ailill sing my songs and give them more
beauty than I knew they had; why then should I feel I had been
robbed?

'Another test!' cried the Queen.

Slaves brought eggs and bowls of water, and she made us do
the old charm of breaking an egg into water and watching the
shape the white took. I had seen my mother do it scores of
times when she chose the Maiden; it was strange to have it used
for ourselves. She nodded and looked wise.

'Give me your swords.'

She laid them together under a cloth and bade her daughter
choose one. The hands of the younger princess, those short-
palmed white hands with the ring-scar on one finger, groped
under the cloth and drew out a polished grey hilt. She looked
at it as if she had expected something else, shook her head,
and sighed.

The Queen said:

'Are these your only swords?'

'Drost has no other—I have a room as big as this full of
swords, in the Fort at home. This happens to have been my
father's and that's why I wear it,' said Ailill.

'There, you're thinking of the wrong one,' said the Queen.
'It is settled; you shall wed the King; he is your destiny. Ilissa
my child, dry your eyes. This younger prince shall be yours.
He is half a priest, and you are half a priestess, and you will
deal very well together.'

She took the hand of the blue-eyed girl and laid it in mine;
it was cold as ice, and trembling. I was torn with pain for her;
why should anyone fear me so? I remembered what I had felt
of my mother's terror on the hill; perhaps it was always so
for them? I tried to smile at her but her head was turned
away.

'You must part now, children, till the night of the Maiden,' the Queen was saying. 'And you, my sweet singer, you must go too, alas! Lead them away with your music, or we shall never be able to separate from you!'

Felim struck up remarkably promptly. The cold fingers drew away from mine and the princesses moved together to the far door.

I stood back for Ailill to follow Felim when our obeisances were made. I looked back over my shoulder down the length of the shadowy room, and I saw her at the far door looking over her shoulder.

The shadows broke into ripples of grey water; birds sang in twisted trees; bells chimed faintly in the twilit air. My dream had come true, I had found her.

Between a note and a note of the song, between a step and a step, I knew her. Her sleeve caught the doorpost and was drawn back, and I saw the golden snake on her forearm. I turned to run to her, and suddenly I faced a stranger, a stranger with dyed hair and painted skin, and behind her the tear-drowned blue eyes of the princess I was to wed.

Ailill plucked at my sleeve.

'Drost, are you mad? What are you thinking of?'

What indeed? What could I find to think of that should comfort me now?

Through the next day's long-drawn ceremonial I passed in a kind of trance. I turned my mind outward and forced myself to put walls between me and the world so that nobody should guess my hurt—least of all that poor child of the trembling hand. If she and I were to be victims of some dreadful jest of the gods, at least we need not show ourselves defeated in public.

For everything was in public; the offerings, the chanting, the processions to and fro, the exchange of gifts—as at our arrival, there was hardly room to move. Perhaps the crowds only wanted to share the blessings that were sung over us, or perhaps they believed a blessing was to be gained by touching us—either way, we were bruised and mauled about. The princesses were masked again, and nobody tried to touch them; guards with drawn swords were ready to lop off any rashly-extended hand.

They brought us at last, after sunset, to a court under the southern ramparts. The ground was freshly swept and sanded, and there were two small huts smelling of new-sawn timber. In the very centre of the court, and raised on a low platform, was a long draped thing; it took me a moment to realise it was a bed.

A thick bank of fog along the eastern skyline was hindering moonrise, and the court was dimly lit by the afterglow and a few faint stars. I stood holding her cold hand in mine, and we heard gates barred behind us.

'Well now,' said the Queen's voice briskly, 'we shall have to wait a little till the moon comes; shall we have music, or shall we just sit and talk?'

I started and looked round. We were not alone, we four, as I had imagined we must be; far from it. Behind us stood the Queen, the fat man, the deeply reluctant Felim, the leader of the Palace Guard, enormous in his wolfskin cloak, and three or four more. Something moved on the ramparts, and I made out a row of heads—living ones—sliding like beads along the top of the wall.

My first reaction was a blush that started somewhere about my liver and spread from my heels to my ears; the second thought was that Ailill would never survive this ordeal. His pride would not submit—his anger would overwhelm him and destroy us all—I must find some way to spare him. But what? What could anyone devise now to prevent disaster?

I had forgotten to tell myself that my bride was, after all, a princess and half a priestess. Her fingers closed strongly on mine. She turned to the Queen—

'With your leave and my sister's,' she said, 'I and the man you have given me will speak to each other apart.'

She gave them no time to answer, but led me over the swept sand to one of the huts. She stood in the doorway as straight as an arrow, her grotesquely red hair hidden by the dull light, her gold mask gleaming faintly, one hand laid on her breast.

'Now,' she said, 'come in here, and I will take off my mask, and we will talk. There! That's better.' She cradled the gold sheath in her hands, and sat on the edge of a bench-bed. 'Now. My name is Ilissa. Tell me your name.'

'Lady, you know my name; it is Drost.'

'I wanted to hear it from your own mouth. Is that your only name, your inner name?'

'It is all the name I know for myself.'

'And your Twin, the King? Has he no other name?'

'Only his titles, Lady, as far as I know.'

'I had hoped—I had still hoped—Drost, are you a priest, as my mother said?'

'No, nothing but the Dark Twin. Nothing else at all.'

She put out her hand and pulled me down to sit by her.

'And why say that? Is your Twin—something else?'

'Lady,' I said urgently, 'he is something else; he carries a wound in his mind that will break open tonight if nobody can go to his aid.'

She gave a little gasp—

'A wound! Tell me quickly then, how was he wounded?'

'A certain ceremony miscarried and we were both hurt, but his wound is the deeper and has never healed.'

She said in a low voice:

'Then I believe I was right after all. At a place of tall columns, under early sunlight—was that it?'

The hair moved on my head.

'And afterwards they ringed him round with enchantments to guard him, and we could not see—was that it?'

'I don't know, Lady,' I said, ashamed, for I should have made it my business long ago to know how Ailill had been healed, and by what arts—'I was sick myself, and walked in dark places.'

'I saw a little,' she said; 'there was a great striped cat that guarded him—my sister was very ill at the same time, and I was not always able to use my eyes for her because I was needed to help hold her in her own body. Tell me where you walked; that may lead us to something.'

I said:

'I dreamed—many things; but not because of my twinhood.'

'Ah!' she said; 'then I was right about you; you have been a priest at some time. Tell me your dream. I'm five years older than you, boy; tell me; it will be safe with me.'

'I cannot tell you my dream,' I said.

'Lean your head on my shoulder and I will tell it.'

Her hands were comforting. A faint moonglow spread softly over the track of our footsteps. Against it I began to see a shining cliff arise, and golden pillars, and a shimmer of woods. I was almost lulled to sleep after the long weary day.

She sat up suddenly.

'Who made the song, then? You?'

I felt again the hurt of that theft.

'A shepherd sang it on a honey-coloured hill; the tune went by me and I caught it as it flew.'

'May the Holy One grant us help! And you taught him?'

I could only nod.

She sprang up and walked back and forth before rounding on me.

'A fine work you have made of it, between the two of you! I told her—over and over again I told her, she must get some token from you so that she would know you when she met you; but no, oh no!—off she went to dream of you in your old meeting-places, in former times and distant lands—once I helped her to send you a token of her own, but you went from her suddenly—'

'The ring? Mother of All, the ring, when she sat spinning— but she isn't wearing the ring now; how was I to know, that day when we came into the presence and her hands were bare?'

'What?' she cried; 'you know, already? And you have done nothing—you have made all this work to marry me instead? What sort of people are you westerners?'

'I know and she knows,' I said miserably. 'We saw each other over the shoulder last night, at the doors.'

'And that was why she wept all night! O Drost, after all these years—why could she not have told me? Why, why, why?'

'It is the Mother's will for us,' said I, forcing the words past my teeth.

'It is not for you to interpret the Mother's will,' she said sharply. 'You prayed to be born in a land where you could find her, and here you are. There must be a way. Trust her.'

Presently she said:

'I wanted to go to the Temple, but they would not allow me —there is nothing I can keep to offer the great ones, not even my virginity. You and I, we must exchange gifts not meant for us. We are the two who stand second in the line.'

I remembered the verse I had made for Melduin—

'The lesser sword, the second spear.'

'Yes,' she said, 'that, exactly.'

As we looked at each other (for I had not spoken aloud) she said again:

'Let me be perfectly sure. What is her name?'

'The Lady—the Lady Yssa.'

'But her true name?'

I told her the true name.

She said:

'Then it is certain. Only one person can help us now.'

'The Queen?' I asked; I dreaded the idea of drawing the Queen into this.

'Oh no; my mother would be no help. Wait a little.'

She went out of the hut.

A moment later a vast shadow fell across the doorway. A squeaky voice said:

'But my dear girl, I really don't think there's time for any more talking—the moon's coming up, and your mother . . .'

'Never mind that; come in and sit down. Drost—here is my father.'

I stood up and saluted the fat man as he waddled in.

The bed groaned under him; I stood beside them as Ilissa knelt and took his hands in hers.

'Father, it is time for you to help us. This is Drost—this is the one Yssa has been looking for, all her life. The other one who is over there with her is the wrong one; Drost told my mother that in his fate there was something about finding the wrong one first, but she was not warned.'

'My dear child, I can't see what I—! Little Yssa! What will she think of her old father if I do nothing? Give me time.'

'You said yourself, there is no time. You must stop them, somehow.'

I forced myself to remember my duty—

205

'Lord, the King my brother is greater than I—if it is the Mother's will for us—but spare him—'

The Queen came into the hut.

She was in a towering rage. She pushed Ilissa aside and came straight for her husband and me.

'What are you men at, hiding in here when you should be out yonder? Do you intend to fail my daughter? There are pits out there full of the bodies of men who have failed to please us —do you want to join them?'

Ilissa caught her hands.

'He is the wrong one; you said it yourself, at the test of the swords; it was not his song; this is the one Yssa seeks.'

The Queen cried:

'They deceived us?'

'Drost knows her name,' said Ilissa.

'Oh, my child, my poor child! What have I done? What can we do?'

'Be quiet,' said the fat man. 'I am making a way.'

'What can you do, now? I should have taken heed of Drost's word!'

'There was another word,' said Ilissa. 'He is to wed young and widow young; if he weds tonight and widows tomorrow, will you let him go to Yssa then?'

'Lady,' I said, 'neither she nor I could accept that offering.'

'Wait,' said her father; 'she is coming to my call.'

We stood in the door of the hut, and as we watched the other hut Yssa came out alone. Her hair flowed over her shoulders, her painted face shone silver, and anger beat out of her like the heat of worked bronze.

'In the good hour you are here, mother!'

'O child, O my child, O my poor child!'

'Do you know what they have done, these western pig-eaters? They have sent us a king who is no man, the shell of a man! How did you come to let him pass you? Don't you know what he is? Don't you, my father? He refuses to come out there—he refuses to offer his worship to the moon—he—oh, to have accepted my fate and then to end with this!'

She threw herself into her father's arms. The Queen rounded on me.

'Is this true? Do you dare to tell me it's true?'

Of course not; it could not be true; but my mind flew to the middle stone where I had so nearly been the tool to make it true.

'No,' I said; 'no, it can't be, no.'

I walked across to the other hut and inside it I heard Ailill whisper in the shadows.

'I am the King,' he said; 'I am the greatest of kings, and I have killed a hundred boars and a thousand stags; I danced down the Smiler for others to kill, and I overcame the priests when I lay on the Stone, and I am stronger than the young gods and wiser than the Old One, and a hundred women will not content me. I am Ailill, son of Ailill, and master of all.'

'Great King,' I whispered; 'Lord of the Boar.'

I heard him start up and fumble for something. 'Drost?'

The moonlight was setting the whole hut aglow; I could see him crouching at the far side, his sword in his hand and his eyes glittering.

'Drost! What, is it so indeed? You have come to tell me that you cannot do what is meant for you tonight? We were afraid of that, I and my Council—we were afraid your wound was worse than the women could heal. Poor Drost, and yet your sacrifice was not acceptable. At last you know it; you are nothing.'

I stood and shuddered. How would they get him home from here? What would become of the People? Would they even be able to keep him safe from himself?

Someone had come over the sand unheard; a hand fell on my arm and drew me back; before I could stop her Ilissa had stooped under the lintel and gone in.

'Great King,' she said, 'I am the elder sister; I have come to the honour of your presence.'

She took him in her arms.

I fell back ashamed and afraid.

'Lady, he may kill her! The moon has possessed him!'

The Queen said quietly:

'Then he is safe in the arms of the moon. Children, here is your moonrise.'

She drew us to the centre of the court.

My hands were held by well-remembered hands, her arms went round me—your arms, Yssa. Your mouth was wine and

207

honey and the salt sweetness of tears. There was no speech between us—what need of speech? One heart in two bodies, a broken circle healed, a fire that leaped to a flame, water poured into a river, two halves made whole—our home-coming. What did we care if others saw us? What did we care though the moon fell from the sky?

Later—much later—we began to talk as we lay.

'Ah, but why did you not send me a sure sign? I would not have forgotten—I do not forget. I watched you so often—at your cattle-driving, and your hunting, and your dancing—and when you faced the bear and the pig—you could have given me some sign? Only your face was hidden; it was hidden from us both. Ilissa is a better seer than I can ever be; she watched for me, and she told me you would wear a gold band on your arm —how was I to know you would both have them? And your song—that was when I was almost certain; when I heard it ringing out over the walls—your mountain song. How could you let him sing it? You have forgotten much more than I have. Have you remembered anything? Tell me what you remember.'

I remembered so much; the dear scent of her, and the spring of the hair above her ears, and the touch of her hands, and bygone times and places past naming; the temple forecourt where the doves' feathers blew in the dust, the snow-capped hills and the pines that sighed below them, hot sands drifting to close the mouths of cliffs where dead kings faced the sunrise and where we had learned our dreaming—so much and so much.

'O Yssa, my little lost Yssa, at last!'

O Yssa. No, not yet; I must not come yet. Wait a little longer, my heart's core; it will not be long now. Wait while I weave the last few strands together; you remember so much more than I do, let me make sure I leave everything ready to waken your memory.

'You were a king and a singer, and you had another sword— don't you remember your sword with the lion-hilt?'

'And your ring—I looked for that, but you didn't wear it.'

'I had to take it off—it grew too small for me—they are making a new one but it wasn't ready in time. Do you remember the dove-feathers—how I used to tuck a feather into the wall of the temple court when I went down to the grove ahead of you?'

I remembered. Later still, it was she who said.

'Three days only, beloved—we have three days; let us use them well.'

'Three days? But when we reach the Lands of the Boar we shall have all our lives; my mother will welcome you gladly; she knows I have sought you—'

I stopped, for I had seen her face in the last of the moonlight.

'I do not ask you to stay here,' she said.

'And I could not stay if you did; I'm Ailill's Twin—and Yssa, I have to get him home safely—I shall be needed there more than ever. You must come and help me—I shall need all your help.'

'You will have my prayers,' she said.

'But your sister—can't she take your place here?'

'Does she deserve nothing for this night? Her heart is set to serve the Mother. The Mother made you a king and me a queen; it may be that her mercy holds a way for us to meet again.'

'Meet again!' I could not say more.

Presently she raised her head from my shoulder to say:

'If there is a way, we shall be shown it. Let us not waste her present mercies.'

Three days later we parted. A great company of the easterners followed us to the boundaries of their country, and when we went up through the passes a line of laden slaves bore food and tents for us. I did not look back.

Ailill talked to Felim all the way and I followed in silence. I needed time to lay the memory of each moment safely in its place where I could find it again.

The spring had begun to turn the hillsides green, and as we came into our own valleys we heard the birds call from the woods. Our own people swarmed out to welcome us with wedding songs; they seemed like strangers to me.

We went to the Great Fort and they made a feast for us. Yssa moved beside me in the firelight and the torchlight. Yssa walked with me in starlit courts. Yssa came to the Hearth-house when I went to offer there.

My mother knew. She took my face between her hands and kissed me, and knelt at the Hearth to give thanks.

I went to the House of the Young Men to find Gerig, for I wanted to take council with him before I spoke to the elder men about Ailill. I did not find Gerig, but I found Arth. He was alight as I was. We touched hands and knew it, as one knows such things.

Time passed, and as I watched Ailill I began to think the danger was over. He held council, and hunted, and went about his daily affairs, his eyes no brighter than they should be and his step light and free. He gave judgment evenly, sometimes calling on me for a word from the laws, more often judging for himself. There was little for me to do but think of Yssa.

Later that spring, old Gerig met me by the gate of the Fort.

'Drost,' he said, 'what's this notion my grandson has taken?'

'What notion, uncle? He hasn't said anything to me.'

'He has gone up to the Hearth-house and made some kind of vow,' said the old man. 'I wish I knew what idea he has in his head. I was afraid at first that he was taking up a feud, but he has sworn to me that it is not so, and I believe him.'

'Of course, if he says so, you must believe him,' I said. 'Gerig is the soul of truth.'

'I'm glad to hear you say so. You think well of him, do you?'

'I would trust him far more than I trust myself,' I said.

That evening in the Young Men's House I saw that Gerig had indeed taken a vow. He had shorn his hair as if he were a boy again, and he had put off all his ornaments except the boar-tooth collar which he could not lay aside. It was not for me to ask what he had vowed; it might be something to do with a woman, perhaps, or with some other desire. Whatever it was, I could feel sure it was honourable.

Felim sat at home all that summer; he said he had had enough of wandering for a time. We never spoke of the days among the easterners, and none of the men questioned me about them; they may have spoken to Felim, perhaps, but not when I was there. I went up and down in a world of my own with you, showing you everything in our valley and about the river-mouth, as I would have shown you if you had come home with me in the body.

We hunted, and went fishing, and worked in the fields—Gerig's vow did not impede him from doing anything that we did—and the year drew towards harvest and on to autumn.

And one autumn evening in the House of the Young Men I found an argument under way when I entered.

They were talking about building the hill-top fires: some of them thought we should not light fires any more, for they honoured gods whom we had disowned; others said that it was the custom, and should be followed. Lan shouted when he saw me at the doorway—

'Here's Drost, boys. He'll tell us. Drost, should we light the winter fires or not?'

I said:

'I can't tell you without thinking a little—give me time.'

Ailill said, cracking a nut as he spoke:

'Drost can't tell you? There's a change for you! Let's leave him to his thinking. Who'll come and net the seapool with me? Gerig? Culla? Lan?'

He called up my friends one by one, eight of them, and led them out laughing. Over his shoulder he said to me:

'We'll leave you to your thoughts, Drost.'

His eyes flashed and he had gone.

Mother of All, I thought, are we to begin all that again? I took my cloak and my sword and went up the hill.

When I was almost at the Hearth-house I knew what they would say to me. Demetroos worshipped all gods, as shadows of great ones beyond his knowing; Felim, if he were there, would laugh and say why not enliven the winter with firelight and shouting? The Old One would darken with anger, and my mother had given her answer already, that nothing men do can part them from the Mother, and that all faiths are one.

I turned away downhill.

I had my answer, then; it was all one, whether we lit the fires or not. But I was not satisfied. Was the New Way only a deceit built up by my father for his own ends? Had he had no priesthood in him?

I walked fast through the darkness, my thoughts whirling darkly round me, going anywhere at random, only keeping away from the river-mouth where the netters were working. When I stopped I found myself close to the sea, on a low cliff with rising ground to the north. I stooped to bring the hill against the stars, and saw a broken line of wall. I was close under the ruins of the Temple.

I had never been back there. If I was to find an answer anywhere, it was here. I wrapped my cloak round me and felt my way to the steps that led up to the gate.

The gateway was open, a sagging barricade lying to one side and the ground rutted with goat-tracks. In the broad level inside there were still low huts scattered about, though some were roofless. I found it more and more easy to see what lay around me, for now the moon was shedding light through thin clouds. Beyond the cliff the sea gleamed like dull metal. On my left the jagged stumps of burnt walls stood up black against the water.

I turned my steps there first. There was hardly anything left; all—passages, cells, the great central space itself—was littered with tumbled stone. I picked my way towards the south end of the point, and there at last I found a pavement clear of rubble. At its far end were three shapeless rocks, all that remained of the bases where the wooden gods had stood.

I went right to the edge and looked over at the surf fretting below. When I turned again, I saw a withered wreath of ivy hanging drunkenly on the middle rock.

I went forward slowly, unbelieving, straining my eyes. The ivy was dead, killed perhaps by the sea-spray, but it had not been there long enough for the leaves to fall. The next stone looked darker; I touched it cautiously; it was faintly sticky. I bent my head and sniffed; it had been anointed with blood.

The stone on the right remained. When I went up to it my foot struck something on the ground, and pushed into the moonlight a saucer filled with curdled milk.

Ivy for the Singer, blood for the Smith, milk for the Long Hand; my knees were trembling as I backed away. Gods are not dead while someone serves them.

The Temple itself had been destroyed; the Mother had shown us what she thought of it. But there was one, at least, who risked the wrath of the Mother to serve these three that most of us hated. I remembered how Naas had come back to Talorc, carrying his life in his hands.

I went out into the middle of the open ground and put off my sword and my bear-tooth necklet and my armlet, and prayed to the Mother for light, for knowledge of right and wrong and for knowledge to tell the People what to do. The moon broke through the torn clouds and shone on the sea beyond the ruins.

I went back to the three stones, and knelt.

I tried to turn my mind to the little I knew of these gods, but most of it came from Naas; I could not be sure that he had taught me truly; perhaps he had sent only what the time required. There were the long golden fingers that reached down to tear out my heart; it seemed as if I had seen them long ago, painted or carved or both, on a wall painted and carved. There was the fire, and the iron, and the anvil, and the great red eye glaring down; I did not think a man could make such dreams out of nothing. And there was the rough-cloaked figure who sat on a stone in a wood and played an air of surpassing beauty.

When I reached the Singer in my thoughts, I stopped. He was true; whether I existed or not, or believed in him or not, he would be there. And it was his likeness I had borrowed to frighten Naas! I trembled at my boldness.

I had come empty-handed into their ruined temple, and I did not know how to pray to them. Much need had I of the Mother's protection. But if they were not gods—if it was all a dream men had dreamed—what had I to fear? No, I said, it is not a dream; the High Gods are beyond falsehood. That had been my own word to the men; if some of the priests had been false, that did not make the gods false, I had said—the Mother putting words into my mouth. If there were a good priest, if one could be found, he might cleanse the place and those who wished to pray to these Sons of the Mother could do so again. They could choose that corner of her mantle.

I stood up stiffly and walked out through the rubble. There might be something here for some men, but there was nothing for me. I took up my sword and my ornaments, and as I put them on I thought I heard a sound from one of the huts. It might have been a sheep or a goat, but it might also have been a man who had coughed.

I went up the slope, hand on sword, to the door of a small round kennel. Stooping low, I could faintly see a heap of rags within.

'Who is there? Is there anyone there?'

Something caught and held its breath.

I knelt and reached in as far as I could, and I touched an arm, skeleton-thin and burning with fever. It jerked away from my hand.

'Who is it? I'm Drost; who are you? Are you ill?'

I took off my cloak and wrapped my sword in it, left them at the door and crawled in. When I had worked my way to the side of the door the moonlight reflected from the wall gave me enough light to see what lay there. A man so terribly emaciated that the bones strained at the skin, lying on his back with a ragged cloak clutched over him—his eyes were huge, and fixed themselves on me as if I were Death come for him at last.

The hut stank of fever.

'Who are you? Why are you here?'

He whispered something through cracked lips. From the way his head turned I thought he asked for water, but there was none in the hut—only a broken cup that had let a dusty trickle run over the floor. I did not know where to find more for him.

He must have help, quickly, if he was to live; I did not know his kinsmen, to call on their aid; I should have to go to my mother. I bent over him and said as clearly as I could:

'I am going for help; I'll come back as quickly as I can.'

I crawled out backwards, caught up my cloak and sword, and set off for the Hearth-house.

I found it ablaze with lights, women everywhere. One of them barred my way to the inner room with a brawny arm—

'King you may be, but in there you do not go!'

'I need her help for a sick man—let me by!'

'Sick man—what's a sick man tonight? There's more than that here! Out of my way!'

Demetroos came out of a side-chamber.

'I am not needed here,' he said. 'May I help you instead?'

I was ashamed that I had not thought of him; it was more seemly for him to enter the Temple than for my mother. I told him quickly what I had found.

'We'll need herbs, and blankets, and a lamp—a horse-load of stuff by the sound of things. I'll come down first and see how bad he is, and then you can get someone to fetch what is wanted. Is he young or old?'

'I don't even know who he is. I only know he's dying—come quickly.'

'I am ready,' said Demetroos. He lit a lamp from the court-yard torches and followed me out.

After one look at the hut and the man inside, he straightened himself—

'This is impossible; we'll have to move him. Are any of the other places any better?'

'I'll go and see.'

The first had a gaping hole in the roof, and the next had been used by goats. The third was bigger, and dry. The moon shone on walls that had once been whitewashed, and there was a good bed-place. I gathered dry ferns along the foot of the cliff for bedding, and went back to Demetroos. Between us we dragged the man out—he whimpered and hid his face from the moon—and I carried him up to the other hut. Demetroos set his lamp on a little shelf in the wall.

'Now,' he said, 'let's see what we need.'

I went up to the Fort by the broken path, and called a couple of slaves away from their gambling at a fireside. They trembled and clung together when I led them to the cliff, and I had to get behind them with my sword out until they were on the path. Demetroos had a string of orders for them; a fire to be lit, bedding to fetch, water to be heated.

'Go on,' he said, 'hurry, and bring firing and blankets first.'

'And come back,' I added, 'for I will remember you tomorrow if you do not.'

'What's the matter with them? Are they afraid of the sickness? It is nothing to fear; he has starved to the edge of death.'

'Not so much the sickness as the place,' I said; 'this is the former Temple ground.'

'I had not known,' he said. He made a sign on the earth. 'Later, when we have finished, I will pray; for now, I must pray working.'

Rather to my surprise the slaves did come back; we set them to building a fire at the door, and when it began to catch they became more cheerful. They sat on our side of it, feeding it with sticks and heating water to bathe the sick man.

At last Demetroos stood back and said:

'We have done what we can. If he dies now it is the Mother's will, not our neglect. He will sleep a little, and when he wakes we must be ready to feed him.'

I looked at the sleeping face in the lamplight, and faint as the last of a chain of echoes among hills a memory stirred—a ledge on the cliffs, and a gull that made me laugh . . .

'Luad!'

A tremor ran over the sleeper; Demetroos caught my arm.

'Not yet; do not rouse him. Let him rest.'

Now there was time to feel weary. We sat with our backs against the wall and stretched our legs. The slaves lay down by the fire. I raised my eyes to the wall and saw a faint mark.

I got up quietly and took the lamp, and crossed the hut, shading the light with my hand. It was as I thought; circles within circles had been scrawled on the whitewash. I set the lamp in its niche and sat down again to think of Mangan.

The man on the bed slept quietly. Demetroos folded his hands and gazed placidly into the fire. One of the slaves snored a little, a gust of air lifted a flame, far off beyond the Fort a dog howled twice.

This had been Mangan's place. Here it would be safe to go free. There was the mark to bring me home, Demetroos was here to help, I could let myself go to see all remembered things —or I could go to Yssa. My longing for her broke all bounds and flooded my heart and mind. I was part of her, I would go to her, neither spell nor symbol should divide us. I leaned my head back and surrendered myself.

After a time I opened my eyes and looked about me. Demetroos' head had sunk a little lower. Luad still slept. The faintest flush of dawn rose against the setting moon.

I tried to force myself out. I thought of her till my hands ached to hold her. I said her name over and over—I beat against invisible walls—I dragged up every memory of all Mangan had done, even the maggots on the water, even the white beast. It was all of no avail.

In angry desperation I stood up and stepped over the sleepers to the open air. If some art of the Old Way was holding me back, I would go to the New Way. I went down to the shattered Temple.

The three stones were naked under the pale light, ugly with their daub of sacrifice, the dead wreath and the stupid little bowl. I knelt between them and raised my arms.

'O Smith,' I cried, 'O Singer, O Swordsman of the Long Hand, set me free!'

The sun sprang clear of the far hills and struck me full in the eyes with his first sword-thrust of the day.

A door opened in my mind and I found words fit to praise him. I found a new voice worthy of the song, and I sang him up the sky. There should have been wine to pour, oil and honey and wheaten cakes to offer, but I had none of these things. Nor can I leave any echo of that song behind, for when I reached its end it departed as suddenly as it had come. Under the strong early light of a mild winter's day, I knelt among the fallen stones and it was shown me that I could sacrifice.

I called on them again by name—

'O Smith and Craftsman, to you I dedicate my armlet;

'O Swordsman, to you my sword;

'O Singer of the Deep Woods, to you my collar of the Smiler's gift; receive my gifts, ye lords, and you, O Mother of gods and men, take me your slave.'

I bowed myself to the ground and lay there, and I went free.

I wandered out of the body, passing remembered places and signs left from former lives. Past the Temple where the Archer stood among his pillars under the shining cliffs—past the oil-bearing trees that rippled like water—past the other temple where dead kings faced the sun—to places long forgotten in far lands, high in the cold hills or low in sea-bound islands. I saw Yssa as she had been, and myself as I had been. Farther and farther I went, until at last there was only a great wide plain of grass, and across it ran a naked boy and a striding chestnut horse side by side, till the boy threw his arm over the tossing head and mingled his wild hair with the wild mane, and horse and boy went from me together, to the sound of laughter and the joy of the beginning of things.

I woke stiff with cold. I got to my feet and looked in wonder at the voiceless and empty place where I had lain, and as I turned to go back to the hut I saw, far up the hill, my mother's house-smoke, and between it and me the strong unshaken forms of the Old Stones, squatting in their places as they had been set. The Hearth, the Temple and the stones; we called this the New Way, where I stood, but what of the time when the Hearth had been new and the stones had held the land?

I met Demetroos coming from under the cliff.

'I've found the water,' he said; 'I was sure they must have had a spring, and there it is, under the rocks and close above the sea-cliff; it's foul now, the gutters are blocked and the water has made a marsh all round; but given a good cleaning and a fish or two put in to keep it right, there would be a fine well. It's sweet enough water; I have drunk it. All it needs is a few bushes for shade—you can see the stumps the goats have killed—and there are marks of half a dozen channels running out to water this ground. A fine well, and strange that it should be here at the very end of the land.'

'Demetroos,' I said hoarsely, 'do you think there was ever a time when people didn't worship the Mother? What did they do?'

He laughed.

'Son of my own country where everyone asks questions day and night! Before the Mother? A dark time that must have been; perhaps they prayed to things rather than to persons, to a tree or a well or any beautiful thing that seemed to hold a secret; if their prayers were honest they would be heard. Why, Drost?'

'Because of the Old Stones,' I said; 'because there they are, we don't even know what they are for, but there they are; we have never heard the names of their builders, or what they did, or how they set their stones there; and then we came, and prayed to the Mother—and then the New Way—and now we return to the Mother, and all the time . . .'

Demetroos said slowly:

'I think the difficulty is in words, not in things. I have sometimes thought that most languages are poor in this, that they lack a—how can I say it to you? Look, you say "he" and "she" and "it", but by "it" you mean, don't you, something less than "he" or "she"? And that's because you mean "neither-he-nor-she", a poor remainder when everything has been taken away.

The word I want is one that would mean "he-and-she-and-more", a great honorific "IT". Then we could begin to be able to talk about God; not the gods, not the Mother, but God, whatever it is that starts them all off like the sun and the stars, coming and going in their seasons. My people have a saying, "Fate is stronger than the gods", but that's only a way of saying that the gods are not God. They are only what he, or it, thinks we can bear to see. Some day we may know better, but till then we can only do our best. That's why, when people ask me, I say I worship all the gods. It's not strictly true, for I am vowed to the service of the Mother of the Grain, as we happen to know her in my country; but it makes no odds to me where I pray. I wouldn't for choice take part again in certain sacrifices I've attended in my travels, but as long as they do what they do because they think it is right and pleasing, and not because they want the fun of tearing some created thing to bits although they can't create it . . . Do you mind telling me how I got into this rigmarole on an empty stomach?'

'I'm sorry,' I said; 'it was my fault; I asked you. And thank you very much indeed. I think I understand now.'

'Do you? Then you have the advantage of me. Let us see how our patient finds himself.'

Luad was awake and bewildered. When he had eaten a little I could not forbear to ask how long he had lived there.

'About ten years, Reverence.'

'I'm not a priest, Luad; I'm Drost; long ago you took care of me one day, on the cliff; I had a green cloak, do you remember? Never mind, it's not important. But—ten years! All the time, then, since—since the others fled?'

'Why not, Reve— master? Where should I go? There were many of us here, once; they went away one at a time, then a few at a time, then at last by companies. The ship came for some of them, the corn-ship. I don't know where they went, the others. The Seer went away to die; he was the first; there was one more great ceremony, but it was not well done—the robes were red . . .'

'Yes, I know, but that was long ago; it's all right now.'

'Then *he* died,' said Luad; 'they wouldn't allow us to make his pyre here; they burned him on the common grounds, on a driftwood fire. We prayed in under-voices for fear of the men

219

'. . . Lurgan stayed for a while and then he went too . . . at last I was alone.'

He struggled to lift himself.

'I have tried!' he shouted. 'I have tried! I gathered the plants in their season, and I begged for you, and stole for you, danced for you, gave you my own blood when there was nothing better—why have you left me behind, now that you have gone?'

Demetroos lifted one thin arm and looked at the knife-scars.

'They have not gone,' he said. 'The High Gods never leave a place where they have faithful service. Rest and grow strong, and you and I will pray to them together.'

I turned my head, for I heard feet on the cliff-path.

'Demetroos, I must go back to the young men soon; but do you think you could make a temple here, one where people could pray to the gods if they want? You could tell them what you were telling me, about doing things because one thinks they're right. I don't believe the Mother would mind; my mother says we can only hold one corner of her mantle.'

'Drost? Drost?' an urgent voice called from the open ground.

'All right, Arth, I'm here; I'm coming.'

I ran out of the hut to meet Arth as he came from the cliff. When he saw me he put down his spear and bent his knee—

'King, forgive the bearer of ill tidings.'

'Arth, don't do that! Have you been looking for me? I'm sorry; I was coming back; I only came here to think about things, and I know the answer now—but we found someone sick here, and . . . Arth, what tidings?'

'The King is dead,' said my friend.

Part Five

THEY HAD brought him in long before Arth found me; he lay on the bier of branches they had made, water still running from his clothes, though the great gash in his neck had ceased to bleed. We laid him by the hearth, before his chair, and stood silently round him. Even Ginetha, when she came from her room, neither wailed nor sobbed but knelt holding one of his drowned hands, and wept.

I stood beside her and presently put my hand on her shoulder, and she leaned her cheek against my wrist.

Culla came and stood by me on the other side and told me what he could, which was little. They had gone to the seapool with the nets, but finding the pool full of strong fish they had decided instead to spear them by torchlight; they and their hounds had both heard and smelt a boar moving above the pool, but in this morning's light they could find no trace of him. Ailill had gone up the bank to the head of the pool to listen, while they stood listening below. Suddenly Gerig's hound had put up his muzzle and given two long howls. A moment later something fell from the rock into the pool, and as they raised their torches to see better, they had seen the water turning red.

I said slowly:

'This was foretold for him. A bar of blood, and a sheet of still water; a quick end instead of a slow one was all the Old One could give him. He is in his peace.'

Regil said: 'What orders, King, concerning the pyre?'

Then I felt the double weight that had fallen on me.

When the death-feast was over, the third for a king that I had seen, I had time to look round me and take order for the continuing things. I gave leave to build the hill-top fires as usual; higher than usual indeed, to light the newly dead on his road. We could not mourn him long; there were only a few days left until the winter feast when we must part with him.

I went up to the Hearth-house to offer in his name, though I was doubtful if I should do so when he had never offered there himself since childhood. My mother came out to meet me. She greeted me as the Twin, not as her son, and I greeted her as the Middle Priestess.

As I came down again I heard Gerig's feet on the road behind me. I had not seen him since the pyre. He was armed and adorned again with his trophies.

He saluted me and told me he had been to the Old One's cave, where she had freed him from his vow. I was glad to have his full companionship again, now most of all in my need.

On the night of the feast, Demetroos came to me—

'King,' he said, 'would it not be well to carry fire from the Hearth to light your hill-fires?'

I told him that the fire must be made there and then, that the logs and the fire-drills lay ready.

'Very well, King; you know your people; but when one splices a rope one must turn in every strand.'

We climbed the highest hill and made our fire, and saw answering lights spring up far and near, even deep in the hills towards the Green Glen. After our own fire had dropped a little, while we were dividing the fire-cake, the night was turned to mystery round us by the shimmering fires of the Dancers in the Sky. They leaped so high that they joined their hands overhead from all sides, leaning over us like a roof. We did not know if that sign was for good or evil.

222

As we returned at daybreak we met women going home with the dark garlands on their heads from the parting-feast at the Hearth. The first we met was Gerig's mother; she came towards us and kissed her son, whispering something as she did so. Then she came to me and did likewise, breathing in my ear:

'The corn is in the basket.'

I gave her the answer:

'Joy be with the harvest.'

As custom required I gave the word to the man next to me, who chanced to be Demetroos. He started back from me in such amazement that he could not utter the reply, so to avert harm I said it for him. Only when the words were spoken did I remember Mangan falling back in Felim's arms, and my fleeting sight of the blue veil drawn aside.

Demetroos left us before we reached the Fort, slipping away like a man who has received a secret message.

Old Gerig came to tell me that it had formerly been the custom for the kings to go to the Hearth-house, when they heard the news, to see for themselves that the harvest was safe. It was the men's desire that I should do so again; I put on fresh clothes and went with some of them, back to the Hearth.

The doors stood open; we went in and knelt by the fire, and the Old One came from the inner room with a closely-wrapped bundle in her arms. She put back the wrappings and showed us a sleeping child. It was not such a red and hideous little thing as I remembered Cardail herself to have been, and I thought it was more than new-born, a few days old perhaps; then all such thoughts were swept away in startled recognition. The little creature's head was covered in soft dark down, his mother's colour, but when the sleepy lids lifted for a breath, and the wide unfixed blue eyes stared over me, the face was Arth's face.

I put out one finger to touch his cheek.

'Joy be with you, you funny little man,' I said.

The Old One clicked her tongue and bore him away to his mother.

After the winter feast the weather turned stormy and wet, so that there was little to do but sit round the logs in the feasting-hall. When the storm eased we went hunting, but as soon as we had the meat we needed we were back to the fireside.

Returned from one such hurried hunt, we were drying our cloaks and greasing our spear-lashings when Neart said :

'There are many yet who do not know how the King died.'

Culla his son answered before anyone else could speak :

'Father, you were here when the King who lives told us it was fated to happen so. And I myself told you how it happened.'

'You told me you were at the other side of the pool, you said you heard a boar and smelt him, yet none of you could track him afterwards. What sort of trackers are you that cannot trail a winter boar ?'

'We could not follow him, uncle,' said Gerig.

'And our king who lives, where was he that night ?'

'We know now where he was,' said Culla; 'he was with the priest Demetroos, enquiring the will of the great ones about the fires. At the time when the—the dead—called us to go with him, he said he didn't want . . . that is, he named us, the eight of us, to go with him.'

'He suggested it ? He named you ?'

Gerig said in a level voice :

'Of what do you accuse us, Neart ? Of carelessness ?'

'No,' said Neart doubtfully. 'No—it's just—I felt that somehow it was strange—no, no, I cannot accuse you; how could you know the boar would be so bold, with your torches, and with nine of you . . . ?'

Dran broke in to say :

'As the animal in question was that certain animal that has been named, do you not think, men, there is no more to be said ?'

There was a mutter round the fire, and though Neart still frowned he leaned back and said no more. I suppose he had feared someone might say his son had failed to guard the King. It was a groundless fear; I could have told him so; we all knew Culla and Gerig too well to think any ill of them. Gerig of the high-jump could never have been guilty of carelessness.

But it did bring to my mind a day in the woods when Ailill had spoken very unwisely about a white boar.

224

There was still another death to come that winter-time. The storm was beating fiercely round the Fort, and sleet lashed the sea, when they brought me word from my mother to come to the Hearth-house.

'Tonight? In this weather?'

I stood up and took my cloak while the hailstones sizzled in the fire below the smokehole.

'Tonight, quickly, if it please you, King; and the word is also for the younger Gerig.'

'What is this? Why are they called?' asked old Gerig.

'The Old One calls them, master,' said Terik.

We wrapped our cloaks over our breasts and shifted the cloak-pins to hold them, and stooped for the slaves to throw leather cloaks over us, the big circular storm-cloaks that withstand all weathers and most weapons; and we went up the hill holding on to each other against the wind and gasping for breath between squalls.

'A night for the Old One!' Gerig grunted as we came under the lee of the Hearth-house. The gate was open and there was a light in the Hearth-room.

A young girl, next year's Maiden, took our cloaks from us. Beyond the white cone of the Hearth, Felim knelt by a bed of furs.

My mother crouched at the wall, supporting a wizened old woman whose grey hair straggled over her seamed face. The whole scene was so shocking, there in the sanctuary, that I fell back a step and almost forgot to salute the Hearth.

'Come quickly, both of you,' said my mother; 'come close. The tide is ebbing, and she wants you. Mother, they are here, the two boys.'

'Where?' Tiny dark eyes, like chips of jet, flashed briefly under the grizzled brows. 'No, not that one—I see him—the other, what d'ye call him? Grath? Ah, there you are.'

'I am here, grandmother,' said Gerig, kneeling by her.

She reached out one knotted hand to lay it on his.

'You remember what I told you once? When you pull out a rotten timber, you must take the strain till another is found.'

'I have not forgotten, grandmother; I will try to take the strain—with your help.'

'Good boy—you have begun well. That was a good leap of

yours—I set you free of your vow, did I not? Did I tell you too that there is no blood-feud left now, either? Go and take the strain—time's scarce these days. You have my blessing.'

He bent low and kissed her cheek. She gave the ghost of a chuckle.

'And there's my last sweetheart's kiss! He's always understood me, that one. Now you, Drost, you listen to me. Your luck's turned. You won't have long to wait. It may be short enough when it comes, so make the best of it.

'You've seen our brat? There's the twin for your own son. Leave it to Gerig there to rear them; he'll do what's right. You'd better tell Cardail's boy to marry her and help with it—they can live here if they like—see to it before you go.'

'Go?' said I, bewildered, thinking she was wandering.

'Aye, go—go to meet her, fool! My head's bad—I don't know what's said and what's to say. Malda—thirsty—ah, that's better. Now. It's you, Drost, still? I had something more for you . . . yes; tell that priest of yours to look after his well now he's found it. It was sweet water . . .

'Felim? Where's Felim? Don't give yourself airs, now, child —though I'm not sorry it fell out this way; she's bred for a queen, at least . . .

'Attend to me, all of you! I'll have no howling and yelling when I'm gone. It's long enough that I've wished for this to come. You can sing "The Love Song of Ennis" for me when the fire takes hold.

'Goodbye, children . . . until the Orchard.'

She closed her eyes, but opened them soon after to say, with another faint chuckle:

'You'll have to knock the old hag on the head before you get rid of her!'

Then she closed her lids again resolutely and lay still.

A log fell in the fire with a little puff of ash; the storm had dropped completely. A last long sough of wind went over the house. She gave a little sigh and was gone.

Felim and I stood in the courtyard under a blaze of stars.

'She was a great old warrior,' he said; 'a great old heart she was. The Fisherman take this water in my eyes! More stick than sweetness I had from her. I remember once, when I was a young blood back from the Green Glen, I went nipping over the back wall yonder, all fur and feathers, to hang a few more claws and teeth on myself before I went courting—and I startled her into dropping a dish. I tell you, she laid me down with one buffet and raised me up with the next, and finely she dusted my buck's hide with her broomstick! I kept my tryst, but I kept it standing . . . oh, a great old warrior. Moon and Stars above, how am I to sing that song?'

' "The Love Song of Ennis"? Do I know it?'

'Of course you do; maybe not by name, but it's the slow love-croon, "Sleep till day—sleep till day." You might tell some of them that she asked for it, if you get the chance; a few folk will raise their eyebrows else.'

'Surely I will,' I said. 'Was—Felim, did you understand all she said?'

'Not the half! But I'm used to that. Keep it in mind and it'll make sense in a month's time—or a year's. The moon knows what she was on to me about, for a start. Ah well, if we live we'll learn. She knew a lot, the old lady. I hope she finds them all, Ennis and the children . . . she buried four of his, did you know? I never saw her shed a tear for him, but the boys . . . aye-aye! Well, King, you'd better go your way; can you spare your bard for a night?'

'Felim, of course; and Felim, may I—what can I say?'

'Nothing!' he said violently, holding up his hand. 'No, King, you mayn't; her orders, not mine. But thank you.'

I went down the hill alone. I had always feared the Old One rather than loved her, but now on the dark hillside I felt immensely lonely without her.

Much further down the hill I realised that I had good cause, for her death made my mother the Old One, and that would take her beyond my daily reach; I would not find her by the fireside whenever I cared to enter the inner room. Instead Cardail would be there; Cardail and . . .

I remembered one part of the Old One's last orders, and quickened my pace to look for Arth.

The winter passed; Demetroos began to clear the ruins of the Temple with Luad's help, and his well flowed strong and clear through its five new channels. My mother came and went about the Hearth-house, helping Cardail with the baby and with preparations for her marriage to Arth. Old Gerig grew very frail in the cold weather, and did not come to the Council often; the men chose young Gerig to sit with them in his place. I was too busy by day, and too tired at night, to dream much, and when I did it was always of meaningless things and never of Yssa.

A short time before the Maiden's Feast ended the winter, Felim came and drew me aside—

'King,' he said, 'you had better come up to the Hearth; there's a young man there with a message for you.'

'Why there? Can he not come here?'

'He has travelled far: it would hardly be courteous to bring him further.'

I sighed, and set off.

Gerig and Arth were talking outside the Hearth-house, leaning on their hunting-spears. They greeted me as I came up, with an odd sidelong look as if they shared a secret. I found nobody in the courtyard, passed through the empty Hearth-room, and drew back the curtain of the inner room.

Cardail sat at the head of the hearth with her baby in her lap: to one side sat my mother and on the other a little dark woman I did not know, her head bound in a red cloth, eastern fashion. I greeted the priestesses, looking about for Felim's young man.

My mother came round the fire to kiss me—

'I am happy for you and for this day,' she said; 'I give you joy of your son.'

She turned to the stranger woman—

'Here he is, my son and the child's father.'

She lifted a bundle of cloth from a cushion beside Cardail. A roar of fury burst from it, and a fist flailed among the wrappings. She clucked and rocked the bundle in her arms.

'Tk, tk, tk! What way is this to greet your father? Here you are, Drost; take him; he is yours.'

She put Yssa's son into my hands.

I trembled so much that I feared I would drop the little

creature. I sat down quickly, holding it like a basket of eggs, but it went on yelling.

'What's wrong? Is it sick?'

'You're not holding him tight enough, that's all; he wants to feel himself safe. That's better; you won't hurt him if you keep a good hold of him. There now, my man! That's your Da!'

Yssa's son!

I tried to see a likeness to her; there was only the usual baby's face that looks so like every other, but the head was crowned by a mass of fiery fluff, unlike anything I had ever seen. I touched it cautiously with one fingertip.

'Aye,' said the woman, 'he has a queen's colour, that one! No need to dye his head! He's strong, too; try his grip, Lord.'

'How did he get here? Did she send him? Is there—oh, is there something wrong?'

My mother said to the nurse:

'Give him the message you have brought; do not fear, this is the right one, this is my son.'

The stranger fumbled among her garments and brought out a torn shred of cloth. There was nothing inside it but one grey dove's feather.

I saw a sun-baked courtyard, a golden wall with the shadow of leaves on it, and fluttering between two stones a feather. This was our sign, our own old sign; it meant one thing only—'Come to me.'

'Where? Where is she? Where shall I find her? At the palace?'

She began to talk very fast, in the clattering way of the easterners: I had to ask her to speak slowly so that I could understand. The lady was in danger, she said; she was no longer the youngest princess. Her elder sister had given her refuge in a temple, and had sent her into the hills with the nurse and the child. And she had bidden the woman push on ahead, for her feet were harder to endure the rough road.

'But why? Is she not your queen-to-be?'

There was another, she said; a new one; they would kill the older to open the way, if they could find her.

'A new one?'

'I think,' said my mother, 'that this might be what the Old

One meant when she spoke to Felim at the end; is it perhaps possible that he is the father of a queen-to-be?'

I stared at her for a moment; that night when we had waited, when he had come back with the shreds of a spell round him— yes, it was very possible. The two children would have been born within days of each other, within days of Cardail's son.

'It seems to me that you should send someone to find her and bring her to safety here as soon as may be,' said my mother. 'I have heard often that they will only keep one or two prin- cesses alive at any time. If there is this elder one who is a virgin and a priestess, that will be enough. Send for her, Drost; send out your young men to bring her here. I have desired to see her for many a long day.'

'No,' I said, 'that will not do; if our men go out armed, they may come to spear-points with the easterners, and that must not happen. Besides, how will she know that they are her friends? No, the sign was to me; I will go. I'll tell the men what I have to do, and I'll fetch her home myself.'

'Well—' she said doubtfully, 'yes, perhaps that is better. I'll keep your little man here till she comes for him. Tell her he is safe and well. Let me have him now; come to me, my hero! There, that's my boy!'

'I'll have to find her—where did you leave her?'

The woman began to clatter again, telling of landmarks I could not know, and of the men of the Bear who had guided her over the high passes. But as she talked I felt Yssa calling. I would find her. I remembered a great pointed peak that looked both ways, to the east and to us, and a side valley we had seen as we returned, where a grove of holy trees grew at the head of a lesser pass. I thought I would aim for that.

'It is cold in the hills,' said my mother. 'Go quickly and find her; go with my blessing, my son.'

I went down and called the men together hurriedly, and told them what I had to do; I gave them little time for talk, but told them what the Old One had commanded, that Gerig should have charge of both boys, and that they were twins. I led them back to the Hearth-house and brought my son out to them.

Regil said:

'King, it would be well if we might see them together, and show the People. Could we not follow the former way in this?'

'What former way? Not as you did to me—to us!'

Old Gerig said huskily, leaning on his grandson's arm:

'No, not that way; that was only a travesty of the way. Here is one who will tell you how it should be done.'

He beckoned behind him, and little Terik the slave pattered out and stood before us.

'Terik,' said old Gerig, 'tell the King how the children ought to be shown.'

'The oldest way was this, master,' said Terik. 'For any bargain, for anything of importance to us all, we gathered in the Prosperous Place, in the Fenced Place; then the bargain was made or the matter declared, over the First-Fruits Stone. We saw it and heard it, and the stones were witnesses that we had seen and heard it; they were there to be witnesses. This was our way, we who were the People of Before.'

We young men stared at him; the Former People were only a name and a mystery to us; I had not thought there had been any living within twenty generations.

'Shall we do this, then? Is it your will?' I asked the men.

'Yes, it is our will; let us do it.'

'Terik,' I said, 'come and walk with me a little, and tell me what we must do. Must we sacrifice? What shall we offer?'

'We have never offered there, any of us alive now,' he said. 'But my grandfather, who was very old, told me what he had heard from his grandfather. Give us leave, and I will gather my brothers and tell them what to do. We will prepare the ground as it ought to be prepared.'

'The New Way used it for their ceremonies, even for—for dark things; have we polluted the ground? Should it be cleansed?'

'Why, master? How can anything dirty that ground? It is the Fenced Place, the Safe Place. Gods and men meet there.'

'Terik, if you know all about it, can you tell me how the place was made? How did your fathers set up those mighty stones?'

He grinned.

'Aha, that was a secret, master! That died with my grandfather's grandfather; but my grandfather told me that our music raised them. We had our own music in the Time of Before. When our people first came from their former places,

231

when they came to land here on the white beaches, there they made their ring and marked it out—'

'How? How did they make the ring?'

'Standing together, all of them from the oldest to the youngest child that could stand, hand to hand, and the old man who led them went round behind their heels and drew the ring on the earth with his digging-stick, thus. Then they dug on the line and threw up the earth to make the bank, as you still see it, and they cut trees from the land as they cleared it, and put a pole in the bank for each fire, for each family that was there. And later, much later when the land was cleared and they grew old, they put a stone in the place of the pole as the heads of the fires died, a stone at a time. The stones yonder, they tell us how many of our people came; more than two hands, more than we can number; so we remember them. The stones remain though the people have gone; but we have not all gone.

'Now I go and see to the preparing?'

'Take anything you need from the stores,' I called after him; 'and, Terik, hurry—there's very little time to give to this. You'd better have a couple of bullocks for yourselves, and make a feast of your own.'

Terik vanished downhill, grinning from ear to ear.

There was very little time. We sent runners to bring in the boys from the Fort of the Girls, and we drummed for all the People to gather. In the late afternoon we gathered everyone to the stones, men, women, slaves and children, and the boys. We stood in a great company within the embanked circle. Terik and his people had been busy; the stones had been cleared of moss and rubbed with red and white clays, so that forgotten symbols leaped out on their faces, and a little way off the graves of the Former People shone with a fresh covering of white pebbles.

I asked if he minded people of other beliefs offering there.

'Why should we mind? They know it all, the stones; they see times change and return; they remain. Why should we mind?'

So we brought the children, the red one and the dark, and we offered to all great ones, to the Mother and to the younger gods; and then it was time for Terik to lead our offerings to the oldest, to the stone-dwellers. He stepped out before us all, resplendent in a fur cloak I had given him, streaked with paint and clay and crowned with feathers, and clapped his hands loudly.

At once, some of the slave-women near the edge of the circle lifted their voices in a curious wailing call, as thrilling as the call of curlews by night; and it was answered from the other side by a clear and beautiful ripple of musical notes. Three men came out of the crowd, playing the little bone flutes to which the slaves sometimes dance.

This was no dancing tune; this was a fountain welling from some dark rock in the beginning of things. They led us from stone to stone, while Terik dashed bowls of offerings at the foot of each, little gifts of honey, and fish, and roots; little enough to end so long a fast.

Behind me I heard Felim sigh—

'After all my singing, at last I have heard song!'

Demetroos answered softly:

'A spring of clear water; music's self and the end of thirst.'

We returned to the middle stone and I climbed on it, under Terik's orders, and held the babies up for everyone to see, and the People cried out to greet them and hail them as kings for the future. They were both wide awake, but neither seemed to mind the noise. The dark one chuckled to himself, and the red man almost lunged out of my arms, so that I made haste to give him back to my mother.

When it was over I took Terik aside and offered him his freedom. He ducked his head, and grinned.

'I thank you, little master, but why should I change? We are here as we have always been, and now we have you and your son to rule us, who are of our own blood. The stones are witnesses that we shall always be here. You great ones and your ways may change, but we, and the land, and the old stones, remain. That was our bargain in the beginning.'

I could see his friends waiting impatiently for him to come and begin their feast; I took leave of him, and then of all my people, and I threw my cloak on my shoulder and went away up the hill road.

When I looked back from the top of the rise I saw them all, little as ants, still standing within the ring. I left them in their safety and went into the hills.

Only much later, in the dusk, did I think of Terik's parting words, that I and my son were of his blood. So the slaves had known, all the time? They, like their old stones, knew more than priests or councillors. 'They'? No; we. I looked up to the hills and began to laugh. Now I could be sure the children were safe. They, and the stones, would remain.

Three days later, travelling as fast as my feet would carry me, I came through a cleft between great rocks, and saw the ground fall below me in a narrow glen to the east. A little stream was born among the rocks and ran down a green strip, and close before me were seven rowans, their branches bare and silver against the sky. I had been seeing this place ahead of me all the way.

I stood quite still and prayed to the Mother, and then I sang the 'Shepherd's Song'.

When I ended, Yssa was standing a few feet from me in the sunlight.

The road I had taken was hard and rough, across mountain ridges and by high bare moors; she feared she might have been tracked towards the pass; a little taint of woodsmoke reached us as we talked. She said she had seen men moving far behind her the evening before. We climbed the south side of the glen, going up steeply between hazels and birches to the ridge, and from the ridge we looked back and saw men in brown cloaks moving up to the pass. She took my hand and we hurried over the hillsides southerly.

We lay that night in a little den among cliffs, wet and weary from our haste and from much fording of rivers to break our scent; but we lay in each other's arms and thought little of weariness. Next day we found ourselves in a bigger valley that led south and east, and it seemed well to follow it, for the pursuers would not expect her to turn east again. As we went on we walked more freely, until by evening we were stepping out down a small track side by side like any two lovers. She was thin, my poor love, but in her plain dress and with her soft hair free of its dye she was more beautiful than ever.

A shepherd gave us food and shelter in his hut; I think he

took us for a pair of runaway slaves, for he promised us next day that he had not seen us.

It was that day, as we walked, that we began to talk of geasa. My sword led us to it, Yssa watching me rub it with my hands to feed the blade, while we wondered how the shepherd would account for a slave carrying a sword. We laughed together, and it was natural to tell her about its geis of rope, and how Talorc had come to tell me of it.

'And is that your only geis? You are more fortunate than I; I have—or I had, when I was what I was, yonder—a cloud of geasa; fish, and nets, and the moon on water, and more of the same.'

'Why should things like that be geasa? They are natural things; must you not eat fish? I had hoped I could catch some for us to eat.'

'I have never tasted one,' she said; 'are they good to eat? As for the reason—why, our greatest enemy is their master; I cannot touch anything that belongs to him—or I could not, when I was what I was. Now that I am nothing, I dare say it is of no importance.'

'Is there one, then, who is an enemy to your people?'

She shivered and drew closer.

'He who sits on a rock; the one whose face is hidden, the one on the edge of the tide; I will not name him even here, far from his kingdom.'

Then I understood that she spoke of Black Arkai the Fisherman, the Shape-changer. I had not known he was still a name of dread in any country. He was only a tale to frighten children at home, I told her, and when we were at home she need not fear him any longer.

We went downhill all next day, and out across a plain. Now where? The hills were falling back on either side; we should have to turn towards the sunset and seek a new pass. We came to a wider river, and I carried her over it on my back.

We had not gone far on the other side when she said:

'I think we should go faster; I think they are near us.'

We stopped to listen; a long way behind us I thought I heard a hound whimper. She looked at me wide-eyed and we hurried on.

We crossed another shallow river, and ahead of us we saw

235

a little creek with boats drawn up on the shore by some poor-looking huts.

'If we go down and get a boat, we can sail down the river and throw off the pursuit,' I said; 'or we could land on the far side and swing round to the west. We need not go straight for home, after all; the weather is warmer, we are all right as we are; aren't we? They will expect us to go straight for home. The longer we delay, the slacker will be the pursuit.'

'Well—' she said, 'it might be so. But let us keep away from houses. One person has seen us today already, and she may guide the hunters.'

'Who? I saw nobody!'

'Oh yes, you must have seen her; that youngish pretty woman who was washing clothes back there at the last river we crossed; I said good-day to her and she smiled and nodded back to me. But she might have gone home by now, and anyway she may be frightened to speak to the men if they do come after us this way.'

I thought she must have mistaken some rock for a woman, as far as I thought at all. I did not think, to be truthful; my mind was wholly on escaping from the easterners; no hint of any other danger touched me. Someone washing clothes at a ford—but what difference could it have made if I had thought?

The creek grew steadily wider and little waves broke on the muddy sand. We kept close to the shore, under a low earth-bank.

'Is that the sea?' she asked. 'Salt water? I have never been so near it.'

'That's the sea; the eastern sea, not our wide friendly water that brings us fish, and weed, and shells for ornaments. Ah, when we get there, what things I shall have to show you!'

She stopped me with a grip on my arm.

'Listen!'

We heard the hound bay, a full-throated cry as he found his quarry, and in the next heart-beat his companions crashed in to join their music to his.

'My father's hounds! They are the best in the world, none steadier on a scent. They know me well—I used to feed them—Drost, what are we to do?'

There was a boat drawn up on the sand a bowshot ahead. I

did not waste one moment, but ran for it. The oars were in her; I lifted Yssa aboard and turned to cast off the painter. Yssa crouched in the stern and began to tremble.

'Quickly, quickly!'

I fumbled with the knot; the dew had swelled the hide and it would not yield. I could hear a man whooping the hounds on the trail.

'Hurry, Drost, hurry!'

I could not lose all now at the last. My blade sang in the air and the two cut ends of the rope sprang apart like snakes.

I thrust the boat down the sand and climbed in over the bow, and behind us over the low meadow we saw three couple of hounds break cover, with a young stag tearing away ahead of them.

There was more wind than I expected. It was hard work rowing against it. A little water slapped into the boat, and I had to tell Yssa how to bale. We were further from the shore than I had meant to be. We would have to cross the estuary, which was growing wider, and make our way up the southern side.

I had been looking over my shoulder at the far shore; when I turned to tell Yssa what I had decided, I found her kneeling in the stern and gazing landwards.

'We're going over the water,' I said.

She did not answer at once. Then I heard her say in a low voice:

'The hounds! Swift, and Certain, and Sure, and dear old Songster! Drost, do you not hear them? Listen to their brave music! How could I leave them—and my father? They know I am here; they are calling me; he is calling me . . . back from the salt water . . .'

How could I know what she would do? She stood up and held out her arms to the distant shore.

The boat heeled crazily; I made a desperate effort to right it; a gust of wind caught us.

We went down into the sea that was geas to her.

Part Six

I CAME up through uncounted ages, through dead time and darkness into pain and grey light and a sound of crying. Fingers plucked me back, ruthless knees rolled me forward, earth refused me and water cast me onwards. I choked on the salt tears of the world, and my hands closed on sliding emptiness. I fell back, helpless as driftwood, into darkness, and again the plucking and pounding began and I had no heart to fight.

At last they left me lying on cold wet sand—nothing colder; the wailing of a thousand women was shrill around me, and tears ran down my smarting face for a sorrow I did not understand. I rose out of the sodden body and looked down on it, a useless hulk lying on the edge of the tide in a grey world. I was almost free of it, free to drift down the wind that sobbed in the sky, but as I hung there a keener pain wrenched me back into the body and made it stir.

I opened my eyes in the grey before dawn, and a huge and gleaming seagull rose from me, its ice-yellow bloody-tipped beak agape with anger. Its fellows lifted after it to the clamour of mourners, and a last pang of life drove me up to shake my arms impotently at their beating wings. All the while I was crying to myself that this was death, that the time had come to lift and be gone. Only the stubborn heart beat on and held me with the bond of the blood that is stronger than the weakened spirit. The blood is strong, but it could not hold much longer.

I opened my eyes again when I felt the sand shake under me, and I looked on strange creatures. I knew them for some sort of humankind by their walking and standing, but they stank and they jabbered, and their faces were flat and wide and grinning as they hung over me. They clutched at my body and lugged it up the beach between them, chattering together, and they rolled it on its breast to get the water out of it, and others of them rubbed my hands and my feet.

I lay in their hands like a log, only lolling my eyes open from time to time as they turned me about. When I fumbled in my mind to know what sort of man I was, I got no answer; not a name, not an echo; only the weight of immense and unknown sorrow and immeasurable loss. Even as I tried to name that loss, tears broke from my eyes and flooded down my face.

At that they gabbled faster, and a youngish woman pulled up her hanging garment and took my feet under her breasts. It was a good and kindly deed to give me her body-heat. Others lay down and stretched their bodies against mine, and kneaded my arms and my chest, until at last warmth began to grow through me. When I stirred of my own accord and tried to sit up, a dozen hands came round to help me; and in the end they had me on my feet between two of them.

One of the men put a garment, his own, on me, over my head and hanging to my thighs; I had not known till then that I was naked. I put my hand to my left side, seeking something I did not find, nor could I tell what I had sought. We stumbled together over a long reach of sand, then through rounded pebbles that slid underfoot, and lastly among salt grasses that cut the legs. I stood head and shoulders above my rescuers.

We came suddenly on their camp, a huddle of rounded tents in a hollow among sandhills. Small children and old people had kept the camp and came crowding round us, staring and reaching out to touch me with suspicious hands. The man whose garment I wore, and who walked beside me in naked dignity, gave an order, and a woman brought a bowl of grey warm liquid and held it for me to drink. It tasted vile, but its warmth was comforting.

240

They were kindly people. They uncovered a small fire and blew it into life and made me sit by it. They hung round me and offered me more soup, held my hands and rubbed them, and when the weight of sorrow fell suddenly on me again, answering tears sprang to their eyes and they rocked themselves and lamented, though they knew as little as I did myself why I wept.

They ran to fetch more firewood, driftwood that burned green and blue with salt. Some of them brought strips of dried meat, chewed it to soften it, and besought me with signs to eat it. When they saw that I did not know how to feed on the stuff they grew frantic and ran about seeking something else to give me; a boy who came with birds' eggs in his hood was greeted with clapping hands. They broke the eggs into a scallop-shell and offered me the raw dish as if it had been a feast. So it was to them, good folk, as I came to know; they were giving me the best of all they had.

At last a very old woman, her face almost black with sun and grime and smoke—but she was not so very old, for these people age fast—hobbled up and gazed on me, and bade the others take me to a tent and let me sleep. So I lay in the dark, in a small space full of savage smells, and I slept.

When I woke, the world was new around me. I could remember nothing before that stranding among the gulls, and I followed these people everywhere for they were my only friends. They went about their business and I blundered after, springing traps, standing on precious nets, scaring birds, eating hard-won food; and never once did any of them say one word of blame or anger. They treated me like one of their children, with whom they were never angry. They lived on the edge of famine, and I am ashamed to think how I took their food and did nothing to gather more.

The men hunted fish with nets and spears, and small game with snares and pitfalls, and the women tended the nets and gathered shells and a few little plants that grew along the strands, and the little children scoured the beaches and the dunes for anything that could be eaten. A day or two after they had found me they had great good fortune and we all ate like kings, for two boys found a young seal on the beach and clubbed it. So we ate raw meat, I as eagerly as any of them, and they took it for a sign that I would bring them hunting-luck.

It would be wrong to say that they thought a god had rewarded them; as far as I could ever learn they knew no gods, but only good luck and bad luck—though when they mended the big net they said charms over it that were something like prayers.

So I stayed with them all summer, and through autumn into the winter, when we put all the tents together and huddled down for warmth—and on into the hungry spring. They drifted along like grazing cattle, here a bite and there a bite; in one place they would find good fishing, and stay until I thought we were settled there, and then overnight they would be up and off to some new beach where they hoped to dive for oysters or set springes for duck. They seemed to move at random, as birds move when the tide turns, but like the birds their purposes were clear to themselves. They knew by ancient knowledge when to expect such and such a food at such and such a place, and when I began to understand their talk I found that every night the elders compared their memories and consulted their feelings about the weather and the season, to decide what to do next.

I have never been able to make out how long I was with those Sea People. We returned to old remembered camps three, perhaps four, times, but then we went as well to many new camps, so that is no way to tell the passage of time. Also we went to the same camp at different times for different reasons; now to gather eggs or nestling birds, now to feed on berries or nuts growing in the woods behind the dunes—for we went up to the woods at times, but cautiously. I could see that they feared the trees, or something in the trees, and not knowing what it was I too was glad when we were safely back among the dunes.

The squalor of the camps was frightful, but I soon forgot to notice it. I would sit between Ungik the leader and Ngu the old woman and chew dried seal meat, as if I had been born in one of those tents.

We seldom saw any other people. Once when we were on the move along a strand there was a gabble of panic from the young men ahead, and we all clapped down behind the nearest sandhill to watch a strangely-dressed group go past. There were three men striding down the sand, an old man and a youth first and another old man following them and carrying a dead deer on his back. The two who walked ahead carried nothing but long sticks with shining tops, a little like our bone-headed fish-spears. They were dressed in short fine garments and flowing cloaks, one blue, the other flame-coloured; the old man with the deer wore a leather loin-cloth.

But what frightened us about them, and made us lie as still as mice, was the two enormous dogs that ranged at the heels of the leaders. I did not know it then, but hounds loathe the smell of the Sea People and hunt them as if they were otters. I only knew that I was deeply afraid of the dogs for some secret reason hidden in my heart.

The men walked past us and the breeze brought us their scent, the smell of cooked food and woodsmoke and cleanliness. The wind was in our favour and the dogs did not scent us, so when they had passed out of sight we could get up and carry on. As we went our young men talked about the strangers, wondering that one man, and he not the youngest, had been left to carry the game. But they settled it to their own satisfaction that he was the successful hunter who was taking it home to show his womenfolk. I knew there was something wrong with that, but as I hardly ever spoke (finding their speech difficult to my tongue) I let it go.

There are times in life when action follows action, pelting in like rain; and times when one hangs between events like a piece of driftwood under a rock in a river. One of these waiting times held me from the day the Sea People found me; when at last I became aware that I was in such a time, I became aware also that it was ending.

First there was the portent of those three men and the dogs. I turned back again and again to the thought of them; I fingered the memory and held it up and gazed at it, but still it told me nothing, and still I felt that it must do so. Then there was the matter of the arrows.

Every time we passed along a certain stretch of coast the

243

children would search a sandy heath behind the beach to pick up certain little shiny stones that they treasured. Because I was useless in all other ways I began to hunt for these stones too, and to ask what purpose they served. Ungik answered that they were of no use to us, but that the Landmen would give food for them. By 'Landmen' he meant a tribe of starvelings who lived further inland than we ever penetrated, but who met us at certain river-crossings and exchanged roots or small game for our fish.

I asked why the Landmen should want these stones, and why they could not find them for themselves; but he only shook his head and said he supposed they did not like to come so near the sea.

The sharp-eyed children had gathered a handful apiece before I found one; but suddenly I came upon it, lying in a patch of sand, and my hand had gone out for it before I knew what I was doing. I picked it up; it was warm and smooth, about as long as my thumbnail, light brown and polished. As I lifted it I said to myself :

'It's a good one; it would flight true.'

In the same instant I wondered what I had said. I went and sat down under a dune and looked at the little stone. It was sharp at one end and at the other it had three points, two sharp and the middle one flattened to go into a split stick. The two long edges leading to the sharp end were most delicately serrated. I turned it round and round and weighed it on my palm. I knew exactly what it was—an arrowhead made by the Former People.

I began to tremble with excitement. What I needed now was a shaft, a branch of willow or elder, and some feathers and a sinew. And I would need a long sapling for a bow, and a stronger sinew for a string, and then I too could hunt and kill game for the people to eat. I stood up and walked away from the children, my treasure tightly clutched in my hand. I was not a useless mouth any more.

I would get the children to find me more arrowheads—I would teach Niah and the other young men to shoot—I would show the women how to drive game past us. I chose my sticks carefully, and hunted again over the sand until I found a worn scraper to fashion my shaft. These sands had been a hunting ground for the Former People, and they had left their tools strewn about as was their custom.

Now for the sinews. I went to Ungik, carrying my finds, and said to him:

'I will show you how I used to hunt. Give me two sinews from Ngu's store, a long one and a little one.'

Ungik said, staring:

'You, a hunter? Why did you not tell us?'

I said:

'The sea washed it away from me; give me the sinews and I will show you.'

'What are they for? What are you holding?'

I opened my hand and held out the flint.

Ungik snatched it up—

'This is not for hunting, this is for giving the Landmen; it is worth a string of fish!'

I said, almost crying in my anxiety:

'Give it back! I know what it's for if you do not.'

He looked at me slily, under his brows, and said nothing, but I saw he was not going to give me my arrowhead. I snatched at it, and the next moment I was locked in his arms and thrown down, and half the tribe came round us gabbling and threatening me. Suddenly I felt their stench and their strangeness, and I jumped up and ran from them as hard as I could till I came to the edge of the woods.

Some of the women were in there looking for nuts and honey —for it was autumn again—and some of the men were with them in case of whatever danger they feared. They had not ventured far, except for two who had followed the flight of some bees from the flowers on the heath. As I stood there, breathing hard, there was a great crash ahead of me. Ngu and two other women came huddling out, clutching their creels of nuts. In the next breath we heard a woman's scream, a thin feeble note suddenly cut off.

I began to run, and as I ran I passed women running the other way. I ran till I came to two young men standing ashen-faced on a pathway. One of them was Ungik's son Niah. He caught my arm to stop me and in a shaking voice he said:

'Get back! It is he; there is nothing we can do. He has killed her.'

245

I shook him off and went on to see what he meant. Presently I saw.

There was a clearing, and at the far side of it a rotten tree where the honey was. The two women had broken open the trunk and begun to pull out the honey; they had smeared themselves with mud to protect them from stings. The bees roared round the stump. One of the women was now clinging to the upper branches of a small tree; the other was lying in the middle of the clearing, with blood pouring from her head and shoulders. And standing over her, swinging his head between her and the other woman, was the Smiler of the Woods.

I knew him, the killer that he was, and I knew I was his brother. The woman was still alive; the pulsing blood told me that. I had felt for my sword at my left side before I remembered it was not there. Niah had followed me with despairing courage. I put my hand back to him, signalling for him to give me his fish-spear.

The woman on the ground was the mother of his children. My fear was that he would rush in himself and be killed, and take that spear out of my reach. I went back a step and caught it out of his hand, and then I went softly forwards and began to dance.

The Smiler saw me at once, and was undecided. He watched me, but he wanted also to watch the women, and he smelt the honey. He turned his head this way and that way. I danced towards him, and he began to give me most of his attention.

My mind was waking; the moment of life or death was coming when he would give me all his mind, and either break me with one flash of his arm, or else join in the dance. I cried with all my heart:

'Mother of All, make him dance!'

He let me come a little closer, and a little closer. I saw him shift his weight on to his hind feet, and I knew the moment was near. I shortened my grip on the spear, that horribly inadequate weapon, and I held my gaze on his eyes, not looking to see what the women were doing (though I too wanted to know). Then he reared up his brown bulk and began to dance.

I stamped and swayed and he stamped with me, and swayed

his great body, and moved a little away from the wounded woman and came nearer me. I found myself singing to him, the song of the dance, the song of the Green Glen. He even answered me a little in his deep voice. We drew near each other and I felt an old weakness, and knew I had felt it before, the pity of killing a brother who was dancing with me, who was nearer to me by that dance than any of those who looked on. We were very close; I could see the short golden hairs on his breast and the coarse hairs over them; he towered above me, shutting out the sky, and still he danced. Then I was too close; at any moment he would smell my strangeness and the arm would flash down, for this time I was not anointed with his fat.

I cried out: 'Brother, forgive me!' and I thrust the spear with all my might under his arm, and sprang clear.

There should have been other spearmen behind me; there should have been men to run in behind him when he fell; there were none. There was only a madman with a fish-spear, standing in a clearing in an unknown country, with a big brown bear slowly dying, sitting down, rolling over, flinging up the great arms that could have crushed his brother and enemy, jerking, kicking once, and lying still.

And there was Niah, and Ungik, and the whole tribe, crowding round the hurt woman and the other, dragging them away, and fleeing from me as if I were the Smiler himself.

I had nothing with which to make offering to my brother whom I had killed. I sat on the ground a little way off, shaking like a leaf in the wind. I could not abandon him without any leave-taking, so at last I took up a sharp stone and cut my wrist, and let a few drops of my blood fall by his blood-flecked muzzle, and said to him:

'Farewell, brother, be at peace, and may your hunting be sweet to you.'

I wondered, as I said it, that I should know how to do such things.

Then I went out of the wood to look for the people. But when I came near the camp the boys were on watch and screamed like gulls, and old Ngu came with a burning stick and waved it at me, and all the men took up stones to throw.

So I knew they had finished with me, and with a heavy heart

I turned and went slowly away inland, going as my feet led me. I was utterly weary in body as in mind, and the pain in my head was piercing. I wandered away from the camp with night drawing in, and at last I went up over a small rise and saw on the far side a cluster of houses.

Houses. All this time there had been houses no further than three good arrow-flights, and I had not known it. I knew that I had once lived in houses, and I wanted more than anything to go to them and be welcome. But when I went nearer, the village dogs winded me and set up such a baying that I fled, along a track that would take me from them and from the sea as well.

I slept that night in the lee of some bushes on an open heath, and next day I passed cautiously by several villages and watched women carrying sheaves of corn on their heads into barns, and men reaping with sickles and old women twisting sheaf-bands, and boys herding cattle on to cleared stubbles. It seemed a strange enough world, and yet not wholly strange. I was hungry now, light-headed with hunger; I ate some berries from the bushes as I passed, and dug up roots with my nails, but still I hungered.

On the second evening as I walked along a track I heard ahead of me a high clear ringing. Without stopping to think what it might mean I stepped off the road into the grass, and knelt there. And round a corner came a little cluster of people.

First there walked a man who carried a rod wrapped round with ears of corn and hung with little bells that chimed continually. Next came young children carrying lights in small clay bowls, and after them a woman all in white. She was neither young nor old; her head was wreathed with poppies and corn, and in her hands she bore a basket. Behind came more people with lights. The sunset made a glory round her and reddened the dust where she trod.

My heart went out to her; I stretched out my hands and cried with all my soul:

'O Mother, O Thou Mother, return and remain with thy sons!'

The bell-bearer frowned on me; the children clung to her skirts and their lights shook with their fear; but she in her hour of joy turned her face to me and smiled.

The smile of the Mother has sent men to madness ere now, but me it sent to sanity. I remembered what I was, and that I was profaning the mysteries with my stinking body and my foul garment, and I sprang up and fled from them as fast as I could, never stopping until I found a little den under some bushes where I could crawl in and hide.

In the morning I woke cold and stiff, and crept out determined to clean myself somehow before I went near people again. I stripped off that half-cured sealskin I had worn so long without considering the smell of it, and only when I turned to hang it on a bush did I realise that I had again committed sacrilege. For, of all places, I had chosen a blackthorn thicket for my hiding-place.

I could have wept with shame; the more my mind wakened, the more I desired the safety of the Mother's goodwill, and the more I seemed fated to incur her anger. She must be very angry with me already, I thought, to pursue me with so many chances of error; and then I rebuked myself and remembered that she does not pursue; it is the guilty spirit that hurls itself deeper and deeper into its own condemnation.

There was a stream at the foot of the slope; at least I could wash there, though how to clothe myself I could not think. I went down to the banks and waded in, and washed all over, and then I came out and lay on the grass and listened to the birds singing their half-song of autumn, and I no longer believed that I was utterly under the cloud of her displeasure.

And then I smelt something.

The most beautiful smell in the world stole down to me, a smell laden with memories of love and home and safety; sweeter than milk or blossom or honey-wine; a smell that unlocked the gates of my heart and brought me round to follow it like a homing bird.

The smell of new-baked bread.

I turned, and she was standing above me, in her robes, and the new harvest-bread in her hands.

There was I, naked, uncouth, untrimmed, a savage from the beaches, and there stood the priestess of the gates of life. I trembled as I knelt; I knew my duty was to flee from her, to take pollution out of her way; I could not stir.

She came down towards me holding out the bread and

smiling. Was this a new trap to make me sin further? No, she does not pursue, I insisted; no, but she offers the choice of good or evil. In confusion and despair I threw myself down at the feet of the priestess.

She knelt beside me; I felt a hand touch my shoulder; a cloak was thrown over me, and into my hand she put the bread.

I could only bow my head still lower to touch the hem of her robe, and tears broke from my heart and blinded me.

When I looked up I thought she had gone, and I was ready to sink back into despair. I got to my feet, and saw her up at the top of the slope, waiting to see what I would do.

I threw the cloak round me—it was a soft brown woollen, such as they keep for guests who come to the Hearth-house—and I took the bread into my breast and went up the hill towards her. She turned as soon as she saw I was coming, and when I topped the crest there she was, a little way off, waiting to make sure I would follow. In this way, ever waiting and looking back, she drew me to the Hearth-house of the place.

It was very early; nobody was astir in the village except the man who had yesterday borne the branch for her. I have only lately seen that those two, who had gone through all the ceremonies of the harvest the day before, must have sat up all night to grind the corn and bake the bread, only to bring me in. The village slept late that morning, and their bread was not ground, let alone baked, until noon; but she and her branch-bearer had not rested.

He got up from a low stone at the door of the Hearth and came down the sleeping street towards us. He held out his hands, and without a word spoken such a tide of welcome enfolded me that I could hardly bear its joy. I saw in his eyes and in his smile that I had come home.

He led me into a little chamber off the court of the Hearth, and there bathed me and trimmed my hair and my beard, and poured sweet oils into my hands for me to rub over myself, and made me as welcome as if I had come like a king. When I was ready he took me into the Hearth-room and he and the priestess waited to see what I would do.

As for me, I fell on my knees before that low grey mound of ash, and I took up branches that lay ready and laid them on the fire; and I stretched out my hands over the flames and gave the Mother thanks with all my heart. And the strangest thing of all (or perhaps it is not at all strange) was that I, who in the stress of the dance against the Smiler had found only one word of prayer, now called on her in my own tongue in phrases I had not known I knew.

When I had finished my thanksgiving the two who stood behind me bowed with me, and then taking my hands they led me into their inner room and sat me down in the guest's place.

Their inner room; as the gates of memory swung open again that was the most wonderful thing, and among the bitterest. It could be done; Malda and Melduin could have done it, my beloved and I might have done it, perhaps Cardail and Arth had achieved it. She was the priestess and he was the king of that place, two parts of one perfect whole. Not one swallowed up by the other, not kingship taken over by priesthood, but a balanced strength to both. The inner room was full of their children, the court crowded with the faithful; the people were prosperous, the faith was strong, all was well. None of the struggle my people had endured had been necessary. It had all sprung from one fault, from one man's greed; Talorc had spoken more truly than he knew.

As they two healed my mind and restored it to me, I yearned for the Land of the Boar; but they wrought with me and made me see that the gate was closed, that I could bring nothing but sorrow and trouble home with me if I returned. I struggled to regain the powers I had had and to reach my people with my thoughts, to know if it was well with them, but at last I understood that all my gifts had gone with my broken geis.

So I shall not know, this side the Orchard, if the red boy lives and thrives; nor my mother, nor Arth, nor Cardail, nor Gerig of the Leap; and I shall not forget this side the Orchard how I broke the geis of my sword and helped my dear love break her own. But those two new friends I had found gave me back many things I had lost, and added to them others I had not known. She taught me some of her healing arts, and something I remembered of Demetroos' skill; and he brought back to me the time when I had been a singer.

251

At first I could not bear to sing; when I tried to begin the 'Shepherd's Song' tears drowned my voice anew; but through time and by careful choosing of songs I came back to such skill as Felim had managed to drive into my head, and I began to make verses.

When I was strong again and my mind was clear, they sent me on my way and gave me their advice, to travel as far as I could towards the sunset and there await the end of things. So I set out with their blessing and left them mine, but when I had gone a few days' journey I came to a place where they were mourning their priest, and it seemed right to me to stay with them until another was old enough to replace him.

In a year or two I set forward again and passed from place to place through the land, sometimes walking all summer, sometimes staying in some village for moons or even years; and at last I came through red valleys rich in the violets that were sacred to your Lady in another place, past the villages of metal-workers who pray to foreign gods, and onward until I understood that there was nothing further westerly without crossing the sea that was geas to you.

I came to the priestesses of this place with a certain name for healing skill—for I had helped to deal with a tin-miner who had neglected to pray before he went underground, and we had kept him alive, little though I expected to do so. And I came too with a name for songs; Felim would have called me a song-smith, I doubt not, but I have made some few songs that pleased the hearers, and even one or two that please me a little. One concerns a meeting in hills and a parting over water, and I have seen people dry their eyes after hearing it, for pity of young lovers.

I came to the priestesses of this place; and immediately I had a sign that the end of things would not be long delayed. They thought well to choose a young girl to attend me, who am grown old, and the name of this child is your name. Till now, in all the length of my travels, I have never found a woman who owned that name, and in having it thus brought back to me I feel a portent and a promise.

So I think it cannot be long now. I have told you all I remember, because you saw what happened to me whether you were with me or not; and you remember much better than I do all that has passed between us in other times and places. I have told you what happened, whether I understood it or not; perhaps some day we shall understand it together. It is not necessary to understand it all, as long as some of it stirs my memory when I return, or stirs your own. I have learnt much of the weaving of this chain, having sought knowledge of it from all the wise ones in my travels; all the women tell me that the surest link in it to touch your memory will be the child—your child. But I can tell you so little about the child— only that he was strong and healthy and had red hair like a crown of fire, and he was bold and brave and unafraid when he met his people for the first time—and that I left him as safe as he could be, in my mother's care and Gerig's charge. He has a Twin, a Twin who is bred of faith and friendship, who will be his friend as his father was mine, or so I pray to the Mother for both of them. And he was certain to live to be King, because the Old One promised I should be the father of kings to come after me, and he was my only child.

One thing, one little thing, troubles me faintly; in my old age I find myself anxious to know the nature of Gerig's vow. It was none of my business, then or now; it was a private matter of his own; it could not have concerned me or mine. It is only the idle curiosity of the old that makes me wonder what it was, and why the Old One told him to pull away a rotten timber and take the strain . . . I shall put it out of my mind and turn back to you, my love, my heart's core.

We who broke out of the circle of things, we shall return. Let us return here, beloved, to this land where no man bars the gates of death against returning lovers, to this land where Credhe the Maiden comes back at the cuckoo's call. Let us remember our lost selves and let us hold hands and walk carefully, offending no gods, breaking no geasa, serving faithfully. And then, if the Mother wills, we shall some day pass out of the opened circle and be together for ever in the Land of the Young.

The sun is going down, cool night is coming, the young moon is watching me yonder; the birds rest on the sea and the cliffs are quiet. The flowers are sleeping, the sea is milky and still; the mist turns to fire as the sunset kisses it, and it draws nearer and nearer, making a soft bank of feathers below the cliff-edge.

253

A ripple runs under it out of the sunset; is it now, my only love?

A red and golden path runs out into the west, and distantly down it I hear the chime of bells. My eyes are dazzled—but here, stepping delicately down the golden path, comes at last the Messenger, the Silver One. She who came for Mangan, for Talorc, comes even for me. The mist is my mounting-block; one moment yet, wait! The chain of memory is complete and I throw it from me—*now*.

Remember, rocks and sea and flowers—remember for me, all ye whom I charge—remember!

Yssa! Ysolda! Ysolda!

Author's Note

This book evolved at a time of deep anxiety and physical exhaustion, out of a series of brief waking dreams. Usually, when I am writing children's adventure-stories, I surround myself with timetables and factual notes; with this one, I floundered through the débris of a cutting-room floor from which there coiled up fragments of scenes and snatches of unintelligible dialogue. I was forced to make notes in order to get rid of these bewildering odds and ends; only after I had gathered a pile of loose-leaf pages could I be sure that the episodes had any connection.

At that stage the characters were still nameless. I found the process of note-taking so tiresome that I assigned names, at random as I thought, to the main actors—gleaning from Pictish and Dalriadic king-lists suitable barbaric sounds. The name 'Yssa' came out of the blue; I began to wonder (correctly, as I found later) whether I was dealing with a primitive version of Tristan and Isolde.

For several years I added more scenes, and at last began to arrange them into a coherent whole (if 'coherent' is the appropriate word). I had completed the section in which a sick man is found in a ruined hut, when I received a jolt which almost made me abandon the whole project; I read, in some review of a work on medieval literature, that 'behind Sir Tristram there stands the shadowy figure of Drust ap Tallwch the Tall'. Of this detail I could recall no conscious knowledge whatever.

Now, nine years after the book's completion, I can try to assess the material setting of the story. Its date is perhaps around 500 B.C. Iron is in use, though bronze is still the prestige metal; the burial-rite is cremation; new tribes have recently introduced new customs. The social organisation of kings, totemic tribes and wealth in cattle, is Celtic, with a substratum of earlier groups enslaved or dispossessed. The 'savages' of the closing section, who seemed grossly anachronistic when I wrote of them, might perhaps be some displaced pre-Celtic group reverting to a debased form of an ancient Mesolithic hunting culture.

Two notions, central to the story and still alive in folk-tradition, need explanation. 'The Apple Orchard' is a translation of *Emain Abhlach*, the Arthurian Avalon. It was a kind of pleasant limbo, where spirits awaited reincarnation; *Tir nan Òg*, the 'Land of the Young', was the Celtic paradise from which there was no return.

The concept of *geas* is more difficult to explain briefly. *Geis* (plural *geasa*) is something tabu; a forbidden act is *geas*. (The word is linked, perhaps, to the Latin *nefas*, 'do not, lest . . .'). Not only is it tabu, it is doomed to happen. A *geis* may seem absurd, a thing one is never in the least likely to encounter, but inevitably some chance will bring about the fated deed or meeting.

This book is in no way an attempt to construct an archaeologically probable picture of prehistoric life; it is a romance, in every sense of the word. I have tried to exclude any comment from a modern standpoint and to adhere to the atmosphere of pre-Christian times; beyond that, I have told the story as it came to me. Like any Celtic tale, the story has as many layers of meaning as an onion has skins; I leave it to the reader to peel off the layers, or not, as he prefers. 'It went by me, and I caught it as it flew.'

October 1972

Kilberry